Praise for *A Gentleman in Moscow*

"Irresistible . . . Towles's tale, as lavishly filigreed as a Fabergé egg, gleams with nostalgia for the golden age of Tolstoy and Turgenev."

—*O, The Oprah Magazine*

"Sly and winning . . . Wonder abounds . . . [Towles] chooses themes that run deeper than mere sociopolitical commentary: parental duty, friendship, romance, the call of home." —*The New York Times Book Review*

"Elegant, old-fashioned, and endlessly winning." —*Entertainment Weekly*

"Entertaining . . . Buzzes with the energy of numerous adventures, love affairs, twists of fate." —*The Wall Street Journal*

"An elegant, wise testimony to the beauty and necessity of human connection." —*The Miami Herald*

"And the intrigue! . . . The novel is laced with sparkling threads (they will tie up) and tokens (they will matter): special keys, secret compartments, gold coins, vials of coveted liquid, old-fashioned pistols, duels and scars, hidden assignations (discreet and smoky), stolen passports, a ruby necklace, mysterious letters on elegant hotel stationery. . . . Backdrop for a downright *Casablanca*-like drama." —*San Francisco Chronicle*

"Marvelous . . . Delightful . . . Count Rostov is a memorable character that you come to care about and root for." —*Chicago Tribune*

"While wars both hot and cold rage in the outside world, Count Rostov finds purpose and people to love within the confines of the Metropol. The count, says author Amor Towles, has a will to joy. No wonder, then, that *A Gentleman in Moscow* is a joyful read." —*NPR*

D0925914

"A tale abundant in humor, history, and humanity, with a poignant message about time passing. That Towles also makes this rollicking good fun is no mean feat."   —*Sunday Telegraph* (London)

"This is an old-fashioned sort of romance, filled with delicious detail. Save this precious book for times you really, really want to escape reality."
                                                                —Louise Erdrich

"In our own allegedly classless society, we seem to have retained only what's deplorable about aristocracy —the oppression, the snobbery, the racism—and thrown out those qualities that were worth retaining. Which makes *A Gentleman in Moscow* an endearing reminder of the graciousness of real class. It has nothing to do with money; it's predicated on the kind of moral discipline that never goes out of style."
                                                            —*The Washington Post*

"Even greater delights, though, are found in Towles's glorious turns of phrase. . . . His first book, *Rules of Civility*, garnered praise for its eloquence befitting the late 1930s setting, and *Gentleman* will not disappoint those fans."   —*The Seattle Times*

"Who will save Rostov from the intrusions of the state if not the seamstresses, chefs, bartenders, and doormen? In the end, Towles's greatest narrative effect is not the moments of wonder and synchronicity but the generous transformation of these peripheral workers, over the course of decades, into confidants, equals, and, finally, friends. With them around, a life sentence in these gilded halls might make Rostov the luckiest man in Russia."   —*The New York Times Book Review*

"Lovely ruminations on the tragicomedies of human endeavor, politics, love, ethics, and art enrich *A Gentleman in Moscow*, as do many terrific riffs about the operatic nature of Russian character (and inextricably, the course of its history)."   —*San Francisco Chronicle*

"It's natural to worry that a second book could never match the brilliance of a debut, but *A Gentleman in Moscow* does not disappoint. Despite being vastly different from *Rules of Civility* in tone, subject, and narrative structure, the same intelligence pulses under the surface of both novels. Continuing in the same epiphany-rich vein, Amor Towles delivers keen observations, quotable moments, and tremendous insights in nearly every other paragraph, making this one of the most lovely and satisfying works of fiction this year, and our pick for best historical fiction."

—Audible.com (Best of 2016: Historical Fiction)

"The Count is a wondrous literary creation—dignified and intelligent . . . the rare protagonist who'll live in your head for years. . . . In the Count, Towles has created a marvelous stand-in for the resilient human spirit."

—*Seattle Weekly*

"Littered with exquisite insights into human behavior."

—*The Austin Chronicle*

PENGUIN BOOKS

A GENTLEMAN IN MOSCOW

Born and raised in the Boston area, Amor Towles graduated from Yale University and received an MA in English from Stanford University. His first novel, *Rules of Civility*, published in 2011, was a *New York Times* bestseller and was named by *The Wall Street Journal* as one of the best books of 2011. His second novel, *A Gentleman in Moscow*, published in 2016, was also a *New York Times* bestseller and was named as one of the best books of 2016 by the *Chicago Tribune*, *The Washington Post*, *The Philadelphia Inquirer*, the *San Francisco Chronicle*, and NPR. Both novels have been translated into over fifteen languages. Having worked as an investment professional for over twenty years, Mr. Towles now devotes himself full-time to writing in Manhattan, where he lives with his wife and two children.

A GENTLEMAN IN MOSCOW

AMOR TOWLES

PENGUIN BOOKS

PENGUIN BOOKS
An imprint of Penguin Random House LLC
375 Hudson Street
New York, New York 10014
penguin.com

First published in the United States of America by Viking Penguin,
an imprint of Penguin Random House LLC, 2016
Published in Penguin Books 2017

ISBN 9780143132462 (paperback)

THE LIBRARY OF CONGRESS HAS CATALOGED THE HARDCOVER EDITION AS FOLLOWS:
Names: Towles, Amor, author.
Title: A gentleman in Moscow / Amor Towles.
Description: New York : Viking, 2016.
Identifiers: LCCN 2016030082 | ISBN 9780670026197 (hardcover) |
ISBN 9780399564048 (e-book) | ISBN 9780735221673 (international edition)
Subjects: | BISAC: FICTION / Historical. | FICTION / Literary. |
FICTION / Political.
Classification: LCC PS3620.O945 G46 2016 | DDC 813/.6—dc23 LC record
available at https://lccn.loc.gov/2016030082

Printed in the United States of America
5   7   9   10   8   6

Set in Dante MT Pro
Designed by Francesca Belanger
Map by Alex Coulter

For Stokley and Esmé

MOSCOW c. 1922

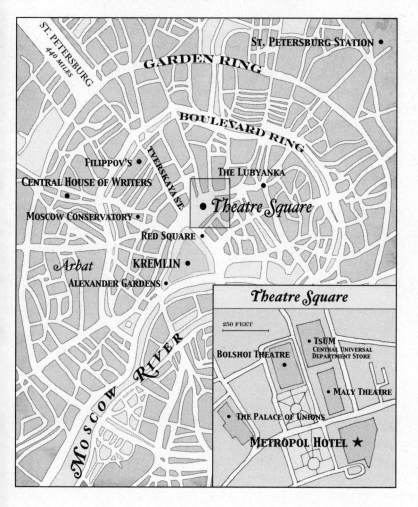

St. Petersburg
440 Miles

St. Petersburg Station •

GARDEN RING

BOULEVARD RING

TVERSKAYA ST.

Filippov's •

Central House of Writers •

The Lubyanka •

Theatre Square

Moscow Conservatory •

Red Square •

Arbat

KREMLIN •

Alexander Gardens •

Moscow River

Theatre Square

250 FEET

Bolshoi Theatre •

• TsUM
Central Universal
Department Store

• Maly Theatre

• The Palace of Unions

METROPOL HOTEL ★

A
GENTLEMAN
IN
MOSCOW

How well I remember

When it came as a visitor on foot
And dwelt a while amongst us
A melody in the semblance of a mountain cat.

Well, where is our purpose now?

Like so many questions
I answer this one
With the eye-averted peeling of a pear.

With a bow I bid goodnight
And pass through terrace doors
Into the simple splendors
Of another temperate spring;

But this much I know:

It is not lost among the autumn leaves on Peter's Square.
It is not among the ashes in the Athenaeum ash cans.
It is not inside the blue pagodas of your fine Chinoiserie.

It is not in Vronsky's saddlebags;
Not in Sonnet XXX, stanza one;
Not on twenty-seven red . . .

Where Is It Now? (Lines 1–19)
Count Alexander Ilyich Rostov
1913

APPEARANCE OF COUNT ALEXANDER ILYICH ROSTOV
BEFORE THE EMERGENCY COMMITTEE OF THE PEOPLE'S
COMMISSARIAT FOR INTERNAL AFFAIRS

Presiding: Comrades V. A. Ignatov,
M. S. Zakovsky, A. N. Kosarev

Prosecuting: A. Y. Vyshinsky

Prosecutor Vyshinsky: State your name.

Rostov: Count Alexander Ilyich Rostov, recipient of the Order of Saint Andrew, member of the Jockey Club, Master of the Hunt.

Vyshinsky: You may have your titles; they are of no use to anyone else. But for the record, are you not Alexander Rostov, born in St. Petersburg, 24 October 1889?

Rostov: I am he.

Vyshinsky: Before we begin, I must say, I do not think that I have ever seen a jacket festooned with so many buttons.

Rostov: Thank you.

Vyshinsky: It was not meant as a compliment.

Rostov: In that case, I demand satisfaction on the field of honor.

[*Laughter.*]

Secretary Ignatov: Silence in the gallery.

Vyshinsky: What is your current address?

Rostov: Suite 317 at the Hotel Metropol, Moscow.

Vyshinsky: How long have you lived there?

Rostov: I have been in residence since the fifth of
    September 1918. Just under four years.

Vyshinsky: And your occupation?

Rostov: It is not the business of gentlemen to have
    occupations.

Vyshinsky: Very well then. How do you spend your
    time?

Rostov: Dining, discussing. Reading, reflecting. The
    usual rigmarole.

Vyshinsky: And you write poetry?

Rostov: I have been known to fence with a quill.

Vyshinsky: [*Holding up a pamphlet*] Are you the author
    of this long poem of 1913: *Where Is It Now?*

Rostov: It has been attributed to me.

Vyshinsky: Why did you write the poem?

Rostov: It demanded to be written. I simply happened
    to be sitting at the particular desk on the
    particular morning when it chose to make its
    demands.

Vyshinsky: And where was that exactly?

Rostov: In the south parlor at Idlehour.

Vyshinsky: Idlehour?

Rostov: The Rostov estate in Nizhny Novgorod.

Vyshinsky: Ah, yes. Of course. How apt. But let us
    return our attention to your poem. Coming as it
    did—in the more subdued years after the failed
    revolt of 1905—many considered it a call to action.
    Would you agree with that assessment?

Rostov: All poetry is a call to action.

Vyshinsky: [*Checking notes*] And it was in the spring
    of the following year that you left Russia for
    Paris . . . ?

Rostov: I seem to remember blossoms on the apple
    trees. So, yes, in all likelihood it was spring.

Vyshinsky: May 16 to be precise. Now, we understand
    the reasons for your self-imposed exile; and we
    even have some sympathy with the actions that
    prompted your flight. What concerns us here is
    your return in 1918. One wonders if you came back
    with the intention of taking up arms and, if so,
    whether for or against the Revolution.

Rostov: By that point, I'm afraid that my days of
    taking up arms were behind me.
Vyshinsky: Why then did you come back?
Rostov: I missed the climate.

[*Laughter.*]

Vyshinsky: Count Rostov, you do not seem to
    appreciate the gravity of your position. Nor do
    you show the respect that is due the men convened
    before you.
Rostov: The Tsarina had the same complaints about me
    in her day.
Ignatov: Prosecutor Vyshinsky. If I may . . .
Vyshinsky: Secretary Ignatov.
Ignatov: I have no doubt, Count Rostov, that many in
    the gallery are surprised to find you so charming;
    but I, for one, am not surprised in the least.
    History has shown charm to be the final ambition
    of the leisure class. What I do find surprising is
    that the author of the poem in question could have
    become a man so obviously without purpose.
Rostov: I have lived under the impression that a
    man's purpose is known only to God.
Ignatov: Indeed. How convenient that must have been
    for you.

[*The Committee recesses for twelve minutes.*]

Ignatov: Alexander Ilyich Rostov, taking into full
    account your own testimony, we can only assume
    that the clear-eyed spirit who wrote the poem
    Where Is It Now? has succumbed irrevocably to the
    corruptions of his class—and now poses a threat to
    the very ideals he once espoused. On that basis,
    our inclination would be to have you taken from
    this chamber and put against the wall. But there
    are those within the senior ranks of the Party who
    count you among the heroes of the prerevolutionary
    cause. Thus, it is the opinion of this committee
    that you should be returned to that hotel of which

you are so fond. But make no mistake: should you
ever set foot outside of the Metropol again, you
will be shot. Next matter.

Bearing the signatures of
V. A. Ignatov
M. S. Zakovsky
A. N. Kosarev

BOOK ONE

BOOK ONE

1922

An Ambassador

A t half past six on the twenty-first of June 1922, when Count Alexander Ilyich Rostov was escorted through the gates of the Kremlin onto Red Square, it was glorious and cool. Drawing his shoulders back without breaking stride, the Count inhaled the air like one fresh from a swim. The sky was the very blue that the cupolas of St. Basil's had been painted for. Their pinks, greens, and golds shimmered as if it were the sole purpose of a religion to cheer its Divinity. Even the Bolshevik girls conversing before the windows of the State Department Store seemed dressed to celebrate the last days of spring.

"Hello, my good man," the Count called to Fyodor, at the edge of the square. "I see the blackberries have come in early this year!"

Giving the startled fruit seller no time to reply, the Count walked briskly on, his waxed moustaches spread like the wings of a gull. Passing through Resurrection Gate, he turned his back on the lilacs of the Alexander Gardens and proceeded toward Theatre Square, where the Hotel Metropol stood in all its glory. When he reached the threshold, the Count gave a wink to Pavel, the afternoon doorman, and turned with a hand outstretched to the two soldiers trailing behind him.

"Thank you, gentlemen, for delivering me safely. I shall no longer be in need of your assistance."

Though strapping lads, both of the soldiers had to look up from under their caps to return the Count's gaze—for like ten generations of Rostov men, the Count stood an easy six foot three.

"On you go," said the more thuggish of the two, his hand on the butt of his rifle. "We're to see you to your rooms."

In the lobby, the Count gave a wide wave with which to simultaneously greet the unflappable Arkady (who was manning the front desk) and sweet Valentina (who was dusting a statuette). Though the Count had greeted them in this manner a hundred times before, both responded with a wide-eyed stare. It was the sort of reception one might have expected when arriving for a dinner party having forgotten to don one's pants.

Passing the young girl with the penchant for yellow who was reading a magazine in her favorite lobby chair, the Count came to an abrupt stop before the potted palms in order to address his escort.

"The lift or the stairs, gentlemen?"

The soldiers looked from one another to the Count and back again, apparently unable to make up their minds.

How is a soldier expected to prevail on the field of battle, the Count wondered, if he cannot be decisive about ascending to an upper floor?

"The stairs," he determined on their behalf, then vaulted the steps two at a time, as had been his habit since the academy.

On the third floor, the Count walked down the red-carpeted hallway toward his suite—an interconnected bedroom, bath, dining room, and grand salon with eight-foot windows overlooking the lindens of Theatre Square. And there the rudeness of the day awaited. For before the flung-open doors of his rooms stood a captain of the guards with Pasha and Petya, the hotel's bellhops. The two young men met the Count's gaze with looks of embarrassment, having clearly been conscripted into some duty they found distasteful. The Count addressed the officer.

"What is the meaning of this, Captain?"

The captain, who seemed mildly surprised by the question, had the good training to maintain the evenness of his affect.

"I am here to show you to your quarters."

"These *are* my quarters."

Betraying the slightest suggestion of a smile, the captain replied, "No longer, I'm afraid."

Leaving Pasha and Petya behind, the captain led the Count and his escort to a utility stair hidden behind an inconspicuous door in the core of the hotel. The ill-lit ascent turned a sharp corner every five steps in the manner of a belfry. Up they wound three flights to where a door opened on a narrow corridor servicing a bathroom and six bedrooms reminiscent of monastic cells. This attic was originally built to house the butlers and ladies' maids of the Metropol's guests; but when the practice of traveling with servants fell out of fashion, the unused rooms had been claimed by the caprices of casual urgency—thenceforth warehousing scraps of lumber, broken furniture, and other assorted debris.

Earlier that day, the room closest to the stairwell had been cleared of all but a cast-iron bed, a three-legged bureau, and a decade of dust. In the corner near the door was a small closet, rather like a telephone box, that had been dropped in the room as an afterthought. Reflecting the pitch of the roof, the ceiling sloped at a gradual incline as it moved away from the door, such that at the room's outer wall the only place where the Count could stand to his full height was where a dormer accommodated a window the size of a chessboard.

As the two guards looked on smugly from the hall, the good captain explained that he had summoned the bellhops to help the Count move what few belongings his new quarters would accommodate.

"And the rest?"

"Becomes the property of the People."

So this is their game, thought the Count.

"Very well."

Back down the belfry he skipped as the guards hurried behind him, their rifles clacking against the wall. On the third floor, he marched along the hallway and into his suite where the two bellhops looked up with woeful expressions.

"It's all right, fellows," the Count assured and then began pointing: "This. That. Those. *All* the books."

Among the furnishings destined for his new quarters, the Count chose two high-back chairs, his grandmother's oriental coffee table, and a favorite set of her porcelain plates. He chose the two table lamps fashioned from ebony elephants and the portrait of his sister, Helena, which Serov had painted during a brief stay at Idlehour in 1908. He did not forget the leather case that had been fashioned especially for him by Asprey in London and which his good friend Mishka had so appropriately christened the Ambassador.

Someone had shown the courtesy of having one of the Count's traveling trunks brought to his bedroom. So, as the bellhops carried the aforementioned upward, the Count filled the trunk with clothes and personal effects. Noting that the guards were eyeing the two bottles of brandy on the console, the Count tossed them in as well. And once the trunk had been carried upstairs, he finally pointed to the desk.

The two bellhops, their bright blue uniforms already smudged from their efforts, took hold of it by the corners.

"But it weighs a ton," said one to the other.

"A king fortifies himself with a castle," observed the Count, "a gentleman with a desk."

As the bellhops lugged it into the hall, the Rostovs' grandfather clock, which was fated to be left behind, tolled a doleful eight. The captain had long since returned to his post and the guards, having swapped their belligerence for boredom, now leaned against the wall and let the ashes from their cigarettes fall on the parquet floor while into the grand salon poured the undiminished light of the Moscow summer solstice.

With a wistful eye, the Count approached the windows at the suite's northwest corner. How many hours had he spent before them? How many mornings dressed in his robe with his coffee in hand had he observed the new arrivals from St. Petersburg disembarking from their cabs, worn and weary from the overnight train? On how many winter eves had he watched the snow slowly descending as some lone silhouette, stocky and short, passed under a street lamp? At that very instant, at the square's northern extreme a young Red Army officer rushed up the steps of the Bolshoi, having missed the first half hour of the evening's performance.

The Count smiled to remember his own youthful preference for arriving *entr'acte*. Having insisted at the English Club that he could only stay for one more drink, he stayed for three. Then leaping into the waiting carriage, he'd flash across the city, vault the fabled steps, and like this young fellow slip through the golden doors. As the ballerinas danced gracefully across the stage, the Count would be whispering his *excusez-moi*'s, making his way to his usual seat in the twentieth row with its privileged view of the ladies in the loges.

Arriving late, thought the Count with a sigh. What a delicacy of youth.

Then he turned on his heels and began to walk his rooms. First, he admired the salon's grand dimensions and its two chandeliers. He admired the painted panels of the little dining room and the elaborate brass mechanics that allowed one to secure the double doors of the bedroom. In short, he reviewed the interior much as would a potential buyer who was seeing the rooms for the very first time. Once in the bedroom, the Count paused before the marble-topped table on which lay an assortment of curios. From among them, he picked up a pair of scissors that had been prized by his sister. Fashioned in the shape of an egret with the long silver blades representing the bird's beak and the small golden screw at the pivot representing its eye, the scissors were so delicate he could barely fit his thumb and finger through the rings.

Looking from one end of the apartment to the other, the Count took a quick inventory of all that would be left behind. What personal possessions, furnishings, and *objets d'art* he had brought to this suite four years before were already the product of a great winnowing. For when word had reached the Count of the Tsar's execution, he had set out from Paris at once. Over twenty days, he had made his way across six nations and skirted eight battalions fighting under five different flags, finally arriving at Idlehour on the seventh of August 1918, with nothing but a rucksack on his back. Though he found the countryside on the verge of upheaval and the household in a state of distress, his grandmother, the Countess, was characteristically composed.

"Sasha," she said without rising from her chair, "how good of you to come. You must be famished. Join me for tea."

When he explained the necessity of her leaving the country and described the arrangements he had made for her passage, the Countess understood that there was no alternative. She understood that although every servant in her employ was ready to accompany her, she must travel with two. She also understood why her grandson and only heir, whom she had raised from the age of ten, would not be coming with her.

When the Count was just seven, he was defeated so soundly by a neighboring boy in a game of draughts that, apparently, a tear was shed, a curse was uttered, and the game pieces were scattered across the floor. This lack of sportsmanship led to a stiff reprimand from the Count's father and a trip to bed without supper. But as the young Count was gripping his blanket in misery, he was visited by his grandmother. Taking a seat at the foot of the bed, the Countess expressed a measure of sympathy: "There is nothing pleasant to be said about losing," she began, "and the Obolensky boy is a pill. But, Sasha, my dear, why on earth would you give him the satisfaction?" It was in this spirit that he and his grandmother parted without tears on the docks in Peterhof. Then the Count returned to the family estate in order to administer its shuttering.

In quick succession came the sweeping of chimneys, the clearing of pantries, and the shrouding of furniture. It was just as if the family were returning to St. Petersburg for the season, except that the dogs were released from their kennels, the horses from their stables, and the servants from their duties. Then, having filled a single wagon with some of the finest of the Rostovs' furniture, the Count bolted the doors and set out for Moscow.

'Tis a funny thing, reflected the Count as he stood ready to abandon his suite. From the earliest age, we must learn to say good-bye to friends and family. We see our parents and siblings off at the station; we visit cousins, attend schools, join the regiment; we marry, or travel abroad. It is part of the human experience that we are constantly gripping a good fellow by the shoulders and wishing him well, taking comfort from the notion that we will hear word of him soon enough.

But experience is less likely to teach us how to bid our dearest possessions *adieu*. And if it were to? We wouldn't welcome the education. For eventually, we come to hold our dearest possessions more closely than we hold our friends. We carry them from place to place, often at considerable expense and inconvenience; we dust and polish their surfaces and reprimand children for playing too roughly in their vicinity—all the while, allowing memories to invest them with greater and greater importance. This armoire, we are prone to recall, is the very one in which we hid as a boy; and it was these silver candelabra that lined our table on Christmas Eve; and it was with this handkerchief that she once dried her tears, et cetera, et cetera. Until we imagine that these carefully preserved possessions might give us genuine solace in the face of a lost companion.

But, of course, a thing is just a thing.

And so, slipping his sister's scissors into his pocket, the Count looked once more at what heirlooms remained and then expunged them from his heartache forever.

One hour later, as the Count bounced twice on his new mattress to identify the key of the bedsprings (G-sharp), he surveyed the furniture that had been stacked around him and reminded himself how, as a youth, he had longed for trips to France by steamship and Moscow by the overnight train.

And why had he longed for those particular journeys?

Because their berths had been so small!

What a marvel it had been to discover the table that folded away without a trace; and the drawers built into the base of the bed; and the wall-mounted lamps just large enough to illuminate a page. This efficiency of design was music to the young mind. It attested to a precision of purpose and the promise of adventure. For such would have been the quarters of Captain Nemo when he journeyed twenty thousand leagues beneath the sea. And wouldn't any young boy with the slightest gumption gladly trade a hundred nights in a palace for one aboard the *Nautilus*?

Well. At long last, here he was.

Besides, with half the rooms on the second floor temporarily commandeered by the Bolsheviks for the tireless typing of directives, at least on the sixth floor a man could hear himself think.*

The Count stood and banged his head on the slope of the ceiling.

"Just so," he replied.

Easing one of the high-back chairs aside and moving the elephant lamps to the bed, the Count opened his trunk. First, he took out the

---

*In fact, it was into the suite directly below the Count's that Yakov Sverdlov, the first chairman of the All-Russian Executive Committee, had locked the constitutional drafting committee—vowing he would not turn the key again until they had completed their work. Thus did the typewriters clack through the night, until that historic document had been crafted which guaranteed for all Russians freedom of conscience (Article 13), freedom of expression (Article 14), freedom of assembly (Article 15), and freedom to have any of these rights revoked should they be "utlitized to the detriment of the socialist revolution" (Article 23)!

photograph of the Delegation and placed it on the desk where it belonged. Then he took out the two bottles of brandy and his father's twice-tolling clock. But when he took out his grandmother's opera glasses and placed them on the desk, a fluttering drew his attention toward the dormer. Though the window was only the size of a dinner invitation, the Count could see that a pigeon had landed outside on the copper stripping of the ledge.

"Why, hello," said the Count. "How kind of you to stop by."

The pigeon looked back with a decidedly proprietary air. Then it scuffed the flashing with its claws and thrust its beak at the window several times in quick succession.

"Ah, yes," conceded the Count. "There is something in what you say."

He was about to explain to his new neighbor the cause of his unexpected arrival, when from the hallway came the delicate clearing of a throat. Without turning, the Count could tell that this was Andrey, the maître d' of the Boyarsky, for it was his trademark interruption.

Nodding once to the pigeon to indicate that they would resume their discussion anon, the Count rebuttoned his jacket and turned to find that it was not Andrey alone who had paid a visit: three members of the hotel's staff were crowded in the doorway.

There was Andrey with his perfect poise and long judicious hands; Vasily, the hotel's inimitable concierge; and Marina, the shy delight with the wandering eye who had recently been promoted from chambermaid to seamstress. The three of them exhibited the same bewildered gaze that the Count had noticed on the faces of Arkady and Valentina a few hours before, and finally it struck him: When he had been carted off that morning, they had all assumed that he would never return. He had emerged from behind the walls of the Kremlin like an aviator from the wreckage of a crash.

"My dear friends," said the Count, "no doubt you are curious as to the day's events. As you may know, I was invited to the Kremlin for a *tête-à-tête*. There, several duly goateed officers of the current regime determined that for the crime of being born an aristocrat, I should be sentenced to spend the rest of my days . . . in this hotel."

In response to the cheers, the Count shook hands with his guests one by one, expressing to each his appreciation for their fellowship and his heartfelt thanks.

"Come in, come in," he said.

Together, the three staff members squeezed their way between the teetering towers of furniture.

"If you would be so kind," said the Count, handing Andrey one of the bottles of brandy. Then he kneeled before the Ambassador, threw the clasps, and opened it like a giant book. Carefully secured inside were fifty-two glasses—or more precisely, twenty-six *pairs* of glasses—each shaped to its purpose, from the grand embrace of the Burgundy glass down to those charming little vessels designed for the brightly colored liqueurs of southern Europe. In the spirit of the hour, the Count picked four glasses at random and passed them around as Andrey, having plucked the cork from the bottle, performed the honors.

Once his guests had their brandy in hand, the Count raised his own on high.

"To the Metropol," he said.

"To the Metropol!" they replied.

The Count was something of a natural-born host and in the hour that ensued, as he topped a glass here and sparked a conversation there, he had an instinctive awareness of all the temperaments in the room. Despite the formality appropriate to his position, tonight Andrey exhibited a ready smile and an occasional wink. Vasily, who spoke with such pointed accuracy when providing directions to the city's sights, suddenly had the lilt of one who may or may not remember tomorrow what he had said today. And at every jest, the shy Marina allowed herself to giggle without placing a hand in front of her lips.

On this of all nights, the Count deeply appreciated their good cheer; but he was not so vain as to imagine it was founded solely on news of his narrow escape. For as he knew better than most, it was in September of 1905 that the members of the Delegation had signed the Treaty of Portsmouth to end the Russo-Japanese War. In the seventeen years since the making of that peace—hardly a generation—Russia had suffered a world war, a civil war, two famines, and the so-called Red Terror. In short, it had been through an era of upheaval that had spared none. Whether one's leanings were left or right, Red or White, whether one's personal circumstances had changed for the better or changed for the worse, surely at long last it was time to drink to the health of the nation.

At ten o'clock, the Count walked his guests to the belfry and bid them goodnight with the same sense of ceremony that he would have exhibited at the door of his family's residence in St. Petersburg. Returning to his quarters, he opened the window (though it was only the size of a postage stamp), poured the last of the brandy, and took a seat at the desk.

Built in the Paris of Louis XVI with the gilded accents and leather top of the era, the desk had been left to the Count by his godfather, Grand Duke Demidov. A man of great white sideburns, pale blue eyes, and golden epaulettes, the Grand Duke spoke four languages and read six. Never to wed, he represented his country at Portsmouth, managed three estates, and generally prized industry over nonsense. But before all of that, he had served alongside the Count's father as a devil-may-care cadet in the cavalry. Thus had the Grand Duke become the Count's watchful guardian. And when the Count's parents succumbed to cholera within hours of each other in 1900, it was the Grand Duke who took the young Count aside and explained that he must be strong for his sister's sake; that adversity presents itself in many forms; and that if a man does not master his circumstances then he is bound to be mastered by them.

The Count ran his hand across the desk's dimpled surface.

How many of the Grand Duke's words did those faint indentations reflect? Here over forty years had been written concise instructions to caretakers; persuasive arguments to statesmen; exquisite counsel to friends. In other words, it was a desk to be reckoned with.

Emptying his glass, the Count pushed his chair back and sat on the floor. He ran his hand behind the desk's right front leg until he found the catch. When he pressed it, a seamless door opened to reveal a velvet-lined hollow that, like the hollows in the other three legs, was stacked with pieces of gold.

An Anglican Ashore

When he began to stir at half past nine, in the shapeless moments before the return to consciousness Count Alexander Ilyich Rostov savored the taste of the day to come.

Within the hour, he would be in the warm spring air striding along Tverskaya Street, his moustaches at full sail. En route, he would purchase the *Herald* from the stand on Gazetny Lane, he would pass Filippov's (pausing only briefly to eye the pastries in the window) and then continue on to meet with his bankers.

But coming to a halt at the curb (in order to let the traffic pass), the Count would note that his lunch at the Jockey Club was scheduled for two o'clock—and that while his bankers were expecting him at half past ten, they were for all intents and purposes in the employ of their depositors, and thus could presumably be kept waiting. . . . With these thoughts in mind, he would double back and, taking his top hat from his head, open Filippov's door.

In an instant, his senses would be rewarded by the indisputable evidence of the baker's mastery. Drifting in the air would be the gentle aroma of freshly baked pretzels, sweet rolls, and loaves of bread so unparalleled they were delivered daily to the Hermitage by train—while arranged in perfect rows behind the glass of the front case would be cakes topped in frostings as varied in color as the tulips of Amsterdam. Approaching the counter, the Count would ask the young lady with the light blue apron for a mille-feuille (how aptly named) and watch with admiration as she used a teaspoon to gently nudge the delicacy from a silver spade onto a porcelain plate.

His refreshment in hand, the Count would take a seat as close as possible to the little table in the corner where young ladies of fashion met each morning to review the previous evening's intrigues. Mindful of their surroundings, the three damsels would initially speak in the hushed voices of gentility; but swept away by the currents of their own emotions, their voices would inevitably rise, such that by 11:15, even the most discreet enjoyer of a pastry would have no choice but to eavesdrop on the thousand-layered complications of their hearts.

By 11:45, having cleaned his plate and brushed the crumbs from his moustaches, having waved a thanks to the girl behind the counter and tipped his hat to the three young ladies with whom he had briefly chatted, he would step back onto Tverskaya Street and pause to consider: *What next?* Perhaps he would stop by Galerie Bertrand to see the latest canvases from Paris, or slip into the hall of the Conservatory where some youthful quartet was trying to master a bit of Beethoven; perhaps he would simply circle back to the Alexander Gardens, where he could find a bench and admire the lilacs as a pigeon cooed and shuffled its feet on the copper flashing of the sill.

On the copper flashing of the sill . . .

"Ah, yes," acknowledged the Count. "I suppose there's to be none of that."

If the Count were to close his eyes and roll to the wall, was it possible that he could return to his bench just in time to remark, *What a lovely coincidence*, when the three young ladies from Filippov's happened by?

Without a doubt. But imagining what might happen if one's circumstances were different was the only sure route to madness.

Sitting upright, the Count put the soles of his feet squarely on the uncarpeted floor and gave the compass points of his moustaches a twist.

On the Grand Duke's desk stood a champagne flute and a brandy snifter. With the lean uprightness of the former looking down upon the squat rotundity of the latter, one could not help but think of Don Quixote and Sancho Panza on the plains of the Sierra Morena. Or of Robin Hood and Friar Tuck in the shadows of Sherwood Forest. Or of Prince Hal and Falstaff before the gates of—

But there was a knock at the door.

The Count stood and hit his head against the ceiling.

"One moment," he called, rubbing his crown and rummaging through his trunk for a robe. Once suitably attired, he opened the door to find an industrious young fellow standing in the hall with the Count's daily breakfast—a pot of coffee, two biscuits, and a piece of fruit (today a plum).

"Well done, Yuri! Come in, come in. Set it there, set it there."

As Yuri arranged the breakfast on top of the trunk, the Count sat at the Grand Duke's desk and penned a quick note to one Konstantin Konstantinovich of Durnovksi Street.

"Would you be so kind as to have this delivered, my boy?"

Never one to shirk, Yuri happily took the note, promised to relay it by hand, and accepted a tip with a bow. Then at the threshold he paused.

"Shall I . . . leave the door ajar?"

It was a reasonable question. For the room was rather stuffy, and on the sixth floor there was hardly much risk of one's privacy being compromised.

"Please do."

As Yuri's steps sounded down the belfry, the Count placed his napkin in his lap, poured a cup of coffee, and graced it with a few drops of cream. Taking his first sip, he noted with satisfaction that young Yuri must have sprinted up the extra three flights of stairs because the coffee was not one degree colder than usual.

But while he was liberating a wedge of the plum from its pit with his paring knife, the Count happened to note a silvery shadow, as seemingly insubstantial as a puff of smoke, slipping behind his trunk. Leaning to his side in order to peer around a high-back chair, the Count discovered that this will-o'-the-wisp was none other than the Metropol's lobby cat. A one-eyed Russian blue who let nothing within the hotel's walls escape his notice, he had apparently come to the attic to review the Count's new quarters for himself. Stepping from the shadows, he leapt from the floor to the Ambassador, from the Ambassador to the side table, and from the side table to the top of the three-legged bureau, without making a sound. Having achieved this vantage point, he gave the room a good hard look then shook his head in feline disappointment.

"Yes," said the Count after completing his own survey. "I see what you mean."

The crowded confusion of furniture gave the Count's little domain the look of a consignment shop in the Arbat. In a room this size, he could have made do with a single high-back chair, a single bedside table, and a single lamp. He could have made do without his grandmother's Limoges altogether.

And the books? *All of them!* he had said with such bravado. But in the light of day, he had to admit that this instruction had been prompted less by good sense than by a rather childish impulse to impress the bellhops and put the guards in their place. For the books were not even to the Count's taste. His personal library of majestic narratives by the likes of Balzac, Dickens, and Tolstoy had been left behind in Paris. The books the bellhops had lugged to the attic had been his father's and, devoted as they were to studies of rational philosophy and the science of modern agriculture, each promised heft and threatened impenetrability.

Without a doubt, one more winnowing was called for.

So, having broken his fast, bathed, and dressed, the Count went about the business. First, he tried the door of the adjacent room. It must have been blocked on the inside by something quite heavy, for under the force of the Count's shoulder it barely budged. In the next three rooms, the Count found flotsam and jetsam from floor to ceiling. But in the last room, amidst tiles of slate and strips of flashing, an ample space had been cleared around a dented old samovar where some roofers had once taken their tea.

Back in his room, the Count hung a few jackets in his closet. He unpacked some trousers and shirts into the back right corner of his bureau (to ensure that the three-legged beast wouldn't topple). Down the hall he dragged his trunk, half of his furniture, and all of his father's books but one. Thus, within an hour he had reduced his room to its essentials: a desk and chair, a bed and bedside table, a high-back chair for guests, and a ten-foot passage just wide enough for a gentleman to circumambulate in reflection.

With satisfaction the Count looked toward the cat (who was busy licking the cream from his paws in the comfort of the high-back chair). "What say you now, you old pirate?"

Then he sat at his desk and picked up the one volume that he had retained. It must have been a decade since the Count had first promised himself to read this work of universal acclaim that his father had held so dear. And yet, every time he had pointed his finger at his calendar and declared: *This is the month in which I shall devote myself to the* Essays *of Michel de Montaigne!* some devilish aspect of life had poked its head in the door. From an unexpected corner had come an expression of romantic interest, which could not in good conscience be ignored. Or his banker had called. Or the circus had come to town.

Life will entice, after all.

But here, at last, circumstance had conspired not to distract the Count, but to present him with the time and solitude necessary to give the book its due. So, with the volume firmly in hand, he put one foot on the corner of the bureau, pushed back until his chair was balanced on its two rear legs, and began to read:

By Diverse Means We Arrive at the Same End

The commonest way of softening the hearts of those we have offended, when, vengeance in hand, they hold us at their mercy, is by submission to move them to commiseration and pity. However, audacity and steadfastness—entirely contrary means—have sometimes served to produce the same effect. . . .

It was at Idlehour that the Count had first formed the habit of reading in a tilted chair.

On those glorious spring days when the orchards were in bloom and the foxtails bobbed above the grass, he and Helena would seek out a pleasant corner to while away the hours. One day it might be under the pergola on the upper patio and the next beside the great elm that overlooked the bend in the river. As Helena embroidered, the Count would tilt back his chair—balancing himself by resting a foot lightly on the lip of the fountain or the trunk of the tree—in order to read aloud from her favorite works of Pushkin. And hour upon hour, stanza upon stanza, her little needle would go round and round.

"Where are all those stitches headed?" he would occasionally demand at the end of a page. "Surely, by now, every pillow in the household has been graced by a butterfly and every handkerchief by a monogram." And when he accused her of unwinding her stitches at night like Penelope just so that he would have to read her another volume of verse, she would smile inscrutably.

Looking up from the pages of Montaigne, the Count rested his gaze on Helena's portrait, which was leaning against the wall. Painted at Idlehour in the month of August, it depicted his sister at the dining room table before a plate of peaches. How well Serov had captured her likeness—with her hair as black as a raven's, her cheeks lightly flushed, her expression tender and forgiving. Perhaps there had been something in those stitches, thought the Count, some gentle wisdom that she was mastering through the completion of every little loop. Yes, with such kindheartedness at the age of fourteen, one could only imagine the grace she might have exhibited at the age of twenty-five. . . .

The Count was roused from this reverie by a delicate tapping. Closing his father's book, he looked back to find a sixty-year-old Greek in the doorway.

"Konstantin Konstantinovich!"

Letting the front legs of his chair land on the floor with a thump, the Count crossed to the threshold and took his visitor's hand.

"I am so glad you could come. We have only met once or twice, so you may not remember, but I am Alexander Rostov."

The old Greek gave a bow to show that no reminder was necessary.

"Come in, come in. Have a seat."

Waving Montaigne's masterpiece at the one-eyed cat (who leapt to the floor with a hiss), the Count offered his guest the high-back chair and took the desk chair for himself.

In the moment that ensued, the old Greek returned the Count's gaze with an expression of moderate curiosity—which was to be expected, perhaps, given that they had never met on a matter of business. After all, the Count was not accustomed to losing at cards. So the Count took it upon himself to begin.

"As you can see, Konstantin, my circumstances have changed."

The Count's guest allowed himself an expression of surprise.

"No, it is true," said the Count. "They have changed quite a bit."

Looking once about the room, the old Greek raised his hands to acknowledge the doleful impermanence of circumstances,

"Perhaps you are looking for access to some . . . capital?" he ventured.

In making this suggestion, the old Greek paused ever so briefly before the word *capital*. And in the Count's considered opinion, it was a perfect pause—one mastered over decades of delicate conversations. It was a pause with which he expressed an element of sympathy for his interlocutor without suggesting for even an instant that there had been a change in their relative stations.

"No, no," assured the Count with a shake of the head to emphasize that borrowing was not a habit of the Rostovs. "On the contrary, Konstantin, I have something that I think will be of interest to you." Then, as if from thin air, the Count produced one of the coins from the Grand Duke's desk, balancing it upright on the tip of a finger and thumb.

The old Greek studied the coin for a second and then, in a sign of appreciation, slowly exhaled. For while Konstantin Konstantinovich was a lender by trade, his *art* was to see an item for a minute, to hold it for a moment, and to know its true worth.

"May I . . . ?" he asked.

"By all means."

He took the coin, turned it once, and handed it back with reverence. For not only was the piece pure in the metallurgical sense, the winking double eagle on the reverse confirmed to the experienced eye that it was one of the five thousand coins minted in commemoration of Catherine the Great's coronation. Such a piece purchased from a gentleman in need could be sold at a reasonable profit to the most cautious of banking houses in the best of times. But in a period of upheaval? Even as the demand for common luxuries collapsed, the value of a treasure like this would be on the rise.

"Excuse my curiosity, Your Excellency, but is that a . . . lonely piece?"

"Lonely? Oh, no," replied the Count with a shake of the head. "It lives like a soldier in a barracks. Like a slave in a galley. Not a moment to itself, I'm afraid."

The old Greek exhaled again.

"Well then . . ."

And in a matter of minutes the two men had struck an arrangement without a hem or haw. What is more, the old Greek said it would be his pleasure to personally deliver three notes, which the Count penned on the spot. Then they shook hands like familiars and agreed to see each other three months hence.

But just as the old Greek was about to step through the door, he paused.

"Your Excellency . . . May I ask a personal question?"

"By all means."

He gestured almost shyly to the Grand Duke's desk.

"Can we expect more verses from you?"

The Count offered an appreciative smile.

"I am sorry to say, Konstantin, that my days of poetry are behind me."

"If your days of poetry are behind you, Count Rostov, then it is we who are sorry."

Tucked discreetly into the northeast corner of the hotel's second floor was the Boyarsky—the finest restaurant in Moscow, if not in all of Russia. With vaulted ceilings and dark red walls reminiscent of a boyar's retreat, the Boyarsky boasted the city's most elegant décor, its most sophisticated waiters, and its most subtle chef de cuisine.

So renowned was the experience of dining at the Boyarsky that on any given night one might have to elbow one's way through a crowd of hopefuls just to catch the eye of Andrey, as he presided over the large black book in which the names of the fortunate were set down; and when beckoned ahead by the maître d', one could expect to be stopped five times in four languages on the way to one's table in the corner, where one would be served flawlessly by a waiter in a white dinner jacket.

That is, one could expect this until 1920 when, having already sealed the borders, the Bolsheviks decided to prohibit the use of rubles in fine restaurants—effectively closing them to 99 percent of the population. So tonight, as the Count began to eat his entrée, water glasses clinked against cutlery, couples whispered awkwardly, and even the best of waiters found himself staring at the ceiling.

But every period has its virtues, even a time of turmoil. . . .

When Emile Zhukovsky was lured to the Metropol as chef de cuisine in 1912, he was given command of a seasoned staff and a sizable kitchen. In addition, he had the most celebrated larder east of Vienna. On his spice shelves was a compendium of the world's predilections and in his cooler a comprehensive survey of birds and beasts hanging from hooks by their feet. As such, one might naturally leap to the conclusion that 1912 had been a perfect year in which to measure the chef's talents. But in a period of abundance any half-wit with a spoon can please a palate. To truly test a chef's ingenuity, one must instead look to a period of want. And what provides want better than war?

In the Revolution's aftermath—with its economic declines, failed crops, and halted trade—refined ingredients became as scarce in Moscow as butterflies at sea. The Metropol's larder was depleted bushel by bushel, pound by pound, dash by dash, and its chef was left to meet the expectations of his audience with cornmeal, cauliflower, and cabbage—that is to say, with whatever he could get his hands on.

Yes, some claimed Emile Zhukovsky was a curmudgeon and others called him abrupt. Some said he was a short man with a shorter temper. But none could dispute his genius. Just consider the dish the Count was finishing at that very moment: a saltimbocca fashioned from necessity. In place of a cutlet of veal, Emile had pounded flat a breast of chicken. In place of prosciutto de Parma, he had shaved a Ukrainian ham. And in place of sage, that delicate leaf that binds the flavors together? He had opted for an herb that was as soft and aromatic as sage, but more bitter to the taste. . . . It wasn't basil or oregano, of that the Count was certain, but he had definitely encountered it somewhere before. . . .

"How is everything this evening, Your Excellency?"

"Ah, Andrey. As usual, everything is perfect."

"And the saltimbocca?"

"Inspired. But I do have one question: The herb that Emile has tucked under the ham—I know it isn't sage. By any chance, is it nettle?"

"Nettle? I don't believe so. But I will inquire."

Then with a bow, the maître d' excused himself.

Without a doubt Emile Zhukovsky was a genius, reflected the Count, but the man who secured the Boyarsky's reputation for excellence by ensuring that all within its walls ran smoothly was Andrey Duras.

Born in the south of France, Andrey was handsome, tall, and graying at the temples, but his most distinguishing feature was not his looks, his height, or his hair. It was his hands. Pale and well manicured, his fingers were half an inch longer than the fingers of most men his height. Had he been a pianist, Andrey could easily have straddled a twelfth. Had he been a puppeteer, he could have performed the sword fight between Macbeth and Macduff as all three witches looked on. But Andrey was neither a pianist nor a puppeteer—or at least not in the traditional sense. He was the captain of the Boyarsky, and one watched in wonder as his hands fulfilled their purpose at every turn.

Having just led a group of women to their table, for instance, Andrey seemed to pull back their chairs all at once. When one of the ladies produced a cigarette, he had a lighter in one hand and was guarding the flame with the other (as if a draft had ever been felt within the walls of the Boyarsky!). And when the woman holding the wine list asked for a recommendation, he didn't point to the 1900 Bordeaux—at least not in the Teutonic sense. Rather, he slightly extended his index finger in a manner reminiscent of that gesture on the Sistine Chapel's ceiling with which the Prime Mover transmitted the spark of life. Then, excusing himself with a bow, he crossed the room and went through the kitchen door.

But before a minute could pass, the door swung open again—and there was Emile.

Five foot five and two hundred pounds, the chef glanced quickly about the room then marched toward the Count with Andrey trailing behind. As he crossed the dining room, the chef knocked into a customer's chair and nearly toppled a busboy with his tray. Coming to an abrupt stop at the Count's table, he looked him up and down as one might measure an opponent before challenging him to a duel.

"Bravo, monsieur," he said in a tone of indignation. *"Bravo!"*

Then he turned on his heels and disappeared back into his kitchen.

Andrey, a little breathless, bowed to express both apologies and congratulations.

"Nettle it was, Your Excellency. Your palate remains unsurpassed."

Though the Count was not a man to gloat, he could not repress a smile of satisfaction.

Knowing that the Count had a sweet tooth, Andrey gestured toward the dessert cart.

"May I bring you a slice of plum tart with our compliments . . . ?"

"Thank you for the thought, Andrey. Normally, I would leap at the chance. But tonight, I am otherwise committed."

Having acknowledged that a man must master his circumstances or otherwise be mastered by them, the Count thought it worth considering how one was most likely to achieve this aim when one had been sentenced to a life of confinement.

For Edmond Dantès in the Château d'If, it was thoughts of revenge that kept him clear minded. Unjustly imprisoned, he sustained himself by plotting the systematic undoing of his personal agents of villainy. For Cervantes, enslaved by pirates in Algiers, it was the promise of pages as yet unwritten that spurred him on. While for Napoleon on Elba, strolling among chickens, fending off flies, and sidestepping puddles of mud, it was visions of a triumphal return to Paris that galvanized his will to persevere.

But the Count hadn't the temperament for revenge; he hadn't the imagination for epics; and he certainly hadn't the fanciful ego to dream of empires restored. No. His model for mastering his circumstances would be a different sort of captive altogether: an Anglican washed ashore. Like Robinson Crusoe stranded on the Isle of Despair, the Count would maintain his resolve by committing to the business of *practicalities*. Having dispensed with dreams of quick discovery, the world's Crusoes seek shelter and a source of fresh water; they teach themselves to make fire from flint; they study their island's topography, its climate, its flora and fauna, all the while keeping their eyes trained for sails on the horizon and footprints in the sand.

It was to this end that the Count had given the old Greek three notes to deliver. Within a matter of hours, the Count had been visited by two messengers: a young lad from Muir & Mirrielees bearing fine linens and a suitable pillow; and another from Petrovsky Passage with four bars of the Count's favorite soap.

And the third respondent? She must have arrived while the Count was at dinner. For waiting on his bed was a light blue box with a single mille-feuille.

An Appointment

Never had the chime of twelve been so welcome. Not in Russia. Not in Europe. Not in all the world. Had Romeo been told by Juliet that she would appear at her window at noon, the young Veronan's rapture at the appointed hour could not have matched the Count's. Had Dr. Stahlbaum's children—Fritz and Clara—been told on Christmas morning that the drawing-room doors would be opened at midday, their elation could not have rivaled the Count's upon the sounding of the first toll.

For having successfully fended off thoughts of Tverskaya Street (and chance encounters with young ladies of fashion), having bathed, dressed, and finished his coffee and fruit (today a fig), shortly after ten the Count had eagerly taken up Montaigne's masterpiece only to discover that at every fifteenth line, his gaze was drifting toward the clock . . .

Admittedly, the Count had felt a touch of concern when he'd first lifted the book from the desk the day before. For as a single volume, it had the density of a dictionary or Bible—those books that one expects to consult, or possibly peruse, but never *read*. But it was the Count's review of the Contents—a list of 107 essays on the likes of Constancy, Moderation, Solitude, and Sleep—that confirmed his initial suspicion that the book had been written with winter nights in mind. Without a doubt, it was a book for when the birds had flown south, the wood was stacked by the fireplace, and the fields were white with snow; that is, for when one had no desire to venture out and one's friends had no desire to venture in.

Nonetheless, with a resolute glance at the time, much as a seasoned sea captain when setting out on an extended journey will log the exact hour he sets sail from port, the Count plowed once again into the waves of the first meditation: "By Diverse Means We Arrive at the Same End."

In this opening essay—in which examples were expertly drawn from the annals of history—the author provided a most convincing argument that when one is at another's mercy one should plead for one's life.

Or remain proud and unbent.

At any rate, having firmly established that either approach might be the right one, the author proceeded to his second meditation: "Of Sadness."

Here, Montaigne quoted an array of unimpeachable authorities from the Golden Age who confirmed conclusively that sadness is an emotion best shared.

Or kept to oneself.

It was somewhere in the middle of the third essay that the Count found himself glancing at the clock for the fourth or fifth time. Or was it the sixth? While the exact number of glances could not be determined, the evidence did seem to suggest that the Count's attention had been drawn to the clock more than once.

But then, what a chronometer it was!

Made to order for the Count's father by the venerable firm of Breguet, the twice-tolling clock was a masterpiece in its own right. Its white enamel face had the circumference of a grapefruit and its lapis lazuli body sloped asymptotically from its top to its base, while its jeweled inner workings had been cut by craftsmen known the world over for an unwavering commitment to precision. And their reputation was certainly well founded. For as he progressed through the third essay (in which Plato, Aristotle, and Cicero had been crowded onto the couch with the Emperor Maximilian), the Count could hear every tick.

Ten twenty and fifty-six seconds, the clock said.

Ten twenty and fifty-seven.

Fifty-eight.

Fifty-nine.

Why, this clock accounted the seconds as flawlessly as Homer accounted his dactyls and Peter the sins of the sinners.

But where were we?

Ah, yes: Essay Three.

The Count shifted his chair a little leftward in order to put the clock out of view, then he searched for the passage he'd been reading. He was almost certain it was in the fifth paragraph on the fifteenth page. But as he delved back into that paragraph's prose, the context seemed utterly unfamiliar; as did the paragraphs that immediately preceded it. In fact, he had to turn back three whole pages before he found a passage that he recalled well enough to resume his progress in good faith.

"Is that how it is with you?" the Count demanded of Montaigne. "One step forward and two steps back?"

Intent upon showing who was master of whom, the Count vowed that he would not look up from the book again until he had reached the twenty-fifth essay. Spurred by his own resolve, the Count made quick work of Essays Four, Five, and Six. And when he dispatched Seven and Eight with even more alacrity, the twenty-fifth essay seemed as close at hand as a pitcher of water on a dining room table.

But as the Count advanced through Essays Eleven, Twelve, and Thir-teen, his goal seemed to recede into the distance. It was suddenly as if the book were not a dining room table at all, but a sort of Sahara. And hav-ing emptied his canteen, the Count would soon be crawling across its sentences with the peak of each hard-won page revealing but another page beyond. . . .

Well then, so be it. Onward crawled the Count.

On past the hour of eleven.

On past the sixteenth essay.

Until, suddenly, that long-strided watchman of the minutes caught up with his bowlegged brother at the top of the dial. As the two embraced, the springs within the clock's casing loosened, the wheels spun, and the miniature hammer fell, setting off the first of those dulcet tones that sig-naled the arrival of noon.

The front feet of the Count's chair fell to the floor with a bang, and Monsieur Montaigne turned twice in the air before landing on the bed-covers. By the fourth chime the Count was rounding the belfry stairs, and by the eighth he was passing the lobby en route to the lower floor for his weekly appointment with Yaroslav Yaroslavl, the peerless barber of the Metropol Hotel.

For over two centuries (or so historians tell us), it was from the St. Peters-burg salons that our country's culture advanced. From those great rooms overlooking the Fontanka Canal, new cuisines, fashions, and ideas all took their first tentative steps into Russian society. But if this was so, it was largely due to the hive of activity beneath the parlor floors. For there, just a few steps below street level, were the butlers, cooks, and footmen who together ensured that when the notions of Darwin or Manet were first bandied about, all went off without a hitch.

And so it was in the Metropol.

Ever since its opening in 1905, the hotel's suites and restaurants had been a gathering spot for the glamorous, influential, and erudite; but the effortless elegance on display would not have existed without the services of the lower floor:

Coming off the wide marble steps that descended from the lobby, one first passed the newsstand, which offered a gentleman a hundred headlines, albeit now just in Russian.

Next was the shop of Fatima Federova, the florist. A natural casualty of the times, Fatima's shelves had been emptied and her windows papered over back in 1920, turning one of the hotel's brightest spots into one of its most forlorn. But in its day, the shop had sold flowers by the acre. It had provided the towering arrangements for the lobby, the lilies for the rooms, the bouquets of roses that were tossed at the feet of the Bolshoi ballerinas, as well as the boutonnieres on the men who did the tossing. What's more, Fatima was fluent in the floral codes that had governed polite society since the Age of Chivalry. Not only did she know the flower that should be sent as an apology, she knew which flower to send when one has been late; when one has spoken out of turn; and when, having taking notice of the young lady at the door, one has carelessly overtrumped one's partner. In short, Fatima knew a flower's fragrance, color, and purpose better than a bee.

Well, Fatima's may have been shuttered, reflected the Count, but weren't the flower shops of Paris shuttered under the "reign" of Robespierre, and didn't that city now abound in blossoms? Just so, the time for flowers in the Metropol would surely come again.

At the very end of the hall, one finally came to Yaroslav's barbershop. A land of optimism, precision, and political neutrality, it was the Switzerland of the hotel. If the Count had vowed to master his circumstances through practicalities, then here was a glimpse of the means: a religiously kept appointment for a weekly trim.

When the Count entered the shop, Yaroslav was attending to a silver-haired customer in a light gray suit while a heavyset fellow in a rumpled jacket bided his time on the bench by the wall. Greeting the Count with a smile, the barber directed him to the empty chair at his side.

As the Count climbed into the chair, he offered a friendly nod to the heavyset fellow, then leaned back and let his eyes settle on that marvel of Yaroslav's shop: his cabinet. Were one to ask Larousse to define the word *cabinet*, the acclaimed lexicographer might reply: *A piece of furniture often adorned with decorative detail in which items may be stowed away from sight.* A serviceable definition, no doubt—one that would encompass everything from a kitchen cupboard in the countryside to a Chippendale in Bucking-ham Palace. But Yaroslav's cabinet would not fit so neatly into such a descrip-tion, for having been made solely of nickel and glass it had been designed not to hide its contents, but to reveal them to the naked eye.

And rightfully so. For this cabinet could be proud of all it contained: French soaps wrapped in waxed papers; British lathers in ivory drums; Italian tonics in whimsically shaped vials. And hidden in the back? That little black bottle that Yaroslav referred to with a wink as the Fountain of Youth.

In the mirror's reflection, the Count now let his gaze shift to where Yaroslav was working his magic on the silver-haired gentleman with two sets of scissors simultaneously. In Yaroslav's hands, the scissors ini-tially recalled the *entrechat* of the *danseur* in a ballet, his legs switching back and forth in midair. But as the barber progressed, his hands moved with increasing speed until they leapt and kicked like a Cossack doing the hopak! Upon the execution of the final snip, it would have been per-fectly appropriate for a curtain to drop only to be raised again a moment later so that the audience could applaud as the barber took a bow.

Yaroslav swung the white cape off his customer and snapped it in the air; he clicked his heels when accepting payment for a job well done; and as the gentleman exited the shop (looking younger and more distin-guished than when he'd arrived), the barber approached the Count with a fresh cape.

"Your Excellency. How are you?"

"Splendid, Yaroslav. At my utmost."

"And what is on the docket for today?"

"Just a trim, my friend. Just a trim."

As the scissors began their delicate snipping, it seemed to the Count that the heavyset customer on the bench had undergone something of a transformation. Although the Count had given his friendly nod just moments before, in the interim the fellow's face seemed to have taken on a rosier hue. The Count was sure of it, in fact, because the color was spreading to his ears.

The Count tried to make eye contact again, intending to offer another friendly nod, but the fellow had fixed his gaze on Yaroslav's back.

"I was next," he said.

Yaroslav, who like most artists tended to lose himself in his craft, continued clipping away with efficiency and grace. So, the fellow was forced to repeat himself, if a little more emphatically.

"*I was next.*"

Drawn from his artistic spell by the sharper intonation, Yaroslav offered a courteous reply:

"I will be with you in just a moment, sir."

"That is what you said when I arrived."

This was said with such unmistakable hostility that Yaroslav paused in his clipping and turned to meet his customer's glare with a startled expression.

Though the Count had been raised never to interrupt a conversation, he felt that the barber should not be put in the position of having to explain the situation on his behalf. So, he interceded:

"Yaroslav meant no offense, my good man. It just so happens that I have a standing appointment at twelve o'clock on Tuesdays."

The fellow now turned his glare upon the Count.

"A standing appointment," he repeated.

"Yes."

Then he rose so abruptly that he knocked his bench back into the wall. At full height, he was no more than five foot six. His fists, which jutted from the cuffs of his jacket, were as red as his ears. When he advanced a step, Yaroslav backed against the edge of his counter. The fellow took another

step toward the barber and wrested one of the scissors from his hand.
Then, with the deftness of a much slighter man, he turned, took the Count
by the collar, and severed the right wing of his moustaches with a single
snip. Tightening his hold, he pulled the Count forward until they were
nearly nose to nose.

"You'll have your appointment soon enough," he said.

Then shoving the Count back in the chair, he tossed the scissors on
the floor and strolled from the shop.

"Your Excellency," exclaimed Yaroslav, aghast. "I have never seen the
man in my life. I don't even know if he resides in the hotel. But he is not
welcome here again, I assure you of that."

The Count, who was standing now, was inclined to echo Yaroslav's
indignation and commend a punishment that fit the crime. But then, what
did the Count know about his assailant?

When he had first seen him sitting on the bench in his rumpled jacket,
the Count had summed him up in an instant as some hardworking sort
who, having stumbled upon the barbershop, had decided to treat himself to
a cut. But for all the Count knew, this fellow could have been one of the
new residents of the second floor. Having come of age in an ironworks, he
could have joined a union in 1912, led a strike in 1916, captained a Red battalion in 1918, and now found himself in command of an entire industry.

"He was perfectly right," the Count said to Yaroslav. "He had been
waiting in good faith. You only wished to honor my appointment. It was
for me to cede the chair and suggest that you attend to him first."

"But what are we to do?"

The Count turned to the mirror and surveyed himself. He surveyed
himself, perhaps, for the first time in years.

Long had he believed that a gentleman should turn to a mirror with
a sense of distrust. For rather than being tools of self-discovery, mirrors
tended to be tools of self-deceit. How many times had he watched as a
young beauty turned thirty degrees before her mirror to ensure that she
saw herself to the best advantage? (As if henceforth all the world would
see her solely from that angle!) How often had he seen a grande dame
don a hat that was horribly out of fashion, but that seemed *au courant* to
her because her mirror had been framed in the style of the same bygone
era? The Count took pride in wearing a well-tailored jacket; but he took

greater pride in knowing that a gentleman's presence was best announced by his bearing, his remarks, and his manners. Not by the cut of his coat.

Yes, thought the Count, the world does spin.

In fact, it spins on its axis even as it revolves around the sun. And the galaxy turns as well, a wheel within a greater wheel, producing a chime of an entirely different nature than that of a tiny hammer in a clock. And when that celestial chime sounds, perhaps a mirror will suddenly serve its truer purpose—revealing to a man not who he imagines himself to be, but who he has become.

The Count resumed his place in the chair.

"A clean shave," he said to the barber. "A clean shave, my friend."

An Acquaintanceship

There were two restaurants in the Hotel Metropol: the Boyarsky, that fabled retreat on the second floor that we have already visited, and the grand dining room off the lobby known officially as the Metropol, but referred to affectionately by the Count as the Piazza.

Admittedly, the Piazza could not challenge the elegance of the Boyarsky's décor, the sophistication of its service, or the subtlety of its cuisine. But the Piazza did not aspire to elegance, service, or subtlety. With eighty tables scattered around a marble fountain and a menu offering everything from cabbage piroghi to cutlets of veal, the Piazza was meant to be an extension of the city—of its gardens, markets, and thoroughfares. It was a place where Russians cut from every cloth could come to linger over coffee, happen upon friends, stumble into arguments, or drift into dalliances—and where the lone diner seated under the great glass ceiling could indulge himself in admiration, indignation, suspicion, and laughter without getting up from his chair.

And the waiters? Like those of a Parisian café, the Piazza's waiters could best be complimented as "efficient." Accustomed to navigating crowds, they could easily seat your party of eight at a table for four. Having noted your preferences over the sound of the orchestra, within minutes they would return with the various drinks balanced on a tray and dispense them round the table in rapid succession without misplacing a glass. If, with your menu in hand, you hesitated for even a second to place your order, they would lean over your shoulder and poke at a specialty of the house. And when the last morsel of dessert had been savored, they would whisk away your plate, present your check, and make your change in under a minute. In other words, the waiters of the Piazza knew their trade to the crumb, the spoon, and the kopek.

At least, that was how things were before the war. . . .

Today, the dining room was nearly empty and the Count was being served by someone who appeared not only new to the Piazza, but new to the art of waiting. Tall and thin, with a narrow head and superior demeanor, he looked rather like a bishop that had been plucked from a chessboard. When the Count took his seat with a newspaper in hand—the international symbol of dining alone—the chap didn't bother to clear the second setting; when the Count closed his menu and placed it beside his plate—the international symbol of readiness to order—the chap needed to be beckoned with a wave of the hand; and when the Count ordered the okroshka and filet of sole, the chap asked if he might like a glass of Sauterne. A perfect suggestion, no doubt, if only the Count had ordered foie gras!

"Perhaps a bottle of the Château de Baudelaire," the Count corrected politely.

"Of course," the Bishop replied with an ecclesiastical smile.

Granted, a bottle of Baudelaire was something of an extravagance for a solitary lunch, but after spending another morning with the indefatigable Michel de Montaigne, the Count felt that his morale could use the boost. For several days, in fact, he had been fending off a state of restlessness. On his regular descent to the lobby, he caught himself counting the steps. As he browsed the headlines in his favorite chair, he found he was lifting his hands to twirl the tips of moustaches that were no longer there. He found he was walking through the door of the Piazza at 12:01 for lunch. And at 1:35, when he climbed the 110 steps to his room, he was already calculating the minutes until he could come back downstairs for a drink. If he continued along this course, it would not take long for the ceiling to edge downward, the walls to edge inward, and the floor to edge upward, until the entire hotel had been collapsed into the size of a biscuit tin.

As the Count waited for his wine, he gazed around the restaurant, but his fellow diners offered no relief. Across the way was a table occupied by two stragglers from the diplomatic corps who picked at their food while they awaited an era of diplomacy. Over there in the corner was a spectacled denizen of the second floor with four enormous documents spread across his table, comparing them word for word. No one appeared particularly gay; and no one paid the Count any mind. That is, except for the young girl with the penchant for yellow who appeared to be spying on him from her table behind the fountain.

According to Vasily, this nine-year-old with straight blond hair was the daughter of a widowed Ukrainian bureaucrat. As usual, she was sitting with her governess. When she realized the Count was looking her way, she disappeared behind her menu.

"Your soup," said the Bishop.

"Ah. Thank you, my good man. It looks delicious. But don't forget the wine!"

"Of course."

Turning his attention to his okroshka, the Count could tell at a glance that it was a commendable execution—a bowl of soup that any Russian in the room might have been served by his grandmother. Closing his eyes in order to give the first spoonful its due consideration, the Count noted a suitably chilled temperature, a tad too much salt, a tad too little kvass, but a perfect expression of dill—that harbinger of summer which brings to mind the songs of crickets and the setting of one's soul at ease.

But when the Count opened his eyes, he nearly dropped his spoon. For standing at the edge of his table was the young girl with the penchant for yellow—studying him with that unapologetic interest peculiar to children and dogs. Adding to the shock of her sudden appearance was the fact that her dress today was in the shade of a lemon.

"Where did they go?" she asked, without a word of introduction.

"I beg your pardon. Where did who go?"

She tilted her head to take a closer look at his face.

"Why, your moustaches."

The Count had not much cause to interact with children, but he had been raised well enough to know that a child should not idly approach a stranger, should not interrupt him in the middle of a meal, and certainly should not ask him questions about his personal appearance. Was the minding of one's own business no longer a subject taught in schools?

"Like swallows," the Count answered, "they traveled elsewhere for the summer."

Then he fluttered a hand from the table into the air in order to both mimic the flight of the swallows and suggest how a child might follow suit.

She nodded to express her satisfaction with his response.

"I too will be traveling elsewhere for part of the summer."

The Count inclined his head to indicate his congratulations.

"To the Black Sea," she added.

Then she pulled back the empty chair and sat.

"Would you like to join me?" he asked.

By way of response, she wiggled back and forth to make herself comfortable then rested her elbows on the table. Around her neck hung a small pendant on a golden chain, some lucky charm or locket. The Count looked toward the young lady's governess with the hopes of catching her attention, but she had obviously learned from experience to keep her nose in her book.

The girl gave another canine tilt to her head.

"Is it true that you are a count?"

"'Tis true."

Her eyes widened.

"Have you ever known a princess?"

"I have known many princesses."

Her eyes widened further, then narrowed.

"Was it terribly hard to be a princess?"

"Terribly."

At that moment, despite the fact that half of the okroshka remained in its bowl, the Bishop appeared with the Count's filet of sole and swapped one for the other.

"Thank you," said the Count, his spoon still in hand.

"Of course."

The Count opened his mouth to inquire as to the whereabouts of the Baudelaire, but the Bishop had already vanished. When the Count turned back to his guest, she was staring at his fish.

"What is that?" she wanted to know.

"This? It is filet of sole."

"Is it good?"

"Didn't you have a lunch of your own?"

"I didn't like it."

The Count transferred a taste of his fish to a side plate and passed it across the table. "With my compliments."

She forked the whole thing in her mouth.

"It's yummy," she said, which if not the most elegant expression was at least factually correct. Then she smiled a little sadly and let out a sigh as she directed her bright blue gaze upon the rest of his lunch.

"Hmm," said the Count.

Retrieving the side plate, he transferred half his sole along with an equal share of spinach and baby carrots, and returned it. She wiggled back and forth once more, presumably to settle in for the duration. Then, having carefully pushed the vegetables to the edge of the plate, she cut her fish into four equal portions, put the right upper quadrant in her mouth, and resumed her line of inquiry.

"How would a princess spend her day?"

"Like any young lady," answered the Count.

With a nod of the head, the girl encouraged him to continue.

"In the morning, she would have lessons in French, history, music. After her lessons, she might visit with friends or walk in the park. And at lunch she would eat her vegetables."

"My father says that princesses personify the decadence of a vanquished era."

The Count was taken aback.

"Perhaps a few," he conceded. "But not all, I assure you."

She waved her fork.

"Don't worry. Papa is wonderful and he knows everything there is to know about the workings of tractors. But he knows absolutely nothing about the workings of princesses."

The Count offered an expression of relief.

"Have you ever been to a ball?" she continued after a moment of thought.

"Certainly."

"Did you dance?"

"I have been known to scuff the parquet." The Count said this with the renowned glint in his eye—that little spark that had defused heated conversations and caught the eyes of beauties in every salon in St. Petersburg.

"Scuff the parquet?"

"Ahem," said the Count. "Yes, I have danced at balls."

"And have you lived in a castle?"

"Castles are not as common in our country as they are in fairy tales," the Count explained. "But I have *dined* in a castle. . . ."

Accepting this response as sufficient, if not ideal, the girl now furrowed her brow. She put another quadrant of fish in her mouth and chewed thoughtfully. Then she suddenly leaned forward.

"Have you ever been in a duel?"

"An *affaire d'honneur*?" The Count hesitated. "I suppose I have been in a duel of sorts. . . ."

"With pistols at thirty-two paces?"

"In my case, it was more of a duel in the figurative sense."

When the Count's guest expressed her disappointment at this unfortunate clarification, he found himself offering a consolation:

"My godfather was a second on more than one occasion."

"A second?"

"When a gentleman has been offended and demands satisfaction on the field of honor, he and his counterpart each appoint seconds—in essence, their lieutenants. It is the seconds who settle upon the rules of engagement."

"What sort of rules of engagement?"

"The time and place of the duel. What weapons will be used. If it is to be pistols, then how many paces will be taken and whether there will be more than one exchange of shots."

"Your godfather, you say. Where did *he* live?"

"Here in Moscow."

"Were his duels in Moscow?"

"One of them was. In fact, it sprang from a dispute that occurred in this hotel—between an admiral and a prince. They had been at odds for quite some time, I gather, but things came to a head one night when their paths collided in the lobby, and the gauntlet was thrown down on that very spot."

"Which very spot?"

"By the concierge's desk."

"Right where I sit!"

"Yes, I suppose so."

"Were they in love with the same woman?"

"I don't think a woman was involved."

The girl looked at the Count with an expression of incredulity.

"A woman is always involved," she said.

"Yes. Well. Whatever the cause, an offense was taken followed by a demand for an apology, a refusal to provide one, and a slap of the glove.

At the time, the hotel was managed by a German fellow named Keffler, who was reputedly a baron in his own right. And it was generally known that he kept a pair of pistols hidden behind a panel in his office, so that when an incident occurred, seconds could confer in privacy, carriages could be summoned, and the feuding parties could be whisked away with weapons in hand."

"In the hours before dawn . . ."

"In the hours before dawn."

"To some remote spot . . ."

"To some remote spot."

She leaned forward.

"Lensky was killed by Onegin in a duel."

She said this in a hushed voice, as if quoting the events of Pushkin's poem required discretion.

"Yes," whispered back the Count. "And so was Pushkin."

She nodded in grave agreement.

"In St. Petersburg," she said. "On the banks of the Black Rivulet."

"On the banks of the Black Rivulet."

The young lady's fish was now gone. Placing her napkin on her plate and nodding her head once to suggest how perfectly acceptable the Count had proven as a luncheon companion, she rose from her chair. But before turning to go, she paused.

"I prefer you without your moustaches," she said. "Their absence improves your . . . countenance."

Then she performed an off-kilter curtsey and disappeared behind the fountain.

An *affaire d'honneur* . . .

Or so thought the Count with a touch of self-recrimination as he sat alone later that night in the hotel's bar with a snifter of brandy.

Situated off the lobby, furnished with banquettes, a mahogany bar, and a wall of bottles, this American-style watering hole was affectionately referred to by the Count as the Shalyapin, in honor of the great Russian opera singer who had frequented the spot in the years before the

Revolution. Once a beehive of activity, the Shalyapin was now more a chapel of prayer and reflection—but tonight that suited the Count's cast of mind.

Yes, he continued in his thoughts, how fine almost any human endeavor can be made to sound when expressed in the proper French. . . .

"May I offer you a hand, Your Excellency?"

This was Audrius, the Shalyapin's tender at bar. A Lithuanian with a blond goatee and a ready smile, Audrius was a man who knew his business. Why, the moment after you took a stool he would be leaning toward you with his forearm on the bar to ask your pleasure; and as soon as your glass was empty, he was there with a splash. But the Count wasn't sure why he was choosing this particular moment to offer a hand.

"With your jacket," the bartender clarified.

In point of fact, the Count did seem to be struggling to get his arm through the sleeve of his blazer—which he couldn't quite remember having taken off in the first place. The Count had arrived at the Shalyapin at six o'clock, as usual, where he maintained a strict limit of one aperitif before dinner. But noting that he had never received his bottle of Baudelaire, the Count had allowed himself a second glass of Dubonnet. And then a snifter or two of brandy. And the next thing he knew, it was . . . , it was . . .

"What time *is* it, Audrius?"

"Ten, Your Excellency."

"Ten!"

Audrius, who was suddenly on the customer side of the bar, was helping the Count off his stool. And as he guided the Count across the lobby (quite unnecessarily), the Count invited him into his train of thought.

"Did you know, Audrius, that when dueling was first discovered by the Russian officer corps in the early 1700s, they took to it with such enthusiasm that the Tsar had to forbid the practice for fear that there would soon be no one left to lead his troops."

"I did not know that, Your Excellency," the bartender replied with a smile.

"Well, it's quite true. And not only is a duel central to the action of *Onegin*, one occurs at a critical juncture in *War and Peace*, *Fathers and Sons*, and *The Brothers Karamazov*! Apparently, for all their powers of invention, the Russian masters could not come up with a better plot device than two central characters resolving a matter of conscience by means of pistols at thirty-two paces."

"I see your point. But here we are. Shall I press for the fifth floor?"

The Count, who found himself standing in front of the elevator, looked at the bartender in shock.

"But, Audrius, I have never taken the lift in my life!"

Then, after patting the bartender on the shoulder, the Count began winding his way up the stairs; that is, until he reached the second-floor landing, where he sat on a step.

"Why is it that our nation above all others embraced the duel so whole-heartedly?" he asked the stairwell rhetorically.

Some, no doubt, would simply dismiss it as a by-product of barbarism. Given Russia's long, heartless winters, its familiarity with famine, its rough sense of justice, and so on, and so on, it was perfectly natural for its gentry to adopt an act of definitive violence as the means of resolving disputes. But in the Count's considered opinion, the reason that dueling prevailed among Russian gentlemen stemmed from nothing more than their passion for the glorious and grandiose.

True, duels were fought by convention at dawn in isolated locations to ensure the privacy of the gentlemen involved. But were they fought behind ash heaps or in scrapyards? Of course not! They were fought in a clearing among the birch trees with a dusting of snow. Or on the banks of a winding rivulet. Or at the edge of a family estate where the breezes shake the blossoms from the trees. . . . That is, they were fought in set-tings that one might have expected to see in the second act of an opera.

In Russia, whatever the endeavor, if the setting is glorious and the tenor grandiose, it will have its adherents. In fact, over the years, as the locations for duels became more picturesque and the pistols more finely manufac-tured, the best-bred men proved willing to defend their honor over lesser and lesser offenses. So while dueling may have begun as a response to high crimes—to treachery, treason, and adultery—by 1900 it had tiptoed down the stairs of reason, until they were being fought over the tilt of a hat, the duration of a glance, or the placement of a comma.

In the old and well-established code of dueling, it is understood that the number of paces the offender and offended take before shooting should be in inverse proportion to the magnitude of the insult. That is, the most reprehensible affront should be resolved by a duel of the fewest paces, to ensure that one of the two men will not leave the field of honor alive. Well, if that was the case, concluded the Count, then in the new era, the duels should have been fought at no less than ten thousand paces. In fact, having thrown down the gauntlet, appointed seconds, and chosen weapons, the offender should board a steamer bound for America as the offended boards another for Japan where, upon arrival, the two men could don their finest coats, descend their gangplanks, turn on the docks, and fire.

Anyway . . .

Five days later, the Count was pleased to accept a formal invitation to tea from his new acquaintance, Nina Kulikova. The engagement was for three o'clock in the hotel's coffeehouse at the northwest corner of the ground floor. Arriving at a quarter till, the Count claimed a table for two near the window. When at five past the hour his hostess arrived in the manner of a daffodil—wearing a light yellow dress with a dark yellow sash—the Count rose and held out her chair.

"*Merci,*" she said.

"*Je t'en prie.*"

In the minutes that followed, a waiter was signaled, a samovar was ordered, and with thunderclouds accumulating over Theatre Square, remarks were exchanged on the bittersweet likelihood of rain. But once the tea was poured and the tea cakes on the table, Nina adopted a more serious expression—intimating the time had come to speak of weightier concerns.

Some might have found this transition a little abrupt or out of keeping with the hour, but not the Count. Quite to the contrary, he thought a prompt dispensing of pleasantries and a quick shift to the business at hand utterly in keeping with the etiquette of tea—perhaps even essential to the institution.

After all, every tea the Count had ever attended in response to a formal invitation had followed this pattern. Whether it took place in a drawing room overlooking the Fontanka Canal or a teahouse in a public garden, before the first cake was sampled the *purpose* of the invitation would be laid upon the table. In fact, after a few requisite pleasantries, the most accomplished of hostesses could signal the transition with a single word of her choosing.

For the Count's grandmother, the word had been *Now*, as in *Now, Alexander. I have heard some very distressing things about you, my boy. . . .* For

Princess Poliakova, a perennial victim of her own heart, it had been *Oh*, as in *Oh, Alexander. I have made a terrible mistake. . . .* And for young Nina, the word was apparently *Anyway*, as in:

"You're absolutely right, Alexander Ilyich. Another afternoon of rain and the lilac blossoms won't stand a fighting chance. Anyway . . ."

Suffice it to say that when Nina's tone shifted, the Count was ready. Resting his forearms on his thighs and leaning forward at an angle of seventy degrees, he adopted an expression that was serious yet neutral, so that in an instant he could convey his sympathy, concern, or shared indignation as the circumstances required.

". . . I would be ever so grateful," Nina continued, "if you would share with me some of the rules of being a princess."

"The rules?"

"Yes. The rules."

"But, Nina," the Count said with a smile, "being a princess is not a game."

Nina stared at the Count with an expression of patience.

"I am certain that you know what I mean. Those things that were *expected* of a princess."

"Ah, yes. I see."

The Count leaned back to give his hostess's inquiry a more appropriate consideration.

"Well," he said after a moment, "setting aside the study of the liberal arts, which we discussed the other day, I suppose the rules of being a princess would begin with a refinement of manners. To that end, she would be taught how to comport herself in society; she would be taught terms of address, table manners, posture . . ."

Having nodded favorably at the various items on the Count's list, Nina looked up sharply at the last one.

"Posture? Is posture a type of manners?"

"Yes," replied the Count, albeit a little tentatively, "it is. A slouching posture tends to suggest a certain laziness of character, as well as a lack of interest in others. Whereas an upright posture can confirm a sense of self-possession, and a quality of engagement—both of which are befitting of a princess."

Apparently swayed by this argument, Nina sat a little more upright.

"Go on."

The Count reflected.

"A princess would be raised to show respect for her elders."

Nina bowed her head toward the Count in deference. He coughed.

"I wasn't referring to me, Nina. After all, I am practically a youth like yourself. No, by 'elders,' I meant the gray haired."

Nina nodded to express her understanding.

"You mean the grand dukes and grand duchesses."

"Well, yes. Certainly them. But I mean elders of every social class. The shopkeepers and milkmaids, blacksmiths and peasants."

Never hesitant to express her sentiments with facial expressions, Nina frowned. The Count elaborated.

"The principle here is that a new generation owes a measure of thanks to *every* member of the previous generation. Our elders planted fields and fought in wars; they advanced the arts and sciences, and generally made sacrifices on our behalf. So by their efforts, however humble, they have earned a measure of our gratitude and respect."

As Nina still looked unconvinced, the Count considered how best to make his point; and it so happened that at that very moment, through the great windows of the coffeehouse could be seen the first hoisting of umbrellas.

"An example," he said.

Thus commenced the story of Princess Golitsyn and the crone of Kudrovo:

One stormy night in St. Petersburg, related the Count, young Princess Golitsyn was on her way to the annual ball at the Tushins'. As her carriage crossed the Lomonosov Bridge, she happened to notice an eighty-year-old woman on foot, hunched against the rain. Without a second thought, she called for her driver to stop the carriage and invited the unfortunate soul inside. The old woman, who was nearly blind, climbed aboard with the footman's help and thanked the Princess profusely. In the back of the Princess's mind may well have been the presumption that her passenger lived nearby. After all, how far was an old, blind woman likely to journey on a night like this? But when the Princess asked where the old woman was headed, she replied that she was going to visit her son, the blacksmith, in Kudrovo—more than seven miles away!

Now, the Princess was already expected at the Tushins'. And in a matter of minutes they would be passing the house—lit from cellar to ceiling with a footman on every step. So, it would have been well within the bounds of courtesy for the Princess to excuse herself and send the carriage on to Kudrovo with the old woman. In fact, as they approached the Tushins', the driver slowed the horses and looked to the Princess for instruction. . . .

Here the Count paused for effect.

"Well," Nina asked, "what did she do?"

"She told him to drive on." The Count smiled with a touch of triumph. "And what is more, when they arrived in Kudrovo and the blacksmith's family gathered round the carriage, the old woman invited the Princess in for tea. The blacksmith winced, the coachman gasped, and the footman nearly fainted. But Princess Golitsyn graciously accepted the old woman's invitation—and missed the Tushins' altogether."

His point expertly made, the Count raised his own cup of tea, nodded once, and drank.

Nina looked at him expectantly.

"And then?"

The Count returned his cup to its saucer.

"And then what?"

"Did she marry the blacksmith's son?"

"Marry the blacksmith's son! Good God. Certainly not. After a glass of tea she climbed into her carriage and headed for home."

Nina mulled this over. Clearly, she thought a marriage to the blacksmith's son a more fitting conclusion. But despite the shortcomings of history, she nodded to acknowledge that the Count had delivered a well-told tale.

Preferring to preserve his success, the Count opted not to share his normal coda to this delightful bit of St. Petersburg lore: that the Countess Tushin had been greeting guests under her portico when Princess Golitsyn's bright blue carriage, known the city over, slowed before the gates and then sped on. This resulted in a rift between the Golitsyns and the Tushins that would have taken three generations to repair—if a certain Revolution hadn't brought an end to their outrage altogether. . . .

"It was behavior befitting a princess," acknowledged Nina.

"Exactly," said the Count.

Then he held out the tea cakes and Nina took two, putting one on her plate and one in her mouth.

The Count was not one to call attention to the social shortcomings of acquaintances, but giddy with his story's reception, he could not resist pointing out with a smile:

"There is another example."

"Where is another example?"

"A princess would be raised to say *please* when she asked for a cake, and *thank you* when she was offered one."

Nina looked taken aback; and then dismissive.

"I can see that *please* would be quite appropriate for a princess to say when she has asked for a cake; but I can see no reason why she should have to say *thank you* when she has been offered one."

"Manners are not like bonbons, Nina. You may not choose the ones that suit you best; and you certainly cannot put the half-bitten ones back in the box. . . ."

Nina eyed the Count with an expression of seasoned tolerance, and then presumably for his benefit, spoke a little more slowly.

"I understand that a princess should say *please* if she is asking for a cake, because she is trying to convince someone to give her the cake. And I suppose, if having asked for a cake, she is given a cake, then she has good reason to say *thank you*. But in the second part of your example, the princess in question didn't ask for the cake; she was *offered* it. And I see no reason why she should have to say *thank you* when she is merely obliging someone by accepting what they've offered."

To punctuate her point, Nina put a lemon tartlet in her mouth.

"I concede that there is some merit to your argument," said the Count. "But I can only tell you from a life of experience that—"

Nina cut him off with a wave of a finger.

"But you have just said that you are quite young."

"Indeed, I am."

"Well then, it seems to me that your claim of 'a life of experience' may be premature."

Yes, thought the Count, as this tea was making perfectly clear.

"I shall work upon my posture," Nina said quite definitively, brushing the crumbs from her fingers. "And I will be sure to say *please* and *thank you* whenever I ask for things. But I have no intention of thanking people for things I never asked for in the first place."

Around and About

On the twelfth of July at seven o'clock, as the Count was crossing the lobby on his way to the Boyarsky, Nina caught his eye from behind one of the potted palms and gave him the signal. It was the first time that she had hailed him for an excursion this late in the day.

"Quick," she explained, when he had joined her behind the tree. "The gentleman has gone out to dine."

The gentleman?

To avoid drawing attention to themselves, the two walked casually up the stairs. But as they turned onto the third floor, they ran smack into a guest who was patting his pockets for his key. On the landing directly across from the elevator, there was a stained-glass window of long-legged birds wading in shallows that the Count had passed a thousand times before. Nina began to study it with care.

"Yes, you were right," she said. "It is some kind of crane."

But as soon as the guest had let himself into his room, Nina forged ahead. Moving at a brisk pace along the carpet, they passed rooms 313, 314, and 315. They passed the little table with the statue of Hermes that stood outside the door of 316. Then with a certain dizziness, the Count realized that they were headed toward his old suite!

But wait.

We are ahead of ourselves. . . .

After the ill-fated night that ended on the second-floor steps, the Count had taken a break from his nightly aperitif, suspecting that the liquor had been an unhealthy influence on his mood. But this saintly abstinence did not prove a tonic to his soul. With so little to do and all the time in the world to do it, the Count's peace of mind continued to be threatened by a sense of ennui—that dreaded mire of the human emotions.

And if this is how desultory one feels after three weeks, reflected the Count, then how desultory can one expect to feel after three years?

But for the virtuous who have lost their way, the Fates often provide a guide. On the island of Crete, Theseus had his Ariadne and her magical ball of thread to lead him safely from the lair of the Minotaur. Through those caverns where ghostly shadows dwell, Odysseus had his Tiresias just as Dante had his Virgil. And in the Metropol Hotel, Count Alexander Ilyich Rostov had a nine-year-old girl by the name of Nina Kulikova.

For on the first Wednesday in July, as the Count sat in the lobby at a loss of what to do with himself, he happened to notice Nina zipping past with an unusually determined expression.

"Hello, my friend. Where are you headed?"

Turning about like one who's been caught in the act, Nina composed herself, then answered with a wave of the hand:

"Around and about . . ."

The Count raised his eyebrows.

"And where is that exactly?"

. . .

"At this moment, the card room."

"Ah. So you like to play at cards."

"Not really . . ."

"Then why on earth are you going there?"

. . .

"Oh, come now," the Count protested. "Surely, there are not going to be secrets between *us*!"

Nina weighed the Count's remark, then looking once to her left and once to her right, she confided. She explained that while the card room was rarely used, at three o'clock on Wednesdays four women met there without fail for a regular game of whist; and if you arrived by two thirty and hid in the cupboard, you could hear their every word—which included a good deal of cursing; and when the ladies left, you could eat the rest of their cookies.

The Count sat upright.

"Where else do you spend your time?"

Again she weighed the Count's remark, looked left and looked right.

"Meet me here," she said, "tomorrow at two."

And thus began the Count's education.

Having lived at the Metropol for four years, the Count considered himself something of an expert on the hotel. He knew its staff by name, its services by experience, and the decorative styles of its suites by heart. But once Nina had taken him in hand, he realized what a novice he had been.

In the ten months that Nina had lived at the Metropol, she had been confronted with her own version of confinement. For, as her father had been posted only "temporarily" to Moscow, he had not bothered to enroll her in school. And as Nina's governess still had one foot set firmly in the hinterlands, she preferred that her charge remain on the hotel's premises where she was less likely to be corrupted by street lamps and trolley cars. So, if the door of the Metropol was known the world over for spinning without stop, it spun not for Nina. But, an enterprising and tireless spirit, the young lady had made the most of her situation by personally investigating the hotel until she knew every room, its purpose, and how it might be put to better use.

Yes, the Count had gone to the little window at the back of the lobby to ask for his mail, but had he been to the sorting room where the incoming envelopes were spilled on a table at ten and at two—including those that were stamped in red with the unambiguous instruction *For Immediate Delivery*?

And yes, he had visited Fatima's in the days when it was open, but had he been inside the cutting room? Through a narrow door at the back of her shop was that niche with a light green counter where stems had been snipped and roses dethorned, where even now one could find scattered across the floor the dried petals of ten perennials essential to the making of potions.

Of course, exclaimed the Count to himself. Within the Metropol there were rooms behind rooms and doors behind doors. The linen closets. The laundries. The pantries. The switchboard!

It was like sailing on a steamship. Having enjoyed an afternoon shooting clay pigeons off the starboard bow, a passenger dresses for dinner, dines at the captain's table, outplays the cocky French fellow at baccarat, and then strolls under the stars on the arm of a new acquaintance—all the while congratulating himself that he has made the most of a journey at sea. But in point of fact, he has only exposed himself to a *glimpse* of life on the ship—having utterly ignored those lower levels that teem with life and make the passage possible.

Nina had not contented herself with the views from the upper decks. She had gone below. Behind. Around. About. In the time that Nina had been in the hotel, the walls had not grown inward, they had grown outward, expanding in scope and intricacy. In her first weeks, the building had grown to encompass the life of two city blocks. In her first months, it had grown to encompass half of Moscow. If she lived in the hotel long enough, it would encompass all of Russia.

To initiate the Count's course of study, Nina quite sensibly began at the bottom—the basement and its network of corridors and cul-de-sacs. Tugging open a heavy steel door, she led him first into the boiler room, where billows of steam escaped from a concertina of valves. With the aid of the Count's handkerchief, she gingerly opened a small cast-iron door in the furnace to reveal the fire that burned day and night, and which happened to be the best place in the hotel to destroy secret messages and illicit love letters.

"You do receive illicit love letters, Count?"

"Most certainly."

Next was the electrical room, where Nina's admonition that the Count touch nothing was quite unnecessary, since the metallic buzzing and sulfurous smell would have counseled caution to the most reckless of adventurers. There, on the back wall amidst a confusion of wires, Nina showed him the very lever that, when pulled, could throw the ballroom into darkness, providing perfect cover for the snatching of pearls.

After a turn to the left and two to the right, they came to a small cluttered room—a sort of cabinet of curiosities—showcasing all the items that the hotel's guests had left behind, such as umbrellas, *Baedekers*, and the weighty novels they had yet to finish but could no longer bear to lug about. While tucked away in the corner, looking no worse for wear, were two small oriental rugs, a standing lamp, and the small satinwood bookcase that the Count had abandoned in his old suite.

At the far end of the basement, as the Count and Nina approached the narrow back stair, they passed a bright blue door.

"What do we have here?" asked the Count.

Nina looked uncharacteristically flummoxed.

"I don't think I've been inside."

The Count tried the knob.

"Ah, well. I'm afraid that it's locked."

But Nina looked left and looked right.

The Count followed suit.

Then she raised her hands under her hair and unhooked the delicate chain that she wore around her neck. Dangling at the bottom of the golden parabola was the pendant the Count had first observed at the Piazza, but it was neither a lucky charm nor locket. It was a passkey for the hotel!

Nina slid the key from its chain and handed it to the Count so that he could do the honors. Slipping it through the skull-shaped hole in the escutcheon, the Count turned gently and listened as the tumblers fell into place with a satisfying click. Then he opened the door and Nina gasped, for inside there was a treasure trove.

Quite literally.

On shelves that lined the walls from floor to ceiling was the hotel's silver service, shimmering as if it had been polished that very morning.

"What is it all for?" she asked in amazement.

"For banquets," replied the Count.

Alongside the stacks of Sèvres plates bearing the hotel's insignia were samovars that stood two feet tall and soup tureens that looked like the goblets of the gods. There were coffeepots and gravy boats. There was an assortment of utensils, each of which had been designed with the greatest care to serve a single culinary purpose. From among them, Nina picked up what looked like a delicate spade with a plunger and an ivory handle. Depressing the lever, Nina watched as the two opposing blades opened and shut, then she looked to the Count in wonder.

"An asparagus server," he explained.

"Does a banquet really need an asparagus server?"

"Does an orchestra need a bassoon?"

As Nina returned it gently to the shelf, the Count wondered how many times he had been served by that implement? How many times had he eaten off these plates? The bicentennial of St. Petersburg had been celebrated in the Metropol's ballroom, as had the centennial of Pushkin's birth and the annual dinner of the Backgammon Club. And then there were the more intimate gatherings that took place in the two private dining rooms adjacent to the Boyarsky: the Yellow and Red Rooms. In their heyday, these retreats were so conducive to frank expressions of sentiment that if one were to eavesdrop at their tables for a month, one would be able to anticipate all of the bankruptcies, weddings, and wars of the year to come.

The Count let his eyes wander over the shelves, then shook his head to express a sense of mystification.

"Surely, the Bolsheviks have discovered this windfall. I wonder why it wasn't carted off?"

Nina responded with the unclouded judgment of a child.

"Perhaps they need it here."

Yes, thought the Count. That is it precisely.

For however decisive the Bolsheviks' victory had been over the privileged classes on behalf of the Proletariat, they would be having banquets soon enough. Perhaps there would not be as many as there had been under the Romanovs—no autumn dances or diamond jubilees—but they were bound to celebrate something, whether the centennial of *Das Kapital* or the silver anniversary of Lenin's beard. Guest lists would be drawn up and shortened. Invitations would be engraved and delivered. Then, having gathered around a grand circle of tables, the new statesmen would nod their heads in order to indicate to a waiter (without interrupting the long-winded fellow on his feet) that, yes, they would have a few more spears of asparagus.

For pomp is a tenacious force. And a wily one too.

How humbly it bows its head as the emperor is dragged down the steps and tossed in the street. But then, having quietly bided its time, while helping the newly appointed leader on with his jacket, it compliments his appearance and suggests the wearing of a medal or two. Or, having served him at a formal dinner, it wonders aloud if a taller chair might not have been more fitting for a man with such responsibilities. The soldiers of the common man may toss the banners of the old regime on the victory pyre, but soon enough trumpets will blare and pomp will take its place at the side of the throne, having once again secured its dominion over history and kings.

Nina was running her fingers over the various serving implements with a blend of admiration and awe. Then she came to a stop.

"What is that?"

On the shelf behind a candelabra stood a three-inch-tall woman fashioned from silver with the hooped skirt and towering hair of a Marie Antoinette.

"It's a summoner," said the Count.

"A summoner?"

"To be placed on the table beside the hostess."

The Count picked up the little lady by her bouffant and when he waggled her to and fro, out from under her skirt came that delightful jangle (at a high C) that had prompted the end of a thousand courses and the clearing of fifty thousand plates.

In the days that followed, Nina presented her curriculum systematically, leading her student from room to room. At the onset, the Count had assumed that all their classes would be held on the hotel's lower levels, where its services were housed. But having visited the basement, the mail room, the switchboard, and all the other nooks of the first floor, one afternoon they proceeded up the staircase to the suites.

Now, admittedly, the exploration of private apartments represents something of a break with decorum, but Nina's interest in visiting the rooms was not thievery. Nor was it snooping per se. It was the views.

Each of the rooms of the Metropol offered an entirely different perspective—one that was shaped not only by altitude and orientation, but by season and time of day. Thus, if by chance one cared to watch the battalions marching toward Red Square on the Seventh of November, one should go no further than room 322. But when one wished to drop snowballs on unsuspecting strollers, this was best accomplished from the deep-ledged windows of 405. Even room 244, a rather depressing little spot overlooking the alley behind the hotel, had its allure: for from there, if one leaned far enough out of the window, one could watch the fruit sellers gather at the kitchen door and catch the occasional apple tossed from below.

But if one wished to watch the arrival of guests at the Bolshoi on a summer night, the best vantage point, without question, was the northwest window of 317. And so . . .

On the twelfth of July at seven o'clock, as the Count was crossing the lobby, Nina caught his eye and gave him the signal. Two minutes later, having joined her on the stairs, he was trailing her past rooms 313, 314, and 315, toward the door of his old suite. And when Nina turned the key and slipped inside, the Count dutifully followed—but with a palpable sense of foreboding.

In a glance the Count reacquainted himself with every inch of the room. The couch and chairs upholstered in red remained, as did the grandfather clock and the large Chinese urns from Idlehour. On the French coffee table (that had been supplied to replace his grandmother's) was a folded copy of *Pravda*, a silver service, and an unfinished cup of tea.

"Quick," she said again, as she padded across the room to the window at the northwest corner.

Across Theatre Square the Bolshoi was lit from portico to pediment. The Bolsheviks who, as usual, were dressed like the cast of *La Bohème*, were taking advantage of the warm night air by mingling among the columns. Suddenly, the lights in the lobby flickered. Scuffing out their cigarettes, the men took their ladies by the elbow. But just as the last of the attendees was disappearing through the doors, a taxi pulled to the curb, the door flung open, and a woman in red dashed up the stairs with the hem of her dress in her hands.

Leaning forward, Nina cupped her palms against the glass and squinted.

"If only I were there and she were here," she sighed.

And there, thought the Count, was a suitable plaint for all mankind.

Later that night, as he sat alone on his bed, the Count mulled over his visit to his old suite.

What had stayed with him was not the sight of his family's clock still ticking by the door, nor the grandeur of the architecture, nor even the view from the northwest window. What had lingered with him was the sight of the tea service on the table beside the folded paper.

That little tableaux, for all its innocence, was somehow suggestive of exactly what had been bearing down on the Count's soul. For he understood every aspect of the scene at a glance. Having returned from some outing at four o'clock and having hung his jacket on the back of a chair, the room's current resident had called for tea and an afternoon edition. Then he had settled himself down on the couch to while away a civilized hour before it was time to dress for dinner. In other words, what the Count had observed in suite 317 was not simply an afternoon tea, but a moment in the daily life of a gentleman at liberty.

In light of these thoughts, the Count reviewed his new room—the one hundred square feet that had been assigned to him. Never had it seemed so small. The bed crowded the coffee table, the coffee table crowded the high-back chair, and the high-back chair had to be shoved aside every time one wished to open the closet. Simply put, there was not enough space to accommodate such a civilized hour.

But as the Count gazed around him with this forlorn thought, a voice only half his own reminded him that in the Metropol there were rooms behind rooms, and doors behind doors. . . .

Rising from his bed, the Count navigated his way around his grandmother's coffee table, set aside the high-back chair, and stood before his telephone box of a closet. Running along the perimeter of where the closet met the wall was an elegant molding. The Count had always thought this flourish a little excessive; but what if the closet had been built in an old doorframe? Opening the door, the Count parted his clothes and tentatively rapped on the back wall. The sound was promisingly thin. With three fingers he gave the barrier a push and could feel it flex. He took all his jackets out and dumped them on the bed. Then holding the jambs of the door he kicked the inner wall with his heel. There came a pleasant crack. Leaning back, he kicked again and again until the barrier splintered. Then he pulled the jagged planks back into his room and slipped through the gap.

He was now inside a dark, narrow space that smelled of dry cedar, presumably the interior of the neighboring closet. Taking a breath, he turned the knob, opened the door, and entered a room that was the mirror image of his own—but in which five unused bedframes had been stored. At some point, two of the frames, which had been leaning against the wall, had fallen, pinning the hallway door shut. Pulling the frames aside, the Count opened the door, dragged everything out of the room, and began to refurnish.

First, he reunited the two high-back chairs with his grandmother's coffee table. Then, taking the belfry stairs, he went down to the basement. From the cabinet of curiosities, he retrieved one of his rugs, the standing lamp, and the small bookcase in three separate trips. Then vaulting the steps two at a time, he made one final visit in order to claim ten of the weighty novels that had been abandoned. Once his new study was furnished, he went down the hall and borrowed the roofer's hammer and five nails.

The Count had not wielded a hammer since he was a boy at Idlehour when he would help Tikhon, the old caretaker, repair the fencing in the first weeks of spring. What a fine feeling it had been to bring the hammer down squarely on the head of a nail, driving it through a plank into a fence post as the impact echoed in the morning air. But on the very first stroke of this hammer what the Count squarely hit was the back of his thumb. (Lest you have forgotten, it is quite excruciating to hammer the back of your thumb. It inevitably prompts a hopping up and down and the taking of the Lord's name in vain.)

But Fortune does favor the bold. So, while the next swing of the hammer glanced off the nail's head, on the third the Count hit home; and by the second nail, he had recovered the rhythm of set, drive, and sink— that ancient cadence which is not to be found in quadrilles, or hexameters, or in Vronsky's saddlebags!

Suffice it to say that within half an hour four of the nails had been driven through the edge of the door into the doorframe—such that from that moment forward the only access to the Count's new room would be through the sleeves of his jackets. The fifth nail he saved for the wall above the bookcase so that he could hang the portrait of his sister.

His work completed, the Count sat down in one of the high-back chairs and felt an almost surprising sense of bliss. The Count's bedroom and this improvised study had identical dimensions, and yet, they exerted a completely different influence on his mood. To some degree, this difference stemmed from the manner in which the two rooms had been furnished. For while the room next door—with its bed, bureau, and desk—remained a realm of practical necessities, the study—with its books, the Ambassador, and Helena's portrait—had been furnished in a manner more essential to the spirit. But in all likelihood, a greater factor in the difference between the two rooms was their provenance. For if a room that exists under the governance, authority, and intent of others seems smaller than it is, then a room that exists in *secret* can, regardless of its dimensions, seem as vast as one cares to imagine.

Rising from his chair, the Count took up the largest of the ten volumes that he had retrieved from the basement. True, it would not be a new venture for him. But need it be? Could one possibly accuse him of nostalgia or idleness, of wasting his time simply because he had read the story two or three times before?

Sitting back down, the Count put one foot on the edge of the coffee table and tilted back until his chair was balanced on its two hind legs, then he turned to the opening sentence:

> *All happy families are alike; each unhappy family is unhappy in its own way.*

"Marvelous," said the Count.

An Assembly

Oh, come along."

"I'd rather not."

"Don't be such a fuddy-duddy."

"I am not a fuddy-duddy."

"Can you be so sure?"

"A man can never be entirely sure that he is not a fuddy-duddy. That is axiomatic to the term."

"Exactly."

In this manner, Nina coerced the Count to join her on one of her favorite excursions: spying from the balcony of the ballroom. The Count was reluctant to accompany Nina on this particular journey for two reasons. First, the ballroom's balcony was narrow and dusty, and to stay out of sight one was forced to remain hunched behind the balustrade—a decidedly uncomfortable position for a grown man over six feet tall. (The last time the Count had accompanied Nina to the balcony, he had torn the seam of his pants and it took three days for him to lose the crick in his neck.) But second, this afternoon's gathering was almost certain to be another Assembly.

Over the course of the summer, the Assemblies had been occurring at the hotel with increasing frequency. At various times of day, small groups of men would come barreling through the lobby, already gesticulating, interrupting, and eager to make their points. In the ballroom, they would join their brethren milling shoulder to shoulder, every other one of them puffing on a cigarette.

As best as the Count could determine, the Bolsheviks assembled whenever possible in whichever form for whatever reason. In a single week, there might be committees, caucuses, colloquiums, congresses, and conventions variously coming together to establish codes, set courses of action, levy complaints, and generally clamor about the world's oldest problems in its newest nomenclature.

If the Count was reluctant to observe these gatherings, it was not because he found the ideological leanings of the attendees distasteful. He would no sooner have crouched behind a balustrade to watch Cicero debating Catiline, or Hamlet debating himself. No, it was not a matter of ideology. Simply put, the Count found political discourse of any persuasion to be tedious.

But then, wasn't that exactly what a fuddy-duddy would argue . . . ?

Needless to say, the Count followed Nina up the stairs to the second floor. Having skirted the entrance to the Boyarsky and ensured the coast was clear, they used Nina's key to open the unmarked door to the balcony.

Down below, a hundred men were already in their chairs and another hundred were conferring in the aisles as three impressive fellows took their seats behind a long wooden table on the dais. Which is to say, the Assembly had nearly Assembled.

As this was the second of August and there had already been two Assemblies earlier that day, the temperature in the ballroom was 91°. Nina skirted out behind the balustrade on her hands and knees. When the Count bent over to do the same, the seam in the back of his pants gave way again.

"*Merde,*" he muttered.

"Shh," said Nina.

The first time the Count had joined Nina on the balcony, he couldn't help but feel some astonishment at how profoundly the life of the ballroom had changed. Not ten years before, all of Moscow society would have been gathered in their finery under the grand chandeliers to dance the mazurka and toast the Tsar. But after witnessing a few of the Assemblies, the Count had come to an even more astonishing conclusion: that despite the Revolution, the room had barely changed at all.

At that very moment, for example, two young men were coming through the doors looking game for the fray; but before exchanging a word with a soul, they crossed the room in order to pay their respects to an old man seated by the wall. Presumably, this elder had taken part in the 1905 revolution, or penned a pamphlet in 1880, or dined with Karl

Marx back in 1852. Whatever his claim to eminence, the old revolutionary acknowledged the deference of the two young Bolsheviks with a self-
assured nod of the head—all the while sitting in the very chair from
which the Grand Duchess Anapova had received the greetings of dutiful
young princes at her annual Easter Ball.

Or consider the charming-looking chap who, in the manner of Prince
Tetrakov, was now touring the room, shaking hands and patting backs.
Having systematically made an impression in every corner—with a weighty
remark here and a witty remark there—he now excused himself "for just a
moment." But once through the door, he will not reappear. For having
ensured that everyone in the ballroom has noted his attendance, he will now
head off to an altogether different sort of Assembly—one that is to take place
in a cozy little room in the Arbat.

Later, no doubt, some dashing young Turk who is rumored to have
Lenin's ear will make a point of arriving when the business of the evening is nearly done—just as Captain Radyanko had when he had the ear
of the Tsar—thus exhibiting his indifference to the smaller conventions
of etiquette while reinforcing his reputation as a man with so much to
attend to and so little time to attend to it.

Of course, there is now more canvas than cashmere in the room,
more gray than gold. But is the patch on the elbow really that much different from the epaulette on the shoulder? Aren't those workaday caps
donned, like the bicorne and shako before them, in order to strike a particular note? Or take that bureaucrat on the dais with his gavel. Surely,
he can afford a tailored jacket and a creased pair of pants. If he is wearing
this ragged fare, it is in order to assure all assembled that he too is a hardened member of the working class!

As if hearing the Count's thoughts, this Secretary suddenly rapped
his gavel on the tabletop—calling to order the Second Meeting of the
First Congress of the Moscow Branch of the All-Russian Union of Railway Workers. The doors were closed, seats were taken, Nina held her
breath, and the Assembly was underway.

In the first fifteen minutes, six different administrative matters were
raised and dispensed with in quick succession—leading one to imagine
that this particular Assembly might actually be concluded before one's
back gave out. But next on the docket was a subject that proved more

contentious. It was a proposal to amend the Union's charter—or more precisely, the seventh sentence of the second paragraph, which the Secretary now read in full.

Here, indeed, was a formidable sentence—one that was on intimate terms with the comma, and that held the period in healthy disregard. For its apparent purpose was to catalog without fear or hesitation every single virtue of the Union including but not limited to: its unwavering shoulders, its undaunted steps, the clanging of its hammers in summer, the shoveling of its coal in winter, and the hopeful sound of its whistles in the night. But in the concluding phrases of this impressive sentence, at the very culmination as it were, was the observation that through their tireless efforts, the Railway Workers of Russia "facilitate communication and trade across the provinces."

After all the buildup, it was a bit of an anticlimax, conceded the Count.

But the objection being raised was not due to the phrase's overall lack of verve; rather it was due to the word *facilitate*. Specifically, the verb had been accused of being so tepid and prim that it failed to do justice to the labors of the men in the room.

"We're not helping a lady put on her jacket!" someone shouted from the rear.

"Or painting her nails!"

"Hear, hear!"

Well, fair enough.

But what verb would better express the work of the Union? What verb would do justice to the sweaty devotion of the engineers, the unflagging vigilance of the brakemen, and the rippling muscles of those who laid the tracks?

A flurry of proposals came from the floor:

To spur.

To propel.

To empower.

The merits and limitations of each of these alternatives were hotly debated. There were three-pointed arguments counted out on fingertips, rhetorical questions, emotional summations, and back-row catcalls punctuated by the banging of the gavel—as the ambient temperature of the balcony rose to 96°.

Then, just as the Count began to sense some risk of riot, a suggestion came from a shy-looking lad in the tenth row that perhaps *to facilitate* could be replaced with *to enable and ensure*. This pairing, the lad explained (while his cheeks grew red as a raspberry), might encompass not only the laying of rails and the manning of engines, but the ongoing mainte- nance of the system.

"Yes, that's it."

"Laying, manning, and maintenance."

"To enable and ensure."

With hearty applause from every corner, the lad's proposal seemed to be barreling toward adoption as quickly and dependably as one of the Union's locomotives barrels across the steppe. But just as it was nearing its terminus, a rather scrawny fellow in the second row stood. Such a wisp of a man was he that one wondered how he had secured a position in the Union in the first place. Once he had the attention of the room, this back- office clerk or accountant, this All-Russian pusher of pencils, asserted in a voice as tepid and prim as the word *facilitate*: "Poetic concision demands the avoidance of a pair of words when a single word will suffice."

"What's that?"

"What did he say?"

Several stood up with the intention of grabbing him by the collar and dragging him from the room. But before they could get their hands on him, a burly fellow in the fifth row spoke without rising to his feet.

"With all due respect to *poetic concision*, the male of the species was endowed with a pair when a single might have sufficed."

Thunderous applause!

The resolution to replace *facilitate* with *enable and ensure* was adopted by a unanimous show of hands and a universal stomping of feet. While in the balcony, a private acknowledgment was made that perhaps politi- cal discourse wasn't always so dull, after all.

At the conclusion of the Assembly, when the Count and Nina had crawled off the balcony and back into the hallway, the Count felt quite pleased with himself. He felt pleased with his little parallels between the respect- payers, back-patters, and latecomers of the present and those of the past. He also had a whole host of entertaining alternatives to the phrase *enable and ensure* ranging from *bustle and trundle* to *carom and careen.* And when Nina inevitably asked what he thought of the day's debate, he was going to reply that it was positively Shakespearean. Shakespearean, that is, in the manner of Dogberry in *Much Ado About Nothing.* Much ado about nothing, indeed. Or so the Count intended to quip.

But by a stroke of luck, he didn't get the chance. For when Nina asked what he thought of the Assembly, unable to wait even a moment for his impressions, she barreled ahead with her own.

"Wasn't that fascinating? Wasn't it fantastic? Have you ever been on a train?"

"The train is my preferred means of travel," said the Count, somewhat startled.

She nodded enthusiastically.

"Mine as well. And when you have traveled by train, have you watched the landscape rolling past the windows, and listened to the conversations of your fellow passengers, and drifted off to the clacking of the wheels?"

"I have done all of those things."

"Exactly. But have you ever, for even one moment, considered how the coal finds its way into the locomotive's engine? Have you considered in the middle of a forest or on a rocky slope how the tracks came to be there in the first place?"

The Count paused. Considered. Imagined. Admitted.

"Never."

She gave him a knowing look.

"Isn't it astounding."

And when seen in that light, who could disagree?

A few minutes later, the Count was knocking on the office door of Marina, the shy delight, while holding a folded newspaper at the back of his pants.

Not long ago, the Count recalled, there had been three seamstresses at work in this room, each before an American-made sewing machine. Like the three Fates, together they had spun and measured and cut—taking in gowns, raising hems, and letting out pants with all of the fateful implications of their predecessors. In the aftermath of the Revolution, all three had been discharged; the silenced sewing machines had, presumably, become the property of the People; and the room? It had been idled like Fatima's flower shop. For those had not been years for the taking in of gowns or the raising of hems any more than they had been for the throwing of bouquets or the sporting of boutonnieres.

Then in 1921, confronted with a backlog of fraying sheets, tattered curtains, and torn napkins—which no one had any intention of replacing—the hotel had promoted Marina, and once again a trustworthy seam was being sewn within the walls of the hotel.

"Ah, Marina," said the Count when she opened the door with needle and thread in hand. "How good to find you stitching away in the stitching room."

Marina looked at the Count with a touch of suspicion.

"What else would I be doing?"

"Quite so," said the Count. Then offering his most endearing smile, he turned ninety degrees, briefly lifted the newspaper, and humbly asked for her assistance.

"Didn't I repair a pair of your pants just last week?"

"I was spying with Nina again," he explained. "From the balcony of the ballroom."

The seamstress looked at the Count with one eye expressing consternation and the other disbelief.

"If you're going to clamber about with a nine-year-old girl, then why do you insist upon wearing pants like those?"

The Count was a little taken aback by the seamstress's tone.

"When I dressed this morning, it was not my plan to go clambering about. But either way, I'll have you know that these pants were custommade on Savile Row."

"Yes. Custom-made for sitting in a sitting room, or drawing in a drawing room."

"But I have never drawn in a drawing room."

"Which is just as well, since you probably would have spilled the ink."

As Marina seemed neither particularly shy nor delightful that day, the Count offered her the bow of one who would now be on his way.

"Oh, enough of that," she said. "Behind the screen and off with your pants."

Without another word the Count went behind the dressing screen, stripped to his shorts, and handed Marina his pants. From the ensuing silence, he could tell that she had found her spool, licked her thread, and was carefully directing it through the eye of the needle.

"Well," she said, "you might as well tell me what you were doing up in the balcony."

So, as Marina began stitching the Count's pants—the laying of locomotive tracks writ small, if you will—he described the Assembly and all his various impressions. Then, almost wistfully, he noted that even as he was seeing the intractability of social conventions and the human tendency to take itself too seriously, Nina was becoming enthralled by the Assembly's energy and its sense of purpose.

"And what is wrong with that?"

"Nothing, I suppose," admitted the Count. "It's just that only a few weeks ago, she was inviting me to tea in order to ask about the rules of being a princess. . . ."

Handing the Count's pants back over the screen, Marina shook her head like one who must now deliver a hard truth to an innocent of mind.

"All little girls outgrow their interest in princesses," she said. "In fact, they outgrow their interest in princesses faster than little boys outgrow their interest in clambering about."

When the Count left Marina's office with a thanks, a wave, and the seat of his pants intact, he practically fell over one of the bellhops, who happened to be standing outside the door.

"Excuse me, Count Rostov!"

"That's quite all right, Petya. No need to apologize. It was my fault, I'm sure."

The poor lad, who looked positively wide-eyed, hadn't even noticed that he'd lost his cap. So, picking it up from the floor and placing it back on the bellhop's head, the Count wished him God's speed in his business and turned to go.

"But my business is with *you*."

"With me?"

"It is Mr. Halecki. He wishes to have a word. In his office."

No wonder the lad was wide-eyed. Not only had the Count never been summoned by Mr. Halecki, in the four years that he had been in residence in the Metropol he had not *seen* the manager on more than five occasions.

For Jozef Halecki was one of those rare executives who had mastered the secret of delegation—that is, having assigned the oversight of the hotel's various functions to capable lieutenants, he made himself scarce. Arriving at the hotel at half past eight, he would head straight to his office with a harried expression, as if he were already late for a meeting. Along the way, he would return greetings with an abbreviated nod, and when he passed his secretary he would inform her (while still in motion) that he was not to be disturbed. Then he would disappear behind his door.

And what happened once he was inside his office?

It was hard to tell, since so few had ever seen it. (Although, those who had caught a glimpse reported that his desk was impressively free of papers, his telephone rarely rang, and along the wall was a burgundy chaise with cushions that were deeply impressed. . . .)

When the manager's lieutenants had no choice but to knock—due to a fire in the kitchen or a dispute about a bill—the manager would open his door with an expression of such fatigue, such disappointment, such moral defeat that the interrupters would inevitably feel a surge of sympathy, assure him that they could see to the matter themselves, then apologetically back out the door. As a result, the Metropol ran as flawlessly as any hotel in Europe.

Needless to say, the Count was both anxious and intrigued by the manager's sudden desire to see him. Without further ado, Petya led him down the hall, through the hotel's back offices, and finally to the manager's door, which predictably was closed. Expecting Petya to formally announce him, the Count paused a few feet short of the office, but the bellhop made a sheepish gesture toward the door and then vanished. With no clear alternative, the Count knocked. There followed a brief rustling, a moment of silence, and a beleaguered call to come in.

When the Count opened the door, he found Mr. Halecki seated at his desk with a pen firmly in hand, but without a piece of paper in sight. And though the Count was not one to draw conclusions, he did note that the manager's hair was matted on one side of his head and his reading glasses were crooked on his nose.

"You wished to see me?"

"Ah. Count Rostov. Please. Come in."

As the Count approached one of the two empty chairs that faced the desk, he noted that hanging above the burgundy chaise was a lovely series of hand-tinted engravings depicting hunting scenes in the English style.

"Those are excellent specimens," said the Count as he took his seat.

"What's that? Oh, yes. The prints. Quite excellent. Yes."

But having said this, the manager removed his glasses and ran a hand over his eyes. Then he shook his head and sighed. And as he did so, the Count felt a welling of that famed sympathy. "How can I be of service to you?" asked the Count, on the edge of his seat.

The manager gave a nod of familiarity, having presumably heard this question a thousand times before, then put both hands on his desk.

"Count Rostov," he began. "You have been a guest of this hotel for many years. In fact, I gather your first visit here dates back to the days of my predecessor. . . ."

"That's right," the Count confirmed with a smile. "It was in August 1913."

"Quite so."

"Room 215, I believe."

"Ah. A delightful room."

The two men were silent.

"It has been brought to my attention," the manager continued, if somewhat haltingly, "that various members of the staff when speaking to you . . . have continued to make use of certain . . . honorifics."

"Honorifics?"

"Yes. More precisely, I gather they have been addressing you as *Your Excellency*. . . ."

The Count considered the manager's assertion for a moment.

"Well, yes. I suppose that some of your staff address me in that fashion."

The manager nodded his head then smiled a little sadly.

"I'm sure you can see the position that this puts me in."

In point of fact, the Count could not see the position that this put the manager in. But given the Count's unmitigated feelings of sympathy, he decidedly did not want to put him in any position. So, he listened attentively as Mr. Halecki went on:

"If it were up to me, of course, it goes without saying. But what with . . ."

Here, just when the manager might have pinpointed the most specific of causes, he instead gave an indefinite twirl of the hand and let his voice drift off. Then he cleared his throat.

"Naturally, I have little choice but to insist that my staff refrain from using such terms when addressing you. After all, I think we can agree without exaggeration or fear of contradiction that the times have changed."

In concluding thus, the manager looked to the Count so hopefully, that the Count took immediate pains to reassure him.

"It is the business of the times to change, Mr. Halecki. And it is the business of gentlemen to change with them."

The manager looked to the Count with an expression of profound gratitude—that someone should understand what he had said so perfectly no further explication was required.

There was a knock at the door and it opened to reveal Arkady, the hotel's desk captain. The manager's shoulders slumped at the sight of him. He gestured toward the Count.

"As you can see, Arkady, I am in the midst of a conversation with one of our guests."

"My apologies, Mr. Halecki, Count Rostov."

Arkady bowed to both men, but did not retreat.

"All right then," said the manager. "What is it?"

Arkady gave a slight gesture of the head to suggest that what he had to relate might best be related in private.

"Very well."

Pushing himself up with both hands, the manager shuffled past his desk, out into the hall, and closed the door, such that the Count found himself alone.

Your Excellency, the Count reflected philosophically. *Your Eminence, Your Holiness, Your Highness.* Once upon a time, the use of such terms was a reliable indication that one was in a civilized country. But now, what with . . .

Here, the Count gave an indefinite twirl of the hand.

"Well. It is probably for the best," he said.

Then rising from his chair, he approached the engravings, which upon closer inspection depicted three phases of a foxhunt: "The Scent," "Tally-ho," and "The Chase." In the second print, a young man in stiff black boots and a bright red jacket was blowing on a brass horn that turned a full

360 degrees from its mouthpiece to its bell. Without a doubt, the horn was a carefully crafted object expressive of beauty and tradition, but was it essential to the modern world? For that matter, did we really need a crew of nattily dressed men, purebred horses, and well-trained dogs to corner a fox in a hole? Without exaggeration or fear of contradiction, the Count could answer his own question in the negative.

For the times do, in fact, change. They change relentlessly. Inevitably. Inventively. And as they change, they set into bright relief not only outmoded honorifics and hunting horns, but silver summoners and mother-of-pearl opera glasses and all manner of carefully crafted things that have outlived their usefulness.

Carefully crafted things that have outlived their usefulness, thought the Count. I wonder . . .

Moving quietly across the room, the Count put an ear to the door, where he could hear the voices of the manager, Arkady, and a third party talking outside. Though muted, their tones suggested they were still a few steps from resolution. Quickly, the Count returned to the wall with the etchings and counted two panels beyond the depiction of "The Chase." Placing his hand in the center of the panel, he gave a firm push. The panel depressed slightly. When a click sounded, the Count pulled back his fingers and the panel popped open, revealing a hidden cabinet. Inside, just as the Grand Duke had described, was an inlaid box with brass fittings. Reaching into the cabinet, the Count gently lifted the lid of the box and there they were, perfectly crafted and peacefully at rest.

"Marvelous," he said. "Simply marvelous."

Archeologies

Pick a card," the Count was saying to the smallest of the three ballerinas.

When he had entered the Shalyapin for his reinstated nightly aperitif, the Count had discovered them standing in a row, their delicate fingers resting on the bar as if they intended to *plié*. But for a solitary drinker hunched over his consolation, the young ladies were alone in the bar; so it seemed only appropriate that the Count should join them in a bit of conversation.

In an instant, he could tell that they were new to Moscow—three of the doves that Gorsky recruited from the provinces every September to join the *corps de ballet*. Their short torsos and long limbs were of the classical style preferred by the director, but their expressions had yet to acquire the aloofness of his more seasoned ballerinas. And the very fact that they were drinking at the Metropol unaccompanied hinted at a youthful naïveté. For while the proximity of the hotel to the Bolshoi made it a natural choice for young ballerinas who wished to slip away at the end of rehearsal, the same proximity also made it a favored spot of Gorsky's whenever he wished to discuss matters of art with his prima ballerina. And should these doves be discovered by the director sipping muscat, they would soon be doing the *pas de deux* in Petropavlosk.

With that in mind, perhaps the Count should have warned them.

But freedom of the will has been a well-established tenet of moral philosophy since the time of the Greeks. And though the Count's days of romancing were behind him, it goes against the nature of even the well-meaning gentleman to recommend that lovely young ladies leave his company on the basis of hypotheses.

So, instead, the Count remarked on the young ladies' beauty, inquired what brought them to Moscow, congratulated them on their achievements, insisted upon paying for their wine, chatted with them about their home-towns, and eventually offered to perform a sleight of hand.

A deck of cards with the Metropol's insignia was produced by the ever-attentive Audrius.

"It has been years since I have done this trick," the Count admitted, "so you must bear with me."

As he began to shuffle the pack, the three ballerinas watched him closely; but like demigods of ancient myth, they watched in three different ways: the first through the eyes of the innocent, the second through the eyes of the romantic, and the third through the eyes of the skeptic. It was the dove with the innocent eyes whom the Count had asked to pick a card.

As the ballerina was making her selection, the Count became aware of someone standing behind his shoulder, but this was to be expected. In the setting of a bar, a sleight of hand will inevitably attract a curious onlooker or two. But when he turned to his left to offer a wink, he found not a curious onlooker, but unflappable Arkady—looking unusually flapped.

"Pardon me, Count Rostov. I am sorry to interrupt. But may I have a moment?"

"Certainly, Arkady."

Smiling apologetically to the ballerinas, the desk captain led the Count a few paces away, then let the facts of the evening speak for themselves: At half past six, a gentleman had knocked at the suite of Secretary Tarakovsky. When the esteemed Secretary opened the door, this gentleman demanded to know who he was and what he was doing there! Taken aback, comrade Tarakovsky explained that he was the current resident of the suite and *that* was what he was doing there. Unconvinced by this logic, the gentleman insisted he be admitted at once. When comrade Tarakovsky refused, the gentleman brushed him aside, crossed the threshold, and commenced searching the rooms one by one, including, ahem, the *salle de bain*—where Mrs. Tarakovsky was seeing to her nightly *toilette*.

This was the point at which Arkady had arrived on the scene, having been summoned urgently by phone. In an agitated state, comrade Tarakovsky waved his cane and demanded "as a regular guest of the Metropol and senior member of the Party" to see the manager at once.

The gentleman, who was now sitting on the couch with his arms crossed, replied that this suited him perfectly—as he had been about to summon the manager himself. And as to Party membership, he asserted that *he* had been a member of the Party since before comrade Tarakovsky was born—which seemed a rather incredible claim given that comrade Tarakovsky is eighty-two. . . .

Now, the Count, who had listened with interest to every word that Arkady had related, would be the first to admit that this was an enthralling tale. In fact, it was just the sort of colorful incident that an international hotel should aspire to have as part of its lore and that he, as a guest of the hotel, would be likely to retell at the first opportunity. But what he could not understand was why Arkady had chosen this particular moment to share this particular story with *him*.

"Why, because comrade Tarakovsky is staying in suite 317; and it is you for whom the gentleman in question was looking."

"Me?"

"I am afraid so."

"What is his name?"

"He refused to say."

. . .

"Then where is he now?"

Arkady pointed toward the lobby.

"He is wearing out the carpet behind the potted palms."

"Wearing out the carpet . . . ?"

The Count stuck his head out of the Shalyapin as Arkady leaned cautiously behind him. And sure enough, there on the other side of the lobby was the gentleman in question, making quick business of the ten feet between the pair of plants.

The Count smiled.

Though a few pounds heavier, Mikhail Fyodorovich Mindich had the same ragged beard and restless pace that he had had when they were twenty-two.

"Do you know him?" asked the desk captain.

"Only like a brother."

When the Count and Mikhail Fyodorovich first met at the Imperial University in St. Petersburg in the fall of 1907, the two were tigers of a very different stripe. While the Count had been raised in a twenty-room mansion with a staff of fourteen, Mikhail had been raised in a two-room apartment with his mother. And while the Count was known in all the salons of the capital as one who could be counted on for his wit, intelligence, and charm, Mikhail was known hardly anywhere as one who preferred to read in his room rather than fritter away the evening on frivolous conversations.

As such, the two young men hardly seemed fated for friendship. But Fate would not have the reputation it has if it simply did what it seemed it would do. Sure enough, while Mikhail was prone to throw himself into a scrape at the slightest difference of opinion, regardless of the number or size of his opponents, it just so happened that Count Alexander Rostov was prone to leap to the defense of an outnumbered man regardless of how ill conceived his cause. Thus, on the fourth day of their first year, the two students found themselves helping each other up off the ground, as they wiped the dust from their knees and the blood from their lips.

While the splendors that elude us in youth are likely to receive our casual contempt in adolescence and our measured consideration in adulthood, they forever hold us in their thrall. Thus, in the days that followed their meeting, the Count listened with as much amazement to Mikhail's impassioned expression of ideals, as Mikhail did to the Count's descriptions of the city's salons. And within the year, they were sharing rented rooms above a cobbler's shop off Sredny Prospekt.

As the Count would later observe, it was fortuitous that they ended up above a cobbler—for no one in all of Russia could wear out a shoe like Mikhail Mindich. He could easily pace twenty miles in a twenty-foot room. He could pace thirty miles in an opera box and fifty in a confessional. For simply put, pacing was Mishka's natural state.

Say the Count secured them invitations to Platonov's for drinks, the Petrovskys' for supper, and Princess Petrossian's for a dance—Mishka would invariably decline on the grounds that in the back of a bookshop he had just discovered a volume by someone named Flammenhescher that demanded to be read from beginning to end without delay. But once alone, having torn through the first fifty pages of Herr Flammenhescher's little monograph, Mikhail would leap to his feet and start pacing from corner to corner in order to voice his fervid agreement or furious dissent with the author's thesis, his style, or his use of punctuation. Such that by the time the Count returned at two in the morning, though Mishka had not advanced beyond the fiftieth page, he had worn out more shoe leather than a pilgrim on the road to St. Paul's.

So, the storming of hotel suites and the wearing out of carpets was not particularly out of character for his old friend. But as Mishka had recently received a new appointment at their alma mater in St. Petersburg, the Count was surprised to have him appear so suddenly, and in such a state.

After embracing, the two men climbed the five flights to the attic. Having been told what to expect, Mishka took in his friend's new circumstances without an expression of surprise. But he paused before the three-legged bureau and tilted his head to give its base a second look.

"The *Essays* of Montaigne?"

"Yes," affirmed the Count.

"I gather they didn't agree with you."

"On the contrary. I found them to be the perfect height. But tell me, my friend, what brings you to Moscow?"

"Nominally, Sasha, I am here to help plan the inaugural congress of RAPP, which is to be held in June. But of greater consequence . . ."

Here Mishka reached into a shoulder satchel and produced a bottle of wine with an image of two crossed keys embossed in the glass above the label.

"I hope I am not too late."

The Count took the bottle in hand. He ran his thumb over the surface of the insignia. Then he shook his head with the smile of the deeply moved.

"No, Mishka. As always, you are right on time." Then he led his old friend through his jackets.

As the Count excused himself to rinse a pair of glasses from the Ambassador, Mishka surveyed his friend's study with a sympathetic gaze. For the tables, the chairs, the *objets d'art*, he recognized them all. And well he knew that they had been culled from the halls of Idlehour as reminders of Elysian days.

It must have been in 1908 that Alexander began inviting him to Idlehour for the month of July. Having traveled from St. Petersburg by a series of consecutively smaller trains, they would finally arrive at that little halt in the high grass on the branch line, where they would be met by a Rostov coach-and-four. With their bags on top, the driver in the carriage, and Alexander at the reins, they would charge across the countryside waving at every peasant girl until they turned onto the road lined with apple trees that led to the family seat.

As they shed their coats in the entry hall, their bags would be whisked to the grand bedrooms of the east wing, where velvet cords could be pulled to summon a cold glass of beer, or hot water for a bath. But first, they would proceed to the drawing room where—at this very table with its red pagoda—the Countess would be hosting some blue-blooded neighbor for tea.

Invariably dressed in black, the Countess was one of those dowagers whose natural independence of mind, authority of age, and impatience with the petty made her the ally of all irreverent youth. She would not only abide, but enjoyed when her grandson would interrupt polite conversation to question the standing of the church or the ruling class. And when her guest grew red and responded in a huff, the Countess would give Mishka a conspiratorial wink, as if they stood arm in arm in the battle against boorish decorum and the outmoded attitudes of the times.

Having paid their respects to the Countess, Mishka and Alexander would head out the terrace doors in search of Helena. Sometimes they would find her under the pergola overlooking the gardens and sometimes under the elm tree at the bend in the river; but wherever they found her, at the sound of their approach she would look up from her book and offer a welcoming smile—not unlike the one captured in this portrait on the wall.

With Helena, Alexander was always his most outlandish, claiming as he collapsed on the grass that they had just met Tolstoy on the train; or that he had decided after careful consideration to join a monastery and take an eternal vow of silence. Immediately. Without a moment's delay. Or, as soon as they'd had lunch.

"Do you really think that silence would suit you?" Helena would ask.

"Like deafness suited Beethoven."

Then, after casting a friendly glance at Mishka, Helena would laugh, look back at her brother, and ask, "What is to become of you, Alexander?"

They all asked that question of the Count. Helena, the Countess, the Grand Duke. *What is to become of you, Alexander?* But they asked it in three different ways.

For the Grand Duke the question was, of course, rhetorical. Confronted with a report of a failed semester or an unpaid bill, the Grand Duke would summon his godson to his library, read the letter aloud, drop it on his desk, and ask the question without expectation of a response, knowing full well that the answer was imprisonment, bankruptcy, or both.

For his grandmother, who tended to ask the question when the Count had said something particularly scandalous, *What is to become of you, Alexander?* was an admission to all in earshot that here was her favorite, so you needn't expect *her* to rein in his behavior.

But when Helena asked the question, she did so as if the answer were a genuine mystery. As if, despite her brother's erratic studies and carefree ways, the world had yet to catch a glimpse of the man he was bound to become.

"What is to become of you, Alexander?" Helena would ask.

"That is the question," the Count would agree. And then he would lie back in the grass and gaze thoughtfully at the figure eights of the dragonflies as if he too were pondering this essential enigma.

Yes, those were Elysian days, thought Mishka. But like Elysium they belonged in the past. They belonged with waistcoats and corsets, with quadrilles and bezique, with the ownership of souls, the payment of tribute, and the stacking of icons in the corner. They belonged in an age of elaborate artifice and base superstition—when a lucky few dined on cutlets of veal and the majority endured in ignorance.

They belong with those, thought Mishka, as he turned his gaze from Helena's portrait to the nineteenth-century novels that lined the familiar little bookcase. All those adventures and romances spun in the fanciful styles that his old friend so admired. But here, on top of the bookcase in its long narrow frame, was a genuine artifact—the black-and-white photograph of the men who signed the Treaty of Portsmouth to end the Russo-Japanese War.

Mishka picked up the picture and surveyed the visages, sober and assured. Standing in formal configuration, the Japanese and Russian delegates all wore high white collars, moustaches, bow ties, and expressions suggestive of some grand sense of accomplishment—having just concluded with the stroke of a pen the war that their likes had started in the first place. And there, just left of center, stood the Grand Duke himself: special envoy from the court of the Tsar.

It was at Idlehour in 1910 that Mishka first witnessed the Rostovs' long-standing tradition—of gathering on the tenth anniversary of a family member's death to raise a glass of Châteauneuf-du-Pape. Two days after the Count and he had arrived for their holiday, the guests began to appear. By four in the afternoon the drive was lined with surreys, britzkas, droshkies, and gigs from Moscow and St. Petersburg and all the neighboring districts. And when the family gathered in the hall at five, it was the Grand Duke who was given the honor of raising the first glass in memory of the Count's parents, who had died just hours apart.

What a formidable figure the Grand Duke had been. Seemingly born in full dress, he rarely sat, never drank, and died on the back of his horse on the twenty-first of September 1912—ten years ago to the day.

"He was a right old soul."

Mishka turned to find the Count standing behind him with two Bordeaux glasses in hand. "A man of another time," Mishka said, not without reverence, returning the picture to its shelf. Then the bottle was opened, the wine was poured, and the two old friends raised their glasses on high.

"What a group we have gathered, Sasha. . . ."

Having toasted the Grand Duke and reminisced of days gone by, the old friends shifted their attention to the upcoming congress of RAPP, which turned out to be the Russian Association of Proletarian Writers.

"It will be an extraordinary assembly. An extraordinary assembly at an extraordinary time. Akhmatova, Bulgakov, Mayakovksy, Mandelstam—the sort of writers who not long ago couldn't have dined at the same table without fear of arrest—will all be there. Yes, over the years they have championed their differing styles, but in June they will gather to forge *novaya poeziya*, a new poetry. One that is universal, Sasha. One that doesn't hesitate and needn't kowtow. One that has the human spirit as its subject and the future as its muse!"

Just before uttering his first *One that*, Mishka had leapt to his feet and now paced the Count's little study from corner to corner, as if formulating his ideas in the privacy of his own apartment.

"You remember, no doubt, that work by the Dane Thomsen. . . ."

(The Count did not remember that work by the Dane Thomsen. But he would no sooner have interrupted Mikhail on his feet than Vivaldi on his violin.)

"As an archeologist, when Thomsen divided the ages of man into Stone, Bronze, and Iron, naturally enough, he did so in accordance with the physical tools that defined each epoch. But what of man's *spiritual* development? What of his *moral* development? I tell you, they progressed along the very same lines. In the Stone Age, the ideas in the caveman's head were as blunt as the club in his hand; they were as rough as the flint from which he struck a spark. In the Age of Bronze, when a canny few discovered the science of metallurgy, how long did it take for them to fashion coins, crowns, and swords? That unholy trinity to which the common man was enslaved for the next one thousand years."

Mishka paused to consider the ceiling.

"Then came the Age of Iron—and with it the steam engine, the printing press, and the gun. Here was a very different trinity, indeed. For while these tools had been developed by the Bourgeoisie to further their own interests, it was through the engine, the press, and the pistol that the Proletariat began to free itself from labor, ignorance, and tyranny."

Mishka shook his head in appreciation of either history's trajectory or his turns of phrase.

"Well, my friend, I think we can agree that a new age has begun: the Age of Steel. We now have the ability to build power stations, skyscrapers, airplanes."

Mishka turned to the Count.

"You have seen the Shukhov Radio Tower?"

The Count had not.

"What a thing of beauty, Sasha. A two-hundred-foot structure of spiraling steel from which we can broadcast the latest news and intelligence—and, yes, the sentimental strains of your Tchaikovsky—into the home of every citizen within a hundred miles. And with each one of these advances, the Russian morality has been keeping step. In our time, we may witness the end of ignorance, the end of oppression, and the advent of the brotherhood of man."

Mishka stopped and waved a hand in the air.

"But what of poetry? you ask. *What of the written word?* Well, I can assure you that it too is keeping pace. Once fashioned from bronze and iron, it is now being fashioned from steel. No longer an art of quatrains and dactyls and elaborate tropes, our poetry has become an art of action. One that will speed across the continents and transmit music to the stars!"

Had the Count overheard such a speech spilling forth from a student in a coffeehouse, he might have observed with a glint in his eye that, apparently, it was no longer enough for a poet to write verse. Now, a poem must spring from a school with its own manifesto and stake its claim on the moment by means of the first-person plural and the future tense, with rhetorical questions and capital letters and an army of exclamation points! And above all else, it must be *novaya*.

But as noted, these would have been the Count's thoughts had he overheard someone *else* speaking. Hearing the speech spill forth from Mishka filled the Count with joy.

For it is a fact that a man can be profoundly out of step with his times. A man may have been born in a city famous for its idiosyncratic culture and yet, the very habits, fashions, and ideas that exalt that city in the eyes of the world may make no sense to him at all. As he proceeds through life, he looks about in a state of confusion, understanding neither the inclinations nor the aspirations of his peers.

For such a fellow, forget any chance of romance or professional success; those are the provenance of men in step with their times. Instead, for this fellow the options will be to bray like a mule or find what solace he can from overlooked volumes discovered in overlooked bookshops. And when his roommate stumbles home at two in the morning, he has little choice but to listen in silent mystification as he is recounted the latest dramas from the city's salons.

This had been Mishka's lot for most of his life.

But events can unfold in such a manner that overnight the man out of step finds himself in the right place at the right time. The fashions and attitudes that had seemed so alien to him are suddenly swept aside and supplanted by fashions and attitudes in perfect sympathy with his deepest sentiments. Then, like a lone sailor adrift for years on alien seas, he wakes one night to discover familiar constellations overhead.

And when this occurs—this extraordinary realignment of the stars— the man so long out of step with his times experiences a supreme lucidity. Suddenly all that has passed comes into focus as a necessary course of events, and all that promises to unfold has the clearest rhyme and reason.

When the twice-tolling clock struck twelve, even Mishka could see the merit in having another glass of wine; and toasts were made not only to the Grand Duke, but to Helena and the Countess, to Russia and Idlehour, to poetry and pacing, and to every other worthy facet of life that they could think of.

Advent

One evening in late December, as he was walking the hallway to the Piazza, the Count distinctly felt a gust of frozen air, despite being fifty yards from the nearest exit to the street. It brushed past him with all the freshness and clarity of a starlit winter's night. After pausing and searching about, he realized that the draft was coming . . . from the coatroom. Which Tanya, the attendant, had left unattended. So, with a look to his left and a look to his right, the Count stepped within.

In the preceding minutes, there must have been such a rush of parties arriving for dinner that the winter air had yet to dissipate from the fabric of their coats. Here was the greatcoat of a soldier with a dusting of snow on shoulders; here the woolen jacket of a bureaucrat still damp; and here was a black mink coat with a collar of ermine (or was it sable?) that was in all probability worn by the mistress of a commissar.

Raising a sleeve to his face, the Count could detect smoke from a fireplace and the hint of an oriental *eau de cologne*. Setting out from some elegant house on the Boulevard Ring, this young beauty presumably arrived in an automobile as black as her coat. Or perhaps she had opted to walk down Tverskaya Street, where Pushkin's statue stood pensive but undaunted in the freshly fallen snow. Or better yet, she had come by sleigh with the hooves of the horses sounding on the cobbled streets and the crack of the whip matching the driver's *Hyah!*

That was how the Count and his sister would brave the cold on Christmas Eve. Promising their grandmother that they would be no later than midnight, the siblings would set out on their troika into the crisp night air to call on their neighbors. With the Count at the reins and the pelt of a wolf on their laps, they would cut across the lower pasture to the village road, where the Count would call: *Who shall it be first? The Bobrinskys? Or the Davidovs?*

But whether they ventured to the one, the other, or somewhere else entirely, there would be a feast, a fire, and open arms. There would be bright dresses, and flushed skin, and sentimental uncles making misty-eyed toasts as children spied from the stairs. And music? There would be songs that emptied your glass and called you to your feet. Songs that led you to leap and alight in a manner that belied your age. Songs that made you reel and spin until you lost your bearings not only between the parlor and the salon, but between heaven and earth.

As midnight approached, the Rostov siblings would stumble from their second or third visit in search of their sleigh. Their laughter would echo under the stars and their steps would weave in wide curves back and forth across the straight tracks that they had made upon their arrival—such that in the morning their hosts would find the giant figure of a G clef transcribed by their boots in the snow.

Back in the troika they would charge across the countryside, cutting through the village of Petrovskoye, where the Church of the Ascension stood not far from its monastery's walls. Erected in 1814 in honor of Napoleon's defeat, the church's campanile was rivaled only by that of the Ivan the Great tower in the Kremlin. Its twenty bells had been forged from cannons that the Interloper had been forced to abandon during his retreat, such that every peal seemed to sound: *Long live Russia! Long live the Tsar!*

But as they came to the bend in the road where the Count would normally give a snap of the reins to speed the horses home, Helena would place a hand on his arm to signal that he should slow the team—for midnight had just arrived, and a mile behind them the bells of Ascension had begun to swing, their chimes cascading over the frozen land in holy canticle. And in the pause between hymns, if one listened with care, above the pant of the horses, above the whistle of the wind, one could hear the bells of St. Michael's ten miles away—and then the bells of St. Sofia's even farther afield—calling one to another like flocks of geese across a pond at dusk.

The bells of Ascension . . .

When the Count had passed through Petrovskoye in 1918 on his hurried return from Paris, he had come upon a gathering of peasants milling in mute consternation before the monastery's walls. The Red Cavalry, it seems, had arrived that morning with a caravan of empty wagons. At the instruction of their young captain, a troop of Cossacks had climbed the campanile and heaved the bells from the steeple one by one. When it came time to heave the Great Bell, a second troop of Cossacks was sent up the stairs. The old giant was hoisted from its hook, balanced on the rail, and tipped into the air, where it somersaulted once before landing in the dust with a thud.

When the abbot rushed from the monastery to confront the captain—demanding in the name of the Lord that they cease this desecration at once—the captain leaned against a post and lit a cigarette.

"One should render unto Caesar what is Caesar's," he said, "and unto God what is God's." With that, he instructed his men to drag the abbot up the belfry steps and hurl him from the steeple into the arms of his Maker.

Presumably, the bells of the Church of the Ascension had been reclaimed by the Bolsheviks for the manufacture of artillery, thus returning them to the realm from whence they came. Though for all the Count knew, the cannons that had been salvaged from Napoleon's retreat to make the Ascension's bells had been forged by the French from the bells at La Rochelle; which in turn had been forged from British blunderbusses seized in the Thirty Years' War. From bells to cannons and back again, from now until the end of time. Such is the fate of iron ore.

"Count Rostov . . . ?"

The Count looked up from his reverie to find Tanya standing in the doorway.

"Sable I should think," said the Count, dropping the sleeve. "Yes, most definitely sable."

December in the Piazza . . .

From the day the Metropol opened its doors, the good people of Moscow had looked to the Piazza to set the tone of the season. For by five o'clock on the first of December, the room had already been festooned in anticipation of the New Year. Evergreen garlands with bright red berries hung from the fountain. Strings of lights fell from the balconies. And revelers? From all across Moscow they came, such that by eight o'clock, when the orchestra struck up its first festive song, every table was spoken for. By nine, the waiters were dragging chairs in from the corridors so that latecomers could hang their arms over the shoulders of friends. And at the center of every table—whether it was hosted by the high or the humble—was a serving of caviar, for it is the genius of this particular delicacy that it may be enjoyed by the ounce or the pound.

As such, it was with a touch of disappointment that the Count entered the Piazza on this winter solstice to find the room ungarlanded, the balustrades unstrung, an accordion player on the bandstand, and two-thirds of the tables empty.

But then, as every child knows, the drumbeat of the season must sound from within. And there, at her usual table by the fountain, was Nina with a dark green ribbon tied around the waist of her bright yellow dress.

"Merry Christmas," said the Count with a bow when he reached the table.

Nina stood and curtsied. "The joys of the season to you, sir."

When they were seated with their napkins in their laps, Nina explained that as she would be meeting her father for dinner a little later, she had taken the liberty of ordering herself an hors d'oeuvre.

"Quite sensible," said the Count.

At that moment, the Bishop appeared, carrying a small tower of ice creams.

"The hors d'oeuvre?"

"*Oui*," Nina replied.

Having placed the dish before Nina with a priestly smile, the Bishop turned and asked if the Count would like a menu (as if he didn't know it by heart!).

"No thank you, my good man. Just a glass of champagne and a spoon."

Systematic in all matters of importance, Nina ate her ice cream one flavor at a time, moving from the lightest to the darkest in shade. Thus, having already dispatched her French vanilla, she was now moving on to a scoop of lemon, which perfectly matched her dress.

"So," said the Count, "are you looking forward to your visit home?"

"Yes, it will be nice to see everyone," said Nina. "But when we return to Moscow in January, I shall be starting school."

"You don't seem very excited by the prospect."

"I fear it will be dreadfully dull," she admitted, "and positively overrun with children."

The Count nodded gravely to acknowledge the indisputable likelihood of children in the schoolhouse; then, as he dipped his own spoon into the scoop of strawberry, he noted that he had enjoyed school very much.

"Everybody tells me that."

"I loved reading the *Odyssey* and the *Aeneid*; and I made some of the finest friends of my life. . . ."

"Yes, yes," she said with a roll of her eyes. "Everybody tells me that too."

"Well, sometimes everybody tells you something because it is true."

"Sometimes," Nina clarified, "everybody tells you something because they are everybody. But why should one listen to everybody? Did *everybody* write the *Odyssey*? Did *everybody* write the *Aeneid*?" She shook her head then concluded definitively: "The only difference between everybody and nobody is all the shoes."

Perhaps the Count should have left it at that. But he hated the idea of his young friend beginning her Moscow school days with such a desolatory view. As she progressed through the dark purple scoop (presumably blackberry), he considered how best to articulate the virtues of a formal education.

"While there are certainly some irksome aspects to school," he conceded after a moment, "I think you will find to your eventual delight that the experience has broadened your horizons."

Nina looked up.

"What do you mean by that?"

"What do I mean by what?"

"By *broadened your horizons*."

The Count's assertion had seemed so axiomatic that he had not prepared an elaboration. So before responding, he signaled the Bishop for another glass of champagne. For centuries champagne has been used to launch marriages and ships. Most assume this is because the drink is so intrinsically celebratory; but, in fact, it is used at the onset of these dangerous enterprises because it so capably boosts one's resolve. When the glass was placed on the table, the Count took a swig large enough to tickle his sinuses.

"By broadening your horizons," he ventured, "what I meant is that education will give you a sense of the world's scope, of its wonders, of its many and varied ways of life."

"Wouldn't travel achieve that more effectively?"

"Travel?"

"We are talking about horizons, aren't we? That horizontal line at the limit of sight? Rather than sitting in orderly rows in a schoolhouse, wouldn't one be better served by working her way toward an *actual* horizon, so that she could see what lay beyond it? That's what Marco Polo did when he traveled to China. And what Columbus did when he traveled to America. And what Peter the Great did when he traveled through Europe *incognito!*"

Nina paused to take a great mouthful of the chocolate, and when the Count appeared about to reply she waved her spoon to indicate that she was not yet finished. He waited attentively for her to swallow.

"Last night my father took me to *Scheherazade.*"

"Ah," the Count replied (grateful for the change of subject). "Rimsky-Korsakov at his best."

"Perhaps. I wouldn't know. The point is: According to the program, the composition was intended to 'enchant' the listeners with 'the world of the Arabian Nights.'"

"That realm of Aladdin and the lamp," said the Count with a smile.

"Exactly. And, in fact, everyone in the theater seemed utterly enchanted."

"Well, there you are."

"And yet, not one of them has any intention of *going* to Arabia—even though that is where the lamp is."

By some extraordinary conspiracy of fate, at the very instant Nina made this pronouncement, the accordion player concluded an old favorite and the sparsely populated room broke into applause. Sitting back, Nina gestured to her fellow customers with both hands as if their ovation were the final proof of her position.

It is the mark of a fine chess player to tip over his own king when he sees that defeat is inevitable, no matter how many moves remain in the game. Thus, the Count inquired:

"How was your hors d'oeuvre?"

"Splendid."

The accordion player now began to play a jaunty little melody reminiscent of an English carol. Taking this as his signal, the Count indicated that he would like to make a toast.

"It is a sad but unavoidable fact of life," he began, "that as we age our social circles grow smaller. Whether from increased habit or diminished vigor, we suddenly find ourselves in the company of just a few familiar faces. So I view it as an incredible stroke of good fortune at this stage in my life to have found such a fine new friend."

With that, the Count reached into his pocket and presented Nina with a gift.

"Here is a little something that I made great use of when I was your age. May it tide you over until you travel *incognito*."

Nina smiled in a manner that suggested (rather unconvincingly) that he absolutely shouldn't have. Then she unwrapped the paper to reveal the Countess Rostova's hexagonal opera glasses.

"They were my grandmother's," said the Count.

For the first time in their acquaintance, Nina was struck dumb. She turned the little binoculars in her hands, admiring the mother-of-pearl scopes and delicate brass fittings. Then she held them to her eyes so she could slowly scan the room.

"You know me better than anyone," she said after a moment. "I shall treasure them to my dying day."

That she had not thought to bring a present for the Count struck him as perfectly understandable. After all, she was only a child; and the days of unwrapping surprises were decidedly behind him.

"It's getting late," said the Count. "I wouldn't want you to keep your father waiting."

"Yes," she admitted regretfully. "It is time for me to go."

Then looking back toward the captain's station, she raised a hand as one who signals for the check. But when the captain approached the table, he did not have the check. Instead, he had a large yellow box tied with dark green ribbon.

"Here," Nina said, "is a little something for you. But you must promise that you will not open it until the stroke of midnight."

When Nina left the Piazza to join her father, the Count's intention had been to settle the check, proceed to the Boyarsky (for an herb-encrusted lamb chop), and then retire to his study with a glass of port to await the chime of twelve. But as the accordion player launched into a second carol, the Count found himself turning his attention to the neighboring table, where a young man seemed to be in the earliest stages of romantic discovery.

In some lecture hall, this lad with a hint of a moustache had presumably admired his fellow student for the sharpness of her intellect and the seriousness of her mien. Eventually, he had worked up the nerve to invite her out, perhaps under the pretense of discussing some matter of ideological interest. And now here she was, sitting before him in the Piazza looking about the room without a smile on her face or a word on her lips.

Attempting to break the silence, the lad remarked on the upcoming conference to unify the Soviet republics—a reasonable gambit given her apparent intensity. Sure enough, the young lady had views on the subject; but as she voiced her opinion on the Transcaucas question, the tenor of the conversation turned decidedly technical. What's more, the young man, having adopted an expression as serious as hers, was clearly out of his depth. Were he to venture his own opinion now, he would almost certainly be revealed as a poseur, as one who was inadequately informed on the crucial issues of the day. From there, the evening could only get worse, and he would end up dragging his hopes behind him in the manner of the chastened child who drags his stuffed bear thumping up the stairs.

But just as the young lady was inviting him to share his thoughts on the matter, the accordion player began a little number with a Spanish flair. It must have struck a chord, because she interrupted herself in order to look at the musician and wonder aloud where that melody was from.

"It is from the *The Nutcracker*," the young man responded without a thought.

"*The Nutcracker* . . . ," she repeated.

Given the prevailing sobriety of her expression, it was unclear what she thought of this music from another era. As such, many a veteran would have counseled the young man to proceed with caution—to wait and hear what associations the music held for her. Instead, he acted; and he acted boldly.

"When I was a boy, my grandmother took me every year."

The young lady turned back from the musician to face her companion.

"I suppose some think the music sentimental," he continued, "but I never fail to attend the ballet when it is performed in December, even if it means attending alone."

Well done, lad.

The expression on the girl's face softened noticeably and her eyes displayed a hint of interest, that here was an unexpected aspect of her new acquaintance, something pure and heartfelt and unapologetic. Her lips parted as she prepared to ask a question—

"Are you ready to order?"

It was the Bishop leaning over their table.

Of course they are not ready to order, the Count wished to shout. *As any fool can see!*

If the young man were wise, he would send the Bishop packing and ask the young lady to go on with her question. Instead, he dutifully picked up the menu. Perhaps he imagined that the perfect dish would leap off the page and identify itself by name. But for a hopeful young man trying to impress a serious young woman, the menu of the Piazza was as perilous as the Straits of Messina. On the left was a Scylla of lower-priced dishes that could suggest a penny-pinching lack of flair; and on the right was a Charybdis of delicacies that could empty one's pockets while painting one pretentious. The young man's gaze drifted back and forth between these opposing hazards. But in a stroke of genius, he ordered the Latvian stew.

While this traditional dish of pork, onions, and apricots was reasonably priced, it was also reasonably exotic; and it somehow harkened back to that world of grandmothers and holidays and sentimental melodies that they had been about to discuss when so rudely interrupted.

"I'll have the same," said our serious young lady.

The same!

And then she glanced at her hopeful young acquaintance with a touch of that tenderness that Natasha had shown Pierre in *War and Peace* at the end of Volume Two.

"And would you like some wine to go with your stew?" asked the Bishop.

The young man hesitated and then picked up the wine list with uncertain hands. It may well have been the first time in his life that he had ordered a bottle of wine. Never mind that he didn't grasp the merits of the 1900 versus the 1901, he didn't know a Burgundy from a Bordeaux.

Giving the young man no more than a minute to consider his options, the Bishop leaned forward and poked the list with a condescending smile.

"Perhaps the Rioja."

The Rioja? Now there was a wine that would clash with the stew as Achilles clashed with Hector. It would slay the dish with a blow to the head and drag it behind its chariot until it tested the fortitude of every man in Troy. Besides, it plainly cost three times what the young man could afford.

With a shake of the head, the Count reflected that there was simply no substitute for experience. Here had been an ideal opportunity for a waiter to fulfill his purpose. By recommending a suitable wine, he could have put a young man at ease, perfected a meal, and furthered the cause of romance, all in a stroke. But whether from a lack of subtlety or a lack of sense, the Bishop had not only failed in his purpose, he had put his customer in a corner. And the young man, clearly unsure of what to do and beginning to feel as if the whole restaurant were watching, was on the verge of accepting the Bishop's suggestion.

"If I may," the Count interjected. "For a serving of Latvian stew, you will find no better choice than a bottle of the Mukuzani."

Leaning toward their table and mimicking the perfectly parted fingers of Andrey, the Count gestured to the entry on the list. That this wine was a fraction of the cost of the Rioja need not be a matter of a discussion between gentlemen. Instead, the Count simply noted: "The Georgians practically grow their grapes in the hopes that one day they will accompany such a stew."

The young man exchanged a brief glance with his companion as if to say, *Who is this eccentric?* But then he turned to the Bishop.

"A bottle of the Mukuzani."

"Of course," replied the Bishop.

Minutes later, the wine had been presented and poured, and the young woman was asking her companion what his grandmother was like. While for his part, the Count cast off any thoughts of herb-encrusted lamb at the Boyarsky. Instead, he summoned Petya to take Nina's present to his room and ordered the Latvian stew and a bottle of the Mukuzani for himself.

And just as he'd suspected, it was the perfect dish for the season. The onions thoroughly caramelized, the pork slowly braised, and the apricots briefly stewed, the three ingredients came together in a sweet and smoky medley that simultaneously suggested the comfort of a snowed-in tavern and the jangle of a Gypsy tambourine.

As the Count took a sip of his wine, the young couple caught his eye and raised their own glasses in a toast of gratitude and kinship. Then they returned to their conversation, which had grown so intimate, it could no longer be heard over the sound of the accordion.

Young love, thought the Count with a smile. There is nothing *novaya* about it.

"Will there be anything else?"

It was the Bishop addressing the Count. He considered for a moment, then he asked for a single scoop of vanilla ice cream.

As the Count entered the lobby, he noticed four men in evening dress coming through the door with black leather cases in hand, clearly one of the string quartets that occasionally played in the private dining rooms upstairs.

Three of the musicians looked as if they had been performing together since the nineteenth century, sharing the same white hair and weary professionalism. But the second violinist stood out from the others as he couldn't have been more than twenty-two and retained a certain brightness to his step. It was only as the quartet approached the elevator that the Count recognized him.

The Count probably hadn't seen Nikolai Petrov since 1914 when the Prince had been no more than a lad of thirteen; and given the passage of time, the Count might not have recognized him at all were it not for his unassuming smile—a distinguishing feature of the Petrov line for generations.

"Nikolai?"

When the Count spoke, the four musicians turned from the elevator and eyed him with curiosity.

"Alexander Ilyich . . . ?" the Prince asked after a moment.

"None other."

The Prince encouraged his colleagues to go ahead and then offered the Count the familial smile.

"It's good to see you, Alexander."

"And you."

They were quiet for a moment, then the Prince's expression changed from one of surprise to curiosity.

"Is that . . . ice cream?"

"What? Oh! Yes, it is. Though not for me."

The Prince nodded in bemusement, but without further remark.

"Tell me," the Count ventured, "have you heard from Dmitry?"

"I believe he is in Switzerland."

"Ah," said the Count with a smile. "The purest air in Europe."

The Prince shrugged, as if to say he had heard something of the sort, but wouldn't know firsthand.

"The last time I saw you," observed the Count, "you were playing Bach at one of your grandmother's dinner parties."

The Prince laughed and held up his case.

"I guess I am still playing Bach at dinner parties."

Then he gestured toward the departed elevator and said with unmistakable fondness:

"That was Sergei Eisenov."

"No!"

At the turn of the century, Sergei Eisenov had given music lessons to half the boys on the Boulevard Ring.

"It's not easy for our likes to find work," said the Prince. "But Sergei hires me when he can."

The Count had so many questions: Were there other members of the Petrov family still in Moscow? Was his grandmother alive? Was he still living in that wonderful house on Pushkin Square? But the two were standing in the middle of a hotel lobby as men and women headed up the stairs—including some in formal clothes.

"They'll be wondering what's become of me," said the Prince.

"Yes, of course. I didn't mean to keep you."

The Prince nodded and turned to mount the stairs, but then turned back.

"We are playing here again on Saturday night," he said. "Perhaps we could meet afterwards for a drink."

"That would be splendid," said the Count.*

---

*Among readers of European fiction, the character names in Russian novels are notorious for their difficulty. Not content to rely on given and family names, we Russians like to make use of honorifics, patronymics, and an array of diminutives— such that a single character in one of our novels may be referred to in four different ways in as many pages. To make matters worse, it seems that our greatest authors, due to some deep-rooted sense of tradition or a complete lack of imagination, constrained themselves to the use of thirty given names. You cannot pick up a work of Tolstoy, Dostoevsky, or Turgenev without bumping into an Anna, an Andrey, or an Alexander. Thus it must be with some trepidation that our Western reader meets any new character in a Russian novel—knowing that in the remote chance this character plays an important role in future chapters, he must now stop and commit the name to memory.

As such, I think it only fair to inform you now that while Prince Nikolai Petrov has agreed to meet the Count on Saturday night for a drink, he will not be keeping the appointment.

For when the quartet finishes their engagement at midnight, young Prince Nikolai will button his overcoat, tighten his scarf, and walk to his family's residence on Pushkin Square. Needless to say, when he arrives at 12:30, there are no footmen to greet him. With his violin in hand, he mounts the staircase headed toward the room on the fourth floor that has been left to his use.

Though the house seems empty, on the second floor Nikolai comes upon two of the house's newer residents smoking cigarettes. Nikolai recognizes one of them as the middle-aged woman who now lives in the nursery. The other is the bus operator with a family of four who lives in his mother's boudoir. When the Prince wishes them a goodnight with the unassuming smile of the house, neither says a word. But when he reaches the fourth floor he understands their reticence and can hardly blame them. For standing in the hallway are three men from the Cheka waiting to search his room.

Upon seeing them, Prince Nikolai does not make a scene or voice some idle protest. After all, it is the third time they have searched his room in six months, and he even recognizes one of the fellows. So, familiar with the procedure and weary from a long day, he offers them the same unassuming smile, lets them inside, and sits at the little table by the window as they go about their business.

The Prince has nothing to hide. Just sixteen years old when the Hermitage fell, he has never read a tract or harbored a grudge. If you asked him to play the imperial anthem, he wouldn't remember how. He even sees some sense in his grand old house being divvied up. His mother and sisters in Paris, his grandparents dead, the family servants scattered to the winds, what was he going to do with thirty rooms? All he really needed was a bed, a washbasin, and a chance to work.

But at two in the morning, the Prince is awakened with a shove by the officer in charge. In his hands is a textbook—a Latin grammar from Nikolai's days at the Imperial Lyceum.

"Is it yours?"

There is no point in lying.

"Yes," he says. "I attended the academy when I was a boy."

The officer opens the book; and there on the front plate looking regal and wise is a picture of Tsar Nicholas II—the possession of which is a crime. The Prince has to laugh, for he had taken such pains to remove all portraits, crests, and royal insignia from his room.

The captain slices the page out of the grammar with the blade of a knife. He marks the back with the time and place and has the Prince undersign it.

The Prince is taken to the Lubyanka, where he is held for several days and questioned once again regarding his loyalties. On the fifth day, all things considered, Fate spares him. For he is not ushered to the courtyard and put against the wall; nor is he shipped off to Siberia. He is merely given a Minus Six: the administrative sentence that allows him to roam Russia at will, as long as he never sets

When the Count arrived on the sixth floor, he clicked his tongue three times then went into his bedroom, leaving the door ajar. On the desk sat Nina's gift where Petya had left it. Taking it under an arm, the Count passed through his jackets into his study, set the present on his grand-mother's table, and put the bowl of melted ice cream on the floor. As the Count poured himself a glass of port, a silvery shadow swerved around his feet and approached the bowl.

"Happy holidays to you, Herr Drosselmeyer."

"Meow," replied the cat.

According to the twice-tolling clock, it was only eleven. So with his port in one hand and *A Christmas Carol* in the other, the Count tilted back his chair and dutifully waited for the chime of twelve. Admittedly, it takes a certain amount of discipline to sit in a chair and read a novel, even a seasonal one, when a beautifully wrapped present waits within arm's reach and the only witness is a one-eyed cat. But this was a disci-pline the Count had mastered as a child when, in the days leading up to

---

foot in Moscow, St. Petersburg, Kiev, Kharkov, Yekaterinburg, and Tibilisi—that is, the country's six largest cities.

About fifty miles from Moscow in Tuchkovo, the young Prince resumes his life; and for the most part, he does so without resentment, indignation, or nostal-gia. In his new hometown, the grass still grows, the fruit trees blossom, and young women come of age. In addition, by virtue of his remoteness, he is spared the knowledge that one year after his sentence, a trio of Cheka will be waiting for his old instructor when he comes home to the small apartment where he lives with his aging wife. When they haul him before a troika, what seals his fate and sends him to the camps is evidence that on multiple occasions he had hired Former Person Nikolai Petrov to play in his quartet despite a clear prohibition against doing so.

But having said that you needn't bother to remember the name of Prince Petrov, I should note that despite the brief appearance of a round-faced fellow with a receding hairline a chapter hence, *he* is someone you should commit to memory, for years later he will have great bearing on the outcome of this tale.

Christmas, he had marched past the closed drawing-room doors with the unflinching stare of a Buckingham Palace guard.

The young Count's self-mastery did not stem from a precocious admiration of military regimentation, nor a priggish adherence to household rules. By the time he was ten, it was perfectly clear that the Count was neither priggish nor regimental (as a phalanx of educators, caretakers, and constables could attest). No, if the Count mastered the discipline of marching past the closed drawing-room doors, it was because experience had taught him that this was the best means of ensuring the splendor of the season.

For on Christmas Eve, when his father finally gave the signal and he and Helena were allowed to pull the doors apart—there was the twelve-foot spruce lit up from trunk to tip and garlands hanging from every shelf. There were the bowls of oranges from Seville and the brightly colored candies from Vienna. And hidden somewhere under the tree was that unexpected gift—be it a wooden sword with which to defend the ramparts, or a lantern with which to explore a mummy's tomb.

Such is the magic of Christmas in childhood, thought the Count a little wistfully, that a single gift can provide one with endless hours of adventure while not even requiring one to leave one's house.

Drosselmeyer, who had retired to the other high-back chair to lick his paws, suddenly turned his one-eyed gaze toward the closet door with his little ears upright. What he must have heard was the whirring of inner wheels, for a second later came the first of midnight's chimes.

Setting his book and his port aside, the Count placed Nina's gift in his lap with his fingers on the dark green bow and listened to the tolling of the clock. Only with the twelfth and final chime did he pull the ribbon's ends.

"What do you think, *mein Herr*? A dapper hat?"

The cat looked up at the Count and in deference to the season began to purr. The Count replied with a nod and then carefully lifted the lid . . . only to discover another box wrapped in yellow and tied with a dark green bow.

Setting the empty box aside, the Count nodded again to the cat, pulled the strands of the second bow, and lifted the second lid . . . only to discover a third box. Dutifully, the Count repeated the debowing and unlidding with the next three boxes, until he held one the size of a match-box. But when he untied the bow and lifted the lid on this box, inside the cozy chamber, strung on a bit of the dark green ribbon, was Nina's pass-key to the hotel.

When the Count climbed into bed with his Dickens at 12:15, he assumed he would only read a paragraph or two before switching off the light; but instead, he found himself reading with the greatest interest.

He had reached the part in the story where Scrooge is being spirited around by that jolly giant, the Ghost of Christmas Present. Over the course of his childhood, the Count had been read *A Christmas Carol* no less than three times. So, he certainly remembered the visit Scrooge and his guide paid to the laughter-filled party at Scrooge's nephew's house; just as he remembered the visit they paid to the humble, yet heartfelt celebration at the Cratchits'. But he had completely forgotten that upon leaving the Cratchits', the Second Spirit had taken Scrooge out of the city of London altogether, to a bleak and deserted moor where a family of miners was celebrating the season in their ramshackle hut at the edge of the mine; and from there to a lighthouse on a rocky outpost where the waves thun-dered as the two craggy keepers of the beacon joined their hands in yule-tide song; and from there, farther and farther the Spirit carried Scrooge, into the howling darkness of the rolling sea, until they alit upon the deck of a ship where every man good or bad had fond thoughts of home and a kinder word for his mates.

Who knows.

Perhaps what stirred the Count were these far-flung figures sharing in the fellowship of the season despite their lives of hard labor in inhospita-ble climes. Perhaps it was the sight earlier in the evening of that modern young couple proceeding toward romance in the age-old fashion. Perhaps it was the chance meeting with Nikolai, who, despite his heritage, seemed to be finding a place for himself in the new Russia. Or perhaps it was the utterly unanticipated blessing of Nina's friendship. Whatever the cause, when the Count closed his book and turned out the light, he fell asleep with a great sense of well-being.

But had the Ghost of Christmas Yet to Come suddenly appeared and roused the Count to give him a glimpse of the future, he would have seen that his sense of well-being had been premature. For less than four years later, after another careful accounting of the twice-tolling clock's twelve chimes, Alexander Ilyich Rostov would be climbing to the roof of the Metropol Hotel in his finest jacket and gamely approaching its parapet in order to throw himself into the street below.

BOOK TWO

1923

An Actress, an Apparition, an Apiary

At five o'clock on the twenty-first of June, the Count stood before his closet with his hand on his plain gray blazer and hesitated. In a few minutes, he would be on his way to the barbershop for his weekly visit, and then to the Shalyapin to meet Mishka, who would probably be wearing the same brown jacket he'd worn since 1913. As such, the gray blazer seemed a perfectly suitable choice of attire. That is, until one considered that it was an anniversary of sorts—for it had been one year to the day since the Count had last set foot outside of the Metropol Hotel.

But how was one to celebrate such an anniversary? And should one? For while house arrest is a definitive infringement upon one's liberty, presumably it is also intended to be something of a humiliation. So both pride and common sense would suggest that such an anniversary might best be left unmarked.

And yet . . .

Even men in the most trying of circumstances—like those lost at sea or confined to prison—will find the means to carefully account the passing of a year. Despite the fact that all the splendid modulations of the seasons and those colorful festivities that recur in the course of normal life have been replaced by a tyranny of indistinguishable days, the men in such situations will carve their 365 notches into a piece of wood or scratch them into the walls of their cell.

Why do they go to such lengths to mark time? When, ostensibly, to do so should matter to them least of all? Well, for one, it provides an occasion to reflect on the inevitable progress of the world they've left behind: *Ah, Alyosha must now be able to climb the tree in the yard; and Vanya must be entering the academy; and Nadya, dear Nadya, will soon be of an age to marry. . . .*

But just as important, a careful accounting of days allows the isolated to note that another year of hardship has been endured; survived; bested. Whether they have found the strength to persevere through a tireless determination or some foolhardy optimism, those 365 hatch marks stand as proof of their indomitability. For after all, if attentiveness should be measured in minutes and discipline measured in hours, then indomitability must be measured in years. Or, if philosophical investigations are not to your taste, then let us simply agree that the wise man celebrates what he can.

Thus, the Count donned his finest smoking jacket (custom-made in Paris from a burgundy velvet) and headed down the stairs.

When the Count reached the lobby, before he could continue to the barbershop his eyes were drawn to a willowy figure coming through the hotel's doors. But then all eyes in the lobby were drawn to her. A tall woman in her midtwenties with arched eyebrows and auburn hair, she was indisputably striking. And as she approached the front desk, she walked with a breezy sureness as seemingly unaware of the feathers projecting from her hat as of the bellhops dragging her luggage behind her. But what guaranteed her position as the natural center of attention were the two borzois she had on leash.

In an instant the Count could see that they were magnificent beasts. Their coats silver, their loins lean, their every sense alert, these dogs had been raised to give chase in the cold October air with a hunting party hot on their heels. And at day's end? They were meant to sit at the feet of their master before a fire in a manor house—not adorn the hands of a willow in the lobby of a grand hotel. . . .

The injustice of this was not lost on the dogs. As their mistress addressed Arkady at the front desk, they tugged every which way, sniffing about for familiar landmarks.

"Stop it!" the willow commanded in a surprisingly husky voice. Then she yanked in a manner that showed she had no more familiarity with the wolfhounds on her leashes than she had with the birds that had feathered her hat.

The Count gave the situation the shake of the head it deserved. But as he turned to go, he noticed with some amusement that a slender shadow suddenly jumped from behind a wingback chair to the edge of one of the potted palms. It was none other than Field Marshal Kutuzov attaining higher ground to take measure of his foes. When the dogs turned their heads in unison with their ears upright, the one-eyed cat slipped behind the trunk of the tree. Then having satisfied himself that the dogs were securely tethered, the cat alit from the palm to the floor and without even bothering to arch his back opened his little jaws and hissed.

With a terrific volley of barking, the dogs leapt to the extent of their leashes, tugging their mistress from the front desk as the ledger pen clattered to the floor.

"Whoa," she shouted. "Whoa!"

Apparently unfamiliar with equine commands, the wolfhounds leapt again and, freeing themselves from the willow's grip, scrambled toward their prey.

Kutuzov was off like a shot. Slipping under the western embankment of lobby chairs, the one-eyed cat dashed toward the front door, as if intending to escape into the street. Without a moment's hesitation, the dogs gave chase. Opting for a pincer movement, they split at the potted palms and pursued the cat on opposite sides of the chairs in the hopes of cutting him off at the door. A lamp that blocked the path of the first hound was knocked to the floor in a shower of sparks, while a standing ashtray that blocked the second was sent head over heels, discharging a cloud of dust.

But just as the dogs were closing ranks, Kutuzov—who like his namesake had the advantage of familiar terrain—suddenly reversed course. Cutting in front of a coffee table, he dashed under the eastern embankment of lobby chairs and headed back toward the staircase.

It took only a few seconds for the borzois to recognize the cat's tactic; but if attentiveness is measured in minutes, discipline in hours, and indomitability in years, then the attaining of the upper hand on the field of battle is measured in the instant. For just as the wolfhounds registered the cat's reversal and attempted to turn, the lobby's expansive oriental carpet came to an end, and the dogs' momentum sent them skidding across the marble floor into the luggage of an arriving guest.

With an advantage over his adversaries of a hundred feet, Kutuzov skipped up the first few steps of the staircase, paused for a moment to admire his handiwork, then disappeared around the corner.

You may accuse a dog of eating without grace or of exhibiting a misplaced enthusiasm for the tossing of sticks, but you may never accuse one of giving up hope. Despite the fact that the cat had a decisive lead and knew every nook and cranny of the hotel's upper floors, once the dogs regained their footing, they charged across the lobby in full chorus with every intention of mounting the stairs.

But the Hotel Metropol was not a hunting ground. It was a residence par excellence, an oasis for the worn and weary. So, with a slight curl of the tongue, the Count gave an upward sloping whistle in G major. At the sound, the dogs broke pursuit and began restlessly circling at the foot of the stairs. The Count gave two more whistles in quick succession and the dogs, resigning themselves to the fact that the day was lost, trotted to the Count and heeled at his feet.

"Well, my boys," he said, giving them a good scratching behind the ears, "where do you hail from?"

"Arf," replied the dogs.

"Ah," said the Count. "How lovely."

After smoothing her skirt and straightening her hat, the willowy one gracefully crossed the lobby to the Count, where, thanks to a pair of French heels, she met him eye to eye. At such proximity the Count could see that she was even more beautiful than he had suspected; and haughtier too. His natural sympathies remained with the dogs.

"Thank you," she said (with a smile that presumed to launch armadas). "I'm afraid that they are quite ill bred."

"On the contrary," replied the Count, "they appear to be perfectly bred."

The willow made a second effort at her smile.

"What I meant to say is that they are ill behaved."

"Yes, perhaps ill behaved; but that is a matter of handling, not breeding."

As the willow studied the Count, he noted that the arches over her eyebrows were very much like the marcato notation in music—that accent which instructs one to play a phrase a little more loudly. This, no doubt, accounted for the willow's preference for issuing commands and the resulting huskiness of her voice. But as the Count was coming to this conclusion, the willow was apparently coming to a conclusion of her own, for she now dispensed with any intent to charm.

"Handling does seem to have a way of eclipsing breeding," she said acerbically. "And for that very reason, I should think that even some of the best-bred dogs belong on the shortest leashes."

"An understandable conclusion," replied the Count. "But I should think the best-bred dogs belong in the surest hands."

One hour later, with his hair neatly trimmed and his chin cleanly shaved, the Count entered the Shalyapin and selected a small table in the corner at which to wait for Mishka, who was in town for the inaugural congress of RAPP.

It was only as he settled in that he realized the willowy beauty, now in a long blue dress, was sitting on the banquette directly opposite his own. She had spared the bar the spectacle of trying to manage her dogs, but in their place she had brought along a round-faced fellow with a receding hairline for whom puppylike devotion seemed to come a little more naturally. While the Count was smiling at his own observation, he happened to meet the willow's gaze. As was only fitting, the two adults immediately acted as if they hadn't seen each other, the one by turning to her puppy and the other by turning to the door. And as luck would have it, there was Mishka right on time—but with a brand-new jacket and a well-groomed beard. . . .

The Count came out from behind the table in order to embrace his friend. Then, rather than reclaim his seat, he offered the banquette to Mishka—an action that seemed at once courteous and opportune, since it allowed the Count to turn his back on the willow.

"Well now," said the Count with a clap of the hands. "What shall it be, my friend? Champagne? Château d'Yquem? A dish of beluga before supper?" But with a shake of the head, Mishka asked for a beer and explained that he could not stay for dinner, after all.

Naturally, the Count was disappointed by the news. After a discreet inquiry, he had learned that the evening's special at the Boyarsky was roasted duck—the perfect dish for two old friends to share. And Andrey had promised to set aside a particular Grand Cru that not only complemented the duck, but would inevitably lead to a retelling of the infamous night when the Count had become locked in the Rothschilds' wine cellar with the young Baroness. . . .

But while the Count was disappointed, he could see from his old friend's fidgeting that he had his own stories to tell. So, as soon as their beers were before them, the Count asked how things were progressing at the congress. Taking a drink, Mishka nodded that here was the topic of the hour—the very conversation that would soon be engrossing all of Russia, if not the world.

"There were no hushed voices today, Sasha. No dozing or fiddling with pencils. For in every corner from every hand there was work being done."

If offering Mishka the banquette had been gracious and opportune, it also had the added benefit of keeping him in his seat. For were he not trapped behind the table, he would already have leapt to his feet and been pacing the bar. And what was the work being done at this congress? As best as the Count could determine, it included the drafting of "Declarations of Intent," "Proclamations of Allegiance," and "Open Statements of Solidarity." Indeed, the Russian Association of Proletarian Writers didn't hesitate to express their solidarity. In fact, they expressed it not only with their fellow writers, publishers, and editors, but with the masons and stevedores, the welders and riveters, even the street sweepers.*

So fevered was the first day of the congress that dinner wasn't served until eleven o'clock. And then at a table set for sixty, they heard from Mayakovsky himself. There were no lecterns, mind you. When the plates had been served, he simply banged on the table and stood on his chair.

---

*Why, *especially* the street sweepers!

Those unsung few who rise at dawn and trod the empty avenues gathering up the refuse of the era. Not simply the matchbooks, candy wrappers, and ticket stubs, mind you; but the newspapers, journals, and pamphlets; the catechisms and hymnals, histories and memoirs; the contracts, deeds, and titles; the treaties and constitutions and all Ten Commandments.

Sweep on, street sweepers! Sweep until the cobblestones of Russia glitter like gold!

In the interests of realism, Mishka tried to stand on the banquette, nearly knocking over his beer. He settled for a seated oration with a finger in the air:

> Suddenly—I
> shone in all my might,
> and morning rang its round.
> Always to shine,
> to shine everywhere,
> to the very depths of the last days,
> to shine—
> and to hell with everything else!
> That is my motto—
> and the sun's!

Naturally, Mayakovsky's poem prompted unrestrained applause and the smashing of glasses. But then, just as everyone had settled down and was preparing to slice into their chicken, some fellow named Zelinsky was up on his chair.

"For, of course, we *must* hear from Zelinsky," muttered Mishka. "As if *he* stands shoulder to shoulder with Mayakovsky. As if he stands shoulder to shoulder with a bottle of milk."

Mishka took another sip.

"You remember Zelinsky. No? The one who was a few years behind us at the university? The one who wore a monocle in '16 and a sailor's cap the following year? Well, anyway, you know the sort, Sasha—the type who must always have their hands on the wheel. At the end of dinner, say two of you are lingering in your chairs to continue a discussion from earlier in the day—well, there is Zelinsky proclaiming that he knows just the place to carry on the conversation. Next thing you know, there are ten of you being crowded around a table in some basement café. When you go to take a seat, he has a hand on your shoulder, steering you to this end of the table or that. And when someone calls for bread, he has a better idea. They have the best zavitushki in Moscow, he says. And before you know it, he's snapping his fingers in the air."

Here Mishka snapped his fingers three times so emphatically that the Count had to wave off the ever-attentive Audrius, who was already halfway across the room.

"And his ideas!" Mishka continued in disdain. "On and on he goes with his declarations, as if he is in a position to enlighten anyone on matters of verse. And what does he have to say to the impressionable young student at his side? That all poets must eventually bow before the haiku. *Bow before the haiku!* Can you imagine."

"For my part," contributed the Count, "I am glad that Homer wasn't born in Japan."

Mishka stared at the Count for a moment then burst out laughing.

"Yes," he said, slapping the table and wiping a tear from his eye. "Glad that Homer wasn't born in Japan. I shall have to remember to tell that one to Katerina."

Mishka smiled in apparent anticipation of telling that one to Katerina.

"Katerina . . . ?" asked the Count.

Mishka casually reached for his beer.

"Katerina Litvinova. Have I not mentioned her before? She's a talented young poet from Kiev—in her second year at the university. We sit on a committee together."

Mishka leaned back in order to drink from his glass. The Count leaned back in order to smile at his companion—as the entire picture came into focus.

A new jacket and a well-groomed beard . . .

A discussion after dinner continued from earlier in the day . . .

And a Zelinsky who, having dragged everyone to his favorite little nightspot, steers an impressionable young poet to one end of the table and a Mishka to the other. . . .

As Mishka continued with his description of the previous evening, the irony of the situation did not escape the Count: that during all those years they had lived above the cobbler's, it was Mishka who had stayed put and the Count who, having apologized that he couldn't join his friend for dinner, had returned hours later with tales of lively toasts and *tête-à-têtes* and impromptu outings to candlelit cafés.

Did the Count take some pleasure in hearing about Mishka's late-night skirmishes? Of course he did. Particularly when he learned that at

the end of the evening, as the group was about to climb into three different cabs, Mishka reminded Zelinsky that he had forgotten his hat; and
when Zelinsky dashed back inside to retrieve it, Katerina from Kiev
leaned from her cab to call: *Here, Mikhail Fyodorovich, why don't you ride
with us. . . .*

Yes, the Count took pleasure in his old friend's romantic skirmish;
but that is not to suggest that he didn't feel the sting of envy.

Half an hour later, after the Count had sent Mishka off to a discussion on
the future of meter (at which Katerina from Kiev would presumably be
in attendance), he headed to the Boyarsky, apparently destined to dine
on duck alone. But just as he was leaving, Audrius beckoned.

Sliding a folded piece of paper across the bar, Audrius explained
under his breath: "I was instructed to relay this to you."

"To me? From whom?"

"Miss Urbanova."

"Miss Urbanova?"

"Anna Urbanova. The movie star."

Since the Count still showed no sign of understanding, the bartender
explained a little more loudly: "The one who was sitting at that table
across from you."

"Ah, yes. Thank you."

As Audrius returned to his work, the Count unfolded the piece of
paper, which bore the following request in a willowy script:

> *Please allow me a second chance*
> *at a first impression*
> *in suite 208*

When the Count knocked on the door of suite 208, it was opened by an
older woman who regarded him with impatience.

"Yes?"

"I am Alexander Rostov. . . ."

"You're expected. Come in. Miss Urbanova will be a moment."

Instinctively, the Count prepared to offer the woman a witty remark about the weather, but when he stepped inside she stepped out and closed the door, leaving him alone in the entryway.

Decorated in the style of a Venetian palazzo, suite 208 was one of the finest accommodations on the floor and looked no worse for wear now that the tireless typers of directives had finally moved to the Kremlin. With a bedroom and drawing room on either side of a grand salon, its ceilings were painted with allegorical figures gazing down from the heavens. On an ornate side table stood two towering arrangements of flowers—one of calla lilies and the other of long-stemmed roses. The fact that the two arrangements matched each other in extravagance while clashing in color suggested they were from competing admirers. One could only imagine what a third admirer would feel obliged to send. . . .

"I'll be right out," called a voice from the bedroom.

"Take your time," called back the Count.

At the sound of his voice, there was a light clacking of nails on the floor as the borzois appeared from the drawing room.

"Hello, boys," he said, giving them another scratch behind the ears.

Having paid their respects, the dogs trotted to the windows overlooking Theatre Square and rested their forepaws on the sills in order to watch the movement of the cars below.

"Count Rostov!"

Turning, the Count found the actress dressed in her third outfit of the day: black pants and an ivory blouse. With the smile of an old acquaintance and her hand extended, she approached.

"I'm so pleased you could come."

"The pleasure is mine, Miss Urbanova."

"I doubt that. But please, call me Anna."

Before the Count could reply, there was a knock at the door.

"Ah," she said. "Here we are."

Swinging the door open, she stepped aside to let Oleg from room service pass. When Oleg caught sight of the Count, he nearly ran his dinner cart into the competing arrangements of flowers.

"Perhaps over there by the window," suggested the actress.

"Yes, Miss Urbanova," said Oleg, who, having regained his composure, set a table for two, lit a candle, and backed out the door.

The actress turned to the Count.

"Have you eaten? I've been in two restaurants and a bar today and haven't had a bite. I'm absolutely starving. Won't you join me?"

"Certainly."

The Count pulled back a chair for his hostess and, as he took his seat on the opposite side of the candle, the borzois looked back from their windows. Presumably, here was a scene that neither of the dogs could have anticipated earlier that day. But having long since lost interest in the fickle course of human affairs, they dropped to the floor and trotted back to the drawing room without a second glance.

The actress watched them retire a little wistfully.

"I confess that I am not a dog lover."

"Then why do you have them?"

"They were . . . a gift."

"Ah. From an admirer."

She responded with a wry smile. "I would have settled for a necklace."

The Count returned the smile.

"Well," she said. "Let's see what we've got."

Removing the silver dome from the serving plate, the actress revealed one of Emile's signature dishes: whole bass roasted with black olives, fennel, and lemon.

"Lovely," she said.

And the Count could not agree more. For by setting his oven to 450°, Emile ensured that the flesh of the fish was tender, the fennel aromatic, and the lemon slices blackened and crisp.

"So, two restaurants and a bar without having a bite to eat . . ."

Thus began the Count, with the natural intention of letting the actress recount her day while he prepared her plate. But before he could lift a finger, she had taken the knife and serving fork in hand. And as she began to relate the professional obligations that had commandeered her afternoon, she scored the fish's spine with the tip of the knife and made diagonal cuts at its head and tail. Then slipping the serving fork between the fish's spine and its flesh, she deftly liberated the filet. In a few succinct movements, she had served portions of the fennel and olives, and topped the filet with the charred lemon. Handing the Count this perfectly prepared plate, she plucked the spine from the fish and served herself the second filet with accompaniments—an operation that took no more than a minute. Then placing the serving utensils on the platter, she turned her attention to the wine.

Good God, thought the Count. So engrossed had he been in watching her technique, he had neglected his own responsibilities. Leaping from his chair, he took the bottle by the neck.

"May I?"

"Thank you."

As the Count poured the wine, he noted it was a dry Montrachet, the perfect complement to Emile's bass and clearly the handiwork of Andrey. The Count raised his glass to his hostess.

"I must say that you deboned that fish like an expert."

She laughed.

"Is that a compliment?"

"Of course it's a compliment! Well. At least, it was intended as one. . . ."

"In that case, thank you. But I wouldn't make too much of it. I was raised in a fishing village on the Black Sea, so I've tied more than my share of knots and filleted more than my share of fish."

"You could do worse than dining on fish every night."

"That's true. But when you live in a fisherman's house, you tend to eat what can't be sold. So more often than not, we dined on flatfish and bream."

"The bounty of the sea . . ."

"The *bottom* of the sea."

And with that disarming memory, Anna Urbanova was suddenly describing how as a girl she would steal away from her mother at dusk and wind her way down the sloping streets of her village so that she could meet her father on the beach and help him mend his nets. And as she talked, the Count had to acknowledge once again the virtues of withholding judgment.

After all, what can a first impression tell us about someone we've just met for a minute in the lobby of a hotel? For that matter, what can a first impression tell us about anyone? Why, no more than a chord can tell us about Beethoven, or a brushstroke about Botticelli. By their very nature, human beings are so capricious, so complex, so delightfully contradictory, that they deserve not only our consideration, but our *reconsideration*—and our unwavering determination to withhold our opinion until we have engaged with them in every possible setting at every possible hour.

Take the simple case of Anna Urbanova's voice. In the context of the lobby, where the actress was struggling to rein in her hounds, the hoarseness of her voice had given the impression of an imperious young lady prone to shouting. Very well. But here in suite 208 in the company of charred lemons, French wine, and memories of the sea, her voice was revealed as that of a woman whose profession rarely allowed her the chance for repose, never mind the enjoyment of a decent meal.

As the Count refilled their glasses, he was struck by a memory of his own that seemed in keeping with the conversation.

"I spent a good part of my youth in the province of Nizhny Novgorod," he said, "which happens to be the world capital of the apple. In Nizhny Novgorod, there are not simply apple trees scattered about the countryside; there are *forests* of apple trees—forests as wild and ancient as Russia itself—in which apples grow in every color of the rainbow and in sizes ranging from a walnut to a cannonball."

"I take it you ate your fair share of apples."

"Oh, we'd find them tucked in our omelets at breakfast, floating in our soups at lunch, and stuffed in our pheasants at dinner. Come Christmas, we had eaten every single variety the woods had to offer."

The Count was about to lift his glass to toast the comprehensiveness of their apple eating, when he waved a self-correcting finger.

"Actually, there was one apple that we did not eat. . . ."

The actress raised one of her bedeviling eyebrows.

"Which?"

"According to local lore, hidden deep within the forest was a tree with apples as black as coal—and if you could find this tree and eat of its fruit, you could start your life anew."

The Count took a generous drink of the Montrachet, pleased to have summoned this little folktale from the past.

"So would you?" the actress asked.

"Would I what?"

"If you found that apple hidden in the forest, would you take a bite?"

The Count put his glass on the table and shook his head.

"There's certainly some allure to the idea of a fresh start; but how could

I relinquish my memories of home, of my sister, of my school years." The Count gestured to the table. "How could I relinquish my memory of this?"

And Anna Urbanova, having put her napkin on her plate and pushed back her chair, came round the table, took the Count by the collar, and kissed him on the mouth.

Ever since reading her note in the Shalyapin Bar, the Count had felt one step behind Miss Urbanova. The casual reception in her suite, the candlelit dinner for two, the deboning of the fish followed by memories of childhood—he had not anticipated any one of these developments. Certainly he had been caught off guard by the kiss. And now, here she was strolling into her bedroom, unbuttoning her blouse, and letting it slip to the floor with a delicate whoosh.

As a young man, the Count had prided himself on being one step ahead. The timely appearance, the apt expression, the anticipation of a need, to the Count these had been the very hallmarks of the well-bred man. But under the circumstances, he discovered that being a step behind had merits of its own.

For one, it was so much more relaxing. To be a step ahead in matters of romance requires constant vigilance. If one hopes to make a successful advance, one must be mindful of every utterance, attend to every gesture, and take note of every look. In other words, to be a step ahead in romance is exhausting. But to be a step behind? To be seduced? Why, that was a matter of leaning back in one's chair, sipping one's wine, and responding to a query with the very first thought that has popped into one's head.

And yet, paradoxically, if being a step behind was more relaxing than being a step ahead, it was also more exciting. From his relaxed position, the one-step-behinder imagines that his evening with a new acquaintance will transpire like any other—with a little chit, a little chat, and a friendly goodnight at the door. But halfway through dinner there is an unexpected compliment and an accidental brushing of fingers against one's hand; there is a tender admission and a self-effacing laugh; then suddenly a kiss.

From here the surprises only grow in power and scope. Such as when one discovers (as the blouse falls to the floor) that a back is as decorated with freckles as the skies are decorated with stars. Or when (having slipped modestly under the covers) the sheets are cast aside and one finds oneself on one's back with a pair of hands pressing on one's chest and a pair of lips issuing breathless instructions. But while each one of these surprises inspires a new state of wonder, nothing can compare to the awe one experiences when at one in the morning a woman rolling on her side utters unambiguously: "As you go, be sure to draw the curtains."

Suffice it to say that once the Count's clothes had been gathered, the curtains were dutifully drawn. What's more, before he had tiptoed to the door half dressed, he took a moment to ensure that the actress's ivory blouse had been picked off the floor and hung on its hanger. After all, as the Count himself had observed just hours before: the best-bred dogs belong in the surest hands.

The sound of the door clicking shut behind you . . .

The Count wasn't sure he had ever heard it before, exactly. In tone it was delicate and unobtrusive; and yet, it had a definitive suggestion of dismissal—which was apt to put one in a philosophical frame of mind.

Even if a person generally frowned upon rude and abrupt behavior, under the circumstances he might have to admit a certain rough justice upon finding himself in an empty hallway with his shoes in his hand and his shirt untucked—as the woman he's just left falls soundly asleep. For if a man has had the good fortune to be plucked from the crowd by an impetuous beauty, shouldn't he expect to be sent on his way without ceremony?

Well, maybe so. But standing in the empty corridor across from a half-eaten bowl of borscht, the Count felt less like a philosopher than a ghost.

Yes, a ghost, thought the Count, as he moved silently down the hall. Like Hamlet's father roaming the ramparts of Elsinore after the midnight watch . . . Or like Akaky Akakievich, that forsaken spirit of Gogol's who in the wee hours haunted the Kalinkin Bridge in search of his stolen coat . . .

Why is it that so many ghosts prefer to travel the halls of night? Ask the living and they will tell you that these spirits either have some unquenched desire or an unaddressed grievance that stirs them from their sleep and sends them out into the world in search of solace.

But the living are so self-centered.

Of course they would judge a spirit's nocturnal wanderings as the product of earthly memories. When, in fact, if these restless souls wanted to harrow the bustling avenues of noon, there is nothing to stop them from doing so.

No. If they wander the halls of night, it is not from a grievance with or envy of the living. Rather, it is because they have no desire to see the living at all. Any more than snakes hope to see gardeners, or foxes the hounds. They wander about at midnight because at that hour they can generally do so without being harried by the sound and fury of earthly emotions. After all those years of striving and struggling, of hoping and praying, of shouldering expectations, stomaching opinions, navigating decorum, and making conversation, what they seek, quite simply, is a little peace and quiet. At least, that is what the Count told himself as he drifted down the hall.

While, as a rule, the Count always took the stairs, when he approached the second-floor landing that night, on some ghostly whim he called for the elevator, assuming he would have it to himself. But when the doors slid open, there was the one-eyed cat.

"Kutuzov!" he exclaimed in surprise.

Taking in every detail of the Count's appearance, the cat responded exactly as the Grand Duke had responded under similar circumstances many years before—that is, with a stern look and a disappointed silence.

"Ahem," said the Count, as he stepped onto the elevator while trying to tuck in his shirt without dropping his shoes.

Parting with the cat on the fifth floor, the Count trudged up the steps of the belfry in woeful acknowledgment that the celebration of his anniversary had been a fiasco. Having set out to gamely etch his mark on the wall, the wall had etched its mark on him. And as experience had taught the Count many years before, when this happens, it is best to wash one's face, brush one's teeth, and pull one's covers over one's head.

But as the Count was about to open the door to his rooms, on the back of his neck he felt a breath of air that was distinctly reminiscent of a summer breeze. Turning to his left, the Count stood motionless. There it was again, coming from the other end of the floor. . . .

Intrigued, the Count walked down the hall only to find that all the doors were tightly shut. At the hallway's end, there seemed to be nothing but a confusion of pipes and flues. But in the farthest corner, in the shadow of the largest pipe, he discovered a wall-mounted ladder that led to a hatch in the roof—which someone had left open. Putting on his shoes, the Count quietly climbed up the ladder and out into the night.

The summer breeze that had beckoned the Count now wrapped him in its full embrace. Warm and forgiving, it called up feelings of summer nights from earlier in his life—from when he was five and ten and twenty on the streets of St. Petersburg or the pastures of Idlehour. Nearly overcome by the surge of old sentiments, he needed to pause a moment before continuing to the western edge of the roof.

Before him lay the ancient city of Moscow, which, after waiting patiently for two hundred years, was once again the seat of Russian governance. Despite the hour, the Kremlin shimmered with electric light from every window, as if its newest denizens were still too drunk with power to sleep. But if the lights of the Kremlin shimmered brightly, like all earthly lights before them they were diminished in their beauty by the majesty of the constellations overhead.

Craning his neck, the Count tried to identify the few that he had learned in his youth: Perseus, Orion, the Great Bear, each flawless and eternal. To what end, he wondered, had the Divine created the stars in heaven to fill a man with feelings of inspiration one day and insignificance the next?

Lowering his gaze to the horizon, the Count looked out beyond the limits of the city—to where that ancient comfort of sailors, the Morning Star, burned brightest in all the firmament.

And then blinked.

"Good morning, Your Excellency."

The Count spun about.

Standing a few feet behind him was a man in his early sixties wearing a canvas cap. When the man took a step forward, the Count recognized him as one of the handymen who battled the hotel's leaky pipes and creaky doors.

"That's the Shukhov all right," he said.

"The Shukhov?"

"The radio tower."

He pointed in the distance toward the comfort of sailors.

Ah, thought the Count with a smile. Mishka's spiraling structure of steel broadcasting the latest news and intelligence . . .

The two men were silent for a moment, as if waiting for the beacon to blink again—which it reliably did.

"Well. The coffee'll be ready. You might as well come along."

The old handyman led the Count to the northeast corner of the roof, where he had established something of a camp between two chimneys. In addition to a three-legged stool, there was a small fire burning in a brazier on which a coffeepot was steaming. The old man had chosen the spot well, for while it was out of the wind he still had a view of the Bolshoi that was only slightly impaired by some old crates stacked at the edge of the roof.

"I don't get many visitors," the handyman said, "so I don't have a second stool."

"That's quite all right," said the Count, picking up a two-foot plank, setting it on end, and balancing himself on its edge.

"Can I pour you a cup?"

"Thank you."

As the coffee was being poured, the Count wondered whether this was the beginning or end of the old man's day. Either way, he figured a cup of coffee would hit the spot. For what is more versatile? As at home in tin as it is in Limoges, coffee can energize the industrious at dawn, calm the reflective at noon, or raise the spirits of the beleaguered in the middle of the night.

"It's perfect," said the Count.

The old man leaned forward.

"The secret is in the grinding." He pointed to a little wooden apparatus with an iron crank. "Not a minute before you brew."

The Count raised his eyebrows with the appreciation of the uninitiated.

Yes, in the open air on a summer night the old man's coffee was perfect. In fact, the only thing that spoiled the moment was a humming in the air—the sort that might be emitted from a faulty fuse or a radio receiver.

"Is that the tower?" the Count asked.

"Is what the tower?"

"The humming."

The old man looked up in the air for a moment then cackled.

"That'll be the girls at work."

"The girls?"

The old man pointed with a thumb to the crates that compromised his view of the Bolshoi. In the predawn light, the Count could just make out a whirl of activity above them.

"Are those . . . bees?"

"Indeed they are."

"What are they doing here?"

"Making honey."

"Honey!"

The old man cackled again.

"Making honey is what bees does. Here."

Leaning forward, the old man held out a roof tile on which there were two slices of black bread slathered with honey. The Count accepted one and took a bite.

The first thing that struck him was actually the black bread. For when was the last time he had even eaten it? If asked outright, he would have been embarrassed to admit. Tasting of dark rye and darker molasses, it was a perfect complement to a cup of coffee. And the honey? What an extraordinary contrast it provided. If the bread was somehow earthen, brown, and brooding, the honey was sunlit, golden, and gay. But there was another dimension to it. . . . An elusive, yet familiar element . . . A grace note hidden beneath, or behind, or within the sensation of sweetness.

"What is that flavor . . . ?" the Count asked almost to himself.

"The lilacs," the old man replied. Without turning, he pointed with his thumb back in the direction of the Alexander Gardens.

Of course, thought the Count. That was it precisely. How could he have missed it? Why, there was a time when he knew the lilacs of the Alexander Gardens better than any man in Moscow. When the trees were in season, he could spend whole afternoons in happy repose under their white and purple blossoms.

"How extraordinary," the Count said with an appreciative shake of the head.

"It is and isn't," said the old man. "When the lilacs are in bloom, the bees'll buzz to the Alexander Gardens and the honey'll taste like the lilacs. But in a week or so, they'll be buzzing to the Garden Ring, and then you'll be tasting the cherry trees."

"The Garden Ring! How far will they go?"

"Some say a bee'll cross the ocean for a flower," answered the old man with a smile. "Though I've never known one to do so."

The Count shook his head, took another bite, and accepted a second cup of coffee. "As a boy, I spent a good deal of time in Nizhny Novgorod," he recalled for the second time that day.

"Where the apple blossoms fall like snow," the old man said with a smile. "I was raised there myself. My father was the caretaker on the Chernik estate."

"I know it well!" exclaimed the Count. "What a beautiful part of the world . . ."

So as the summer sun began to rise, the fire began to die, and the bees began to circle overhead, the two men spoke of days from their childhoods when the wagon wheels rattled in the road, and the dragonflies skimmed the grass, and the apple trees blossomed for as far as the eye could see.

Addendum

At the very moment that the Count heard the door to suite 208 clicking shut, Anna Urbanova was, in fact, falling asleep; but she did not sleep soundly.

When the actress first dismissed the Count (having rolled onto her side with a languid sigh), she watched with cool pleasure as he gathered his clothes and drew the curtains. She even took some satisfaction when he paused to pick up her blouse and hang it in the closet.

But at some point during the night, this image of the Count picking up her blouse began to trouble her sleep. On the train back to St. Petersburg, she found herself muttering about it. And by the time she returned home, it positively infuriated her. In the week that followed, if she had the slightest break in her demanding schedule, the image rushed forth, and her famous alabaster cheeks grew red with rage.

"Who does he think he is, this Count Rostov? Pulling out chairs and whistling at dogs? Putting on airs and looking down noses, is more like it. But by what right? Who gave him permission to pick up a blouse and hang it on its hanger? If I drop my blouse on the floor, what of it? It's my clothing and I can treat it as I please!"

Or so she would find herself reasoning to no one in particular.

One night, returning from a party, the very thought of the Count's precious little gesture was so infuriating that when she undressed she not only threw her red silk gown on the floor, she instructed her staff that it was not to be touched. Each night that followed, she dumped another outfit on the floor. Dresses and blouses of velvet and silk from London and Paris, the more expensive the better. Dumped here on the bathroom floor and there by the dustbin. In a word, wherever it suited her.

After two weeks, her boudoir began to look like an Arabian tent with fabrics of every color underfoot.

Olga, the sixty-year-old Georgian who had met the Count at the door of suite 208 and who had faithfully served as the actress's dresser since 1920, initially eyed her mistress's behavior with seasoned indifference. But one night, when Anna had dropped a blue backless dress on top of a white silk gown, Olga observed matter-of-factly:

"My dear, you are acting like a child. If you do not pick up your clothes, I shall have no choice but to give you a spanking."

Anna Urbanova turned as red as a jar of jam.

"Pick up my clothes?" she shouted. "You want me to pick up my clothes? Then I shall pick them up!"

Gathering up twenty outfits in her arms, she marched to the open window and cast them into the street below. With the greatest satisfaction, the actress watched as they fluttered and coasted to the ground. When she wheeled about to confront her dresser in triumph, Olga coolly observed how entertained the neighbors would be by this evidence of the famous actress's petulance, then she turned and left the room.

Switching off the lights and climbing into bed, Anna sputtered like a candle.

"What do I care what the neighbors will say about my petulance. What do I care what St. Petersburg will say, or all of Russia!"

But at two in the morning, having tossed and turned, Anna Urbanova tiptoed down the grand staircase, slipped out into the street, and gathered up her garments one by one.

1924

Anonymity

Dreams of invisibility are as old as folklore. By means of some talisman or potion, or with the help of the gods themselves, the corporeal presence of the hero is rendered insubstantial, and for the duration of the spell he may wander among his fellow men unseen.

The advantages of having such a power can be rattled off for you by any child of ten. Whether slipping past dragons, eavesdropping on intriguers, and sneaking into treasuries, or plucking a pie from the pantry, knocking the cap off a constable, and lighting the schoolmaster's coattails on fire, suffice it to say that a thousand tales have been told in acknowledgment of invisibility's bounty.

But the tale that has less often been told is the one in which the spell of invisibility is cast upon the unknowing hero in the form of a curse. Having lived his life in the heat of battle, at the crux of conversation, and in the twentieth row with its privileged view of the ladies in the loges— that is, in the very thick of things—suddenly, he finds himself invisible to friend and foe alike. And the spell that had been cast over the Count by Anna Urbanova in 1923 was of this very sort.

On that fateful night when the Count had dined with the enchantress in her suite, she presumably had the power to render him invisible on the spot. Instead, to toy with his peace of mind, she had cast her spell to manifest itself over the course of a year, bit by bit.

In the weeks that followed, the Count suddenly noticed that he was disappearing from view for a few minutes at a time. He could be dining in the Piazza when a couple would approach his table with the clear intention of taking it as their own; or he could be standing near the front desk when a harried guest would nearly knock him off his feet. By winter, those prone to greet him with a wave or a smile often failed to see him until he was ten feet away. And now a year later? When he crossed the lobby, it often took a full minute for his closest friends to notice that he was standing right in front of them.

"Oh," said Vasily, returning the telephone receiver to its cradle. "Excuse me, Count Rostov. I didn't see you there. How can I be of service?"

The Count gave the concierge's desk a delicate tap.

"You wouldn't happen to know where Nina is?"

In asking Vasily for Nina's whereabouts, the Count was not making a passing inquiry of the first chap he happened to meet; for Vasily had an uncanny awareness of where people were at any given time.

"She is in the card room, I believe."

"Ah," said the Count with a knowing smile.

Turning about, he walked down the hall to the card room and quietly opened the door, assuming he would find four middle-aged ladies exchanging cookies and profanities over tricks of whist—as an attentive spirit held her breath in a cupboard. Instead, he found the object of his search sitting at the card table alone. With two stacks of paper in front of her and a pencil in hand, she appeared the very model of scholastic enthusiasm. The pencil was moving so brightly it looked like an honor guard—parading across the page with its head held high then pivoting at the margin to make the quick march back.

"Greetings, my friend."

"Hello, Your Countship," Nina replied without looking up from her work.

"Would you like to join me for an excursion before dinner? I was thinking of visiting the switchboard."

"I'm afraid I can't at the moment."

The Count claimed the seat opposite Nina as she put a completed sheet of paper on one stack and took a fresh sheet of paper from the other. Out of habit, he picked up the deck of cards that sat on the corner of the table and shuffled it twice.

"Would you like to see a trick?"

"Some other time, perhaps."

Neatening the deck, the Count replaced it on the table. Then he picked up the topmost sheet from the stack of completed papers. In carefully aligned columns, he found all of the cardinal numbers from 1,100 to 1,199.

In accordance with some unknown system, thirteen of the numbers had been circled in red.

Needless to say, the Count was intrigued.

"What are we up to here?"

"Mathematics."

"I see you are addressing the subject with vigor."

"Professor Lisitsky says that one must wrestle with mathematics the way that one wrestles with a bear."

"Is that so? And which species of bear are we wrestling with today? More polar than panda, I suspect."

Nina looked up at the Count with her glint-extinguishing stare.

The Count cleared his throat and adopted a more serious tone.

"I take it the project involves some subset of integers. . . ."

"Do you know what a prime number is?"

"As in two, three, five, seven, eleven, thirteen . . . ?"

"Exactly," said Nina. "Those whole numbers that are *indivisible* by any number other than one and itself."

Given the dramatic manner with which she had said *indivisible*, one might have imagined Nina was speaking of the impregnability of a fortress.

"At any rate," she said, "I am making a list of them all."

"Them all!"

"It is a Sisyphean task," she admitted (though with an enthusiasm that prompted one to wonder if she had a complete command of the term's etymology).

She pointed to the already inscribed pages on the table.

"The list of prime numbers begins with two, three, and five, as you say. But prime numbers grow increasingly rare the larger they become. So it is one thing to land upon a seven or eleven. But to land upon a one thousand and nine is another thing altogether. Can you imagine identifying a prime number in the hundreds of thousands . . . ? In the millions . . . ?"

Nina looked off in the distance, as if she could see that largest and most impregnable of all the numbers situated on its rocky promontory where for thousands of years it had withstood the onslaughts of fire-breathing dragons and barbarian hordes. Then she resumed her work.

The Count took another look at the sheet in his hands with a heightened sense of respect. After all, an educated man should admire any course of study no matter how arcane, if it be pursued with curiosity and devotion.

"Here," he said in the tone of one chipping in. "This number is not prime."

Nina looked up with an expression of disbelief.

"Which number?"

He laid the paper in front of her and tapped a figure circled in red.

"One thousand one hundred and seventy-three."

"How do you know it isn't prime?"

"If a number's individual digits sum to a number that is divisible by three, then it too is divisible by three."

Confronted with this extraordinary fact, Nina replied:

"*Mon Dieu.*"

Then she leaned back in her chair and appraised the Count in a manner acknowledging that she may have underestimated him.

Now, when a man has been underestimated by a friend, he has some cause for taking offense—since it is our friends who should *overestimate* our capacities. They should have an exaggerated opinion of our moral fortitude, our aesthetic sensibilities, and our intellectual scope. Why, they should practically imagine us leaping through a window in the nick of time with the works of Shakespeare in one hand and a pistol in the other! But in this particular instance, the Count had to admit he had little grounds for taking offense. Because, for the life of him, he could not imagine from what dark corner of his adolescent mind this extraordinary fact had materialized.

"Well," said Nina, pointing to the stack of completed papers in front of the Count. "You'd better hand me those."

Leaving Nina to her work, the Count consoled himself that he was to meet Mishka for dinner in fifteen minutes; and besides, he had yet to read the daily papers. So, returning to the lobby, he picked up a copy of *Pravda* from the coffee table and made himself comfortable in the chair between the potted palms.

After scanning the headlines, the Count delved into an article on a Moscow manufacturing plant that was exceeding its quotas. He then read a sketch on various improvements in Russian village life. When he shifted his attention to a report on the grateful schoolchildren of Kazan, he couldn't help but remark on the repetitiveness of the new journalistic style. Not only did the Bolsheviks seem to dwell on the same sort of subject matter day to day, they celebrated such a narrow set of views with such a limited vocabulary that one inevitably felt as if one had read it all before.

It wasn't until the fifth article that the Count realized he *had* read it all before. For this was yesterday's paper. With a grunt, he tossed it back on the table and looked at the clock behind the front desk, which indicated that Mishka was now fifteen minutes late.

But then, the measure of fifteen minutes is entirely different for a man in step than for a man with nothing to do. If for the Count the prior twelve months could be characterized politely as uneventful, the same could not be said for Mishka. The Count's old friend had left the 1923 RAPP congress with a commission to edit and annotate a multivolume anthology of the Russian short story. That alone would have provided him with a reasonable excuse for being late; but there was a second development in Mishka's life that earned him even more latitude with his appointments. . . .

As a boy, the Count had a well-deserved reputation for marksmanship. He had been known to hit the schoolhouse bell with a rock while standing behind the bushes on the other side of the yard. He had been known to sink a kopek into an inkwell from across the classroom. And with an arrow and bow, he could pierce an orange at fifty paces. But he had never hit a tighter mark from a greater distance than when he noted his friend's interest in Katerina from Kiev. In the months after the 1923 congress, her beauty became so indisputable, her heart so tender, her demeanor so kind, that Mishka had no choice but to barricade himself behind a stack of books at the old Imperial Library in St. Petersburg.

"She's a firefly, Sasha. A pinwheel." Or so said Mishka with the wistful amazement of one who has been given only a moment to admire a wonder of the world.

But then one autumn afternoon, she appeared in his alcove in need of a confidant. Behind his volumes, they whispered for an hour, and when the library sounded its closing bell, they took their conversation out onto

Nevsky Prospekt and wandered all the way to Tikhvin Cemetery where, on a spot overlooking the Neva River, this firefly, this pinwheel, this wonder of the world had suddenly taken his hand.

"Ah, Count Rostov," exclaimed Arkady in passing. "There you are. I believe I have a message for you. . . ." Returning to the front desk, Arkady quickly rifled through some notes. "Here."

The message, which had been taken down by the hotel's receptionist, conveyed Mishka's apologies and explained that as Katerina was under the weather, he was returning to St. Petersburg earlier than planned. Taking a moment to mask his disappointment, the Count looked up from the note to thank Arkady, but the desk captain had already turned his attention to another guest.

"Good evening, Count Rostov." Andrey took a quick look in the Book. "A party of two tonight, isn't it?"

"I'm afraid it's going to be a party of one, Andrey."

"Nonetheless, it is our pleasure to have you. Your table should be ready in just a few minutes."

With the recent recognition of the USSR by Germany, England, and Italy, a wait of a few minutes had become increasingly common at the Boyarsky; but such was the price of being welcomed back into the sisterhood of nations and the brotherhood of trade.

As the Count stepped aside, a man with a pointed beard came marching down the hallway with a protégé in tow. Though the Count had only seen him once or twice before, the Count could tell he was the Commissar of Something-or-Other, for he walked with urgency, talked with urgency, and even came to a stop with urgency.

"Good evening, comrade Soslovsky," said Andrey with a welcoming smile.

"Yes," pronounced Soslovsky—as if he'd just been asked whether he wanted to be seated immediately.

With a nod of understanding, Andrey signaled a waiter, handed him two menus, and directed him to lead the gentlemen to table fourteen.

Geometrically speaking, the Boyarsky was a square at the center of which was a towering arrangement of flora (today forsythia branches in bloom), around which were twenty tables of various sizes. If one considered the tables in respect to the cardinal points of a compass, then, at Andrey's instruction, the waiter was now leading the Commissar and his protégé to the table for two at the northeast corner—right next to where a jowly-faced Belarusian was dining.

"Andrey, my friend . . ."

The maître d' looked up from his Book.

"Isn't he the chap who had an exchange of words with that bulldog of a fellow a few days ago?"

An "exchange of words" was something of a polite diminution of the facts. For on the afternoon in question, when this Soslovsky had wondered aloud to his luncheon companions why the Belarusians seemed particularly slow to embrace the ideas of Lenin, the bulldog (who had been sitting at a neighboring table) had cast his napkin on his plate and demanded to know "the meaning of this!" With a disregard as pointed as his beard, Soslovsky suggested there were three reasons, and he began to tick them off:

"First, there is the relative laziness of the population—a trait for which the Belarusians are known the world over. Second, there is their infatuation with the West, which presumably stems from their long history of intermarriage with the Poles. But third, and above all else—"

Alas, the restaurant was never to hear the above-all-else. For the bulldog, who had knocked back his chair at the word *intermarriage*, now hoisted Soslovsky off his seat. In the scramble that ensued, it took three waiters to separate the various hands from the various lapels, and two busboys to sweep the chicken Maréchal from the floor.

Recalling the scene in a flash, Andrey looked back toward table thirteen, where the bulldog in question was currently seated with a woman of such similar aspect that any seasoned logician would conclude she was his wife. Spinning on his heels, Andrey rounded the forsythia blossoms, headed off Soslovsky and his protégé, and led them back to table three—a lovely spot at south-southeast, which could comfortably accommodate a party of four.

"*Merci beaucoup*," said Andrey upon his return.

"*De rien*," replied the Count.

. . . .

In replying *It is nothing* to Andrey, the Count was not simply resorting to a Gallic figure of speech. In point of fact, the Count deserved as much thanks for his little intervention as a swallow deserves for its trill. For since the age of fifteen, Alexander Rostov had been a master of seating tables.

Whenever he was home for the holidays, his grandmother would inevitably call him into the library, where she liked to knit by the fireplace in a solitary chair.

"Come in, my boy, and sit with me a moment."

"Certainly, Grandmother," replied the Count, balancing himself on the edge of the fire grate. "How can I be of assistance?"

"The prelate is coming for dinner on Friday night—as are the Duchess Obolensky, Count Keragin, *and* the Minsky-Polotovs. . . ."

Here she would let her voice trail off without further explanation; but no further explanation was needed. The Countess was of a mind that dinner should provide one with respite from life's trials and tribulations. Thus, she could not countenance discussions of religion, politics, or personal sorrows at her table. Further complicating matters, the prelate was deaf in his left ear, partial to Latin epigrams, and prone to stare at décolletage whenever he drank a glass of wine; while the Duchess Obolensky, who was particularly caustic in summer, frowned upon pithy sayings and could not abide discussions of the arts. And the Keragins? Their great-grandfather had been called a Bonapartist by Prince Minsky-Polotov in 1811, and they had not exchanged a word with a Minsky-Polotov since.

"How many will be in attendance?" asked the Count.

"Forty."

"The usual assembly?"

"More or less."

"The Osipovs?"

"Yes. But Pierre is in Moscow. . . ."

"Ah," said the Count with the smile of the chess champion who has been confronted with a new gambit.

The Nizhny Novgorod Province had a hundred prominent families, which over the course of two centuries had intermarried and divorced, borrowed and lent, accepted and regretted, offended, defended, and dueled—while championing an array of conflicting positions that varied by generation, gender, and house. And at the center of this maelstrom was the Countess Rostova's dining room with its two tables for twenty standing side by side.

"Not to worry, *Grand-mère*," assured the Count. "A solution is close at hand."

Out in the garden, as the Count closed his eyes to begin moving through the individual permutations one by one, his sister enjoyed making light of his task.

"Why do you furrow your brow so, Sasha? However the table is arranged, we always have such delightful conversations when we dine."

"However the table is arranged!" the Count would exclaim. "Delightful conversations! I'll have you know, dear sister, that careless seating has torn asunder the best of marriages and led to the collapse of the longest-standing *détentes*. In fact, if Paris had not been seated next to Helen when he dined in the court of Menelaus, there never would have been a Trojan War."

A charming rejoinder, no doubt, reflected the Count, from across the years. But where were the Obolenskys and the Minsky-Polotovs now?

With Hector and Achilles.

"Your table is ready, Count Rostov."

"Ah. Thank you, Andrey."

Two minutes later, the Count was comfortably seated at his table with a glass of champagne (a small gesture of thanks from Andrey for his timely intervention).

Taking a sip, the Count reviewed the menu in reverse order as was his habit, having learned from experience that giving consideration to appetizers before entrées can only lead to regrets. And here was a perfect example. For the very last item on the menu was the evening's sole necessity: osso buco—a dish that was best preceded by a light and lively appetizer.

Closing his menu, the Count surveyed the restaurant. Undeniably, he had felt a little low when he had climbed the stairs to the Boyarsky; but here he was with a glass of champagne in hand, osso buco in the offing, and the satisfaction that he had been of service to a friend. Perhaps the

Fates—who of all their children loved Reversal most—were set upon lifting his spirits.

"Do you have any questions?"

Thus came an inquiry from behind the Count's back.

Without hesitation, the Count began to reply that he was ready to order, but as he turned in his chair, he was struck dumb to discover that it was the Bishop who was leaning over his shoulder—in the white jacket of the Boyarsky.

Now admittedly, with the recent return of international guests to the hotel, the Boyarsky had become a little understaffed. So the Count could well appreciate why Andrey had decided to bolster his crew. But of all the waiters at the Piazza, of all the waiters in the world, why would he choose *this* one?

The Bishop seemed to be following the Count's train of thought, for his smile became especially smug. *Yes*, he seemed to be saying, *here I am in your famed Boyarsky, one of the chosen few who pass with impunity through the doors of Chef Zhukovsky's kitchen.*

"Perhaps you need more time . . . ?" the Bishop suggested, his pencil poised over his pad.

For an instant, the Count considered sending him on his way and asking for a new table. But the Rostovs had always prided themselves on admitting when their behavior lacked charity.

"No, my good man," replied the Count. "I am ready to place my order. I will have the fennel and orange salad to start, and the osso buco to follow."

"Of course," said the Bishop. "And how will you be having the osso buco?"

The Count almost betrayed his amazement. *How will I be having it? Does he expect me to dictate the temperature of a piece of stewed meat?*

"As the chef prepares it," replied the Count magnanimously.

"Of course. And will you be having wine?"

"Absolutely. A bottle of the San Lorenzo Barolo, 1912."

"Will you be having the red or the white?"

"A Barolo," the Count explained as helpfully as he could, "is a full-bodied red from northern Italy. As such, it is the perfect accompaniment to the osso buco of Milan."

"So then, you will be having the red."

The Count studied the Bishop for a moment. *The fellow gives no evidence of being deaf,* he reflected; *and his accent would suggest that Russian is his native tongue. So surely, by now, he should have been on his way to the kitchen?* But as the Countess Rostova liked to remark: *If patience wasn't so easily tested, then it would hardly be a virtue. . . .*

"Yes," said the Count after counting to five. "The Barolo is a *red*."

The Bishop continued to stand there with his pencil poised over his pad.

"I apologize," he said unapologetically, "if I am not being clear. But for your selection of a wine tonight, there are only *two* options: white and red."

The two men stared at each other.

"Perhaps you could ask Andrey to stop by for a moment."

"Of course," said the Bishop, backing away with an ecclesiastical bow.

The Count drummed the tabletop with his fingers.

Of course, he says. Of course, of course, of course. Of course what? Of course you are there and I am here? Of course you have said something and I have replied? Of course a man's time on earth is finite and may come to an end at any moment!

"Is something the matter, Count Rostov?"

"Ah, Andrey. It's about your new man. I'm quite familiar with him from his work downstairs. And in that venue I suppose a certain lack of experience is to be tolerated, or even expected. But here at the Boyarsky . . ."

The Count opened both hands to gesture toward the hallowed room and then looked to the maître d' with an expectation of understanding.

No one who knew Andrey in the slightest would ever describe his demeanor as gay. He was not some barker at a carnival, or an impresario of light entertainments. His position as the maître d' of the Boyarsky called for judiciousness, tact, decorum. So the Count was quite accustomed to Andrey having a solemn expression. But in all his years of dining at the Boyarsky, he had never seen Andrey appear *this* solemn.

"He was promoted at the instruction of Mr. Halecki," explained the maître d' quietly.

"But why?"

"I am not certain. I presume he has a friend."

"A friend?"

Uncharacteristically, Andrey shrugged.

"A friend with influence. Someone within the Table Servers Union, perhaps; or at the Commissariat of Labor; or in the upper echelons of the Party. These days, who can tell?"

"My sympathies," said the Count.

Andrey bowed in gratitude.

"Well, you certainly can't be held accountable if they foist the fellow upon you; and I will adjust my expectations accordingly. But before you go, can you do me a small service? For some incomprehensible reason, he will not let me order my wine. I was just hoping to get a bottle of the San Lorenzo Barolo to accompany the osso buco."

If such a thing could be imagined, Andrey's expression grew even more solemn.

"Perhaps you should come with me. . . ."

Having followed Andrey across the dining room, through the kitchen, and down a long, winding stair, the Count found himself in a place that even Nina had never been: the wine cellar of the Metropol.

With its archways of brick and its cool, dark climate, the Metropol's wine cellar recalled the somber beauty of a catacomb. Only, instead of sarcophagi bearing the likenesses of saints, receding into the far reaches of the chamber were rows of racks laden with bottles of wine. Here was assembled a staggering collection of Cabernets and Chardonnays, Rieslings and Syrahs, ports and Madeiras—a century of vintages from across the continent of Europe.

All told, there were almost ten thousand cases. More than a hundred thousand bottles. And every one of them without a label.

"What has happened!" gasped the Count.

Andrey nodded in grim acknowledgment.

"A complaint was filed with comrade Teodorov, the Commissar of Food, claiming that the existence of our wine list runs counter to the ideals of the Revolution. That it is a monument to the privilege of the nobility, the effeteness of the intelligentsia, and the predatory pricing of speculators."

"But that's preposterous."

For the second time in an hour, the unshrugging Andrey shrugged.

"A meeting was held, a vote was taken, an order was handed down. . . . Henceforth, the Boyarsky shall sell only red and white wine with every bottle at a single price."

With a hand that was never meant to serve such a purpose, Andrey gestured to the corner, where beside five barrels of water a confusion of labels lay on the floor. "It took ten men ten days to complete the task," he said sadly.

"But who on earth would file such a complaint?"

"I am not certain; though I have been told it may have originated with your friend. . . ."

"My friend?"

"Your waiter from downstairs."

The Count looked at Andrey in amazement. But then a memory presented itself—a memory of a Christmas past when the Count had leaned from his chair to correct a certain waiter's recommendation of a Rioja to accompany a Latvian stew. How smugly the Count had observed at the time that there was no substitute for experience.

Well, thought the Count, here is your substitute.

With Andrey a few paces behind him, the Count began walking the cellar's center aisle, much as a commander and his lieutenant might walk through a field hospital in the aftermath of battle. Near the end of the aisle, the Count turned down one of the rows. With a quick accounting of columns and shelves, the Count determined that in this row alone, there were over a thousand bottles—a thousand bottles virtually identical in shape and weight.

Picking up one at random, he reflected how perfectly the curve of the glass fit in the palm of the hand, how perfectly its volume weighed upon the arm. But inside? Inside this dark green glass was what exactly? A Chardonnay to complement a Camembert? A Sauvignon Blanc to go with some chèvre?

Whichever wine was within, it was decidedly not identical to its neighbors. On the contrary, the contents of the bottle in his hand was the product of a history as unique and complex as that of a nation, or a man. In its color, aroma, and taste, it would certainly express the idiosyncratic geology and prevailing climate of its home terrain. But in addition, it would express all the natural phenomena of its *vintage*. In a sip, it would evoke the timing of that winter's thaw, the extent of that summer's rain, the prevailing winds, and the frequency of clouds.

Yes, a bottle of wine was the ultimate distillation of time and place; a poetic expression of individuality itself. Yet here it was, cast back into the sea of anonymity, that realm of averages and unknowns.

And suddenly, the Count had his own moment of lucidity. Just as Mishka had come to understand the present as the natural by-product of the past, and could see with perfect clarity how it would shape the future, the Count now understood *his* place in the passage of time.

As we age, we are bound to find comfort from the notion that it takes generations for a way of life to fade. We are familiar with the songs our grandparents favored, after all, even though we never danced to them ourselves. At festive holidays, the recipes we pull from the drawer are routinely decades old, and in some cases even written in the hand of a relative long since dead. And the objects in our homes? The oriental coffee tables and well-worn desks that have been handed down from generation to generation? Despite being "out of fashion," not only do they add beauty to our daily lives, they lend material credibility to our presumption that the passing of an era will be glacial.

But under certain circumstances, the Count finally acknowledged, this process can occur in the comparative blink of an eye. Popular upheaval, political turmoil, industrial progress—any combination of these can cause the evolution of a society to leapfrog generations, sweeping aside aspects of the past that might otherwise have lingered for decades. And this must be especially so, when those with newfound power are men who distrust any form of hesitation or nuance, and who prize self-assurance above all.

For years now, with a bit of a smile, the Count had remarked that this or that was behind him—like his days of poetry or travel or romance. But in so doing, he had never really believed it. In his heart of hearts, he had imagined that, even if unattended to, these aspects of his life were lingering somewhere on the periphery, waiting to be recalled. But looking at the bottle in his hand, the Count was struck by the realization that, in fact, it *was* all behind him. Because the Bolsheviks, who were so intent upon recasting the future from a mold of their own making, would not rest until every last vestige of his Russia had been uprooted, shattered, or erased.

Returning the bottle to its slot, the Count went to join Andrey at the foot of the stairs. But as he passed among the shelves, it occurred to him that it was *almost* all behind him. For he had one last duty to attend to.

"Just a moment, Andrey."

Starting at the end of the cellar, the Count began weaving back and forth through the rows systematically, scanning the racks from top to bottom, until Andrey must have thought he'd lost his reason. But in the sixth row he came to a stop. Reaching down to a shelf at the height of his knee, the Count carefully took a bottle from among the thousands. Holding it up with a wistful smile, he ran his thumb over the insignia of the two crossed keys that was embossed on the glass.

On the twenty-second of June 1926—the tenth anniversary of Helena's death—Count Alexander Ilyich Rostov would drink to his sister's memory. Then he would shed this mortal coil, once and for all.

1926

Adieu

It is a fact of human life that one must eventually choose a philosophy. Or such was the opinion of the Count, as he stood before his old windows in suite 317, having slipped inside with the help of Nina's key.

Whether through careful consideration spawned by books and spirited debate over coffee at two in the morning, or simply from a natural proclivity, we must all eventually adopt a fundamental framework, some reasonably coherent system of causes and effects that will help us make sense not simply of momentous events, but of all the little actions and interactions that constitute our daily lives—be they deliberate or spontaneous, inevitable or unforeseen.

For most Russians, the philosophical consolations had been found for centuries under the eaves of the church. Whether they favored the unflinching hand of the Old Testament or the more forgiving hand of the New, their submission to the will of God helped them to understand, or at least accept the inescapable course of events.

In keeping with the fashion of the times, most of the Count's schoolmates had turned their backs on the church; but they had only done so in favor of alternative consolations. Some who preferred the clarity of science adhered to the ideas of Darwin, seeing at every turn the mark of natural selection; while others opted for Nietzsche and his eternal recurrence or Hegel and his dialectic—each system quite sensible, no doubt, when one had finally arrived at the one-thousandth page.

But for the Count, his philosophical leanings had always been essentially meteorological. Specifically, he believed in the inevitable influence of clement and inclement weathers. He believed in the influence of early frosts and lingering summers, of ominous clouds and delicate rains, of fog and sunshine and snowfall. And he believed, most especially, in the reshaping of destinies by the slightest change in the thermometer.

By way of example, one need only look down from this window. Not three weeks before—with the temperature hovering around 45° Fahrenheit—Theatre Square had been empty and gray. But with an increase in the average temperature of just five degrees, the trees had begun to blossom, the sparrows had begun to sing, and couples young and old were lingering on the benches. If such a slight change in temperature was all it took to transform the life of a public square, why should we think the course of human history any less susceptible?

Napoleon would have been the first to admit that after assembling an intrepid corps of commanders and fifteen divisions, after assessing the enemy's weaknesses, studying his terrain, and carefully formulating a plan of attack, one must finally contend with temperature. For the reading on the thermometer will not only govern the pace of advance, but will also determine the adequacy of supplies, and either bolster or betray the courage of one's men. (Ah, Napoleon, perhaps you would never have prevailed in your quest for Mother Russia; but ten degrees warmer and at least you might have reached home with half your forces intact, instead of losing another three hundred thousand men between the gates of Moscow and the banks of the Neman River.)

But if examples from the field of battle are not to your taste, then consider instead a party in late autumn to which you and a loose-knit band of friends and acquaintances have been invited to celebrate the twenty-first birthday of the charming Princess Novobaczky. . . .

At five o'clock, when you look from your dressing room window, the weather seems certain to weigh upon the festivities. For with the temperature at 34°, clouds as far as the eye can see, and the onset of a drizzling rain, the Princess's guests will be arriving at her party cold, wet, and a little worse for wear. But by the time you set out at six, the temperature has dropped just enough that what begins to land on your shoulders is not a gray, autumnal rain, but the season's first snowfall. Thus, the very precipitation that might have soured the evening, instead lends it an aura of magic. In fact, so mesmerizing is the manner in which the snowflakes spiral through the air that you are run from the road when a troika passes at full gallop—with a young officer of the Hussars standing at the reins like a centurion in his chariot.

Having spent an hour freeing your carriage from a ditch, you arrive at the Princess's late but, as luck would have it, so does a portly old friend from your days at the academy. In fact, you get to watch as he alights from his droshky, throws back his shoulders, fills out his chest, and then tests the formality of the footmen—by slipping on a patch of ice and landing on his rump. Helping him up, you hook your arm under his and lead him into the house just as the rest of the party is spilling from the drawing room.

In the dining room, you make a quick circle of the table in search of your name, assuming that—given your reputation as a raconteur—you will once again be placed beside some awkward cousin. But lo and behold, you have been seated at the right hand of the guest of honor. While on the Princess's left . . . is none other than the dashing young Hussar who had run you from the road.

With a glance, you can see that he fancies himself the natural recipient of the Princess's attention. Clearly, he expects to regale her with tales of the regiment while occasionally refilling her glass with wine. When the meal is over, he will offer his arm and lead her into the ballroom, where he will display his talents at the mazurka. And when the orchestra plays Strauss, he will not need to waltz the Princess across the floor, because he will be on the terrace in her arms.

But just as the young lieutenant is about to tell his first anecdote, the doors to the kitchen open and three footmen appear bearing platters. All eyes turn to see what Mrs. Trent has prepared for the occasion, and when the three silver domes are lifted simultaneously there are gasps of appreciation. For in honor of the Princess, she has cooked her specialty: English roast with Yorkshire pudding.

In the history of man, no military commissary has raised envy. Due to a combination of efficiency, disinterest, and the lack of a feminine touch, all of the food in an army kitchen is boiled until the tops rattle off the pots. So, having made do with cabbage and potatoes for three months straight, the young lieutenant is unprepared for the arrival of Mrs. Trent's beef. Seared for fifteen minutes at 450° and then roasted for two hours at 350°, her roast is tender and red at the center yet crispy and brown at the crust. Thus, our young Hussar sets aside his regimental tales in favor of extra helpings and the refilling of his own glass with wine; while in accordance with the established rules of etiquette, it is you who must entertain the Princess with a few amusing stories of your own.

Having cleaned the gravy from his plate with the last crust of the pudding, the young lieutenant finally turns his attention to his hostess; but at that very same moment, the orchestra begins tuning in the ballroom and the guests push back their chairs. So he simply holds out his arm for the Princess, as your portly friend appears at your side.

Now, there is nothing your friend loves better than a good quadrille; and despite his physique, he has been known to hop like a rabbit and prance like a buck. But placing his hand on his tailbone, he explains that his spill on the drive has left him too sore to gallivant. He wonders, instead, if you'd like to play a few hands of cards and you respond it would be your pleasure. But it just so happens that the lieutenant overhears this exchange and, in a boisterous frame of mind, imagines that here is a perfect opportunity to teach some dandies a thing or two about games of chance. Besides, he reasons to himself, the orchestra will be playing for hours and the Princess is going nowhere. So without further thought, he passes her arm to the nearest gentleman and invites himself to join you at the card table—while signaling the butler for another glass of wine.

Well.

Perhaps it was that extra glass of wine. Perhaps it was the lieutenant's tendency to underestimate a well-dressed man. Or perhaps it was simply bad luck. Whatever the cause, suffice it to say that after two hours, it is the lieutenant who has lost one thousand rubles and you who hold his marker.

But however recklessly the fellow drives his troika, you have no wish to put him in a spot. "It is the Princess's birthday," you say. "In her honor, let us call it even." And with that, you tear the lieutenant's marker in two and toss the halves on the baize. In appreciation, he sweeps his wine glass to the floor, knocks back his chair, and stumbles out the terrace doors into the night.

Although in the course of the game there were only five players and three observers, the story of the torn IOU quickly makes its way around the ballroom, and suddenly the Princess has sought you out in order to express her gratitude for this act of gallantry. As you bow and reply *It is nothing*, the band strikes up a waltz and you have no choice but to take her in your arms and spirit her across the floor.

The Princess waltzes divinely. She is light on her feet and spins like a top. But with more than forty couples dancing and the fires in the two fireplaces built unusually high, the ambient temperature in the ballroom reaches 80°, prompting the Princess's cheeks to flush and her bosom to heave. Concerned that she may be feeling faint, naturally, you inquire if she would like some air. . . .

You see?

If Mrs. Trent had not so perfectly mastered the art of roasting, the young lieutenant might have kept his attention on the Princess instead of washing down a third helping of beef with an eighth glass of wine. If the temperature that night had not dropped six degrees in as many hours, the ice might not have formed in the drive, your portly friend might not have fallen, and the card game might not have been played. And if the sight of snow hadn't prompted the footmen to build the fires so high, you might not have ended up on the terrace in the arms of the birthday girl—as a young Hussar returned his supper to the pasture from whence it came.

And what is more, thought the Count with a grave expression, all the sorry events that followed might never have come to pass. . . .

"What is this? Who are you?"

Turning from the window, the Count discovered a middle-aged couple standing in the doorway with the key to the suite in their hands.

"What are you doing here?" the husband demanded.

"I am . . . from the drapers," the Count replied.

Turning back to the window, he took hold of the curtain and gave it a tug.

"Yes," he said. "Everything seems in order."

Then he doffed the cap he wasn't wearing and escaped into the hall.

"Good evening, Vasily."

"Oh. Good evening, Count Rostov."

The Count gave the desk a delicate tap.

"Have you seen Nina about?"

"She is in the ballroom, I believe."

"Ah. Just so."

The Count was pleasantly surprised to hear that Nina was back in one of her old haunts. Now thirteen, Nina had all but given up her youthful pastimes in favor of books and professors. To have set aside her studies, there must have been quite an Assembly assembled.

But when the Count opened the door, there was no shuffling of chairs or pounding of podiums. Nina was sitting alone at a small table under the central chandelier. The Count noted that her hair was tucked behind her ears, an unfailing indication that something of significance was in the works. Sure enough, on the pad before her was a six by three grid, while on the table sat a set of scales, a measuring tape, and a sprinter's watch.

"Greetings, my friend."

"Oh, hello, Your Countship."

"What, pray tell, are you up to?"

"We are preparing for an experiment."

The Count looked around the ballroom.

"We?"

Nina pointed with her pencil to the balcony.

Looking up, the Count discovered a boy Nina's age crouching in their old perch behind the balustrade. Simply though neatly dressed, the boy had wide eyes and an expression that was earnest and attentive. Along the balustrade were lined a series of objects of different shapes and sizes.

Nina made the introductions.

"Count Rostov, Boris. Boris, Count Rostov."

"Good afternoon, Boris."

"Good afternoon, sir."

The Count turned back to Nina.

"What is the nature of this endeavor?"

"We intend to test the hypotheses of two renowned mathematicians in a single experiment. Specifically, we will be testing Newton's calculation of the speed of gravity and Galileo's principle that objects with different mass fall at an equivalent rate."

From the balustrade, wide-eyed Boris nodded earnestly and attentively.

By way of illustration, Nina pointed her pencil to the first column of her grid, in which six objects were listed in ascending order of size.

"Where did you get the pineapple?"

"From the fruit bowl in the lobby," Boris called down with enthusiasm.

Nina set down her pencil.

"Let's start with the kopek, Boris. Remember to hold it *precisely* at the top of the balustrade, and drop it *exactly* when I tell you to do so."

For a moment, the Count wondered if the height of the balcony was sufficient to measure the influence of mass on the descent of varying objects. After all, hadn't Galileo climbed the Tower of Pisa when he executed his experiment? And surely, the balcony wasn't high enough to calculate the acceleration of gravity. But it is hardly the role of the casual observer to call into question the methodology of the seasoned scientist. So, the Count kept his wonderings where they belonged.

Boris took up the kopek and, showing due consideration for the seriousness of his task, he carefully arranged himself so that he could hold the designated object *precisely* at the top of the balustrade.

After making a notation on her pad, Nina picked up her watch.

"On the count of three, Boris. One. Two. Three!"

Boris released the coin and after a moment of silence, it pinged against the floor.

Nina looked at her watch.

"One point two five seconds," she called to Boris.

"Check," he replied.

Carefully noting the datum in its corresponding square, on a separate sheet of paper Nina divided the figure by a factor, carried its remainder, subtracted the difference, and so on and so forth, until she rounded the solution to the second decimal. Then she shook her head in apparent disappointment.

"Thirty-two feet per second per second."

Boris responded with an expression of scientific concern.

"The egg," Nina said.

The egg (which presumably had been liberated from the Piazza's kitchen) was held precisely, released exactly, and timed to the centisecond.

The experiment continued with a teacup, a billiard ball, a dictionary, and the pineapple, all of which completed their journey to the dance floor in the same amount of time. Thus, in the ballroom of the Metropol Hotel on the twenty-first of June 1926, was the heretic, Galileo of Galilei, vindicated by a ping, a splat, a smash, a thunk, a thump, and a thud.

Of the six objects, the teacup was the Count's personal favorite. It not only made a satisfying smash upon impact, but in the immediate aftermath one could hear the shards of porcelain skidding across the floor like acorns across the ice.

Having completed her tally, Nina observed a little sadly:

"Professor Lisitsky said that these hypotheses have been tested over time. . . ."

"Yes," said the Count. "I imagine they have. . . ."

Then to lighten her spirits, he suggested that as it was almost eight o'clock, perhaps she and her young friend might join him for supper at the Boyarsky. Alas, she and Boris had another experiment to perform—one that involved a bucket of water, a bicycle, and the perimeter of Red Square.

On this of all nights, was the Count disappointed that Nina and her young friend couldn't join him for supper? Of course he was. And yet, the Count had always been of the opinion that God, who could easily have split the hours of darkness and light right down the middle, had chosen instead to make the days of summer longer for scientific expeditions of just this very sort. In addition, the Count had a pleasant inkling that Boris might prove to be the first in a long line of earnest and attentive young men who would be dropping eggs from balustrades and riding bikes with buckets.

"Then I leave you to it," said the Count with a smile.

"All right. But had you come for something in particular?"

"No," the Count replied after a pause, "nothing in particular." But as he turned toward the door, something did occur to him. "Nina . . ."

She looked up from her work.

"Even though these hypotheses have been tested over time, I think you were perfectly right to test them again."

Nina studied the Count for a moment.

"Yes," she said with a nod. "You have always known me the best."

At ten o'clock the Count was seated in the Boyarsky with an empty plate and a nearly empty bottle of White on the table. With the day drawing rapidly to a close, he took some pride in knowing that everything was in order.

That morning, having received a visit from Konstantin Konstanti-novich, the Count had brought his accounts up to date at Muir & Mirri-elees (now known as the Central Universal Department Store), Filippov's (the First Moscow Bakery), and, of course, the Metropol. At the Grand Duke's desk, he had written a letter to Mishka, which he had then entrusted to Petya with instructions it be mailed on the following day. In the after-noon, he had paid his weekly visit to the barber and tidied up his rooms. He had donned his burgundy smoking jacket (which, to be perfectly frank, was disconcertingly snug), and in its pocket he placed a single gold coin for the undertaker with instructions that he be dressed in the freshly pressed black suit (which had been laid out on his bed), and that his body be buried in the family plot at Idlehour.

But if the Count took pride in knowing that everything was in order, he took comfort in knowing that the world would carry on without him—and, in fact, already had. The night before, he had happened to be standing at the concierge's desk when Vasily produced a map of Moscow for one of the hotel's guests. As Vasily drew a zigzagging line from the center of the city to the Garden Ring, more than half of the streets he named were unfa-miliar to the Count. Earlier that day, Vasily had informed him that the famed blue-and-gold lobby of the Bolshoi had been painted over in white, while in the Arbat Andreyev's moody statue of Gogol had been plucked from its pedestal and replaced with a more uplifting one of Gorky. Just like that, the city of Moscow could boast new street names, new lobbies, and new statues—and neither the tourists, the theatergoers, nor the pigeons seemed particularly put out.

The staffing trend that had begun with the appointment of the Bishop had continued unabated—such that any young man with more influence than experience could now don the white jacket, clear from the left, and pour wine into water glasses.

Marina, who once had welcomed the Count's company as she stitched in the stitching room, now had a junior seamstress to watch over as well as a toddler at home (God bless).

Nina, who had taken her first steps into the modern world and found it just as worthy of her unblinking intelligence as the study of princesses, was moving with her father to a large apartment in one of the new buildings designated for the use of Party officials.

And as it was the third week of June, the Fourth Annual Congress of RAPP was underway, but Mishka was not in attendance, having taken a leave from his post at the university in order to finish his short story anthology (now in five volumes) and to follow his Katerina back to Kiev, where she was teaching in an elementary school.

On occasion, the Count still shared a cup of coffee on the roof with the handyman, Abram, where they would talk of summer nights in Nizhny Novgorod. But the old man was now so nearsighted and uncertain on his feet that one morning earlier that month, as if in anticipation of his retirement, the bees had disappeared from their hives.

So, yes, life was rolling along, just as it always had.

Looking back, the Count recalled how on the first night of his house arrest, in the spirit of his godfather's old maxim, he had committed himself to mastering his circumstances. Well, in retrospect, there was another story his godfather told that was just as worthy of emulation. It entailed the Grand Duke's close friend, Admiral Stepan Makarov, who commanded the Imperial Russian Navy during the Russo-Japanese War. On the thirteenth of April 1904, with Port Arthur under attack, Makarov led his battleships into the fray and drove the Japanese fleet back into the Yellow Sea. But upon returning to port on calm seas, the flagship struck a Japanese mine and began to take on water. So, with the battle won and the shores of his homeland in sight, Makarov ascended to the helm in full military dress and went down with his ship.

The Count's bottle of White (which he was fairly certain was a Chardonnay from Burgundy and best served at 55°) sat sweating on the table. Reaching across his plate, he picked up the bottle and served himself. Then having made a toast of gratitude to the Boyarsky, the Count emptied his glass and headed to the Shalyapin for one last snifter of brandy.

When the Count arrived at the Shalyapin, his plan had been to enjoy the brandy, pay Audrius his respects, then retire to his study to await the chime of twelve. But as he neared the bottom of his glass, he couldn't help but overhear a conversation taking place farther down the bar between a high-spirited young Brit and a German traveler for whom travel had obviously lost all its charms.

What had first drawn the Count's attention was the Brit's enthusiasm for Russia. In particular, the young man was taken with the whimsical architecture of the churches and the rambunctious tenor of the language. But with a dour expression, the German replied that the only contribution the Russians had made to the West was the invention of vodka. Then, presumably to drive home his point, he emptied his glass.

"Come now," said the Brit. "You can't be serious."

The German gave his younger neighbor the look of one who had no experience being anything but serious. "I will buy a glass of vodka," he said, "for any man in this bar who can name three more."

Now, vodka was not the Count's preferred spirit. In point of fact, despite his love for his country, he rarely drank it. What's more, he had already polished off a bottle of White and a snifter of brandy, and he still had his own rather pressing business to attend to. But when a man's country is dismissed so offhandedly, he cannot hide behind his preferences or his appointments—*especially* when he has drunk a bottle of White and a snifter of brandy. So, having sketched a quick instruction for Audrius on the back of a napkin and tucked it under a one-ruble note, the Count cleared his throat.

"Excuse me, gentlemen. I couldn't help but overhear your exchange. I have no doubt, *mein Herr*, that your remark regarding Russia's contributions to the West was a form of inverted hyperbole—an exaggerated diminution of the facts for poetic effect. Nonetheless, I will take you at your word and happily accept your challenge."

"I'll be damned," said the Brit.

"But I do have one condition," added the Count.

"And what is that?" asked the German.

"That for each of the contributions I name, we three shall drink a glass of vodka *together*."

The German, who was scowling, waved a hand in the air as if he were about to dismiss the Count, much as he had dismissed the country. But ever-attentive Audrius had already set three empty glasses on the bar and was filling them to the brim.

"Thank you, Audrius."

"My pleasure, Your Excellency."

"Number one," said the Count, adding a pause for dramatic effect: "Chekhov and Tolstoy."

The German let out a grunt.

"Yes, yes. I know what you're going to say: that every nation has its poets in the pantheon. But with Chekhov and Tolstoy, we Russians have set the bronze bookends on the mantelpiece of narrative. Henceforth, writers of fictions from wheresoever they hail, will place themselves on the continuum that begins with the one and ends with the other. For who, I ask you, has exhibited better mastery of the shorter form than Chekhov in his flawless little stories? Precise and uncluttered, they invite us into some corner of a household at some discrete hour in which the entire human condition is suddenly within reach, if heartbreakingly so. While at the other extreme: Can you conceive of a work greater in scope than *War and Peace*? One that moves so deftly from the parlor to the bat-tlefield and back again? That so fully investigates how the individual is shaped by history, and history by the individual? In the generations to come, I tell you there will be no new authors to supplant these two as the alpha and omega of narrative."

"I daresay he has something there," said the Brit. Then he raised his glass and emptied it. So the Count emptied his, and after a grumble, the German followed suit.

"Number two?" asked the Brit, as Audrius refilled the glasses.

"Act one, scene one of *The Nutcracker*."

"Tchaikovsky!" the German guffawed.

"You laugh, *mein Herr*. And yet, I would wager a thousand crowns that you can picture it yourself. On Christmas Eve, having celebrated with family and friends in a room dressed with garlands, Clara sleeps soundly on the floor with her magnificent new toy. But at the stroke of midnight, with the one-eyed Drosselmeyer perched on the grandfather clock like an owl, the Christmas tree begins to grow. . . ."

As the Count raised his hands slowly over the bar to suggest the growth of the tree, the Brit began to whistle the famous march from the opening act.

"Yes, exactly," said the Count to the Brit. "It is commonly said that the English know how to celebrate Advent best. But with all due respect, to witness the essence of winter cheer one must venture farther north than London. One must venture above the fiftieth parallel to where the course of the sun is its most elliptical and the force of the wind its most unforgiving. Dark, cold, and snowbound, Russia has the sort of climate in which the spirit of Christmas burns brightest. And that is why Tchaikovsky seems to have captured the sound of it better than anyone else. I tell you that not only will every European child of the twentieth century know the melodies of *The Nutcracker*, they will imagine their Christmas just as it is depicted in the ballet; and on the Christmas Eves of their dotage, Tchaikovsky's tree will grow from the floor of their memories until they are gazing up in wonder once again."

The Brit gave a sentimental laugh and emptied his glass.

"The story was written by a Prussian," said the German, as he begrudgingly lifted his drink.

"I grant you that," conceded the Count. "And but for Tchaikovsky, it would have remained in Prussia."

As Audrius refilled the glasses, the ever-attentive tender at bar noted the Count's look of inquiry and replied with a nod of confirmation.

"Third," said the Count. Then in lieu of explanation, he simply gestured to the Shalyapin's entrance where a waiter suddenly appeared with a silver platter balanced on the palm of his hand. Placing the platter on the bar between the two foreigners, he lifted the dome to reveal a generous serving of caviar accompanied by blini and sour cream. Even the German could not help but smile, his appetite getting the better of his prejudices.

Anyone who has spent an hour drinking vodka by the glass knows that size has surprisingly little to do with a man's capacity. There are tiny men for whom the limit is seven and giants for whom it is two. For our German friend, the limit appeared to be three. For if the Tolstoy dropped him in a barrel, and the Tchaikovsky set him adrift, then the caviar sent him over the falls. So, having wagged a chastising finger at the Count, he moved to the corner of the bar, laid his head on his arms, and dreamed of the Sugar Plum Fairy.

Taking this as a signal, the Count prepared to push back his stool, but the young Brit was refilling his glass.

"The caviar was a stroke of genius," he said. "But how did you manage it? You never left our sight."

"A magician never reveals his secrets."

The Brit laughed. Then he studied the Count as if with renewed curiosity.

"Who are you?"

The Count shrugged.

"I am someone you have met in a bar."

"No. That's not quite it. I know a man of erudition when I meet one. And I heard how the bartender referred to you. Who are you, really?"

The Count offered a self-deprecating smile.

"At one time, I was Count Alexander Ilyich Rostov—recipient of the Order of Saint Andrew, member of the Jockey Club, Master of the Hunt. . . ."

The young Brit held out his hand.

"Charles Abernethy—presumptive heir to the Earl of Westmorland, financier's apprentice, and bowman of the losing Cambridge crew at Henley in 1920."

The two gentlemen shook hands and drank. And then the presumptive heir to the Earl of Westmorland studied the Count again. "This must have been quite a decade for you. . . ."

"You could put it that way," said the Count.

"Did you try to leave after the Revolution?"

"On the contrary, Charles; I came back because of it."

Charles looked at the Count in surprise.

"You came back?"

"I was in Paris when the Hermitage fell. I had left the country before the war due to certain . . . circumstances."

"You weren't an anarchist, were you?"

The Count laughed.

"Hardly."

"Then what?"

The Count looked into his empty glass. He hadn't spoken of these events in so many years.

"It is late," he said. "And the story is long."

By way of response, Charles refilled their glasses.

So the Count took Charles all the way back to the fall of 1913, when on an inclement night he had set out for the twenty-first birthday of the Princess Novobaczky. He described the ice on the driveway, and Mrs. Trent's roast, and the torn IOU—and how a few degrees here and there had landed him on the terrace in the arms of the Princess while the rash lieutenant retched in the grass.

Charles laughed.

"But, Alexander, that sounds splendid. Surely, it's not the reason you left Russia."

"No," admitted the Count, but then he continued with his fateful tale: "Seven months pass, Charles. It is the spring of 1914, and I return to the family estate for a visit. Having paid my respects to my grandmother in the library, I venture outside in search of my sister, Helena, who likes to read under the great elm at the bend in the river. From a hundred feet away, I can tell that she is not herself—that is, I can tell that she is *more* than herself. Upon seeing me she sits up with a sparkle in her eye and a smile on her lips, clearly eager to share some piece of news, which I am now equally eager to hear. But just as I cross the lawn toward her, she looks over my shoulder and smiles even more brightly to see a lone figure approaching on a steed—a lone figure in the uniform of the Hussars. . . .

"You see the dilemma the fox had put me in, Charles. While I had been carousing back in Moscow, he had sought my sister out. He had arranged an introduction and then courted her carefully, patiently, *successfully*. And when he swung down from the saddle and our eyes met, he could barely keep the twist of mirth from his lips. But how was I to explain the situation to Helena? This angel of a thousand virtues? How was I to tell her that the man she has fallen in love with has sought her affections not due to an appreciation of her qualities, but to settle a score?"

"What did you do?"

"Ah, Charles. What did I do? I did nothing. I thought surely his true nature would find occasion to express itself—much as it had at the Novo-baczkys'. So in the weeks that followed, I hovered at the edge of their courtship. I suffered through lunches and teas. I ground my teeth as I watched them stroll through the gardens. But as I bided my time, his self-control surpassed my wildest expectations. He pulled out her chair; he picked blossoms; he read verses; he *wrote* verses! And always when he caught my eye there was that little twist in his smile.

"But then on the afternoon of my sister's twentieth birthday, when he was off on maneuvers and we were paying a visit to a neighbor, we returned at dusk to find his troika in front of our house. From a glance at Helena, I could sense her elation. He has rushed back all the way from his battalion, she was thinking, to wish me well on my day. She nearly jumped from her horse and ran up the steps; and I followed her like a condemned man to the noose."

The Count emptied his glass and slowly set it back onto the bar.

"But there inside the entry hall, I did not find my sister in his arms. I found her two steps from the door, trembling. Against the wall was Nadezhda, my sister's handmaiden. Her bodice torn open, her arms across her chest, her face scarlet with humiliation, she looked briefly at my sister then ran up the stairs. In horror, my sister stumbled across the hall, collapsed in a chair, and covered her face with her hands. And our noble lieutenant? He grinned at me like a cat.

"When I began to express my outrage, he said: 'Oh, come now, Alexander. It is Helena's birthday. In her honor, let us call it even.' Then roaring with laughter, he walked out the door without giving my sister a glance."

Charles whistled softly.

The Count nodded.

"But at this juncture, Charles, I did not do nothing. I crossed the entry-way to the wall where a pair of pistols hung beneath the family crest. When my sister grabbed at my sleeve and asked where I was going, I too walked out the door without giving her a glance."

The Count shook his head in condemnation of his own behavior.

"He had a one-minute head start, but he hadn't used it to put distance between us. He had casually climbed into his troika and set his horses moving at little more than a trot. And there you have him in a nutshell, my friend: a man who raced toward parties, and trotted from his own misdeeds."

Charles refilled their glasses and waited.

"Our drive was a grand circle that connected the house to the main road by two opposing arcs lined with apple trees. My horse was still tied at its post. So, when I saw him riding away, I mounted and set off in the opposite direction at a gallop. In a matter of minutes, I had reached the point where the two arcs of the drive met the road. Dismounting, I stood and waited for his approach.

"You can picture the scene—me alone in the drive with the sky blue, the breeze blowing, and the apple trees in bloom. Though he had left the house at little more than a trot, when he saw me, he rose to his feet, raised his whip, and began driving his horses at full speed. There was no question as to what he intended to do. So without a second thought, I raised my arm, steadied my aim, and pulled the trigger. The impact of the bullet knocked him off his feet. The reins flew free and the horses careened off the drive, rolling the troika, and tossing him into the dust—where he lay unmoving."

"You killed him?"

"Yes, Charles. I killed him."

The presumptive heir to the Earl of Westmorland slowly nodded his head.

"Right there in the dust . . ."

The Count sighed and took a drink.

"No. It was eight months later."

Charles looked confused.

"Eight months later . . . ?"

"Yes. In February 1915. You see, ever since my youth I had been known for my marksmanship, and I had every intention of shooting the brute in the heart. But the road was uneven . . . and he was whipping his reins . . . and the apple blossoms were blowing about in the wind . . . In a word, I missed my mark. I ended up shooting him here."

The Count touched his right shoulder.

"So, then you didn't kill him. . . ."

"Not at that moment. After binding his wound and righting his troika, I drove him home. Along the way he cursed me at every turn of the wheel, and deservedly so. For while he survived the gunshot wound, with his right arm now lame, he was forced to surrender his commission in the Hussars. And when his father filed an official complaint, my grandmother sent me to Paris, as was the custom at the time. But later that summer when the war broke out, despite his injury he insisted upon resuming his place at the head of his regiment. And in the Second Battle of the Masurian Lakes, he was knocked from his horse and run through with a bayonet by an Austrian dragoon."

There was a moment of silence.

"Alexander, I am sorry that this fellow died in battle; but I think I can safely say that you have assumed more than your share of guilt for these events."

"But there is one more event to relate: Ten years ago tomorrow, while I was biding my time in Paris, my sister died."

"Of a broken heart . . . ?"

"Young women only die of broken hearts in novels, Charles. She died of scarlet fever."

The presumptive earl shook his head in bewilderment.

"But don't you see?" explained the Count. "It is a chain of events. That night at the Novobaczkys' when I magnanimously tore his marker, I knew perfectly well that word of the act would reach the Princess; and I took the greatest satisfaction in turning the tables on the cad. But if I had not so smugly put him in his place, he would not have pursued Helena, he would not have humiliated her, I would not have shot him, he might not have died in Masuria, and ten years ago I would have been where I belonged— at my sister's side—when she finally breathed her last."

Having capped off his snifter of brandy with six glasses of vodka, when the Count emerged from the attic hatch shortly before midnight, he weaved across the hotel's roof. With the wind a little wild and the building shifting back and forth, one could almost imagine one was crossing the deck of a ship on high seas. How fitting, thought the Count, as he paused to steady himself at a chimney stack. Then picking his way among the irregular shadows that jutted here and there, he approached the building's northwest corner.

For one last time, the Count looked out upon that city that was and wasn't his. Given the frequency of street lamps on major roads, he could easily identify the Boulevard and Garden Rings—those concentric circles at the center of which was the Kremlin and beyond which was all of Russia.

As long as there have been men on earth, reflected the Count, there have been men in exile. From primitive tribes to the most advanced societies, someone has occasionally been told by his fellow men to pack his bags, cross the border, and never set foot on his native soil again. But perhaps this was to be expected. After all, exile was the punishment that God meted out to Adam in the very first chapter of the human comedy; and that He meted out to Cain a few pages later. Yes, exile was as old as mankind. But the Russians were the first people to master the notion of sending a man into exile at home.

As early as the eighteenth century, the Tsars stopped kicking their enemies out of the country, opting instead to send them to Siberia. Why? Because they had determined that to exile a man from Russia as God had exiled Adam from Eden was insufficient as a punishment; for in another country, a man might immerse himself in his labors, build a house, raise a family. That is, he might begin his life anew.

But when you exile a man into his *own* country, there is no beginning anew. For the exile at home—whether he be sent to Siberia or subject to the Minus Six—the love for his country will not become vague or shrouded by the mists of time. In fact, because we have evolved as a species to pay the utmost attention to that which is just beyond our reach, these men are likely to dwell on the splendors of Moscow more than any Muscovite who is at liberty to enjoy them.

But enough of all that.

Having retrieved a Bordeaux glass from the Ambassador, the Count set it on a chimney top. He wrested the cork from the labelless bottle of Châteauneuf-du-Pape that he had taken from the Metropol's cellar back in 1924. Even as he poured the wine, he could tell it was an excellent vintage. Perhaps a 1900 or 1921. With his glass filled, he raised it in the direction of Idlehour.

"To Helena Rostov," he said, "the flower of Nizhny Novgorod. Lover of Pushkin, defender of Alexander, embroiderer of every pillowcase within reach. A life too brief, a heart too kind." Then he drank to the bottom of the glass.

Though the bottle was far from empty, the Count did not refill the glass; nor did he toss it over his shoulder. Rather, he placed it with care on the chimney top and then approached the parapet, where he stood to his full height.

Before him sprawled the city, glorious and grandiose. Its legions of lights shimmered and reeled until they mixed with the movement of the stars. In one dizzy sphere they spun, confusing the works of man with the works of heaven.

Placing his right foot on the parapet's edge, Count Alexander Ilyich Rostov said, "Good-bye, my country."

As if in reply, the beacon on Mishka's tower blinked.

It was now the simplest of matters. Like one who stands on a dock in spring preparing to take the first plunge of the season, all that remained was a leap. Starting just six stories off the ground and falling at the speed of a kopek, a teacup, or a pineapple, the entire journey would only take a matter of seconds; and then the circle would be complete. For as sunrise leads to sunset and dust to dust, as every river returns to the sea, just so a man must return to the embrace of oblivion, from whence—

"Your Excellency!"

Turning in dismay at the interruption, the Count discovered Abram standing behind him in a state of excitement. In fact, Abram was in such a state of excitement that he showed not the slightest surprise at finding the Count poised on the spot where the roof met the ether.

"I thought I heard your voice," said the old handyman. "I'm so glad you're here. You must come with me at once."

"Abram, my friend," the Count began to explain, but the old man continued unabated:

"You will not believe it, if I tell you. You will have to see it for yourself." Then without waiting for a response, he hurried with surprising agility toward his encampment.

The Count let out a sigh. Assuring the city that he would be back in a moment, he followed Abram across the roof to the brazier, where the old man stopped and pointed to the northeast corner of the hotel. And there, against the brightly lit backdrop of the Bolshoi, one could just make out a frenzy of tiny shadows darting through the air.

"They've returned!" Abram exclaimed.

"The bees . . . ?"

"Yes. But that is not all. Sit, sit." Abram gestured toward the plank of wood that had so often served as the Count's chair.

As the Count stood the plank on end, Abram bent over his makeshift table. On it was a tray from one of the hives. He cut into the comb with a knife, spread the honey on a spoon, and handed it to the Count. Then he stood back with a smile of anticipation.

"Well?" he prompted. "Go ahead."

Dutifully, the Count put the spoon in his mouth. In an instant, there was the familiar sweetness of fresh honey—sunlit, golden, and gay. Given the time of year, the Count was expecting this first impression to be followed by a hint of lilacs from the Alexander Gardens or cherry blossoms from the Garden Ring. But as the elixir dissolved on his tongue, the Count became aware of something else entirely. Rather than the flowering trees of central Moscow, the honey had a hint of a grassy riverbank . . . the trace of a summer breeze . . . a suggestion of a pergola. . . . But most of all, there was the unmistakable essence of a thousand apple trees in bloom.

Abram was nodding his head.

"Nizhny Novgorod," he said.

And it was.

Unmistakably so.

"All these years, they must have been listening to us," Abram added in a whisper.

The Count and the handyman both looked toward the roof's edge where the bees, having traveled over a hundred miles and applied themselves in willing industry, now wheeled above their hives as pinpoints of blackness, like the inverse of stars.

It was nearly two in the morning when the Count bid Abram goodnight and returned to his bedroom. Taking the gold coin from his pocket, he placed it back on the stack inside the leg of his godfather's desk—where it would remain untouched for another twenty-eight years. And the following evening at six, when the Boyarsky opened, the Count was the first one through its doors.

"Andrey," he said to the maître d'. "Can you spare a moment . . . ?"

BOOK THREE

BOOK THREE

1930

Count Alexander Ilyich Rostov stirred at half past eight to the sound of rain on the eaves. With a half-opened eye, he pulled back his covers and climbed from bed. He donned his robe and slipped on his slippers. He took up the tin from the bureau, spooned a spoonful of beans into the Apparatus, and began to crank the crank.

Even as he turned the little handle round and round, the room remained under the tenuous authority of sleep. As yet unchallenged, somnolence continued to cast its shadow over sights and sensations, over forms and formulations, over what has been said and what must be done, lending each the insubstantiality of its domain. But when the Count opened the small wooden drawer of the grinder, the world and all it contained were transformed by that envy of the alchemists—the aroma of freshly ground coffee.

In that instant, darkness was separated from light, the waters from the lands, and the heavens from the earth. The trees bore fruit and the woods rustled with the movement of birds and beasts and all manner of creeping things. While closer at hand, a patient pigeon scuffed its feet on the flashing.

Easing the little drawer from the Apparatus, the Count poured its contents into the pot (which he had mindfully primed with water the night before). He lit the burner and shook out the match. As he waited for the coffee to brew, he did thirty squats and thirty stretches and took thirty deep breaths. From the little cupboard in the corner, he took a small pitcher of cream, a pair of English biscuits, and a piece of fruit (today an apple). Then having poured the coffee, he began to enjoy the morning's sensations to their fullest:

The crisp tartness of the apple . . .

The hot bitterness of the coffee . . .

The savory sweetness of the biscuit with its hint of spoiled butter . . .

So perfect was the combination that upon finishing, the Count was tempted to crank the crank, quarter the apple, dole out the biscuits, and enjoy his breakfast all over again.

But time and tide wait for no man. So, having poured the remnants of the coffee from its pot, the Count brushed the biscuit crumbs from his plate onto the window ledge for his feathered friend. Then he emptied the little pitcher of cream into a saucer and turned toward the door with the intention of placing it in the hall—and that was when he saw the envelope on the floor.

Someone must have slipped it under his door in the middle of the night.

Setting the saucer down for his one-eyed friend, he picked up the envelope and discovered that it had an unusual feel, as if something quite different than a letter had been enclosed. On the back, it bore the dark blue moniker of the hotel, while on the front, in place of a name and address, was written the query: *Four o'clock?*

The Count sat on his bed and took the last sip of coffee. Then he tucked the point of his paring knife under the envelope's flap, slit it from corner to corner, and gazed within.

"*Mon Dieu,*" he said.

Arachne's Art

History is the business of identifying momentous events from the comfort of a high-back chair. With the benefit of time, the historian looks back and points to a date in the manner of a gray-haired field marshal pointing to a bend in a river on a map: *There it was,* he says. *The turning point. The decisive factor. The fateful day that fundamentally altered all that was to follow.*

There on the third of January 1928, the historians tell us, was the launch of the First Five-Year Plan—that initiative which would begin the transformation of Russia from a nineteenth-century agrarian society into a twentieth-century industrial power. There on the seventeenth of November 1929, Nikolai Bukharin, founding father, editor of *Pravda*, and last true friend of the peasant, was outmaneuvered by Stalin and ousted from the Politburo—clearing the way for a return to autocracy in all but name. And there on the twenty-fifth of February 1927, was the drafting of Article 58 of the Criminal Code—the net that would eventually ensnare us all.

There on the twenty-seventh of May, or there on the sixth of December; at eight or nine in the morning.

There it was, they say. As if—like at the opera—a curtain has closed, a lever has been pulled, one set has been whisked to the rafters and another has dropped to the stage, such that when the curtain opens a moment later the audience will find itself transported from a richly appointed ballroom to the banks of a wooded stream. . . .

But the events that transpired on those various dates did not throw the city of Moscow into upheaval. When the page was torn from the calendar, the bedroom windows did not suddenly shine with the light of a million electric lamps; that Fatherly gaze did not suddenly hang over every desk and appear in every dream; nor did the drivers of a hundred Black Marias turn the keys in their ignitions and fan out into the shadowy streets. For the launch of the First Five-Year Plan, Bukharin's fall from grace, and the expansion of the Criminal Code to allow the arrest of anyone even countenancing dissension, these were only tidings, omens, underpinnings. And it would be a decade before their effects were fully felt.

No. For most of us, the late 1920s were not characterized by a series of momentous events. Rather, the passage of those years was like the turn of a kaleidoscope.

At the bottom of a kaleidoscope's cylinder lie shards of colored glass in random arrangement; but thanks to a glint of sunlight, the interplay of mirrors, and the magic of symmetry, when one peers inside what one finds is a pattern so colorful, so perfectly intricate, it seems certain to have been designed with the utmost care. Then by the slightest turn of the wrist, the shards begin to shift and settle into a new configuration—a configuration with its own symmetry of shapes, its own intricacy of colors, its own hints of design.

So it was in the city of Moscow in the late 1920s.

And so it was at the Metropol Hotel.

In fact, if a seasoned Muscovite were to cross Theatre Square on the last day of spring in 1930, he would find the hotel much as he remembered it.

There on the front steps still stands Pavel Ivanovich in his greatcoat looking as stalwart as ever (though his hip now gives him some trouble on foggy afternoons). On the other side of the revolving doors are the same eager lads in the same blue caps ready to whisk one's suitcases up the stairs (though they now answer to Grisha and Genya rather than Pasha and Petya). Vasily, with his uncanny awareness of whereabouts, still mans the concierge's desk directly across from Arkady, who remains ready to spin the register and offer you a pen. And in the manager's office, Mr. Halecki still sits behind his spotless desk (though a new assistant manager with the smile of an ecclesiastic is prone to interrupt his reveries over the slightest infraction of the hotel's rules).

In the Piazza, Russians cut from every cloth (or at least those who have access to foreign currency) gather to linger over coffee and happen upon friends. While in the ballroom, the weighty remarks and late arrivals that once characterized the Assemblies now characterize Dinners of

State (though no one with a penchant for yellow spies from the balcony anymore).

And the Boyarsky?

At two o'clock its kitchen is already in full swing. Along the wooden tables the junior chefs are chopping carrots and onions as Stanislav, the sous-chef, delicately debones pigeons with a whistle on his lips. On the great stoves, eight burners have been lit to simmer sauces, soups, and stews. The pastry chef, who seems as dusted with flour as one of his rolls, opens an oven door to withdraw two trays of brioches. And in the center of all this activity, with an eye on every assistant and a finger in every pot, stands Emile Zhukovsky, his chopping knife in hand.

If the kitchen of the Boyarsky is an orchestra and Emile its conductor, then his chopping knife is the baton. With a blade two inches wide at the base and ten inches long to the tip, it is rarely out of his hand and never far from reach. Though the kitchen is outfitted with paring knives, boning knives, carving knives, and cleavers, Emile can complete any of the various tasks for which those knives were designed with his ten-inch chopper. With it he can skin a rabbit. He can zest a lemon. He can peel and quarter a grape. He can use it to flip a pancake or stir a soup, and with the stabbing end he can measure out a teaspoon of sugar or a dash of salt. But most of all, he uses it for pointing.

"You," he says to the saucier, waving the point of his chopper. "Are you going to boil that to nothing? What are you going to use it for, eh? To pave roads? To paint icons?

"You," he says to the conscientious new apprentice at the end of the counter. "What are you doing there? It took less time for that parsley to grow than for you to mince it!"

And on the last day of spring? It is Stanislav who receives the tip of the knife. For in the midst of trimming the fat from racks of lamb, Emile suddenly stops and glares across the table.

"You!" he says, pointing the chopper at Stanislav's nose. "What is that?"

Stanislav, a lanky Estonian who has dutifully studied his master's every move, looks up from his pigeons with startled eyes.

"What is what, sir?"

"What is that you're whistling?"

Admittedly, there has been a melody playing in Stanislav's head—a little something that he had heard the night before while passing the entrance of the hotel's bar—but he had not been conscious of whistling it. And now that he faces the chopper, he cannot for the life of him remember what the melody was.

"I am not certain," he confesses.

"Not certain! Were you whistling or weren't you?"

"Yes, sir. It was I who must have been whistling. But I assure you it was just a ditty."

"Just a ditty?"

"A little song."

"I know what a ditty is! But under what authority are you whistling one? Eh? Has the Central Committee made you Commissar of Ditty Whistling? Is that the Grand Order of Dittyness I see pinned to your chest?"

Without looking down, Emile slams his chopper to the counter, splitting a lamb chop from its rack as if he were severing the melody from Stanislav's memory once and for all. The chef raises his chopper again and points its tip, but before he can elaborate, that door which separates Emile's kitchen from the rest of the world swings open. It is Andrey, as prompt as ever, with his Book in hand and a pair of spectacles resting on the top of his head. Like a brigand after a skirmish, Emile slips his chopper under the tie of his apron and then looks expectantly at the door, which a moment later swings again.

With the slightest turn of the wrist the shards of glass tumble into a new arrangement. The blue cap of the bellhop is handed from one boy to the next, a dress as yellow as a canary is stowed in a trunk, a little red guidebook is updated with the new names of streets, and through Emile's swinging door walks Count Alexander Ilyich Rostov—with the white dinner jacket of the Boyarsky draped across his arm.

One minute later, sitting at the table in the little office overlooking the kitchen were Emile, Andrey, and the Count—that Triumvirate which met each day at 2:15 to decide the fate of the restaurant's staff, its customers, its chickens and tomatoes.

As was customary, Andrey convened the meeting by resting his reading glasses on the tip of his nose and opening the Book.

"There are no parties in the private rooms tonight," he began, "but every table in the dining room is reserved for two seatings."

"Ah," said Emile with the grim smile of the commander who prefers to be outnumbered. "But you're not going to rush them, eh?"

"Absolutely not," assured the Count. "We'll simply see to it that their menus are delivered promptly and their orders taken directly."

Emile nodded in acknowledgment.

"Are there any complications?" asked the Count of the maître d'.

"Nothing out of the ordinary."

Andrey spun the Book so that his headwaiter could see for himself.

The Count ran a finger down the list of reservations. As Andrey had said, there was nothing out of the ordinary. The Commissar of Transport loathed American journalists; the German ambassador loathed the Commissar of Transport; and the deputy head of the OGPU was loathed by all.* The most delicate matter was that two different members of the Politburo were hosting tables during the second seating. As both were relatively new to their positions, it was not essential that either have the best tables in the house. What *was* essential was that their treatment be identical in every respect. They must be served with equal attention at tables of equal size equidistant from the kitchen door. And ideally, they would be on opposite sides of the centerpiece (tonight an arrangement of irises).

"What do you think?" asked Andrey, with his pen in hand.

As the Count made his suggestions of who should sit where, there

---

*Established in 1923, the OGPU replaced the Cheka as Russia's cental organ of the secret police. In 1934, the OGPU would be replaced by the NKVD, which in turn would be replaced by the MGB in 1943 and the KGB in 1954. On the surface, this may seem confusing. But the good news is that unlike political parties, artistic movements, or schools of fashion—which go through such sweeping reinventions—the methodologies and intentions of the secret police never change. So you should feel no need to distinguish one acronym from the next.

came a delicate knock on the door. Stanislav entered, carrying a serving bowl and platter.

"Good day, gentlemen," the sous-chef said to Andrey and the Count with a friendly smile. "In addition to our normal fare, tonight we have cucumber soup and—"

"Yes, yes," said Emile with a scowl. "We know, we know."

Stanislav apologetically placed the bowl and platter on the table, even as Emile waved him from the room. Once he was gone, the chef gestured at the offering. "In addition to our normal fare, tonight we have cucumber soup and rack of lamb with a red wine reduction."

On the table were three teacups. Emile ladled the soup into two of the cups and waited for his colleagues to sample it.

"Excellent," said Andrey.

Emile nodded and then turned to the Count with his eyebrows raised.

A puree of peeled cucumber, thought the Count. Yogurt, of course. A bit of salt. Not as much dill as one might expect. In fact, something else entirely . . . Something that speaks just as eloquently of summer's approach, but with a little more flair . . .

"Mint?" he asked.

The chef responded with the smile of the bested.

"*Bravo, monsieur.*"

". . . To anticipate the lamb," the Count added with appreciation.

Emile bowed his head once and then, slipping the chopper from his waist, he carved four chops from the rack and stacked two on each of his colleagues' plates.

The lamb, which had been encrusted with rosemary and bread-crumbs, was savory and tender. Both maître d' and headwaiter sighed in appreciation.

Thanks to a member of the Central Committee, who had tried unsuccessfully to order a bottle of Bordeaux for the new French ambassador in 1927, wines with labels could once again be found in the Metropol's cellar (after all, despite its considerable size, the neck of a dragon has been known to whip about like that of an asp). So, turning to the Count, Andrey asked what he thought they should recommend with the lamb.

"For those who can afford it, the Château Latour '99."

The chef and maître d' nodded.

"And for those who cannot?"

The Count considered.

"Perhaps a Côtes du Rhône."

"Excellent," said Andrey.

Picking up his chopper, Emile pointed at the rest of the rack and cautioned the Count: "Tell your boys that my lamb is served rare. If someone wants it medium, they can go to a canteen."

The Count expressed his comprehension and willingness to comply. Then Andrey closed the Book and Emile wiped his chopper. But as they began pushing back their chairs, the Count remained where he was.

"Gentlemen," he said. "Just one more thing before we adjourn. . . ."

Given the expression on the Count's face, the chef and the maître d' pulled their chairs back to the table.

The Count looked through the window into the kitchen to confirm that the staff were consumed with their work. Then from his jacket pocket he took the envelope that had been slipped under his door. When he tipped it over Emile's unused teacup, out poured filaments of a red and golden hue.

The three men were silent for a moment.

Emile sat back.

"*Bravo*," he said again.

"May I?" asked Andrey.

"Certainly."

Andrey picked up the teacup and tipped it back and forth. Then he replaced it so gently on its saucer that the porcelain didn't make a sound.

"Is it enough?"

Having watched the filaments spill from the envelope, the chef didn't need a second look.

"Without a doubt."

"Do we still have the fennel?"

"There are a few bulbs at the back of the larder. We'll have to discard the outer leaves, but otherwise they're fine."

"Did you hear back about the oranges?" asked the Count.

With a somber look, the chef shook his head.

"How many would we need?" asked Andrey.

"Two. Maybe three."

"I think I know where some can be found. . . ."

"Can they be found today?" asked the chef.

Andrey pulled the pocket watch from his vest and consulted it in the palm of his hand.

"With any luck."

Where would Andrey be able to acquire three oranges on such short notice? Another restaurant? One of the special stores for hard currencies? A patron in the upper echelons of the Party? Well, for that matter, where did the Count acquire a quarter of an ounce of saffron? Such questions had stopped being asked years ago. Suffice it to say, the saffron was in hand and the oranges within reach.

The three conspirators exchanged satisfied glances and then pushed back their chairs. Andrey put his glasses back on his head as Emile turned to the Count.

"You'll get the menus in their hands directly and their orders taken promptly, eh? No malingering?"

"No malingering."

"Well then," concluded the chef. "We meet at half past twelve."

When the Count left the Boyarsky with his white jacket draped across his arm, there was a smile on his lips and a jauntiness to his step. In fact, there was a brightness in his whole demeanor.

"Greetings, Grisha," he said as he passed the bellhop (who was on his way up the stairs with a vase of tiger lilies two feet tall).

"*Guten tag*," he said to the lovely young Fraulein in the lavender blouse (who was waiting by the elevator door).

The Count's good humor was due in part, no doubt, to the reading on the thermometer. Over the previous three weeks, the temperature had climbed four and a half degrees, setting in motion that course of natural and human events which culminates in hints of mint in cucumber soups, lavender blouses at elevator doors, and midday deliveries of tiger lilies two feet tall. Also lightening his step were the promises of an afternoon assignation and a midnight rendezvous. But the factor that most directly contributed to the Count's good humor was the double *bravo* from Emile. This was something that had occurred only once or twice in four years.

Passing through the lobby, the Count returned the friendly wave from the new fellow at the mail window and hailed Vasily, who was hanging up his phone (having undoubtedly secured another two tickets for some sold-out performance).

"Good afternoon, my friend. Hard at work I see."

In acknowledgment, the concierge gestured to the lobby, which bustled almost as much as it had in its prewar prime. As if on cue, the telephone on his desk began to ring, the bellhop's bell triple-chimed, and someone called out, "Comrade! Comrade!"

Ah, *comrade*, thought the Count. Now, there was a word for the ages. . . .

When the Count was a boy in St. Petersburg, one rarely bumped into it. It was always prowling at the back of a mill or under the table in a tavern, occasionally leaving its paw marks on the freshly printed pamphlets that were drying on a basement floor. Now, thirty years later, it was the most commonly heard word in the Russian language.

A wonder of semantic efficiency, *comrade* could be used as a greeting, or a word of parting. As a congratulations, or a caution. As a call to action, or a remonstrance. Or it could simply be the means of securing someone's attention in the crowded lobby of a grand hotel. And thanks to the word's versatility, the Russian people had finally been able to dispense with tired formalities, antiquated titles, bothersome idioms—even names! Where else in all of Europe could one shout a single word to hail any of one's countrymen be they male or female, young or old, friend or foe?

"Comrade!" someone called again—this time with a little more urgency. And then he tugged on the Count's sleeve.

Startled, the Count turned to find the new fellow from the mail window at his elbow.

"Well, hello there. How can I be of service to you, young man?"

The fellow looked perplexed at the Count's question, having assumed that it was his position to be of service to someone else.

"There is a letter for you," he explained.

"For me?"

"Yes, comrade. It came yesterday."

The young fellow pointed back toward the window to indicate where the letter remained.

"Well, in that case, after you," said the Count.

Civil servant and customer proceeded to their appropriate stations on either side of that small window which separates the written from the read.

"Here it is," he said, after a moment of sorting.

"Thank you, my good man."

Taking the envelope in hand, the Count was half expecting to find it addressed to *Comrade*, but there (under two postage stamps bearing the likeness of Lenin) was the Count's full name—written in an indifferently groomed, relatively reclusive, occasionally argumentative script.

When the Count had come down to the lobby from the Boyarsky, he had been on his way to the office of the shy delight, where he hoped to secure a length of white thread for a button that had been compromised on his jacket. But he had not seen Mishka in almost half a year; and at the very moment that he recognized his old friend's script, a lady with a lap-dog rose from his favorite chair between the potted palms. Ever respectful of Fate, the Count postponed his visit to the seamstress, claimed his seat, and opened the letter.

Leningrad
June 14, 1930

Dear Sasha,

At four this morning, unable to sleep, I ventured out into the old city. As the revelers of the white nights had already stumbled home and the tram conductors had yet to don their caps, I strolled along Nevsky Prospekt through a stillness of spring that seemed stolen from another province, if not another time.

Nevsky, like the city itself, bears a new name: October 25th Prospekt—a worthy day staking its claim on a storied street. But at this hour, it was just as you remember it, my friend. And with no destination in mind, I crossed the Moika and Fontanka Canals, I passed the shops, and the rose-hued facades of the grand old homes until, at last, I reached Tikhvin Cemetery, where the bodies of

Dostoevsky and Tchaikovsky slumber a few feet apart. (Do you
remember how late into the night we would debate the genius of the one
over the other?)

And suddenly it struck me that walking the length of Nevsky
Prospekt was like walking the length of Russian literature. Right there
at the beginning—just off the avenue on the Moika embankment—is
the house where Pushkin ended his years. A few paces on are the rooms
where Gogol began Dead Souls. *Then the National Library, where*
Tolstoy scoured the archives. And here, behind the cemetery walls, lies
brother Fyodor, our restless witness of the human soul entombed
beneath the cherry trees.

As I was standing lost in thought, the sun rose above the cemetery
walls, shining its light down the Prospekt and, nearly overcome, I
recalled that great affirmation, that proclamation, that promise:

> *Always to shine,*
> *to shine everywhere,*
> *to the very depths of the last days . . .*

Before turning to the second page of his old friend's letter, the Count
found himself looking up, deeply moved.

It was not the memories of St. Petersburg that affected him so—not
some nostalgia for his youth among the rose-hued facades, or for his
years with Mishka in the apartment above the cobbler's. Nor was it Mishka's sentimental reminders of Russia's literary greatness. What moved
the Count was the thought of his old friend venturing out into this stolen
spring barely aware of where he was headed. For from the letter's first
line, the Count had known exactly where Mishka was headed.

It had been four years since Mishka had moved to Kiev with Katerina; it had been one year since she had left him for another man; and six
months since he had returned to St. Petersburg to barricade himself once
again behind his books. Then one spring night at four in the morning,
unable to sleep, he finds himself on Nevsky Prospekt following the very
same route that he had walked with Katerina on the day that she had
first taken his hand. And there, as the sun begins to rise, he is overcome
with thoughts of an affirmation, a proclamation, a promise—a promise

to shine everywhere and always to very depths of the last days—which, after all, is all that anyone has ever asked of love.

As these thoughts passed through the Count's mind, was he concerned that Mishka still pined for Katerina? Was he concerned that his old friend was morbidly retracing the footsteps of a lapsed romance?

Concerned? Mishka would pine for Katerina the rest of his life! Never again would he walk Nevsky Prospekt, however they chose to rename it, without feeling an unbearable sense of loss. And that is just how it should be. That sense of loss is exactly what we must anticipate, prepare for, and cherish to the last of our days; for it is only our heartbreak that finally refutes all that is ephemeral in love.

The Count picked up Mishka's letter with the intention of reading on, but as he turned the page, three youths leaving the Piazza happened to stop on the other side of one of the potted palms to carry on some weighty conversation.

The trio was made up of a good-looking Komsomol type in his early twenties, and two younger women—one blonde, one brunette. The three were apparently headed for the Ivanovo Province in some official capacity and the young man, who was their captain, now warned his compatriots of the privations they would inevitably face while assuring them of their work's historical significance.

When he finished, the brunette asked how large the province was, but before he could answer, the blonde obliged: "It is over three hundred square miles with a population of half a million. And while the region is largely agricultural, it has only eight machine tractor stations and six modern mills."

The handsome captain did not seem the least put out by his younger comrade answering on his behalf. On the contrary, it was plain from the expression on his face that he held her in the highest regard.

As the blonde concluded her geography lesson, a fourth member of the party jogged up from the direction of the Piazza. Shorter and younger than the leader, he was wearing the sailor's cap that had been favored among landlocked youth ever since *Battleship Potemkin*. In his hand he had a canvas jacket, which he now held out to the blonde.

"I took the liberty of getting your coat," he said eagerly, "when I picked up mine."

The blonde accepted the coat with a nod, and without a word of thanks.

Without a word of thanks . . . ?

The Count rose to his feet.

"Nina?"

All four youths turned toward the potted palm.

Leaving his white jacket and Mishka's letter in his chair, the Count stepped from behind the fronds.

"Nina Kulikova!" he exclaimed. "What a delightful surprise."

And that is exactly what it was for the Count: a delightful surprise. For he had not seen Nina in over two years; and many had been the time that he had passed the card room or the ballroom and found himself wondering where she was and what she was doing.

But in an instant, the Count could see that for Nina his sudden appearance was less opportune. Perhaps she'd rather not have to explain to her comrades about her acquaintance with a Former Person. Perhaps she hadn't mentioned that she had lived as a child in such a fine hotel. Or perhaps she simply wanted to carry on this purposeful conversation with her purposeful friends.

"I'll be just a minute," she told them, then crossed over to the Count.

Naturally, after such a long separation the Count's instinct was to embrace little Nina like a bear; but she seemed to dissuade his impulse with her posture.

"It is good to see you, Nina."

"And you, Alexander Ilyich."

The old friends took each other in for a moment; then Nina made a gesture toward the white jacket hanging over the arm of the chair.

"I see you are still presiding over tables at the Boyarsky."

"Yes," he said with a smile, though unsure from her businesslike tone whether he should take the remark as a compliment or criticism. . . . He was tempted in turn to ask (with a glint in his eye) if she had had an "hors d'oeuvre" at the Piazza, but thought better of it.

"I gather you are on the verge of an adventure," he said instead.

"I suppose there will be adventurous aspects," she replied. "But mostly there will be a good deal of work."

The four of them, she explained, were leaving the next morning with ten other cadres of local Komsomol youth for the Kady District—an ancient agricultural center in the heart of the Ivanovo Province—to aid the *udarniks*, or "shock workers," in the collectivization of the region. At the end of 1928, only 10 percent of the farms in Ivanovo had been operating as collectives. By the end of 1931, nearly all of them would be.

"For generations the kulaks have farmed the land for themselves, organizing the local peasant labor to their own ends. But the time has come for the common land to serve the common good. It is a historical necessity," she added matter-of-factly, "an inevitability. After all, does a teacher only teach his own children? Does a physician only care for his parents?"

As Nina began this little speech, the Count was taken aback for a moment by her tone and terminology—by her exacting assessment of kulaks and the "inevitable" need for collectivization. But when she tucked her hair behind her ears, he realized that her fervor shouldn't have come as a surprise. She was simply bringing to the Komsomol the same unwavering enthusiasm and precise attention to detail that she had brought to the mathematics of Professor Lisitsky. Nina Kulikova always was and would be a serious soul in search of serious ideas to be serious about.

Nina had told her comrades that she would only be a minute, but as she elaborated on the work that lay ahead, she seemed to forget that they were still standing on the other side of the potted palm.

With an inward smile, the Count noted over her shoulder that the handsome captain, having volunteered to wait for Nina, was sending the others on ahead—a reasonable gambit under any ideology.

"I should go," she said, after drawing her remarks to a close.

"Yes. Absolutely," replied the Count. "You must have a great deal to see to."

In sober acknowledgment, she shook his hand; and when she turned, she barely seemed to notice that two of her comrades had already left—as if having a handsome fellow wait for her was something to which she had already become accustomed.

As the two young idealists left the hotel, the Count watched through the revolving doors. He watched as the young man spoke to Pavel, and Pavel signaled a taxi. But when the taxi appeared and the young man opened the door, Nina gestured across Theatre Square, indicating that she was headed in another direction. The handsome captain made a similar gesture, presumably offering to accompany her, but Nina shook his hand just as soberly as she had shaken the Count's and then walked across the square in the general direction of historical necessity.

"Isn't that more of a cream than a pearl?"

Together, the Count and Marina were staring at a spool that she had just taken from a drawer filled with threads in every possible shade of white.

"I am so sorry, Your Excellency," Marina replied. "Now that you bring it to my attention, it does seem more creamy than pearly."

The Count looked up from the spool into Marina's stationary eye, which was filled with concern; but her wandering eye seemed filled with mirth. Then she laughed like a schoolgirl.

"Oh, give me that," he said.

"Here," she said in a conciliatory tone. "Let me."

"Absolutely not."

"Oh, come now."

"I'm perfectly capable of doing it myself, thank you."

But to the Count's credit, he was not simply making a peevish point. He was, in fact, perfectly capable of doing it himself.

It stands to reason that if you wish to be a good waiter you must be master of your own appearance. You must be clean, well groomed, and graceful. But you must also be neatly dressed. You certainly can't wander around the dining room with fraying collars or cuffs. And God forbid you should presume to serve with a dangling button—for next thing you knew, it would be floating in a customer's vichyssoise. So, three weeks after joining the staff of the Boyarsky, the Count had asked Marina to teach him Arachne's art. To be conservative, the Count had set aside an hour for the lesson. It ended up taking eight hours over the course of four weeks.

Who knew that there was such a plethora of stitches? The backstitch, cross-stitch, slip stitch, topstitch, whipstitch. Aristotle, Larousse, and Diderot—those great encyclopedists who spent their lives segmenting, cataloging, and defining all manner of phenomena—would never have imagined that there were so many, and each one suited to a different purpose!

With his creamy thread in hand, the Count settled himself into a chair; and when Marina held out her pincushion, he surveyed the needles as a child surveys chocolates in a box.

"This one," he said.

Licking the thread and closing an eye (just as Marina had taught him), the Count threaded the needle faster than saints enter the gates of heaven. Forming a double loop, tying off a knot, and snipping the thread from the spool, the Count sat upright and set about his work as Marina set about hers (the repair of a pillowcase).

As with any sewing circle since the beginning of time, the two in this one were accustomed to sharing observations from their day as they stitched. Most of these observations were met with a *Hmm*, or an *Is that so?* without a break in the rhythm of the work; but occasionally, some item that warranted greater attention would bring the stitching to a stop. Just so, having exchanged remarks on the weather, and Pavel's handsome new topcoat, Marina's needle suddenly froze in midstitch when the Count mentioned that he had run into Nina.

"Nina Kulikova?" she asked in surprise.

"None other."

"Where?"

"In the lobby. She had been having lunch with three of her comrades."

"Did you speak?"

"At some length."

"What did she have to say for herself?"

"It seems they are off to Ivanovo to rationalize kulaks and collectivize tractors, and what have you."

"Never mind that, Alexander. How *was* she?"

Here the Count stopped his stitching.

"She was every bit herself," he said after a moment. "Still full of curiosity and passion and self-assurance."

"Wonderful," Marina said with a smile.

The Count watched as she resumed her stitching.

"And yet . . ."

Marina stopped again and met his gaze.

"And yet?"

. . .

"It's nothing."

"Alexander. There is clearly something on your mind."

. . .

"It's just that to hear Nina talk of her upcoming journey, she is so passionate, so self-assured, and perhaps so single-minded, that she seems almost humorless. Like some dauntless explorer, she seems ready to place her flag in a polar ice cap and claim it in the name of Inevitability. But I can't help suspecting that all the while, her happiness may be waiting in another latitude altogether."

"Come now, Alexander. Little Nina must be nearly eighteen. Surely, when you were that age you and your friends spoke with passion and self-assurance."

"Of course we did," said the Count. "We sat in cafés and argued about ideas until they mopped the floors and doused the lights."

"Well, there you are."

"It's true that we argued about ideas, Marina; but we never had any intention of doing anything about them."

Marina rolled one of her eyes.

"Heaven forbid you should do something about an idea."

"No, I am serious. Nina is so determined, I fear that the force of her convictions will interfere with the joys of her youth."

Marina put her sewing in her lap.

"You have always been fond of little Nina."

"Of course I have."

"And in part, that is because she is such an independent spirit."

"Precisely."

"Then you must trust in her. And even if she is single-minded to a fault, you must trust that life will find her in time. For eventually, it finds us all."

The Count nodded for a moment, reflecting on Marina's position. Then returning to his task, he looped through the button's holes, wound the shank, tied off the knot, and snapped the thread with his teeth. Poking

Marina's needle back into its cushion, he noted it was already 4:05, a fact that confirmed once again how quickly time flies when one is immersed in a pleasant task accompanied by pleasant conversation.

Wait a moment . . . , thought the Count.

Already 4:05?

"Great Scott!"

Thanking Marina, the Count grabbed his jacket, dashed to the lobby, and vaulted up the stairs two by two. When he arrived at suite 311, he found the door ajar. Looking left and looking right, he slipped inside and closed the door.

On the side table before an ornate mirror were the two-foot tiger lilies that had passed him earlier in the day. After taking a quick look around, the Count crossed the empty sitting room and entered the bedchamber, where a willowy figure stood in silhouette before one of the great windows. At the sound of his approach, she turned and let her dress slip to the floor with a delicate whoosh. . . .

An Afternoon Assignation

After taking a quick look around, the Count crossed the empty sitting room and entered the bedchamber, where a willowy figure stood in silhouette before one of the great windows. At the sound of his approach, she turned and let her dress slip to the floor with a delicate whoosh. . . .

What's this!

When we last left this pair in 1923, did not Anna Urbanova dismiss the Count with a definitive instruction to "draw the curtains"? And when he closed the door behind him with a click, did he not assume the aspect of a ghost before drifting forlornly to the roof? And now, as she slips beneath the bedcovers, this once haughty figure offers a smile suggestive of patience, tenderness, even gratitude—traits that are mirrored almost exactly in the smile of her former adversary as he hangs the white jacket of the Boyarsky on the back of a chair and begins to unbutton his shirt!

What possibly could have happened to reunite these contrary souls? What twisting path could have led them to suite 311 and back into each other's arms?

Well, it was not the path of the Count that twisted. For Alexander Rostov had spent the intervening years traveling up and down the Metropol's staircase from his bedroom to the Boyarsky and back again. No, the path that twisted, turned, veered, and doubled back was not the Count's; it was Anna's.

When we first encountered Miss Urbanova in the Metropol's lobby in 1923, the haughtiness the Count noted in her bearing was not without foundation, for it was a by-product of her unambiguous celebrity. Discovered in a regional theater on the outskirts of Odessa in 1919 by Ivan

Rosotsky, Anna was cast as leading lady in his next two films. Both of these were historical romances that celebrated the moral purity of those who toiled, while disparaging the corruption of those who did not. In the first, Anna played an eighteenth-century kitchen maid for whom a young nobleman abandons the trappings of court. In the second, she was a nineteenth-century heiress who turns her back on her legacy to wed a blacksmith's apprentice. Setting his fables in the palaces of yesteryear, Rosotsky lit them in the hazy aura of dreams, shot them in the soft focus of memories, and capped the first, second, and third acts with close-ups of his starlet: Anna aspiring; Anna distraught; Anna at long last in love. Both of the films were popular with the public, both found favor with the Politburo (which was eager to give the People some respite from the war years through suitably themed diversions), and our young starlet reaped the effortless rewards of fame.

In 1921, Anna was given membership in the All-Russian Film Union and access to its dedicated stores; in 1922 she was given use of a dacha near Peterhof; and in 1923 she was given the mansion of a former fur merchant furnished with gilded chairs, painted armoires, and a Louis Quatorze dresser—all of which could easily have been props in one of Rosotsky's films. It was at her soirées in this house that Anna mastered the ancient art of descending a staircase. With one hand on the banister and the train of a long silk dress behind her, she descended step by step while painters, authors, actors, and senior members of the Party waited at the foot of the stair. *

But art is the most unnatural minion of the state. Not only is it created by fanciful people who tire of repetition even more quickly than they tire

---

*In those early years of the Soviet Union, how did the Bolsheviks countenance the idea of gilded chairs and Louis Quatorze dressers in the mansions of starlets? For that matter, how did they stomach them in their own apartments? Simple. Nailed to the bottom of every piece of fine furniture was a small copper plate embossed with a number. This number served to identify the piece as part of the vast inventory of the People. Thus, a good Bolshevik could sleep soundly in the knowledge that the mahogany bed he was lying on was not his; and despite the fact that his apartment was furnished with priceless antiques, he had fewer possessions than a pauper!

of being told what to do, it is also vexingly ambiguous. Just when a care-fully crafted bit of dialogue is about to deliver a crystal-clear message, a hint of sarcasm or the raising of an eyebrow can spoil the entire effect. In fact, it can give credence to a notion that is the exact opposite of that which was intended. So, perhaps it is understandable that governing authorities are bound to reconsider their artistic preferences every now and then, if for no other reason than to keep themselves fit.

Sure enough, at the Moscow premiere of Rosotsky's fourth film with Anna as leading lady (in which, playing the part of a princess mistaken for an orphan, she falls in love with an orphan mistaken for a prince), it was noted by the savvy in the orchestra section that General Secretary Stalin, who was known so endearingly in his youth as Soso, was not smiling as wholeheartedly at the screen as he had in the past. Instinctively, they restrained their own enthusiasm, which tempered the enthusiasm of those in the mezzanine, which in turn tempered those in the balcony—until everyone in the house could sense that something was afoot.

Two days after the premiere, an open letter was written to *Pravda* by an up-and-coming apparatchik (who had been sitting just a few seats behind Soso). The film was entertaining in its way, he conceded, but what was one to make of Rosotsky's incessant return to the era of princes and princesses? Of waltzing and candlelight and marble stairs? Had not his fascination with the past begun to smell suspiciously of nostalgia? And once again, does not his story line seem centered on the trials and triumphs of the individual? A predilection that he reinforces by his rather excessive reliance on the close-up? Yes, we have another beautiful woman in another beautiful gown, but where is the historical immediacy? And where the collective struggle?

Four days after the letter appeared in *Pravda*, Soso took a moment before addressing the Plenum to approach this new film critic and com-pliment him on his turns of phrase. Two weeks after the Plenum, the substance of the letter (and a few of its turns of phrase) were echoed in three more newspapers and a journal of the arts. The film received lim-ited distribution to second-rate theaters, where it was met with muted applause. By that autumn, not only was Rosotsky's next project up in the air, his political reliability had come into question. . . .

An ingénue in film but not in life, Anna understood that Rosotsky's fall from grace was a stone that could quickly drag her to the depths. She began avoiding public appearances in his company, while openly praising the aesthetics of other directors; and this stratagem might well have succeeded in securing her a new avenue of stardom but for an unfortunate development across the Atlantic: the talking picture. While Anna's face was still one of the most alluring on screen, audiences who for years had imagined her speaking in dulcet tones were not prepared to hear her husky tenor. Thus, in the spring of 1928, at the sprightly age of twenty-nine, Anna Urbanova was what the Americans would have called a has-been.

Alas, while the copper plate on the bottom of a priceless antique may allow a good comrade to sleep soundly, it is the nature of objects with serial numbers set down in ledgers that they may be reclaimed and put to new use at the stroke of a pen. In a matter of months, the gilded chairs, painted armoires, and Louis Quatorze dresser were all gone—as was the fur merchant's mansion and the Peterhof dacha—and Anna found herself with two trunks of clothing in the street. In her purse she still had train fare to her hometown outside Odessa. Instead, she moved into a one-room apartment with her sixty-year-old dresser, for Anna Urbanova had no intention of going home ever again.

The second time the Count saw Anna was in November 1928, about eight months after she had lost her mansion. He was just pouring water into the glass of an Italian importer when she walked through the door of the Boyarsky wearing a red sleeveless dress and high-heeled shoes. As the Count apologized to the importer and attempted to mop his lap with a napkin, he overheard the actress explain to Andrey that she would be joined by a guest at any moment.

Andrey led her to a table for two in the corner.

Forty minutes later her guest arrived.

From his vantage point on the other side of the Boyarsky's centerpiece (an arrangement of sunflowers), the Count could tell that the actress and her guest knew each other only by reputation. He was a good-enough-looking fellow, a few years younger than Anna and wearing a tailored jacket, but plainly something of a cad. For having taken his seat, even as he apologized for being late he was already scanning the menu; and when she assured him that it was quite all right, he was already signaling their waiter. For her part, Anna appeared to be perfectly charming. She related her stories with a sparkle in her eye and listened to his with a ready laugh; and she was the very image of patience whenever their conversation was interrupted by someone who had approached the table to fawn over his latest picture.

A few hours later, when the Boyarsky was empty and the kitchen was closed, the Count passed through the lobby just as Anna and her guest emerged from the Shalyapin Bar. As he paused to put on his overcoat, Anna gestured to the elevator, clearly inviting him upstairs for one more drink. But he continued putting his arms through his sleeves. It was a pleasure meeting, he assured her with a glance at his watch; unfortunately, he was expected elsewhere. Then he made a beeline for the door.

As the young director crossed the lobby, the Count was of the opinion that Anna looked every bit as radiant as she had in 1923. But the moment the director disappeared into the street, the actress's smile and shoulders drooped. Then having passed a hand across her brow, she turned from the door—only to meet the gaze of the Count.

In an instant, she drew back her shoulders, raised her chin, and strolled toward the staircase. But having mastered the art of descending the stairs to a gathering of admirers, she had yet to master the art of ascending the stairs alone. (Perhaps no one has.) On the third step, she stopped. She stood motionless. Then she turned, came back down, and crossed to where the Count was standing.

"Whenever I am in this lobby with you," she said, "it seems that I am destined to be humiliated."

The Count looked surprised.

"Humiliated? You have no cause to feel humiliated, as far as I can see."

"I gather you're blind."

She looked toward the revolving door as if it were still spinning from the young director's exit.

"I invited him for a nightcap. He said he had an early start."

"I have never had an early start in my life," said the Count.

Offering her first genuine smile of the evening, she waved a hand at the stairs.

"Then you might as well come on up."

At the time, Anna was staying in room 428. It was not the finest room on the fourth floor, nor was it the worst. Off the small bedroom, it had a small sitting area with a small couch, a small coffee table, and two small windows looking over the trolley tracks on Teatralny Proyezd. It was the room of one who hoped to make an impression when she could not easily afford to do so. On the coffee table were two glasses, a serving of caviar, and a bottle of vodka in a bucket of melting ice.

As they looked over this little *mise-en-scène*, she shook her head.

"That'll cost me a pretty penny."

"Then we mustn't let it go to waste."

The Count drew the bottle from the ice and poured them both a glass.

"To old times," he said.

"To old times," she conceded with a laugh. And they emptied their glasses.

When one experiences a profound setback in the course of an enviable life, one has a variety of options. Spurred by shame, one may attempt to hide all evidence of the change in one's circumstances. Thus, the merchant who gambles away his savings will hold on to his finer suits until they fray, and tell anecdotes from the halls of the private clubs where his membership has long since lapsed. In a state of self-pity, one may retreat from the world in which one has been blessed to live. Thus, the long-suffering husband, finally disgraced by his wife in society, may be the one who leaves his home in exchange for a small, dark apartment on the other side of town. Or, like the Count and Anna, one may simply join the Confederacy of the Humbled.

Like the Freemasons, the Confederacy of the Humbled is a close-knit brotherhood whose members travel with no outward markings, but who know each other at a glance. For having fallen suddenly from grace, those in the Confederacy share a certain perspective. Knowing beauty, influence, fame, and privilege to be borrowed rather than bestowed, they are not easily impressed. They are not quick to envy or take offense. They certainly do not scour the papers in search of their own names. They remain committed to living among their peers, but they greet adulation with caution, ambition with sympathy, and condescension with an inward smile.

As the actress poured some more vodka, the Count looked about the room.

"How are the dogs?" he asked.

"Better off than I am."

"To the dogs then," he said, lifting his glass.

"Yes," she agreed with a smile. "To the dogs."

And so it began.

Over the next year and a half, Anna would visit the Metropol every few months. In advance, she would reach out to some director she'd known. Admitting with some relief that her days of appearing in films were behind her, she'd invite him to be her guest at the Boyarsky. Having learned her lesson in 1928, she no longer arrived at the restaurant first. By means of a small gratuity to the girl in the coatroom, she ensured that she would arrive two minutes *after* her guest. Over dinner, she would confess that she was one of the director's greatest fans. She would recall favorite elements from several of his films and then dwell on a particular scene—one that was easily overlooked because it involved a secondary character and just a few lines of dialogue, but that had been rendered with such obvious nuance and care. And when Anna had walked her guest to the lobby, she would not suggest a nightcap in the Shalyapin; she certainly wouldn't invite him for one in her room. She would say, instead, what a pleasure it had been to see him, and then bid him goodnight.

Donning his coat, the director would pause. Watching the elevator doors close, he would acknowledge that Anna Urbanova's days of stardom were probably behind her—and yet, he would find himself wondering if she might not be perfect for that little role in the second act.

And having let herself into her room on the fourth floor, Anna would change into a simple dress (after hanging her gown in the closet), make herself comfortable with a book, and wait for the Count to arrive.

In the aftermath of one such dinner with an old director friend, Anna was cast for a single scene as a middle-aged worker in a factory that was struggling to meet its quota. With two weeks left in the quarter, the workers gather to compose a letter to the Party leadership that details the causes of their inevitable shortfall. But as they begin to enumerate the various obstacles they have faced, Anna—her hair drawn back in a kerchief—rises to give a short, impassioned speech in favor of pushing on.

As the camera draws closer to this unnamed character, one can see that she is a woman who is no longer young or ravishing, but who remains proud and unbent. And her voice?

Ah, her voice . . .

From the very first words of her speech, the audience can tell that here was no idler. For her voice was that of a woman who has breathed the dust of unpaved roads; who has screamed during childbirth; who has called out to her sisters on the factory floor. In other words, it was the voice of my sister, my wife, my mother, my friend.

Needless to say, it is her speech that prompts the women to redouble their efforts until they have exceeded their quota. But more important, when the film is premiered, there is a round-faced fellow with a receding hairline in the fifteenth row who'd once held Anna in awe; and while he'd only been the director of the Moscow Department of Cinematographic Arts when he had the pleasure of meeting her in the Shalyapin back in 1923, he was now a senior official in the Ministry of Culture and rumored to be the likely successor to its current chief. So moved was he by her speech in the factory that he would soon be asking every director within earshot whether they hadn't seen her astounding performance; and whenever she was in Moscow, he would send an arrangement of lilies to her room. . . .

Ah, you may say with a knowing smile. *So that is how it happened. That is how she regained her footing.* . . . But Anna Urbanova was a genuine artist trained on the stage. What is more, as a member of the Confederacy of the Humbled, she had become an actress who appeared on time, knew her lines, and never complained. And as official preference shifted toward movies with a sense of realism and a spirit of perseverance, there was often a role for a woman with seasoned beauty and a husky voice. In other words, there were many factors within and without Anna's control that contributed to her resurgence.

Perhaps you are still skeptical. Well then, what about you?

No doubt there have been moments when your life has taken a bit of a leap forward; and no doubt you look back upon those moments with self-assurance and pride. But was there really no third party deserving of even a modicum of credit? Some mentor, family friend, or schoolmate who gave timely advice, made an introduction, or put in a complimentary word?

So, let us not dissect the hows and whys. It is enough to know that Anna Urbanova was once again a star with a house on the Fontanka Canal and copper ovals nailed to her furniture; though now when she has guests, she greets them at the door.

Suddenly, at 4:45 in the afternoon, wheeling before the Count was the five-starred constellation of Delphinus.

If one drew a line with one's finger through its two lowest stars and followed its trajectory across the heavens, one would reach Aquila, the Eagle; while if one drew a line through its uppermost stars, one would reach Pegasus, Bellerophon's flying stallion; and if one drew a line in the opposite direction, one would reach what appeared to be a brand-new star—a sun that may have flared out a thousand years ago, but the light of which had just reached the Northern Hemisphere in order to provide guidance to weary travelers, sojourners, and adventurers for another millennia to come. . . .

"What are you doing?"

Anna rolled back toward the Count.

"I think you have a new freckle," he said.

"What!"

Anna tried to look over her own shoulder.

"Don't worry," he assured. "It's nice."

"Where is it?"

"A few degrees east of Delphinus."

"Delphinus?"

"You know. The constellation of the dolphin. You have it between your shoulder blades."

"How many freckles do I have?"

"How many stars are in the sky . . . ?"

"Good God."

Anna rolled flat on her back.

The Count lit a cigarette and took a puff.

"Don't you know the story of Delphinus?" he asked, handing her the cigarette.

"Why would I know the story of Delphinus?" she replied with a sigh.

"As a fisherman's daughter."

. . .

"Why don't you tell it to me."

"All right. There was a wealthy poet named Arion. A great player of the lyre and the inventor of the dithyramb."

"The dithyramb?"

"An ancient type of verse. Anyway, one day he was returning from the island of Sicily when his crew decided to relieve him of his fortune. Specifically, they gave him the option of killing himself or being thrown into the sea. As Arion weighed these unattractive alternatives, he sang a sorrowful song; and so beautiful was his singing, that a pod of dolphins gathered around the ship; and when he finally leapt into the sea, one of the dolphins carried him safely to shore. As a reward, Apollo placed this charitable creature among the stars to shine for all eternity."

"That's lovely."

The Count nodded, retrieving the cigarette from Anna and rolling on his back.

"It's your turn," he said.

"My turn for what?"

"To tell a tale of the sea."

"I don't know any tales of the sea."

"Oh, come now. Your father must have told you one or two. There isn't a fisherman in Christendom who doesn't tell tales of the sea."

. . .

"Sasha, I have a bit of a confession. . . ."

"A confession?"

"I wasn't raised on the Black Sea."

"But what about your father? And meeting him at dusk by the shore to mend his nets?"

"My father was a peasant from Poltava."

. . .

"But why would you fabricate such a ridiculous story?"

"I think I thought it would appeal to you."

"You think you thought?"

"Exactly."

The Count reflected for a moment.

"What about the deboning of the fish!"

"I worked in a tavern in Odessa after I ran away from home."

The Count shook his head.

"How dispiriting."

Anna rolled on her side to face the Count.

"You told me that preposterous story about the apples of Nizhny Novgorod."

"But that story's true!"

"Oh, come on. Apples as big as cannonballs? In every color of the rainbow?"

The Count was silent for a moment. Then he tamped out the cigarette in the ashtray on the bedside table.

"I should be going," he said, and began climbing out of bed.

"All right," she said, pulling him back. "I remember one."

"One what?"

"A sea story."

He rolled his eyes.

"No. I'm serious. It's a story my grandmother used to tell me."

"A sea story."

"With a young adventurer, and a deserted island, and a fortune in gold . . ."

Begrudgingly, the Count lay back on the pillows and gestured for her to begin.

Once upon a time, Anna related, there was a rich merchant with a fleet of ships and three sons, the youngest of whom was rather small in stature. One spring, the merchant gave his older sons ships laden down with furs, carpets, and fine linens, instructing one to sail east and one to sail west in search of new kingdoms with which to trade. When the youngest son asked where his boat was, the merchant and the older boys laughed. In the end, the merchant gave his youngest son a rickety sloop with raggedy sails, a toothless crew, and empty sacks for ballast. When the young man asked his father in which direction he should sail, the merchant replied that he should sail until the sun never set in December.

So the son sailed southward with his scurvy crew. After three times three months on the open seas, they reached a land where the sun never set in December. There, they landed on an island that appeared to have a mountain of snow, but which turned out to have a mountain of salt. Salt was so plentiful in his homeland that housewives cast it over their shoulders for good luck without a second thought. Nonetheless, the young man instructed his crew to fill the sacks in the hull with the salt, if for no other reason than to add to the ship's ballast.

Sailing truer and faster than before, they soon came upon a great kingdom. The king received the merchant's son in his court and asked what he had to trade. The young man replied that he had a hull full of salt. Remarking that he had never heard of it, the king wished him well and sent him on his way. Undaunted, the young man paid a visit to the king's kitchens, where he discreetly sprinkled salt onto the mutton, into the soup, over the tomatoes, and into custard.

That night, the king was amazed at the flavor of his food. The mutton was better, the soup was better, the tomatoes were better, even the custard was better. Calling his chefs before him, he excitedly asked what new technique they were using. Befuddled, the chefs admitted they had done nothing different; although they had been visited in the kitchen by the young stranger from the sea. . . .

The next afternoon, the merchant's son set sail for home in a ship laden with one bag of gold for every sack of salt.

. . .

"Your grandmother told you that?"

"She did."

. . .

"It is a good story. . . ."

"Yes, it is."

. . .

"But it doesn't absolve you."

"I should think not."

An Alliance

At 5:45, with his five waiters standing at their stations, the Count made his nightly rounds of the Boyarsky. Beginning in the northwest corner, he circulated through the twenty tables to ensure that every setting, every saltcellar, every vase of flowers was in its proper place.

At table four a knife was realigned to be parallel with its fork. At table five a water glass was moved from midnight to one o'clock. At table six a wine glass that had a remnant of lipstick was whisked away, while at table seven the soap spots on a spoon were polished until the inverted image of the room could be clearly seen on the surface of the silver.

This, one might be inclined to observe, is exactly how Napoleon must have appeared when in the hour before dawn he walked among his ranks, reviewing everything from the stores of munitions to the dress of the infantry—having learned from experience that victory on the field of battle begins with the shine on a boot.

But many of Napoleon's greatest battles lasted only a day and were never to be fought again. . . .

As such, the more apt analogy might be that of Gorsky at the Bolshoi. Having studied the intent of the composer, collaborated closely with his conductor, trained his dancers, overseen the design of the costumes and sets, Gorsky also walked his ranks in the minutes before battle. But once the curtain fell and the audience departed, there would be no parade along the Champs-Élysées. For in less than twenty-four hours, his ballerinas, musicians, and technicians would reassemble to execute the same performance to the same standard of perfection. Now *that* was the life of the Boyarsky—a battle that must be waged with exacting precision while giving the impression of effortlessness, every single night of the year.

Confident that all was in order in the dining room, at 5:55 the Count turned his attention, if briefly, to Emile's kitchen. Peering through the little round window in the door, the Count could see that the chef's assistants were standing at the ready in their freshly bleached coats; he could see that the sauces were simmering on the stovetop and the garnishes ready for plating. But what of that notorious misanthrope of a chef? With the opening of the Boyarsky's doors just minutes away, wasn't he railing against his staff, his customers, and all his fellow men?

In point of fact, Emile Zhukovsky began his days in a state of the blackest pessimism. The very moment he looked out from under his covers, he met existence with a scowl, knowing it to be a cold and unforgiving condition. Having had his worst suspicions confirmed by the morning papers, at eleven o'clock he would be waiting at the curb for a crowded tram to rattle him to the hotel while muttering, "What a world."

But as the day unfolded, hour by hour Emile's pessimism would slowly give way to the possibility that all was not lost. This rosier perspective would begin building quietly around noon, when he came into his kitchen and saw his copper pots. Hanging from their hooks, still shining from the previous night's scrubbing, they seemed to suggest an indisputable sense of possibility. Stepping into the cooler, he would hoist a side of lamb over his shoulder, and when he dropped it on the counter with a satisfying thump, his worldview would brighten by another hundred lumens. Such that by 3:00, when he heard the sound of root vegetables being chopped and smelled the aroma of garlic being sizzled, Emile might begrudgingly acknowledge that existence had its consolations. Then at 5:30, if everything seemed in order, he might allow himself to sample the wine that he'd been cooking with—just to polish off the bottle, you understand; waste not want not; neither a borrower nor a lender be. And at around 6:25, that dark humor which had seemed at dawn to be the very foundation of Emile's soul, would become irreversibly sanguine when the first order was delivered to his kitchen.

So, what did the Count see when he looked through the window at 5:55? He saw Emile dip a spoon into a bowl of chocolate mousse and lick it clean. With that confirmation, the Count turned to Andrey and nodded. Then he assumed his station between table one and table two as the maître d' threw the bolts to open the Boyarsky's doors.

Around nine o'clock, the Count reviewed the restaurant from corner to corner, satisfied that the first seating had gone without a hitch. Menus had been delivered and orders taken according to plan. Four inclinations toward overcooked lamb had been narrowly averted, more than five bottles of Latour had been poured, and the two members of the Politburo had been equitably seated and equitably served. But then Andrey (who had just led the Commissar of Transport to the opposite side of the room from the American journalists) signaled the Count with an expression of apparent distress.

"What has happened?" asked the Count when he reached the maître d's side.

"I have just been notified that there is to be a private function in the Yellow Room, after all."

"How large?"

"They weren't specific, other than to say it would be small."

"Then we can send Vasenka. I'll take tables five and six; Maxim can take tables seven and eight."

"But that's just it," said Andrey. "We cannot send Vasenka."

"Why not?"

"Because they have asked for you by name."

Standing at attention in front of the Yellow Room was a Goliath that would have given any David pause. As the Count approached, the giant barely seemed to take note of his surroundings; then without a sign of acknowledgment, he suddenly stepped aside and deftly opened the door.

It was not particularly surprising for the Count to find a giant at the door of a private function in the Metropol; what was surprising was how the dining room had been arranged within. For the majority of furniture had been cleared to the periphery, leaving a single table set for two under the chandelier—at which a middle-aged man in a dark gray suit sat alone.

Though much smaller than the guard at the door and substantially better dressed, the man at the table struck the Count as one who was no stranger to brute force. His neck and wrists were as thick as a wrestler's and his close-cropped hair revealed a scar above the left ear, which was presumably the result of a glancing blow that had hoped to cleave his skull. Apparently unhurried, the man was playing with his spoon.

"Good evening," said the Count with a bow.

"Good evening," replied the man with a smile, returning his spoon to the table.

"May I bring you something to drink while you wait?"

"There will be no one else coming."

"Ah," said the Count. He began clearing the second place setting.

"You needn't clear those."

"I'm sorry. I thought you weren't expecting anyone else."

"I am not expecting anyone else. I am expecting you, Alexander Ilyich."

The two men studied each other for a moment.

"Please," said the man. "Have a seat."

The Count hesitated to take the offered chair.

Under the circumstances, one might leap to the conclusion that the Count hesitated due to a suspicion or even dread about this stranger. But principally, he hesitated because as a matter of decorum, it seemed utterly inappropriate for one to sit at a table when one is dressed to wait upon it.

"Come now," the stranger said amiably. "You wouldn't refuse a solitary diner the pleasure of your company."

"Certainly not," replied the Count.

But having accepted the chair, he did not place the napkin in his lap.

After a rap at the door, it opened to admit the Goliath. Without looking at the Count, he approached the table and held out a bottle for the stranger's consideration.

The host leaned forward and squinted at the label.

"Excellent," he said. "Thank you, Vladimir."

Presumably, Vladimir could simply have broken the top off the bottle, but with surprising agility he produced a corkscrew from a pocket, spun it in his hand, and pulled the cork. Then, having received a nod from his superior, he placed the open bottle on the table and retreated back to the hall. The stranger poured a glass for himself. Then, with the bottle hovering over the table at a forty-five-degree angle, he looked to the Count.

"Won't you join me?"

"With pleasure."

After the stranger poured, they both raised their glasses and drank.

"Count Alexander Ilyich Rostov," he said after returning his glass to the table. "Recipient of the Order of Saint Andrew, member of the Jockey Club, Master of the Hunt . . ."

"You have me at a disadvantage."

"You don't know who I am?"

"I know that you are a man who can secure one of the Boyarsky's private rooms in which to dine alone while a behemoth waits at the door."

The stranger laughed.

"Very good," he said, leaning back in his chair. "What else do you see?"

The Count studied his host more indiscreetly and then shrugged.

"I'd say you were a man of forty and were a soldier once. I suspect you joined the infantry, but were a colonel by the end of the war."

"How would you know that I became a colonel?"

"It is the business of a gentleman to distinguish between men of rank."

"The business of a gentleman," the colonel repeated with a smile, as if he appreciated the turn of phrase. "And can you tell where I'm from?"

The Count dismissed the question with a wave of the hand.

"The surest way to insult a Walloon is to mistake him for a Frenchman, though they live but a few miles apart and share the same language."

"I suppose that's true," the colonel conceded. "Nonetheless. I'm interested in your guesswork; and I promise I won't be insulted."

The Count took a sip of his wine and returned the glass to the table.

"You are almost certainly from eastern Georgia."

The colonel sat up with an expression of enthusiasm.

"Extraordinary. Do I have an accent?"

"Not that's distinguishable. But then armies, like universities, are where accents are most commonly shed."

"Then why eastern Georgia?"

The Count gestured to the wine.

"Only an eastern Georgian would start his meal with a bottle of Rkatsiteli."

"Because he's a hayseed?"

"Because he misses home."

The colonel laughed again.

"What a canny fellow you are."

There was another rap at the door and it opened to admit the giant pushing a Regency cart.

"Ah. Excellent. Here we are."

When Vladimir had wheeled the cart to the table, the Count began to push back his chair, but his host gestured that he should remain seated. Vladimir removed the dome and placed a platter at the center of the table. As he left the room, the colonel picked up a carving knife and fork.

"Let's see. What do we have here? Ah, roasted duck. I've been told the Boyarsky's is unparalleled."

"You are not misinformed. Make sure you take a few cherries and some of the skin."

The colonel doled out a portion for himself, including cherries and skin, and then served the Count.

"Absolutely delicious," he said, when he had taken his first bite.

The Count bowed his head to accept the compliment on Emile's behalf.

The colonel gestured to the Count with his fork.

"You have a very interesting file, Alexander Ilyich."

"I have a file?"

"I'm sorry. A terrible habit of speech. What I meant to say is that you have an interesting *background*."

"Ah, yes. Well. Life has been generous to me in its variety."

The colonel smiled. Then he commenced in the tone of one who is trying to do justice to the facts.

"You were born in Leningrad. . . ."

"I was born in St. Petersburg."

"Ah, yes, of course. In St. Petersburg. As your parents died when you were young, you were raised by your grandmother. You attended the academy and then the Imperial University in . . . *St. Petersburg.*"

"All correct."

"And you have traveled broadly, I gather."

The Count shrugged.

"Paris. London. Firenze."

"But when you last left the country in 1914, you went to France?"

"On the sixteenth of May."

"That's right. A few days after the incident with Lieutenant Pulonov. Tell me, why did you shoot the fellow? Wasn't he an aristocrat like yourself?"

The Count showed an expression of mild shock.

"I shot him *because* he was an aristocrat."

The colonel laughed and waved his fork again.

"I hadn't thought of it that way. But yes, that's an idea that we Bolsheviks should understand. So you were in Paris at the time of the Revolution, and shortly thereafter you made your way home."

"Exactly."

"Now, I think I understand why you hurried back: to help your grandmother safely from the country. But having arranged for her escape, why did you choose to stay?"

"For the cuisine."

"No, I am serious."

. . .

"My days of leaving Russia were behind me."

"But you didn't take up arms with the Whites."

"No."

"And you don't strike me as a coward. . . ."

"I should hope not."

"So why didn't you join in the fray?"

The Count paused, then shrugged.

"When I left for Paris in 1914, I swore I would never shoot another one of my countrymen."

"And you count the Bolsheviks as your countrymen."

"Of course I do."

"Do you count them as gentlemen?"

"That's another thing entirely. But certainly some of them are."

"I see. But even from the manner in which you say that, I can tell that you do not count *me* a gentleman. Now, why is that?"

The Count responded with a light laugh, as much as to say that no gentleman would ever answer such a question.

"Come now," the colonel persisted. "Here we two are dining together on the Boyarsky's roasted duck with a bottle of Georgian wine, which practically makes us old friends. And I am genuinely interested. What is it about me that makes you so sure that I am not a gentleman?"

As a sign of encouragement, the colonel leaned across the table to refill the Count's glass.

"It isn't any one thing," the Count said after a moment. "It is an assembly of small details."

"Like in a mosaic."

"Yes. Like in a mosaic."

"So, give me an example of one of these smaller details."

The Count took a sip from his glass and replaced it on the table at one o'clock.

"As a host, it was perfectly appropriate for you to take up the serving tools. But a gentleman would have served his guest before he served himself."

The colonel, who had just taken a bite of duck, smiled at the Count's first example and waved his fork.

"Continue," he said.

"A gentleman wouldn't gesture at another man with his fork," said the Count, "or speak with his mouth full. But perhaps most importantly, he would have introduced himself at the beginning of a conversation—particularly when he had the advantage over his guest."

The colonel put his utensils down.

"And I ordered the wrong wine," he added with a smile.

The Count put a finger in the air.

"No. There are many reasons for ordering a particular bottle of wine. And memories of home are among the best."

"Then allow me to introduce myself: I am Osip Ivanovich Glebnikov—former colonel of the Red Army and an officer of the Party, who as a boy in eastern Georgia dreamed of Moscow, and who as a man of thirty-nine in Moscow dreams of eastern Georgia."

"It is a pleasure meeting you," said the Count, reaching across the table. The two men shook hands and then resumed eating. After a moment, the Count ventured:

"If I may be so bold, Osip Ivanovich: What is it exactly that you *do* as an officer of the Party?"

"Let's just say that I am charged with keeping track of certain men of interest."

"Ah. Well, I imagine that becomes rather easy to achieve when you place them under house arrest."

"Actually," corrected Glebnikov, "it is easier to achieve when you place them in the ground. . . ."

The Count conceded the point.

"But by all accounts," continued Glebnikov, "you seem to have reconciled yourself to your situation."

"As both a student of history and a man devoted to living in the present, I admit that I do not spend a lot of time imagining how things might otherwise have been. But I do like to think there is a difference between being resigned to a situation and reconciled to it."

Glebnikov let out a laugh and gave the table a light slap.

"There you go. That's just the sort of nuance that has brought me begging to your door."

Setting his silverware down, the Count looked to his host with interest.

"As a nation, Alexander Ilyich, we are at a very intriguing juncture. We have had open diplomatic relations with the French and British for seven years, and there is talk that we will soon have them with the Americans. Since the time of Peter the Great, we have acted the poor cousin of the West—admiring their ideas as much as we admired their clothes. But we are about to assume a very different role. Within a matter of years, we will be exporting more grain and manufacturing more steel than any other country in Europe. And we are leaps ahead of them all in ideology. As a result, for the first time, we are on the verge of taking our rightful place on the world stage. And when we do so, it will behoove us to listen with care and speak with clarity."

"You would like to learn French and English."

Osip raised his glass in confirmation.

"Yes, sir. But I don't simply want to learn the languages. I want to understand those who speak them. And most especially, I would like to understand their privileged classes—for that's who remains at the helm. I would like to understand how they view the world; what they are likely to count as a moral imperative; what they would be prone to value and what to disdain. It's a matter of developing certain diplomatic skills, if you will. But for a man in my position, it is best to foster one's skills . . . discreetly."

"How do you propose that I help?"

"Simple. Dine with me once a month in this very room. Speak with me in French and English. Share with me your impressions of Western societies. And in exchange . . ."

Glebnikov let his sentence trail off, not to imply the paucity of what he could do for the Count, but rather to suggest the abundance.

But the Count raised a hand to stay any talk of exchanges.

"If you are a customer of the Boyarsky, Osip Ivanovich, then I am already at your service."

Absinthe

As the Count approached the Shalyapin at 12:15, what emanated from this onetime chapel of prayer and reflection was a sound that would have been unthinkable ten years before. It was a sound characterized by fits of laughter, a mélange of languages, the bleat of a trumpet, and the clinking of glasses—in other words, the sound of gay abandon.

What development could have brought about such a transformation? In the case of the Shalyapin, there were three. The first was the rather breathless return of the American musical form known as jazz. Having squelched the craze on the grounds of its intrinsic decadence, in the mid-1920s the Bolsheviks had begun to countenance it again. This was presumably so that they could study more closely how a single idea can sweep the globe. Whatever the cause, here it was zipping and zinging and rat-a-tat-tatting on its little stage at the back of the room.

The second development was the return of foreign correspondents. In the aftermath of the Revolution, the Bolsheviks had ushered them straight to the door (along with divinities, doubts, and all the other troublemakers). But correspondents are a wily bunch. Having stashed their typewriters, crossed the border, changed their clothes, and counted to ten, they began slipping back into the country one by one. So in 1928, the Foreign Press Office was opened anew on the top floor of a six-story walk-up conveniently located halfway between the Kremlin and the offices of the secret police—a spot that just happened to be across the street from the Metropol. Thus, on any given night you could now find fifteen members of the international press in the Shalyapin ready to bend your ear. And when there were no listeners to be found, they lined up at the bar like gulls on the rocks and squawked all at once.

And then there was that extraordinary development of 1929. In April of that year, the Shalyapin suddenly had not one, not two, but three hostesses—all young, beautiful, and wearing black dresses hemmed above the knee. With what charm and elegance they moved among the patrons of the bar, gracing the air with their slender silhouettes, delicate laughter, and hints of perfume. If the correspondents at the bar were inclined to talk more than they listened, in an instance of perfect symbiosis the hostesses were inclined to listen more than they talked. In part, of course, this was because their jobs depended upon it. For once a week, they were required to visit a little gray building on the corner of Dzerzhinsky Street where some little gray fellow behind a little gray desk would record whatever they had happened to hear word for word.*

Did this obligation of the hostesses cause the journalists to be more cautious or tight-lipped for fear that some careless remark would be passed along?

On the contrary. The foreign press corps had a standing wager of ten American dollars to any of their number who could get summoned to the Commissariat of Internal Affairs. To that end, they crafted outrageous provocations and wove them into their chatter. One American let

---

*Yes, this little gray fellow behind his little gray desk was charged not only with recording the information the waitresses gathered, but with ensuring their willing participation by reminding them of their duty to their country, by suggesting how easy it would be for them to lose their positions, and, when necessary, by making some other more ominous innuendo. But let us not condemn the fellow too quickly.

For he has never been to the Shalyapin Bar. Nor has he dined at the Boyarsky. He has been allotted a vicarious life—a life in which all experiences are at arm's length, all sensations secondhand. No bleat of the trumpet, no clink of the glass, no sight of a young woman's knee for him. Like a scientist's assistant, his lot was simply to record the data and then relay a summary to his superiors without embellishment or elaboration.

To be fair, he was no slouch in this endeavor and was even known throughout his department as something of a prodigy. For no one in all of Moscow could write a report to such drab perfection. With limited instruction, he had perfected the art of withholding his insights, forgoing his witticisms, curbing the use of metaphors, similes, and analogies—in essence, exercising every muscle of poetic restraint. In fact, if the reporters whom he was dutifully transcribing had only seen his handiwork, they would have taken off their hats, bowed their heads, and acknowledged that here was a master of objectivity.

slip that in the backyard of a certain dacha a disenchanted engineer was building a balloon from specifications he'd found in Jules Verne. . . . Another relayed that an unnamed biologist was crossing a peep of chickens with a flock of pigeons to breed a bird that could lay an egg in the morning and deliver a message at night. . . . In sum, they would say anything within earshot of the hostesses—that is, anything that might be underscored in a report and land with a thud on a desk in the Kremlin.

As the Count stood at the Shalyapin's entrance, he could see that tonight there was even more cavorting than usual. The jazz ensemble in the corner, which was charged with setting the tempo, was scrambling to keep up with the eruptions of laughter and the slaps on the back. Working his way through the hubbub, the Count approached the more discreet end of the bar (where an alabaster pillar fell from the ceiling to the floor). A moment later, Audrius was leaning toward the Count with his forearm on the bar.

"Good evening, Count Rostov."

"Good evening, Audrius. It seems like quite a celebration tonight."

The bartender gestured with his head toward one of the Americans.

"Mr. Lyons was taken to the office of the OGPU today."

"The OGPU! How so?"

"It seems that a letter written in his hand was found on the floor of Perlov's Tea House—a letter that included descriptions of troop movements and artillery placements on the outskirts of Smolensk. But when the letter was laid on the desk and Mr. Lyons was asked to explain himself, he said that he'd simply been transcribing his favorite passage from *War and Peace*."

"Ah, yes," said the Count with a smile. "The Battle of Borodino."

"For this accomplishment, he collected the kitty and now he's buying everyone a round. But what can we do for you this evening?"

The Count tapped twice on the bar.

"You wouldn't happen to have any absinthe, would you?"

Ever so slightly, Audrius raised an eyebrow.

How well this tender of bar knew the Count's preferences. He knew that before dinner the Count enjoyed a glass of champagne or dry vermouth. He knew that after dinner he enjoyed a snifter of brandy until the average nightly temperature fell below 40°, at which point he would switch to a glass of whiskey or port. But absinthe? In the decade that they had known each other, the Count had not asked for a single glass. In fact, he rarely indulged in any of the syrupy liqueurs—and certainly not those that were colored green and reported to cause madness.

But ever the professional, Audrius confined his surprise to the movement of his eyebrow.

"I believe I may have one bottle left," he said. Then opening a seamless door in the wall, he disappeared into the cabinet where he kept his more expensive and esoteric spirits.

On the platform in the opposite corner of the bar, the jazz ensemble was playing a perky little tune. Admittedly, when the Count had first encountered jazz, he hadn't much of an affinity for it. He had been raised to appreciate music of sentiment and nuance, music that rewarded patience and attention with crescendos and diminuendos, allegros and adagios artfully arranged over four whole movements—not a fistful of notes crammed higgledy-piggledy into thirty measures.

And yet . . .

And yet, the art form had grown on him. Like the American correspondents, jazz seemed a naturally gregarious force—one that was a little unruly and prone to say the first thing that popped into its head, but generally of good humor and friendly intent. In addition, it seemed decidedly unconcerned with where it had been or where it was going—exhibiting somehow simultaneously the confidence of the master and the inexperience of the apprentice. Was there any wonder that such an art had failed to originate in Europe?

The Count's reverie was broken by the sound of a bottle being placed on the bar.

"Absinthe Robette," said Audrius, tilting the bottle so that the Count could read the label. "But I'm afraid there's only an ounce or two left."

"It will have to do."

The bartender emptied the bottle into a cordial glass.

"Thank you, Audrius. Please add it to my account."

"No need. It is on Mr. Lyons."

As the Count turned to go, an American who had commandeered the piano began performing a jaunty little number that celebrated a lack of bananas, a lack of bananas today. A moment later, all the journalists were singing along. On another night, the Count might have lingered to observe the festivities, but he had his own celebration to attend to. So with his precious cargo in hand, he navigated through the crowd of elbows, being careful not to spill a drop.

Yes, thought the Count as he climbed the stairs to the second floor, this evening the Triumvirate has its own cause for celebration. . . .

The Plan had been hatched almost three years before, springing from a wistful comment of Andrey's, which had been echoed by Emile.

"Sadly, it's impossible," the maître d' had lamented.

"Yes," the chef had conceded with a shake of the head.

But was it?

All told, there were fifteen ingredients. Six of them could be plucked from the pantry of the Boyarsky at any time of year. Another five were readily available in season. The nut of the problem was that, despite the overall improvement in the general availability of goods, the last four ingredients remained relatively rare.

From the outset, it was agreed that there would be no skimping—no shortcuts or substitutions. It was the symphony or silence. So the Triumvirate would have to be patient and watchful. They would have to be willing to beg, barter, collude, and if necessary, resort to chicanery. Three times the dream had been within their grasp, only to be snatched away at the last moment by unforeseen circumstances (once by mishap, once by mold, and once by mice).

But earlier that week, it seemed that the stars were wheeling into alignment once again. With nine elements already in Emile's kitchen, four whole haddock and a basket of mussels meant for the National Hotel had been delivered to the Metropol by mistake. That was ten and eleven in a single stroke. The Triumvirate convened and conferred. A favor could be called in by Andrey, a swap negotiated by Emile, and Audrius approached by the Count. Thus, the twelfth, thirteenth, and fourteenth ingredients. But the fifteenth? This would require access to a store with the rarest of luxuries—that is, one which served the highest members of the Party. A discreet inquiry was made by the Count of a certain actress with certain connections. And *mirabile dictu*, an unsigned envelope had been slipped under his door. With all fifteen ingredients now at hand, the Triumvirate's patience was on the verge of being rewarded. Within the hour, they would once again experience that intricacy of flavors, that divine distillation, that impression as rich and elusive as—

"Good evening, comrade."

The Count stopped in his tracks.

For a moment he hesitated. Then he slowly turned around—as from the shadows of an alcove the hotel's assistant manager emerged.

Like his counterpart on the chessboard, the Bishop of the Metropol never moved along the rank or file. With him it was always on the bias: slipping diagonally from corner to corner, skirting past a potted plant, sliding through a crack in the door. One caught sight of him at the periphery of one's vision, if one caught sight of him at all.

"Good evening," replied the Count.

The two men took each other in from heel to hair—both practiced at confirming in a glance their worst suspicions of each other. Leaning a little to his right, the Bishop adopted an expression of idle curiosity.

"What do we have here . . . ?"

"What do we have where?"

"Why, there. Behind your back."

"Behind my back?"

The Count slowly brought his hands in front of him and turned his palms upright to show that they were empty. The right upper corner of the Bishop's smile twitched, turning it ever so briefly into a smirk. The Count reciprocated in kind and with a polite bow of the head turned to walk away.

"Headed to the Boyarsky . . . ?"

The Count stopped and turned back.

"Yes. That's right. The Boyarsky."

"Isn't it closed . . . ?"

"It is. But I think I may have left my pen in Emile's office."

"Ah. The man of letters has lost his pen. *Where is it now . . .* , hmm? If not in the kitchen, perhaps you should look in the blue pagoda of your fine Chinoiserie." And turning with his smirk, the Bishop slipped diagonally down the hall.

The Count waited until he was out of sight, then hurried in the opposite direction, muttering as he went:

"*Where is it now . . . ? Perhaps in your blue pagoda.* . . . Very witty, I'm sure. Coming from a man who couldn't rhyme *cow* with *plow*. And what's with all that dot-dot-dotting?"

Ever since the Bishop had been promoted, he had taken to adding an ellipsis at the end of every question. But what was one to infer from it . . . ? That this particular punctuation mark should be fended off . . . ? That an interrogative sentence should never end . . . ? That even though he is asking a question, he has no need of an answer because he has already formed an opinion . . . ?

Of course.

Coming through the Boyarsky's doors, which Andrey had left unbolted, the Count crossed the empty dining room and passed through the swinging door into the kitchen. There he found the chef at his counter slicing a bulb of fennel, as four stalks of celery lying in an orderly row waited like Spartans to meet their fate. To the side were the filets of haddock and the basket of mussels, while on the stove sat a great copper pot from which small clouds of steam graced the air with other intimations of the sea.

Looking up from the fennel, Emile met the eye of the Count and smiled. In an instant the Count could see that the chef was in rosy form. Having sensed at two that all might not be lost, at half past midnight the chef hadn't the slightest doubt that the sun would shine tomorrow, that most people were generous at heart, and that, when all was said and done, things tended to work out for the best.

The chef wasted no time on salutations. Instead, without pausing his chopper, he tilted his head toward the little table, which had been moved from his office into the kitchen and which had been waiting patiently to be set.

But first things first.

Carefully, the Count removed the little cordial glass from his back pocket and placed it on the counter.

"Ah," said the chef, wiping his hands on his apron.

"Is it enough?"

"It is only meant to be a hint. An aside. An innuendo. If it is the real thing, it should be plenty."

Emile dipped his pinkie in the absinthe and gave it a lick.

"Perfect," he said.

Selecting an appropriate tablecloth from the linen closet, the Count unfurled it with a snap and let it billow to the table. As he set the places, the chef began to whistle a tune and the Count smiled to realize it was the very same song that he had heard in the Shalyapin regarding the absence of bananas. As if on cue, the door to the back stair opened and in rushed Andrey with a pile of oranges about to tumble from his arms. Reaching Emile's side, he bowed at the waist and spilled them onto the counter.

With the instincts of convicts who discover the gates of their prison open, the individual oranges rolled in every direction to maximize their chances of escape. In a flash, Andrey had extended his arms in a grand circumference to fence them in. But one of the oranges dodged the maître d's reach and shot across the counter—headed straight for the absinthe! Dropping his chopper, Emile lunged and plucked the glass from the counter in the nick of time. The orange, which was gaining in confidence, dashed behind the fennel, jumped from the counter, thudded to the floor, and made a break for the exit. But at the last moment, that door that separated Emile's kitchen from the rest of the world swung inward, sending the orange spinning back across the floor in the opposite direction—while in the doorway stood the Bishop.

The three members of the Triumvirate froze.

Advancing two paces north by northwest, the Bishop took in the scene.

"Good evening, gentlemen," he said in his friendliest tone. "What brings you all to the kitchen at this hour . . . ?"

Andrey, who'd had the presence of mind to step in front of the simmering pot, gestured with a hand toward the food on the counter.

"We are taking inventory."

"Inventory . . . ?"

"Yes. Our quarterly inventory."

"Of course," the Bishop replied with his ecclesiastical smile. "And at whose request are you taking a quarterly inventory . . . ?"

As this exchange between the Bishop and the maître d' unfolded, the Count noticed that Emile, who had grown pale at the inward swinging of the door, was regaining his color second by second. It had begun with a slight pinkness of the cheeks when the Bishop had crossed the threshold. It turned to rose when the Bishop asked *What brings you all to the kitchen* . . . ? But when he asked *At whose request* . . . ? the chef's cheeks, neck, and ears took on a purple of such moral indignation, it made one wonder if the presence of a question mark in his kitchen was itself a capital crime.

"At whose request?" the chef asked.

The Bishop turned his gaze from Andrey to Emile and was clearly struck by the chef's transformation. He seemed to waver.

"At whose request?" the chef repeated.

Without taking his eyes off the Bishop, Emile suddenly reached for his chopper.

"At whose request!"

When Emile took a step forward while raising his chopping arm high above his head, the Bishop grew as white as the haddock. Then the kitchen door was swinging on its hinge and the Bishop was nowhere to be seen.

Andrey and the Count turned their gaze from the door to Emile. Then in wide-eyed amazement, Andrey pointed a delicate finger at Emile's raised hand. For in the heat of outrage, the chef had grabbed not his chopper but a celery stalk, whose little green fronds now trembled in the air. And to a man, the Triumvirate burst into laughter.

At one in the morning, the conspirators took their seats. On the table before them were a single candle, a loaf of bread, a bottle of rosé, and three bowls of bouillabaisse.

After exchanging a glance, the three men dipped their spoons into the stew in unison, but for Emile, the gesture was a sleight of hand. For when Andrey and the Count raised their spoons to their mouths, Emile let his hover above his bowl—intent upon studying his friends' expressions at the very first taste.

Fully aware that he was being watched, the Count closed his eyes to attend more closely to his impressions.

How to describe it?

One first tastes the broth—that simmered distillation of fish bones, fennel, and tomatoes, with their hearty suggestions of Provence. One then savors the tender flakes of haddock and the briny resilience of the mussels, which have been purchased on the docks from the fisherman. One marvels at the boldness of the oranges arriving from Spain and the absinthe poured in the taverns. And all of these various impressions are somehow collected, composed, and brightened by the saffron—that essence of summer sun which, having been harvested in the hills of Greece and packed by mule to Athens, has been sailed across the Mediterranean in a felucca. In other words, with the very first spoonful one finds oneself transported to the port of Marseille—where the streets teem with sailors, thieves, and madonnas, with sunlight and summer, with languages and life.

The Count opened his eyes.

"*Magnifique*," he said.

Andrey, who had put down his spoon, brought his elegant hands together in a respectful show of silent applause.

Beaming, the chef bowed to his friends and then joined them in their long-awaited meal.

Over the next two hours, the three members of the Triumvirate each ate three bowls of the bouillabaisse, each drank a bottle of wine, and each spoke openly in turn.

And what did these old friends talk about? What did they *not* talk about! They talked of their childhoods in St. Petersburg, Minsk, and Lyon. Of their first and second loves. Of Andrey's four-year-old son and Emile's four-year-old lumbago. They spoke of the once and the was, of the wishful and the wonderful.

Rarely awake at this hour, Emile was in an unprecedented state of euphoria. As youthful stories were told, he laughed so heartily that his head rolled on his shoulders, and the corner of his napkin was raised to his eyes twice as often as it was raised to his lips.

And the *pièce de résistance*? At three in the morning, Andrey referred briefly, offhandedly, almost parenthetically to his days under the big top.

"Eh? What's that? Under what?"

"Did you say 'the big top'?"

Yes. In point of fact: the circus.

Raised by a widowed father who was prone to drunken violence, at the age of sixteen Andrey had run away to join a traveling circus. It was with this troupe that he had come to Moscow in 1913 where, having fallen in love with a bookseller in the Arbat, he had bid the circus *adieu*. Two months later, he was hired as a waiter at the Boyarsky, and he had been there ever since.

"What did you do in the circus?" asked the Count.

"An acrobat?" suggested Emile. "A clown?"

"A lion tamer?"

"I juggled."

"No," said Emile.

In lieu of a response, the maître d' rose from the table and gathered three of the unused oranges from the countertop. With the fruit in his hands, he stood perfectly erect. Or rather, he stood at a slight tilt induced by the wine, a sort of 12:02. Then after a brief pause, he set the spheres in motion.

In all honesty, the Count and Emile had been skeptical of their old friend's claim; but as soon as he began, they could only wonder that they had not guessed at it before. For Andrey's hands had been crafted by God to juggle. So deft was his touch that the oranges seemed to move of their own accord. Or better yet, they moved like planets governed by a force of gravity that simultaneously propelled them forward and kept them from flinging off into space; while Andrey, who was standing before these planets, seemed to be simply plucking them from their orbits and releasing them a moment later to pursue their natural course.

So gentle and rhythmic was the motion of Andrey's hands that one was at constant risk of falling under hypnosis. And, in fact, without Emile or the Count noticing, another orange had suddenly joined the solar system. And then with a courtly flourish, Andrey caught all four spheres and bowed at the waist.

Now it was the Count and Emile's turn to applaud.

"But surely, you didn't juggle oranges," said Emile.

"No," Andrey admitted, as he carefully returned the oranges to the counter. "I juggled knives."

Before the Count and Emile could express their disbelief, Andrey had taken three blades from a drawer and set them in motion. These were no planets. They spun through the air like the parts of some infernal machine, an effect that was heightened by the flashes of light from whenever the candle's flame was reflected on the surface of the blades. And then, just as suddenly as the knives had been set in motion, their hilts were fixed in Andrey's hands.

"Ah, but can you do four of *those*?" teased the Count.

Without a word, Andrey moved back toward the knife drawer; but before he could reach inside, Emile had risen to his feet. With the expression of a boy enthralled by a street magician, he shyly stepped from the crowd and held out his chopper—that blade which had not been touched by another human hand in almost fifteen years. With an appropriate sense of ceremony, Andrey bowed from the waist to accept it. And when he set the four knives in motion, Emile leaned back in his chair and with a tear in his eye watched as his trusted blade tumbled effortlessly through space, feeling that this moment, this hour, this universe could not be improved upon.

At half past three in the morning, the Count swayed up the stairs, veered to his room, lurched through his closet, emptied his pockets onto the bookcase, poured himself a brandy, and with a sigh of satisfaction dropped into his chair. While from her place on the wall, Helena took him in with a tender, knowing smile.

"Yes, yes," he admitted. "It is a little late, and I am a little drunk. But in my defense, it has been an eventful day."

As if to make his point, the Count suddenly rose from his chair and tugged at one of the folds of his jacket.

"Do you see this button? I'll have you know that I sewed it on myself." Then dropping back in his chair, the Count picked up his brandy, took a sip, and reflected. "She was perfectly right, you know. Marina, I mean. Absolutely, positively, perfectly right." The Count sighed again. Then he shared with his sister a notion.

Since the beginning of storytelling, he explained, Death has called on the unwitting. In one tale or another, it arrives quietly in town and takes a room at an inn, or lurks in an alleyway, or lingers in the marketplace, surreptitiously. Then just when the hero has a moment of respite from his daily affairs, Death pays him a visit.

This is all well and good, allowed the Count. But what is rarely related is the fact that Life is every bit as devious as Death. It too can wear a hooded coat. It too can slip into town, lurk in an alley, or wait in the back of a tavern.

Hadn't it paid such a visit to Mishka? Hadn't it found him hiding behind his books, lured him out of the library, and taken his hand on a secluded spot overlooking the Neva?

Hadn't it found Andrey in Lyon and beckoned him to the big top?

Emptying his glass, the Count rose from his chair and stumbled into the bookcase as he reached for the brandy.

"Excusez-moi, monsieur."

The Count poured himself a tad, just a drop, no more than a sip, and fell back into his seat. Then waving a finger gently in the air, he continued:

"The collectivization of collectives, Helena, and the dekulaking of kulaks—in all probability, these are quite probable. They're even likely to be likely. But *inevitable?*"

With a knowing smile, the Count shook his head at the very sound of the word.

"Allow me to tell you what is inevitable. What is inevitable is that Life will pay Nina a visit too. She may be as sober as St. Augustine, but she is too alert and too vibrant for Life to let her shake a hand and walk off alone. Life will follow her in a taxi. It will bump into her by chance. It will work its way into her affections. And to do so, it will beg, barter, collude, and if necessary, resort to chicanery.

"What a world," the Count sighed at last, before falling asleep in his chair.

On the following morning, with his eyes a little blurry and his head a little sore, the Count poured a second cup of coffee, settled himself in his chair, and leaned to his side in order to retrieve Mishka's letter from his jacket.

But it wasn't there.

The Count distinctly remembered tucking the letter in the inside pocket when he was leaving the lobby the day before; and it had definitely been there when he had repaired the button in Marina's office. . . .

It must have fallen out, he thought, when he draped the jacket over the back of Anna's chair. So, after finishing his coffee, the Count went down to suite 311—only to find the door open, the closets empty, and the bottom of the dustbins bare.

But Mishka's half-read letter had not fallen from the Count's jacket in Anna's room. Having emptied his pockets at half past three, when the Count had stumbled reaching for the brandy, he had knocked the letter into the gap between the bookcase and the wall, where it was destined to remain.

Though perhaps this was just as well.

For while the Count had been so moved by Mishka's bittersweet walk along Nevsky Prospekt and his romantic lines of verse, the lines of verse were not written by Mishka at all. They were from the poem that Mayakovsky had delivered while standing on his chair back in 1923. And what had prompted Mishka to quote them had nothing to do with the day that Katerina had first taken his hand. What had prompted the citation, and the writing of the letter, for that matter, was the fact that on the fourteenth of April, Vladimir Mayakovsky, the poet laureate of the Revolution, had shot himself through the heart with a prop revolver.

Addendum

On the morning of the twenty-second of June, even as the Count was looking through his pockets for Mishka's letter, Nina Kulikova and her three confederates were boarding a train headed east for Ivanovo full of energy, excitement, and a clear sense of purpose.

Since the launch of the First Five-Year Plan in 1928, tens of thousands of their comrades in the urban centers had been working tirelessly to build power stations, steel mills, and manufacturing plants for heavy machinery. As this historic effort unfolded, it would be essential for the country's grain-producing regions to do their part—by meeting the increased demand for bread in the cities with leaps in agricultural production.

But to pave the way for this ambitious effort, it was deemed necessary to exile a million kulaks—those profiteers and enemies of the common good, who also happened to be the regions' most capable farmers. The remaining peasants, who viewed newly introduced approaches to agriculture with resentment and suspicion, proved antagonistic to even the smallest efforts at innovation. Tractors, which were meant to usher in the new era by the fleet, ended up being in short supply. These challenges were compounded by uncooperative weather resulting in a collapse of agricultural output. But given the imperative of feeding the cities, the precipitous decline in the harvest was met with increased quotas and requisitions enforced at gunpoint.

In 1932, the combination of these intractable forces would result in widespread hardship for the agricultural provinces of old Russia, and death by starvation for millions of peasants in Ukraine.*

---

*While many of the young loyalists (like Nina) who joined the *udarniks* in the countryside would have their faith in the Party tested by what they witnessed, most of Russia, and for that matter the world, would be spared the

But, as noted, all of this was still in the offing. And when Nina's train finally arrived in the far reaches of Ivanovo, where the fields of young wheat bent in the breeze for as far as the eye could see, she was almost overwhelmed by the beauty of the landscape, and by the sense that her life had just begun.

---

spectacle of this man-made disaster. For just as peasants from the countryside were forbidden to enter the cities, journalists from the cities were forbidden to enter the countryside; delivery of personal mail was suspended; and the windows of passenger trains were blackened. In fact, so successful was the campaign to contain awareness of the crisis, when word leaked out that millions were starving in Ukraine, Walter Duranty, the lead correspondent for *The New York Times* in Russia (and one of the ringleaders in the Shalyapin Bar), would report that these rumors of famine were grossly exaggerated and had probably originated with anti-Soviet propagandists. Thus, the world would shrug. And even as the crime unfolded, Duranty would win the Pulitzer Prize.

1938

An Arrival

Let us concede that the early thirties in Russia were unkind.

In addition to starvation in the countryside, the famine of '32 eventually led to a migration of peasants to the cities, which, in turn, contributed to overcrowded housing, shortages of essential goods, even hooliganism. At the same time, the most stalwart workers in the urban centers were wearying under the burden of the continuous workweek; artists faced tighter constraints on what they could or could not imagine; churches were shuttered, repurposed, or razed; and when revolutionary hero Sergei Kirov was assassinated, the nation was purged of an array of politically unreliable elements.

But then, on the seventeenth of November 1935, at the First All-Union Conference of Stakhanovites, Stalin himself declared: *Life has improved, comrades. Life is more joyous. . . .*

Yes, generally speaking such a remark falling from the lips of a statesman should be swept from the floor with the dust and the lint. But when it fell from the lips of Soso, one had good reason to lend it credence. For it was often through secondary remarks in secondary speeches that the General Secretary of the Central Committee of the Communist Party signaled the shifts in his thinking.

In point of fact, a few days before giving this speech, Soso had seen a photograph in the *Herald Tribune* of three healthy young Bolshevik girls standing before a factory gate—dressed in the tunic and kerchief long favored by the Party. Normally, such a picture would have warmed the cockles of his heart. But in the context of the Western press, it struck the Secretary of Secretaries that this simple attire might suggest to the world that after eighteen years of Communism, Russian girls still lived like peasants. Thus, the fateful sentences were slipped into the speech—and the direction of the country veered.

For upon reading in *Pravda* that life had improved, the attentive apparatchiks understood that a turning point had been reached—that given the Revolution's unqualified success, the time had come for the Party not only to countenance but to encourage a little more glamour, a little more luxury, a little more laughter. Within a matter of weeks, the Christmas tree and Gypsy music, both long in exile, were given a warm welcome home; Polina Molotova, wife of the foreign minister, was entrusted with the launch of the first Soviet perfumes; the New Light Factory (with the help of some imported machinery) was charged with producing champagne at the rate of ten thousand bottles a day; members of the Politburo traded in their military uniforms for tailored suits; and those hardworking girls exiting their factories were now encouraged to look not like peasants, but like the girls along the Champs-Élysées.*

So, not unlike that fellow in Genesis who said *Let there be this*, or *Let there be that*, and there was this or that, when Soso said *Life has improved, comrades*, life—in fact—improved!

Case in point: At this very moment, two young ladies are strolling down Kuznetsky Most wearing brightly colored dresses fitted at the waist and hemmed at the calf. One of them even sports a yellow hat with a brim that slopes seductively over a long-lashed eye. With the rumble of the brand-new Metro underfoot, they pause before three of the great windows at TsUM, the Central Universal Department Store, which respectively showcase a pyramid of hats, a pyramid of watches, and a pyramid of high-heeled shoes.

Granted, the girls still live in crowded apartments and wash their pretty dresses in a common sink, but do they look through the store's windows with resentment? Not in the least. With envy, perhaps, or wide-eyed wonder, but not resentment. For the doors of TsUM are no longer closed to them. Having long served foreigners and high Party officials, the store

---

*True, there was still one more purge to see to, but this one was to be directed at high Party officials and members of the secret police. In fact, Genrikh Yagoda, the dreaded head of the NKVD, was about to get his. Accused of treason, conspiracy, and diamond smuggling, Yagoda would be tried publicly in the Palace of Unions—right across the square from the Metropol Hotel—found guilty, and summarily shot. So, this too would be regarded by many as a harbinger of brighter days. . . .

had been opened to the citizenry in '36—as long as they could pay the cashier in foreign currencies, silver, or gold. In fact, on TsUM's lower level there is a nicely appointed office where a discreet gentleman will give you store credit for half the value of your grandmother's jewelry.

You see? Life *is* more joyous.

So, having admired the contents of the windows and imagined the day when they too might have an apartment with closets in which to stow their hats, watches, and shoes, our fetching pair resumes their stroll, all the while chatting about the two well-connected young men they are on their way to meet for dinner.

At Teatralny Proyezd, they wait at the curb for a break in the flow of automobiles. Then skipping across the street, they enter the Metropol Hotel where, as they pass the concierge's desk en route to the Piazza, they are admired by a distinguished-looking man with a touch of gray in his hair. . . .

"Ah, the end of spring," observed the Count to Vasily (who was sorting through the night's reservations). "By the hems of the skirts on those young ladies, I'd wager it must be almost 70° along Tverskaya, despite being seven o'clock at night. In another few days, the boys will be stealing posies from the Alexander Gardens and Emile will be scattering peas across his plates. . . ."

"No doubt," said the concierge, in the manner of a librarian agreeing with a scholar.

Earlier that day, in fact, the first strawberries of the season had arrived in the kitchen and Emile had slipped a handful to the Count for his breakfast the following morning.

"Without question," concluded the Count, "summer is now at the gates and the days that ensue are sure to be long and carefree. . . ."

"Alexander Ilyich."

At the unexpected sound of his own name, the Count turned to find another young lady standing right behind him, though this one was in a pair of pants. Five and a half feet tall, she had straight blond hair, light blue eyes, and a rare sense of self-possession.

"Nina!" he exclaimed. "What a sight for sore eyes. We haven't heard from you in ages. When did you get back to Moscow?"

"May I speak with you a moment?"

"Certainly . . ."

Sensing that something personal must have prompted the visit, the Count followed Nina a few paces from the concierge's desk.

"It is my husband—" she began.

"Your husband," the Count interjected. "You've gotten married!"

"Yes," she said. "Leo and I have been married for six years. We worked together in Ivanovo—"

"Why, I remember him!"

Frustrated by the Count's interruptions, Nina shook her head.

"You would not have met."

"You're quite right. We did not meet, per se; but he was here with you in the hotel just before you left."

The Count couldn't help but smile to recall the handsome Komsomol captain who had sent the others on ahead so that he could wait for Nina alone.

Nina tried for a moment to recollect this visit with her husband to the Metropol; but then waved a hand as if to say whether or not they had been in the hotel all those years ago was of no consequence.

"Please, Alexander Ilyich. I don't have much time. Two weeks ago, we were recalled from Ivanovo to attend a conference on the future of agricultural planning. On the first day of the meetings, Leo was arrested. After some effort, I tracked him to the Lubyanka, but they wouldn't let me see him. Naturally, I began to fear the worst. But yesterday, I received word that he has been sentenced to five years corrective labor. They are putting him on a train tonight for Sevvostlag. I'm going to follow him there. What I need is for someone to watch over Sofia while I get myself settled."

"Sofia?"

The Count followed Nina's glance across the lobby to where a girl of five or six with black hair and ivory skin was in a high-back chair, her feet dangling a few inches from the floor.

"I can't take her with me now as I will need to find work and a place to live. It may take a month or two. But once I have established myself, I'll come back for her."

Nina had explained these developments as one reports a series of scientific outcomes—a succession of facts that warranted our fear and indignation as much as would the laws of gravity or motion. But the Count could no longer contain some sense of shock, if only due to the speed at which the particulars were unfolding: a husband, a daughter, an arrest, the Lubyanka, corrective labor . . .

Interpreting the Count's expression as one of hesitation, Nina—that most self-reliant of souls—gripped the Count by the arm.

"I have no one else to turn to, Alexander." Then after a pause she added: "Please."

Together, the Count and Nina crossed the lobby to this child of five or six with black hair, white skin, and dark blue eyes. Had the Count been introduced to Sofia under different circumstances, he might have observed with quiet amusement the signs of Nina's rugged practicality on display: that Sofia wore simple clothes; that her hair was almost as short as a boy's; and that the linen doll she hugged by the neck didn't even have a dress.

Nina knelt so that she could see her daughter eye to eye. She put a hand on Sofia's knee and began to speak in a tenor the Count had never heard her speak in before. It was the tenor of tenderness.

"Sonya, this is your Uncle Sasha whom I have told you so much about."

"The one who gave you the pretty binoculars?"

"Yes," said Nina with a smile. "The very same."

"Hello, Sofia," said the Count.

Nina then explained that while Mama went to prepare their new home, Sofia would be staying for a few weeks in this lovely hotel. Nina told her that until Mama returned, she must be strong and respectful and listen to her uncle.

"And then we will take the long train to Papa," the girl said.

"That's right, my sweet. Then we will take the long train to Papa."

Sofia was doing her best to match her mother's fortitude; but she did not yet have her mother's command over her own emotions. So while she did not question, or plead, or act dismayed, when she nodded to show that she understood, tears fell down her cheeks.

Nina used her thumb to wipe the tears away from one side of her daughter's face as Sofia used the back of her hand to wipe them away from the other. Nina looked Sofia in the eye until she was sure the tears had stopped. Then nodding once, she gave her daughter a kiss on the forehead and led the Count a few yards away.

"Here," she said, handing him a canvas pack with shoulder straps, the sort that might have been worn on the back of a soldier. "These are her things. And you should probably take this too." Nina handed him a small photograph without a frame. "It may be better to keep it to yourself. I don't know. You will have to decide."

Nina gripped the Count on the arm again; then she walked across the lobby at the pace of one who hopes to leave herself no room for second thoughts.

The Count watched her exit the hotel and head across Theatre Square, just as he had eight years before. When she was gone, he looked down at the photograph in his hand. It was a picture of Nina and her husband, Sofia's father. From Nina's face, the Count could tell that the picture had been taken some years before. He could also tell that he had only been half right. For while he had seen her husband all those years ago in the lobby of the Metropol, Nina had not married the handsome captain—she had married the hapless young fellow with the sailor's cap who had so eagerly retrieved her coat.

This entire exchange—from Nina's saying the Count's name to her passing through the hotel's doors—had taken less than fifteen minutes. So, the Count had little more than a moment to consider the nature of the commitment he was being asked to make.

Granted it was only for a month or two. He would not be responsible for the girl's education, her moral instruction, or her religious upbringing. But her health and comfort? He would be responsible for those even were he to care for her for one night. What was she to eat? Where was she to sleep? And, while it was his night off tonight, what was he to do with her the following evening, when he had to don the white jacket of the Boyarsky?

But let us imagine that before committing himself, the Count had had the time to see the problem in its full scope, to consider every challenge and obstacle, to acknowledge his own lack of experience, to concede that in all likelihood he was the least fitting, least well-equipped, and most poorly situated man in Moscow to care for a child. Had he the time and presence of mind to weigh all of this, would he have denied Nina her request?

He would not even have attempted to dissuade her.

How could he?

This was the very woman who, as a child herself, had crossed the Piazza without hesitation in order to become his friend; who had shown him the hidden corners of the hotel and bestowed upon him, quite literally, the key to its mysteries. When such a friend has sought one out to ask for aid—particularly one for whom asking favors in a time of need does not come naturally—then there is only one acceptable response.

The Count slipped the photograph in his pocket. He composed himself. Then he turned to find his new charge looking up at him.

"Well, Sofia. Are you hungry? Would you like something to eat?"

She shook her head.

"Then why don't we head upstairs and get ourselves situated."

The Count helped Sofia down from the chair and led her across the lobby. But as he was about to mount the stairs, he noticed her staring when the elevator doors opened to let off two of the hotel's guests.

"Have you ever ridden on an elevator before?" he asked.

Gripping her doll by the neck, Sofia shook her head again.

"In that case . . ."

Holding the doors open, the Count gestured for Sofia to proceed. With an expression of cautious curiosity, she stepped onto the elevator, made room for the Count, and then watched as the doors slid shut.

With a theatrical flourish and the command of *Presto!* the Count pressed the button for the fifth floor. The elevator lurched and began to move. Sofia steadied herself; then she leaned a little to her right so that she could watch the floors pass by through the caging.

"*Voilà*," said the Count when they arrived a moment later at their destination.

Leading Sofia down the hall and into the belfry, the Count gestured again for her to proceed. But having looked up the narrow twisting stair, Sofia turned to the Count and raised both hands in the air in the international symbol of *Pick me up*.

"Hmm," said the Count. Then despite his age, he picked her up.

She yawned.

Once in his room, the Count sat Sofia on his bed, put her knapsack on the Grand Duke's desk, and then told her he would be right back. He walked down the hall and retrieved a winter blanket from his trunk. His plan was to make her a small bed on the floor beside his own and lend her one of his pillows. He would just have to be careful not to step on her, should he wake in the night.

But the Count needn't have worried about stepping on Sofia. For when he returned to his room with the blanket, she had already climbed under his covers and fallen asleep.

Adjustments

Never had the toll of a bell been so welcome. Not in Moscow. Not in Europe. Not in all the world. When the Frenchman Carpentier faced the American Dempsey, he could not have felt more relief upon hearing the clang that signaled the end of the third round than the Count felt upon hearing his own clock strike twelve. Nor could the citizens of Prague upon hearing the church bells that signaled the end of their siege at the hands of Frederick the Great.

What was it about this child that prompted a grown man to count so carefully the minutes until lunch? Did she prattle on nonsensically? Did she flit about giggling? Did she dissolve into tears or launch into tantrums at the slightest provocation?

On the contrary. She was quiet.

Unsettlingly so.

Upon waking she rose, dressed, and made her bed without a word. When the Count served breakfast, she nibbled her biscuits like a Trappist. Then, having quietly cleared her plate, she climbed up onto the Count's desk chair, sat on her hands, and gazed at him in silence. And what a gaze it was. With irises as dark and foreboding as the deep, it was positively unnerving. Without shyness or impatience, it seemed simply to say: *What now, Uncle Alexander?*

What now, indeed. For having made their beds and nibbled their biscuits, the two of them had the whole day before them. 16 hours. 960 minutes. 57,600 seconds!

The notion was indisputably daunting.

But who was Alexander Rostov, if not a seasoned conversationalist? At weddings and name-day celebrations from Moscow to St. Petersburg, he had inevitably been seated beside the most recalcitrant of dinner guests. The prudish aunts and pompous uncles. The mirthless, mordant, and shy. Why? Because Alexander Rostov could be counted upon to draw his dinner companions into a lively conversation, whatever their dispositions.

If he had happened to be seated beside Sofia at a dinner party—or, for that matter, in the compartment of a train traveling across the countryside—what would he do? Naturally, he would ask about her life: *Where are you from, my friend? Ivanovo, you say. I have never been, but always wanted to go. What is the best season to visit? And what should one see whilst one is there?*

"So, tell me . . . ," the Count began with a smile, as Sofia's eyes opened wide.

But even as the words were leaving his lips, the Count was having second thoughts. For he was decidedly not seated beside Sofia at a dinner party, or in a railway car. She was a child who, with little explanation, had been uprooted from her home. To pursue a line of inquiry about the sights and seasons of Ivanovo or daily life with her parents was almost certain to raise a host of sad associations, spurring feelings of longing and loss.

"So, tell me . . . ," he said again, feeling the onset of dizziness, as her eyes opened wider. But just in time, he had a flash of inspiration:

"What is your dolly's name?"

A sure step, that one, thought the Count, with an inward pat on the back.

"Dolly doesn't have a name."

"What's that? No name? But surely, your doll *must* have a name."

Sofia stared at the Count for a moment then tilted her head like a raven. "Why?"

"Why?" repeated the Count. "Why, so that she can be addressed. So that she can be invited for tea; called to from across the room; discussed in conversation when absent; and included in your prayers. That is, for all the very reasons that *you* benefit from having a name."

As Sofia considered this, the Count leaned forward, ready to elaborate on the matter to the smallest detail. But nodding once, the girl said, "I shall call her Dolly." Then she looked to the Count with her big blue eyes as if to say: *Now that that's decided, what next?*

The Count leaned back in his chair and began to sort through his vast catalog of casual questions, discarding one after another. But as luck would have it, he noticed that Sofia's gaze had shifted almost furtively toward something behind him.

Discreetly, the Count glanced back.

The ebony elephant, he realized with a smile. Raised her entire life in a rural province, the child had probably never even imagined that such an animal existed. *What sort of fantastical beast is that?* she must be wondering. *Is it mammal or reptile? Fact or fable?*

"Have you ever seen one of those before?" the Count asked with a backward gesture and a smile.

"An elephant?" she asked. "Or a lamp?"

The Count coughed.

"I meant an elephant."

"Only in books," she admitted a little sadly.

"Ah. Well. It is a magnificent animal. A wonder of creation."

Sofia's interest piqued, the Count launched into a description of the species, animating each of its characteristics with an illustrative flourish of the arms. "A native of the Dark Continent, the mature example can weigh over ten thousand pounds. Its legs are as thick as tree trunks, and it bathes itself by drawing water into its proboscis and spraying it into the air—"

"So, you have seen one?" she interrupted brightly. "On the Dark Continent?"

The Count fidgeted.

"Not exactly on the Dark Continent . . ."

"Then where?"

"In various books . . ."

"Oh," said Sofia, bringing the topic to a close with the efficiency of the guillotine.

. . .

. . .

The Count considered for a moment what other sort of wonder might capture her imagination, but which he had actually seen in person.

"Would you like to hear a story about a princess?" he suggested.

Sofia sat upright.

"The age of the nobility has given way to the age of the common man," she said with the pride of one who has recited her times tables correctly. "It was historically inevitable."

"Yes," said the Count. "So I've been told."

. . .

. . .

"Do you enjoy pictures?" he asked, picking up an illustrated guide to the Louvre that he had borrowed from the basement. "Here is a lifetime's supply. While I wash up, why don't you delve in?"

Sofia moved a little in order to set Dolly at her side and then accepted the book in a ready and determined manner.

Retreating to the safety of the washroom, the Count took off his shirt, bathed his upper body, and lathered his cheeks, all the while muttering the principal riddle of the day:

"She is no more than thirty pounds; no more than three feet tall; her entire bag of belongings could fit in a single drawer; she rarely speaks unless spoken to; and her heart beats no louder than a bird's. So how is it possible that she takes up so much space?!"

Over the years, the Count had come to think of his rooms as rather ample. In the morning, they easily accommodated twenty squats and twenty stretches, a leisurely breakfast, and the reading of a novel in a tilted chair. In the evenings after work, they fostered flights of fancy, memories of travel, and meditations on history all crowned by a good night's sleep. Yet somehow, this little visitor with her kit bag and her rag doll had altered every dimension of the room. She had simultaneously brought the ceiling downward, the floor upward, and the walls inward, such that anywhere he hoped to move she was already there. Having roused himself from a fitful night on the floor, when the Count was ready for his morning calisthenics, she was standing in the calisthenics spot. At breakfast, she ate more than her fair share of the strawberries; then when he was about to dip his second biscuit in his second cup of coffee, she was staring at it with such longing that he had no choice but to ask if she wanted it. And when, at last, he was ready to lean back in his chair with his book, she was already sitting in it, staring up at him expectantly.

But having caught himself waving his shaving brush emphatically at his own reflection, the Count stopped cold.

Good God, he thought. Is it possible?

Already?

At the age of forty-eight?

"Alexander Rostov, could it be that you have become settled in your ways?"

As a young man, the Count would *never* have been inconvenienced by a fellow soul. He sought out congenial company the moment he awoke.

When he had read in his chair, no interruption could be counted as a disturbance. In fact, he preferred to read with a little racket in the background. Like the shouts of a vendor in the street; or the scales of a piano in a neighboring apartment; or best of all, footsteps on the stair—footsteps that having quickly ascended two flights would suddenly stop, bang on his door, and breathlessly explain that two friends in a coach-and-four were waiting at the curb. (After all, isn't that why the pages of books are numbered? To facilitate the finding of one's place after a reasonable interruption?)

As to possessions, he hadn't cared a whit about them. He was the first to lend a book or an umbrella to an acquaintance (never mind that no acquaintance since Adam had returned a book or an umbrella).

And routines? He had prided himself on never having one. He would breakfast at 10:00 A.M. one day and 2:00 P.M. the next. At his favorite restaurants, he had never ordered the same dish twice in a season. Rather, he traveled across their menus like Mr. Livingstone traveled across Africa and Magellan the seven seas.

No, at the age of twenty-two, Count Alexander Rostov could not be inconvenienced, interrupted, or unsettled. For every unexpected appearance, comment, or turn of events had been welcomed like a burst of fireworks in a summer sky—as something to be marveled at and cheered.

But apparently, this was no longer the case. . . .

The unanticipated arrival of a thirty-pound package had torn the veil from his eyes. Without his even noticing—without his acknowledgment, input, or permission—routine had established itself within his daily life. Apparently, he now ate his breakfast at an appointed hour. Apparently, he must sip his coffee and nibble his biscuits without interruption. He must read in a particular chair tilted at a particular angle with no more than the scuffing of a pigeon's feet to distract him. He must shave his right cheek, shave his left, and only then move on to the underside of his chin.

To that end, the Count now tilted back his head and raised his razor, but the change in the angle of his gaze revealed two fathomless eyes staring back at him from the reflection in the mirror.

"Egads!"

"I have finished looking at the pictures," she said.

"Which ones?"

"All of them."

"All of them!" It was now the Count's eyes that opened wide. "Well, isn't that splendid."

"I think this is for you," she said, holding out a small envelope.

"Where did that come from?"

"It was slipped under your door. . . ."

Taking the envelope in hand, the Count could tell that it was empty; but in place of an address, the query *Three o'clock?* was written in a willowy script.

"Ah, yes," said the Count, stuffing it in his pocket. "A small matter of business." Then he thanked Sofia in a manner indicating that she could now be on her way.

And she replied, "You're welcome," in a manner indicating that she had no intention of going anywhere.

Thus had the Count leapt from his bed and clapped his hands at the first chime of the noon hour.

"Right," he said. "How about some lunch? You must be famished. I think you will find the Piazza positively delightful. More than simply a restaurant, the Piazza was designed to be an extension of the city—of its gardens, markets, and thoroughfares."

But as the Count continued with his description of the Piazza's advantages, he noticed that Sofia was staring at his father's clock with an expression of surprise. And when they passed over the threshold to go downstairs, she took another look back then hesitated—as if on the verge of asking how such a delicate device could generate such a lovely sound.

Well, thought the Count as he began to close the door, if she wanted to know the secrets of the twice-tolling clock, she had come to the right place. For not only did the Count know something of chronometry, he knew absolutely everything there was to know about this particular—

"Uncle Alexander," Sofia said in the tender tone of one who must deliver unhappy news. "I fear your clock is broken."

Taken aback, the Count released his grip on the doorknob.

"Broken? No, no, I assure you, Sofia, my clock keeps *perfect* time. In fact, it was made by craftsmen known the world over for their commitment to precision."

"It isn't the timekeeper that is broken," she explained. "It is the chime."

"But it just chimed beautifully."

"Yes. It chimed at *noon*. But it failed to chime at nine and ten and eleven."

"Ah," the Count said with a smile. "Normally, you would be perfectly right, my dear. But, you see, this is a twice-tolling clock. It was made many years ago to my father's specifications to toll only twice a day."

"But why?"

"Why indeed, my friend, why indeed. I'll tell you what. Let us adjourn to the Piazza where—having placed our order and made ourselves comfortable—we shall investigate all the whys and wherefores of my father's clock. For there is nothing more essential to the enjoyment of a civilized lunch than to have a lively topic of conversation."

At 12:10 the Piazza was not yet bustling; but perhaps this was just as well, as the Count and Sofia received an excellent table and prompt attention from Martyn—a capable new waiter who pulled back Sofia's chair with an admirable sense of politesse.

"My niece," explained the Count, as Sofia looked around the room in amazement.

"I have a six-year-old of my own," Martyn replied with a smile. "I'll give you a moment."

Granted, Sofia was not so unworldly as to be unfamiliar with elephants, but she had never seen anything quite like the Piazza. Not only was she marveling at the room's scale and elegance, but at each of the individual elements that seemed to turn common sense on its head: A ceiling made of glass. A tropical garden indoors. A fountain in the middle of a room!

When Sofia completed her survey of the Piazza's paradoxes, she seemed to understand instinctively that such a setting deserved an elevated standard of behavior. For she suddenly took her doll off the table and placed it on the empty chair to her right; when the Count slipped his napkin out from under his silverware to place it in his lap, Sofia followed suit, taking particular care not to jangle her fork and knife; and when, having placed their order with Martyn, the Count said *Thank you so much, my good man*, Sofia echoed the Count word for word. Then she looked to the Count, expectantly.

"Now?" she asked.

"Now what, my dear?"

"Is now when you will tell me about the twice-tolling clock?"

"Oh, yes. Precisely."

But where to start?

Naturally enough, at the beginning.

The twice-tolling clock, the Count explained, had been commissioned by his father from the venerable firm of Breguet. Establishing their shop in Paris in 1775, the Breguets were quickly known the world over not only for the precision of their chronometers (that is, the accuracy of their clocks), but for the elaborate means by which their clocks could signal the passage of time. They had clocks that played a few measures of Mozart at the end of the hour. They had clocks that chimed not only at the hour but at the half and the quarter. They had clocks that displayed the phases of the moon, the progress of the seasons, and the cycle of the tides. But when the Count's father visited their shop in 1882, he posed a very different sort of challenge for the firm: a clock that tolled only twice a day.

"*Why* would he do so?" asked the Count (in anticipation of his young listener's favorite interrogative).

Quite simply, the Count's father had believed that while a man should attend closely to life, he should not attend too closely to the clock. A student of both the Stoics and Montaigne, the Count's father believed that our Creator had set aside the morning hours for industry. That is, if a man woke no later than six, engaged in a light repast, and then applied himself without interruption, by the hour of noon he should have accomplished a full day's labor.

Thus, in his father's view, the toll of twelve was a moment of reckoning. When the noon bell sounded, the diligent man could take pride in having made good use of the morning and sit down to his lunch with a clear conscience. But when it sounded for the frivolous man—the man who had squandered his morning in bed, or on breakfast with three papers, or on idle chatter in the sitting room—he had no choice but to ask for his Lord's forgiveness.

In the afternoon, the Count's father believed that a man should take care not to live by the watch in his waistcoat—marking the minutes as if the events of one's life were stations on a railway line. Rather, having been suitably industrious before lunch, he should spend his afternoon in wise liberty. That is, he should walk among the willows, read a timeless text, converse with a friend beneath the pergola, or reflect before the fire—engaging in those endeavors that have no appointed hour, and that dictate their own beginnings and ends.

And the second chime?

The Count's father was of the mind that one should never hear it. If one had lived one's day well—in the service of industry, liberty, and the Lord—one should be soundly asleep long before twelve. So the second chime of the twice-tolling clock was most definitely a remonstrance. *What are* you *doing up?* it was meant to say. *Were you so profligate with your daylight that you must hunt about for things to do in the dark?*

"Your veal."

"Ah. Thank you, Martyn."

Quite appropriately, Martyn placed the first dish before Sofia and the second before the Count. Then he lingered a little closer to the table than was necessary.

"Thank you," the Count said again in a polite sign of dismissal. But as the Count took up his silverware and began recalling for Sofia's benefit how he and his sister would sit by the twice-tolling clock on the last night of December in order to ring in the New Year, Martyn took a step even closer.

"Yes?" asked the Count, somewhat impatiently.

Martyn hesitated.

"Shall I . . . cut the young lady's meat?"

The Count looked across the table to where Sofia, fork in hand, was staring at her plate.

Mon Dieu, thought the Count.

"No need, my friend. I shall see to it."

As Martyn backed away with a bow, the Count circled the table and in a few quick strokes had cut Sofia's veal into eight pieces. Then, on the verge of setting down her cutlery, he cut the eight pieces into sixteen. By the time he had returned to his seat, she had already eaten four.

Having regained her energy through sustenance, Sofia now unleashed a cavalcade of *Whys*. Why was it better to commune with work in the morning and nature in the afternoon? Why would a man read three newspapers? Why should one walk under the willows rather than some other sort of tree? And what was a pergola? Which in turn led to additional inquiries regarding Idlehour, the Countess, and Helena.

In principle, the Count generally regarded a barrage of interrogatives as bad form. Left to themselves, the words *who, what, why, when,* and *where* do not a conversation make. But as the Count began to answer Sofia's litany of queries, sketching the layout of Idlehour on the tablecloth with the tines of his fork, describing the personalities of family members and referencing various traditions—he noticed that Sofia was entirely, absolutely, and utterly engaged. What elephants and princesses had failed to accomplish, the life at Idlehour had apparently achieved. And just like that, her veal was gone.

When the plates had been cleared away, Martyn reappeared to inquire if they would be having dessert. The Count looked to Sofia with a smile, assuming that she would leap at the chance. But she bit her lower lip and shook her head.

"Are you quite sure?" the Count asked. "Ice cream? Cookies? A piece of cake?"

But shifting a bit in her chair, she shook her head again.

Enter the new generation, thought the Count with a shrug, while returning the dessert menu to Martyn.

"Apparently, we are done."

Martyn accepted the menu, but once again lingered. Then, turning his back slightly to the table, he actually leaned over with the clear intention of whispering in the Count's ear.

For goodness sake, thought the Count. What now?

"Count Rostov, I believe that your niece . . . may need to go."

"Go? Go where?"

Martyn hesitated.

"To the privy . . ."

The Count looked up at the waiter and then at Sofia.

"Say no more, Martyn."

The waiter bowed and excused himself.

"Sofia," the Count suggested tentatively, "shall we visit the ladies' room?"

Still biting her lip, Sofia nodded.

"Do you need me to . . . accompany you inside?" he asked, after leading her down the hallway.

Sofia shook her head and disappeared behind the washroom door.

As he waited, the Count chastised himself for his lug-headedness. Not only had he failed to cut her meat and bring her to the ladies' room, he clearly hadn't thought to help her unpack, because she was wearing the exact same clothes she had worn the day before.

"And you call yourself a waiter . . . ," he said to himself.

A moment later, Sofia emerged, looking relieved. But then, despite her readily apparent love of interrogatives, she hesitated like one who is struggling with whether to ask a question.

"What is it, my dear? Is there something on your mind?"

Sofia struggled for another moment, then worked up the nerve:

"Can we still have dessert, Uncle Alexander?"

Now, it was the Count who looked relieved.

"Without a doubt, my dear. Without a doubt."

Ascending, Alighting

At two o'clock, when Marina answered her office door to find the Count at the threshold in the company of a little girl with a rag doll gripped tightly by the neck, she was so surprised her eyes almost came into alignment.

"Ah, Marina," said the Count, raising his eyebrows meaningfully. "You remember Nina Kulikova? May I present her daughter, Sofia. She will be staying with us in the hotel for a bit. . . ."

As a mother of two, Marina did not need the Count's signal to tell her that something weighty had occurred in the life of the child. But she could also see that the girl was curious about the whirring sound coming from the other end of the room.

"What a pleasure to meet you, Sofia," she said. "I knew your mother well when she was just a few years older than you are now. But tell me: Have you ever seen a sewing machine?"

Sofia shook her head.

"Well then. Come and let me show you one."

Offering Sofia her hand, Marina led the girl to the other side of the room, where her assistant was mending a royal blue drape. Dropping down so that she would be at Sofia's level, Marina pointed to various parts of the machine and explained their use. Then, asking the young seamstress to show Sofia their collection of fabrics and buttons, she came back to the Count with an expression of inquiry.

In a hushed voice, he quickly recounted the events of the previous day.

"You can see the predicament that I'm in," concluded the Count.

"I can see the predicament that Sofia is in," corrected Marina.

"Yes. You're absolutely right," the Count admitted contritely. Then, just as he was about to continue, he had a notion—a notion so inspired, it was incredible he hadn't thought of it before. "I came, Marina, to see if you'd be willing to watch Sofia for an hour while I am at the Boyarsky's daily meeting. . . ."

"Of course I will," said Marina.

"As I say, I came with that intention. . . . But as you have so rightly pointed out, it is Sofia who deserves our support and consideration. And watching you together just now, seeing your instinctive tenderness, and seeing the way that she felt instantly at ease in your company, it was suddenly so obvious that what she needs, especially at this juncture in her life, is a mother's touch, a mother's way, a mother's—"

But Marina cut him off. And from the bottom of her heart, she said:

"Do not ask that of me, Alexander Ilyich. Ask it of yourself."

I can do this, said the Count to himself as he skipped up the stairs to the Boyarsky. After all, it was really just a matter of making some minor adjustments—a rearranging of some furniture and a shifting of some habits. Since Sofia was too young to be left alone, he would eventually need to find someone who could sit with her while he was at work. For tonight, he would simply request an evening off, suggesting that his tables be divided between Denis and Dmitry.

But in an extraordinary example of a friend anticipating the needs of a friend, when the Count arrived at the meeting of the Triumvirate a few minutes late, Andrey said:

"There you are, Alexander. Emile and I were just discussing that Denis and Dmitry can share your tables tonight."

Collapsing into his chair, the Count let out a sigh of relief.

"Perfect," he said. "By tomorrow, I shall have come up with a longer-term solution."

The chef and the maître d' looked at the Count in confusion.

"A longer-term solution?"

"Weren't you splitting my tables so that I could be free for the evening?"

"Free for the evening!" gasped Andrey.

Emile guffawed.

"Alexander, my friend, it's the third Saturday of the month. You'll be expected in the Yellow Room at ten. . . ."

Mein Gott, thought the Count. He had completely forgotten.

". . . What's more, the GAZ dinner is in the Red Room at half past seven."

The director of *Gorkovsky Avtomobilny Zavod*, the state's leading automotive manufacturing agency, was hosting a formal dinner to commemorate their fifth anniversary. In addition to key staff members, the event was to be attended by the Commissar of Heavy Industry, and three representatives of the Ford Motor Company—who didn't speak a word of Russian.

"I shall see to it personally," said the Count.

"Good," said the maître d'. "Dmitry has already set up the room."

Then he slid two envelopes across the table to the Count.

In accordance with Bolshevik custom, the tables in the Red Room had been laid out in the shape of a long U with chairs arranged on the outer perimeter—such that all the men seated could watch the head of the table without craning their necks. Satisfied that the settings were in order, the Count turned his attention to the envelopes that Andrey had given him. Unsealing the smaller of the two, he removed the seating chart, which had presumably been prepared in some office in the Kremlin. Then he opened the larger envelope, spilled out the place cards, and began positioning them accordingly. Having circled the table a second time in order to double-check the precision of his own execution, the Count stuffed the two envelopes into the pocket of his pants—only to discover another envelope. . . .

Removing the third envelope, the Count considered it with a furrowed brow. That is, until he turned it over and saw the willowy script.

"Great Scott!"

According to the clock on the wall, it was already 3:15.

The Count dashed out of the Red Room, down the hall, and up a flight of stairs. Finding the door to suite 311 ajar, he slipped inside, closed the door, and crossed the grand salon. In the bedroom, a silhouette turned from the window as her dress fell to the floor with a delicate whoosh.

The Count replied with a slight cough.

"Anna, my love . . ."

Noting the expression on the Count's face, the actress pulled her dress back up toward her shoulders.

"I'm terribly sorry, but due to a confluence of unexpected events, I am not going to be able to keep our appointment today. In fact, for related reasons, I may need to ask a small favor. . . ."

In the fifteen years that they had known each other, the Count had only asked Anna for one favor, and that had weighed less than two ounces.

"Of course, Alexander," she replied. "What is it?"

"How many suitcases do you travel with?"

A few minutes later, the Count was hurrying down the staff stairwell—two Parisian traveling cases in hand. With renewed respect, he thought of Grisha and Genya and all their predecessors. For though Anna's cases had been fashioned from the finest materials, they seemed to have been designed without the slightest consideration for having to be carried. The little leather handles were so small one could barely slip two fingers through them; and the cases' dimensions were so generous that at every step they banged from the banister into one's knee. How could the bell-hops possibly manage to carry these things around so effortlessly? And often with a hatbox thrown in for good measure!

Arriving at the subfloor, the Count pushed his way through the staff doors into the laundry. In the first suitcase, he stowed two sheets, a bed-cover, and a towel. In the second, he packed a pair of pillows. Then back up six flights he went, banging his knees at every turn of the belfry stairs. In his room, he unloaded the linens and then went down the hall to get a second mattress from one of the abandoned rooms.

This had seemed an excellent idea to the Count when it had struck him, but the mattress was decidedly against it. When he bent over to lift the mattress from the bedsprings, it crossed its arms, held its breadth, and refused to budge. When he managed to get it upright, it immediately flopped over his head, nearly knocking him off his feet. And when he'd finally dragged it down the hall and flumped it in his room, it spread out its limbs, claiming every spare inch of the floor.

This will not do, thought the Count with his hands on his hips. If he left the mattress there, how were they to move about? And he certainly wasn't going to drag it in and out of the room on a daily basis. But in a flash of inspiration, the Count was reminded of that morning sixteen years before, when he had consoled himself that living in this room would provide the satisfactions of traveling by train.

Yes, he thought. That is it, exactly.

Lifting the mattress onto its edge, he leaned it against the wall and warned it to stay put, if it knew what was good for it. Then he took Anna's suitcases and ran down four flights to the pantry of the Boyarsky, where the canned tomatoes were stored. With an approximate height of eight inches and a diameter of six, they were perfectly suited to the task. So having lugged them back upstairs (with a healthy measure of huffing and puffing), he stacked, hoisted, pulled, and perched until the room was ready. Then, having returned Anna's cases, he dashed down the stairs.

When the Count arrived at Marina's office (more than an hour late), he was relieved to find the seamstress and Sofia seated on the floor in close consultation. Bounding up, Sofia held out her doll, which was now in a royal blue dress with little black buttons down the front.

"Do you see what we made for Dolly, Uncle Alexander?"

"How lovely!"

"She is quite a seamstress," said Marina.

Sofia hugged Marina and then skipped into the hall with her newly attired companion. The Count began to follow his charge, but Marina called him back.

"Alexander: What arrangements have you made for Sofia while you are at work tonight . . . ?"

The Count bit his lip.

"All right," she said. "I will stay with her this evening. But tomorrow, you need to find someone else. You should speak with one of the younger chambermaids. Perhaps Natasha. She is unmarried and would be good with children. But you have to pay her a reasonable wage."

"Natasha," confirmed the Count with gratitude. "I'll speak to her first thing tomorrow. And a reasonable wage, absolutely. Thank you so much, Marina. I'll send you and Sofia dinner from the Boyarsky around seven; and if last night is any indication, she will be sound asleep by nine."

The Count turned to go, then turned back again.

"And, I'm sorry about earlier. . . ."

"It's all right, Alexander. You were anxious because you haven't spent time with children before. But I am certain that you are up to the challenge. If you are ever in doubt, just remember that unlike adults, children *want* to be happy. So they still have the ability to take the greatest pleasure in the simplest things." By way of example, the seamstress placed something small and seemingly insignificant in the Count's hand with an assurance and a few words of instruction.

As a result, when the Count and Sofia had climbed the five flights back to their rooms and she had turned her deep blue gaze of expectation upon him, the Count was ready.

"Would you like to play a game?" he asked.

"I would," she said.

"Then come this way."

With a touch of ceremony, the Count ushered Sofia through the closet door into the study.

"Ooo," she said as she emerged on the other side. "Is this your secret room?"

"It is *our* secret room," the Count replied.

Sofia nodded gravely to show that she understood.

But then children understand the purpose of secret rooms better than they understand the purpose of congresses, courtrooms, and banks.

Somewhat shyly, Sofia pointed at the painting.

"Is that your sister?"

"Yes. Helena."

"I like peaches too." She ran a hand along the coffee table. "Is this where your grandma had tea?"

"Exactly."

Sofia nodded gravely again.

"I am ready for the game."

"All right then. Here's how we play. You will go back into the bedroom and count to two hundred. I shall remain in order to hide *this* within the boundaries of the study." Then, as if from thin air, the Count produced the silver thimble that Marina had given him. "Sofia, you do know how to count to two hundred?"

"No," she admitted. "But I can count to one hundred twice."

"Well done."

Sofia exited through the closet, pulling the door shut behind her.

The Count glanced about the room in search of an appropriate spot—one that would prove reasonably challenging for the child without taking unfair advantage of her age. After a few minutes of consideration, he approached the little bookcase and carefully placed the thimble on top of *Anna Karenina*; then he took a seat.

At the count of two hundred, the closet door opened a crack.

"Are you ready?" she asked.

"Indeed, I am."

When Sofia came in, the Count expected her to scamper about the room willy-nilly, looking every which way. Instead, she remained in the doorway and quietly, almost unsettlingly, studied the room from quadrant to quadrant. Upper left, lower left, upper right, lower right. Then without a word, she walked straight to the bookcase and picked the thimble off the top of Tolstoy. This had occurred in less time than it would have taken for the Count to count to one hundred once.

"Well done," said the Count, not meaning it. "Let's play again."

Sofia handed the Count the thimble. But as soon as she left the room, the Count chastised himself for not having considered his next hiding place before initiating the second round. Now he had only two hundred seconds to find a suitable spot. As if to unnerve him further, Sofia began counting so loudly that he could hear her through the closed closet door.

"Twenty-one, twenty-two, twenty-three . . ."

Suddenly it was the Count who was scampering about willy-nilly and looking every which way—discarding this spot for being too easy and that spot for being too hard. In the end, he tucked the thimble under the handle of the Ambassador—on the other side of the room from the bookcase.

When Sofia returned, she followed the same procedure as before. Although, as if anticipating the Count's petty little trick, this time she began her survey in the corner opposite from where she had found the thimble in the first round. It took her all of twenty seconds to pluck it from its hiding place.

Clearly, the Count had underestimated his adversary. But by placing the thimble in such low locations, he had been playing to Sofia's natural strengths. In the next round, he would take advantage of her limitations by hiding it six or seven feet off the ground.

"Again?" he said with the smile of a fox.

"It's your turn."

"What's that?"

"It is your turn to look, and my turn to hide."

"No, you see, in this game I always do the hiding and you always do the hunting."

Sofia studied the Count as her mother would have.

"If you *always* do the hiding and I *always* do the hunting, then it wouldn't be a game at all."

The Count frowned at the indisputability of this point of view. And when she held out her hand, he dutifully placed the thimble in her palm. As if this turnabout weren't enough, when he reached for the doorknob, she tugged at his sleeve.

"Uncle Alexander, you won't peek, will you?"

Won't peek? The Count had a mind to say a word or two about the integrity of the Rostovs. Instead, he composed himself.

"No, Sofia. I will not peek."

"You promise . . . ?"

. . .

"I promise."

The Count went out into the bedroom muttering something about his word being his bond and never having cheated at cards or welched on a wager, and then he began to count. As he proceeded past 150, he could hear Sofia moving around the study, and when he reached 175, he heard a chair being pushed across the floor. Well aware of the difference between a gentleman and a cad, the Count counted until the room fell silent—that is, all the way to 222.

"Ready or not," he called.

When he came into the room, Sofia was sitting in one of the high-back chairs.

With a bit of theatricality, the Count put his hands behind his back and circled the room while saying *hmmm*. But after two circuits, the little silver thimble had yet to reveal itself. So he began to search a bit more in earnest. Taking a page from Sofia's book, he divided the room into quadrants and reviewed them systematically, but to no avail.

Recalling that he had heard one of the chairs being moved, and accounting for Sofia's height and arm extension, the Count estimated that she could have reached a spot at least five feet off the ground. So, he looked behind the frame of his sister's portrait; he looked under the mechanics of the little window; he even looked above the doorframe.

Still no thimble.

Occasionally, he would look back at Sofia in the hopes that she would give herself away by glancing at her hiding place. But she maintained an infuriatingly disinterested expression, as if she hadn't the slightest awareness of the hunt that was underway. And all the while, swinging her little feet back and forth.

As a student of psychology, the Count decided he must attempt to solve the problem from his opponent's point of view. Just as he had wanted to take advantage of her limited height, perhaps she had taken advantage of his stature. *Of course,* he thought. The sound of moving furniture didn't have to mean that she was climbing up on a chair; it could have been her pulling something aside in order to hide something *beneath* it. The Count dropped to the floor and crawled like a lizard from the bookcase to the Ambassador and back again.

And still she sat there swinging her little feet.

The Count stood to his full height, banging his head against the slope of the ceiling. What's more, his kneecaps hurt from the hardwood floor, and his jacket was covered in dust. Suddenly, as he looked a little wildly around the room, he became aware of a quietly encroaching eventuality. It was slinking slowly toward him like a cat across the lawn; and the name of this cat was Defeat.

Could it be?

Was he, a Rostov, preparing to surrender?

Well, in a word: Yes.

There were no two ways about it. He had been bested and he knew it. Naturally, there would have to be a word or two of self-recrimination, but first he cursed Marina and the alleged pleasures of simple games. He breathed deeply and exhaled. Then he presented himself to Sofia as General Mack had presented himself to Napoleon, having let the Russian army slip through his grasp.

"Well done, Sofia," he said.

Sofia looked directly at the Count for the first time since he'd come into the room.

"Are you giving up?"

"I am conceding," said the Count.

"Is that the same as giving up?"

. . .

"Yes, it is the same as giving up."

"Then you should say so."

Naturally. His humiliation must be brought to its full realization.

"I give up," he said.

Without a hint of gloating, Sofia accepted his surrender. Then she jumped off her chair and walked toward him. He stepped a little out of her way, assuming that she must have hid the thimble somewhere in the bookcase. But she didn't approach the bookcase. Instead, she stopped in front of him, reached into his jacket pocket, and withdrew the thimble.

The Count was aghast.

In fact, he actually sputtered.

"But, but, but, Sofia—that's not fair!"

Sofia studied the Count with curiosity.

"Why is it not fair?"

Always with that damnable Why.

"Because it's not," replied the Count.

"But you said we could hide it anywhere in the room."

"That's just it, Sofia. My pocket wasn't in the room."

"Your pocket was in the room when I hid the thimble; and it was in the room when you hunted. . . ."

And as the Count gazed into her innocent little face, it all became clear. He, a master of nuance and sleight of hand, had been played at every turn. When she had called him back to insist he not peek and had so sweetly tugged at his sleeve, that was a ploy to mask the slipping of the thimble into his pocket. And the moving of the furniture as the two-hundredth second approached? Pure theater. A ruthless case of dissembling. And even as he searched, there she sat, clutching her little Dolly in its bright blue dress, without ever once betraying her wiles.

The Count took one step back and bowed at the waist.

At six o'clock, having descended to the ground floor to deliver Sofia into Marina's care, returned up to the sixth floor to retrieve Sofia's doll, and then down to the ground floor to deliver it, the Count proceeded to the Boyarsky.

Apologizing to Andrey for being late, he quickly assessed his team, reviewed the tables, adjusted the glasses, aligned the silver, took a peek at Emile, and finally gave the signal that the restaurant could be opened. At half past seven, he went to the Red Room to oversee the GAZ dinner. Then at ten, he headed down the hall to where the doors of the Yellow Room were being guarded by a Goliath.

Ever since 1930, the Count and Osip had been dining together on the third Saturday of the month in order to further the former Red Army colonel's understanding of the West.

Having dedicated the first several years to a study of the French (covering their idioms and forms of address, the personalities of Napoleon, Richelieu, and Talleyrand, the essence of the Enlightenment, the genius of Impressionism, and their prevailing aptitude for *je ne sais quoi*), the Count and Osip spent the next few years studying the British (covering the necessity of tea, the implausible rules of cricket, the etiquette of foxhunting, their relentless if well-deserved pride in Shakespeare, and the all-encompassing, overriding importance of the pub). But more recently, they had shifted their attention to the United States.

To that end, tonight on the table beside their nearly empty plates were two copies of Alexis de Tocqueville's masterpiece, *Democracy in America*. Osip had been somewhat intimidated by its length, but the Count had assured him that there was no better text with which to establish a fundamental understanding of American culture. So, the former colonel had burned the midnight oil for three weeks and arrived in the

Yellow Room with the eagerness of the well-prepared schoolboy at his baccalaureate. And having seconded the Count's fondness for summer nights, echoed his compliments on the *sauce au poivre*, and shared his appreciation of the claret's nose, Osip was itching to get down to business.

"It is indeed a lovely wine, a lovely steak, and a lovely summer night," he said. "But shouldn't we be shifting our attention to the book?"

"Yes, certainly," said the Count, setting down his glass. "Let us turn our attention to the book. Why don't you start us off. . . ."

"Well, first I'd have to say that it's no *Call of the Wild*."

"No," said the Count with a smile. "It is certainly no *Call of the Wild*."

"And I have to admit, that while I appreciated de Tocqueville's attention to detail, on the whole I found the first volume, on the Americans' political system, rather slow in going."

"Yes." The Count nodded sagely. "The first volume may well be characterized as detailed to a fault. . . ."

"But the second volume—on the characteristics of their society—I found to be absolutely fascinating."

"In that, you are not alone."

"In fact, right from the first line . . . Wait. Where is it? Here we are: *There is not, I think, a single country in the civilized world where less attention is paid to philosophy than in the United States*. Ha! That should tell us a thing or two."

"Quite so," said the Count with a chuckle.

"And here. A few chapters later, he singles out their unusual passion for material well-being. The minds of Americans, he says, *are universally preoccupied with meeting the body's every need and attending to life's little comforts*. And that was in 1840. Imagine if he had visited them in the 1920s!"

"Ha. Visited them in the 1920s. Well put, my friend."

"But tell me, Alexander: What are we to make of his assertion that democracy is particularly suited to industry?"

The Count leaned back in his chair and moved about his utensils.

"Yes. The question of industry. That is an excellent place to dig in, Osip. Right at the heart of it. What do you make of it?"

"But I was asking what you made of it, Alexander."

"And you shall hear what I think without fail. But as your tutor, I would be remiss were I to skew your impressions before you had the chance to formulate them yourself. So let us begin with the freshness of your thoughts."

Osip studied the Count, who in turn reached for his glass of wine.

"Alexander . . . You have read the book. . . ."

"Of course I have read the book," confirmed the Count, putting down his glass.

"I mean, you have read both volumes—to the very last page."

"Osip, my friend, it is a fundamental rule of academic study that whether a student has read every word of a work matters less than whether he has established a reasonable familiarity with its essential material."

"And to which page does your reasonable familiarity extend in this particular work?"

"Ahem," said the Count, opening to the table of contents. "Let me see now. . . . Yes, yes, yes." He looked up at Osip. "Eighty-seven?"

Osip considered the Count for a moment. Then he picked up de Tocqueville and hurled him across the room. The French historian crashed headfirst into a framed photograph of Lenin leaning over a podium—shattering the glass and falling to the floor with a thud. The door to the Yellow Room flew open and the Goliath leapt inside with his firearm drawn.

"Gadzooks!" exclaimed the Count, raising his hands above his head.

Osip, on the verge of commanding his bodyguard to shoot his tutor, took a deep breath, then simply shook his head.

"It's all right, Vladimir."

Vladimir nodded once and returned to his station in the hall.

Osip folded his hands on the table and looked at the Count, waiting for an explanation.

"I am so sorry," the Count said in genuine embarrassment. "I meant to finish it, Osip. In fact, I had cleared my calendar today in order to read the rest, when . . . circumstances intervened."

"Circumstances."

"Unexpected circumstances."

"What sort of unexpected circumstances?"

"A young lady."

"A young lady!"

"The daughter of an old friend. She appeared out of the blue, and will be staying with me for a spell."

Osip looked at the Count as if dumbfounded, then let out a laugh.

"Well, well, well. Alexander Ilyich. A young lady staying with you. Why didn't you say so. You are utterly absolved, you old fox. Or at least, mostly so. We shall have our de Tocqueville, mind you; and you shall read every last page. But for now, don't let me keep you another second. It's not too late for some caviar in the Shalyapin. Then you can whisk her to the Piazza for a little dancing."

"Actually . . . she's a very young lady."

. . .

"How young a lady?"

"Five or six?"

"Five or six!"

"I'd say almost certainly six."

"You are hosting an almost certainly six-year-old."

"Yes . . ."

"In your room."

"Precisely."

"For how long?"

"A few weeks. Maybe a month. But no more than two . . ."

Osip smiled and nodded his head.

"I see."

"To be perfectly honest," the Count admitted, "so far her visit has been a little disruptive to the daily routine. But that's to be expected, I suppose, given that she has only just arrived. Once we've made some minor adjustments and she has had a chance to acclimatize, then everything should go back to running without a hitch."

"Without a doubt," agreed Osip. "In the meantime, don't let me keep you."

Promising to read his de Tocqueville by their very next meeting, the Count excused himself and slipped out the door while Osip picked up the claret. Finding the bottle empty, he reached across the table for the Count's unfinished glass and poured it into his.

Did he remember those days when his children were almost certainly six? When there was a pitter-pat in the hallways an hour before dawn?

When every object smaller than an apple was nowhere to be found, until it was right underfoot? When books went unread, letters unanswered, and every train of thought was left incomplete? He remembered them as if they were yesterday.

"Without a doubt," he said again with a smile on his face: "Once they have made some minor adjustments, everything should go back to running without a hitch . . ."

The Count was generally of a mind that grown men should not run in hallways. But when he left Osip it was nearly eleven, and he had already taken ample advantage of Marina's good nature. So, making an exception just this once, he sprinted down the hall, around the corner, and ran smack into some fellow with a ragged beard who was pacing at the top of the stairs.

"Mishka!"

"Ah. There you are, Sasha."

The instant the Count recognized his old friend, his first thought was that he would have to send him on his way. What else was he to do? There were no two ways about it.

But when he got a good look at Mishka's face, he could tell that this was impossible. Something of significance had clearly occurred. So, instead of sending him on his way, the Count led him back up to his study where, having taken a seat, Mishka turned his hat in his hands.

"Weren't you scheduled to arrive in Moscow tomorrow?" the Count ventured after a brief silence.

"Yes," said Mishka with a careless wave of his hat. "But I came a day early at Shalamov's request. . . ."

An acquaintance from their university days, Viktor Shalamov was now the senior editor at *Goslitizdat*. It was his idea to have Mishka edit their forthcoming volumes of Anton Chekhov's collected letters—a project that Mishka had been slaving over since 1934.

"Ah," said the Count brightly. "You must be nearly done."

"Nearly done," Mishka repeated with a laugh. "You're quite right, Sasha. I am nearly done. In fact, all that remains is to remove a word."

Here is what had unfolded:

Early that morning, Mikhail Mindich had arrived in Moscow on the overnight train from Leningrad. With the galleys on their way to the printer, Shalamov had said he wanted to take Mishka to the Central House of Writers for a celebratory lunch. But when Mishka arrived in the publisher's reception room shortly before one o'clock, Shalamov asked him to come back to his office.

Once they were settled, Shalamov congratulated Mishka on a job well done. Then he patted the galleys that, as it turned out, were not on their way to the printer, but were lying right there on the editor's desk.

Yes, it was a job of nuance and erudition, Shalamov said. A paragon of scholarship. But there was one small matter that needed to be addressed before printing. It was an elision in the letter of the sixth of June 1904.

Mishka knew the letter well. It was the bittersweet missive written by Chekhov to his sister, Maria, in which he predicts his full recovery just a few weeks before his death. During typesetting, a word must have been dropped—which just shows that no matter how many times you review a galley, you will never catch every flaw.

"Let's see to it," said Mishka.

"Here," said Shalamov, rotating the galley so that Mishka could review the letter for himself.

Berlin,
June 6, 1904

Dear Masha,

I am writing you from Berlin. I've been here a whole day now. It turned very cold in Moscow and even snowed after you left; the bad weather must have given me a cold, I began having rheumatic pains in my arms and legs, I couldn't sleep at night, lost a great deal of weight, had morphine injections, took thousands of different kinds of medicine, and recall with gratitude only the heroin Altschuller once prescribed for me. Nonetheless, toward departure time I began to recover my strength. My appetite returned, I began giving myself arsenic injections, and so on and so forth, and finally on Thursday I left the country very thin, with very thin, emaciated legs. I had a fine, pleasant trip. Here in Berlin, we've taken a comfortable room in the best hotel. I am very much enjoying the life here and haven't eaten so

well and with such an appetite in a long time. The bread here is amazing,
I've been stuffing myself with it, the coffee is excellent, and the dinners are
beyond words. People who have never been abroad don't know how good
bread can be. There's no decent tea (we have our own kind) and none of our
hors d'oeuvres, but everything else is superb, even though it's cheaper here
than in Russia. I've already put on weight, and today, despite the chill in
the air, I even took the long ride to the Tiergarten. And so you can tell
Mother and anyone else who's interested that I'm on my way to recovery or
even that I've already recovered . . . Etc., etc.

Yours,
A. Chekhov

Mishka read the passage once, then read it again while calling up in his
mind's eye an image of the original letter. After four years, he knew most of
them by heart. But as hard as he tried, he could not identify the discrepancy.

"What is missing?" he asked, at last.

"Oh," said Shalamov, in the tone of one who suddenly understands a
simple misapprehension between friends. "It is not that something is
missing. It is that something must be taken out. Here."

Shalamov reached across the desk in order to point to the lines in
which Chekhov had shared his first impressions of Berlin, but particularly
his praise for their amazing bread, and his observations that Russians who
hadn't traveled had no idea how good bread could be.

"This part should be taken out?"

"Yes. That's right."

"As in stricken."

"If you wish."

"And why, might I ask?"

"In the interests of concision."

"So it is to save paper! And once I have taken out this little passage of
the sixth of June, where shall you have me put it? In the bank? In a dresser
drawer? In Lenin's tomb?"

As Mishka had been relating this exchange to the Count, his voice
had grown increasingly loud, as if with a renewed sense of outrage; but
then he suddenly fell silent.

"And then Shalamov," he continued after a moment, "this Shalamov from our youth, he tells me that I can shoot the passage from a cannon for all he cares, but it must be taken out. So do you know what I did, Sasha? Can you even imagine?"

One might well draw the conclusion, that a man prone to pacing is a man who will act judiciously—given the unusual amount of time he has allocated to the consideration of causes and consequences, of ramifications and repercussions. But it had been the Count's experience that men prone to pace are always on the verge of acting impulsively. For while the men who pace are being whipped along by logic, it is a multifaceted sort of logic, which brings them no closer to a clear understanding, or even a state of conviction. Rather, it leaves them at such a loss that they end up exposed to the influence of the merest whim, to the seduction of the rash or reckless act—almost as if they had never considered the matter at all.

"No, Mishka," the Count admitted with some sense of foreboding. "I can't imagine. What did you do?"

Mishka ran a hand across his forehead.

"What is a man supposed to do when confronted with such madness? I struck the passage out. Then I walked from the room without a word."

Upon hearing this denouement, the Count felt a great sense of relief. Were it not for the defeated appearance of his old friend, he might even have smiled. For one must admit, there was something genuinely comic about the circumstances. It could have been a tale from Gogol with Shalamov playing the part of a well-fed privy councillor impressed by his own rank. And the offending passage, hearing of its pending fate, could have climbed out a window and escaped down an alley never to be heard from again—that is, until it reappeared ten years later on the arm of a French countess, wearing a pince-nez and the *Légion d'honneur*.

But the Count maintained a solemn expression.

"You were perfectly right," he consoled. "It was just a matter of a few sentences. Fifty words out of a few hundred thousand."

The Count pointed out that on the balance, Mikhail had so much to be proud of. An authoritative collection of Chekhov's letters was long overdue. It promised to inspire a whole new generation of scholars and students, readers and writers. And Shalamov? With his long nose and little eyes, the Count had always found him to be something of a ferret, and one mustn't let a ferret spoil one's sense of accomplishment, or one's cause for celebration.

"Listen, my friend," the Count concluded with a smile, "you arrived on the overnight train and missed your lunch. That's half the problem right there. Go back to your hotel. Take a bath. Have something to eat and a glass of wine. Get a good night's sleep. Then tomorrow night, we shall meet at the Shalyapin as planned, raise a glass to brother Anton, and have a good laugh at the ferret's expense."

In this manner, the Count attempted to comfort his old friend, buoy his spirits, and move him gently toward the door.

At 11:40, the Count finally descended to the ground floor and knocked at Marina's.

"I'm so sorry I'm late," he said in a whisper when the seamstress answered the door. "Where is Sofia? I can carry her upstairs."

"There's no need to whisper, Alexander. She's awake."

"You kept her up!"

"I didn't keep anybody anything," Marina retorted. "She insisted upon waiting for you."

The two went inside, where Sofia was sitting on a chair with perfect posture. At the sight of the Count, she leapt to the floor, walked to his side, and took him by the hand.

Marina raised an eyebrow, as if to say: *You see* . . .

The Count raised his own eyebrows, as if to reply: *Imagine that* . . .

"Thank you for dinner, Aunt Marina," Sofia said to the seamstress.

"Thank you for coming, Sofia."

Then Sofia looked up at the Count.

"Can we go now?"

"Certainly, my dear."

When they left Marina's, it was obvious enough to the Count that little Sofia was ready for bed. Without letting go of his hand, she led him straight to the lobby, onto the elevator, and pressed the button for the fifth floor with the command of *Presto*. When they reached the belfry, rather than asking to be carried, she practically dragged him up the last flight of stairs. And when he introduced her to the ingenious design of their new bunk bed, she barely took notice. Instead, she hurried down the hall to brush her teeth and get into her nightgown.

But when she returned from the bathroom, instead of slipping under the covers, she climbed onto the desk chair.

"Aren't you ready for bed?" the Count asked in surprise.

"Wait," she replied, putting up a hand to silence him.

Then she leaned a little to her right in order to look around his torso. Mystified, the Count stepped aside and turned—just in time to see the long-strided watchman of the minutes catch up with his bowlegged brother of the hours. As the two embraced, the springs loosened, the wheels spun, and the miniature hammer of the twice-tolling clock began to signal the arrival of midnight. As Sofia listened, she sat perfectly still. Then, with the twelfth and final chime, she leapt down from the chair and climbed into bed.

"Goodnight, Uncle Alexander," she said; and before the Count could tuck her in, she had fallen fast asleep.

It had been a long day for the Count, one of the longest in memory. On the verge of exhaustion, he brushed his teeth and donned his pajamas almost as quickly as Sofia had. Then, returning to their bedroom, he put out the light and eased himself onto the mattress under Sofia's bedsprings. True, the Count had no bedsprings of his own, and the stacked tomato cans barely suspended Sofia's bed high enough for him to turn on his side; but it was a decided improvement upon the hardwood floor. So, having lived a day that his father would have been proud of, and hearing Sofia's delicate respirations, the Count closed his eyes and prepared to drift into a dreamless sleep. But, alas, sleep did not come so easily to our weary friend.

Like in a reel in which the dancers form two rows, so that one of their number can come skipping brightly down the aisle, a concern of the Count's would present itself for his consideration, bow with a flourish, and then take its place at the end of the line so that the next concern could come dancing to the fore.

What exactly were the Count's concerns?

He was worried about Mishka. Although he had been genuinely

relieved to discover that his friend's distress stemmed from the elision of four sentences on the three-hundredth page of the third volume, he couldn't help but feel with a certain sense of foreboding that the matter of the fifty words was not entirely behind them. . . .

He was worried about Nina and her journey east. The Count had not heard much about Sevvostlag, but he had heard enough about Siberia to comprehend the inhospitability of the road that Nina had chosen for herself. . . .

He was worried about little Sofia—and not simply over the cutting of her meat and the changing of her clothes. Whether dining in the Piazza or riding the elevator to the fifth floor, a little girl in the Metropol would not go unnoticed for long. Though Sofia was only staying with the Count for a matter of weeks, there was always the possibility that, before Nina's return, some bureaucrat would become aware of her residency and forbid it. . . .

And finally, in the interests of being utterly forthright, it should be added that the Count was worried about the following morning—when, having nibbled her biscuit and stolen his strawberries, Sofia would once again climb into his chair and look back at him with her dark blue eyes.

Perhaps it is inescapable that when our lives are in flux, despite the comfort of our beds, we are bound to keep ourselves awake grappling with anxieties—no matter how great or small, how real or imagined. But in point of fact, Count Rostov had good reason to be concerned about his old friend Mishka.

When he left the Metropol late on the night of the twenty-first of June, Mikhail Mindich followed the Count's advice to the letter. He went straight to his hotel, bathed, ate, and tucked himself in for a good night's sleep. And when he awoke, he looked upon the events of the previous day with more perspective.

In the light of morning, he saw that the Count was perfectly right—that it was only a matter of fifty words. And it was not as if Shalamov had asked him to cut the last lines of *The Cherry Orchard* or *The Seagull*. It was a passage that might have appeared in the correspondence of any traveler in Europe and that Chekhov himself had, in all probability, composed without a second thought.

But after dressing and eating a late breakfast, when Mishka headed to the Central House of Writers, he happened to pass that statue of Gorky on Arbatskaya Square, where the brooding statue of Gogol once had stood. Other than Mayakovsky, Maxim Gorky had been Mishka's greatest contemporary hero.

"Here was a man," said Mishka to himself (as he stood in the middle of the sidewalk ignoring the passersby), "who once wrote with such fresh and unsentimental directness that his memories of youth became *our* memories of youth."

But having settled in Italy, he was lured back to Russia by Stalin in '34 and set up in Ryabushinsky's mansion—so that he could preside over the establishment of Socialist Realism as the sole artistic style of the entire Russian people. . . .

"And what has been the fallout of that?" Mishka demanded of the statue.

All but ruined, Bulgakov hadn't written a word in years. Akhmatova had put down her pen. Mandelstam, having already served his sentence, had apparently been arrested again. And Mayakovsky? Oh, Mayakovsky . . .

Mishka pulled at the hairs of his beard.

Back in '22, how boldly he had predicted to Sasha that these four would come together to forge a new poetry for Russia. Improbably, perhaps. But in the end, that is exactly what they had done. They had created the poetry of silence.

"Yes, silence can be an opinion," said Mishka. "Silence can be a form of protest. It can be a means of survival. But it can also be a school of poetry—one with its own meter, tropes, and conventions. One that needn't be written with pencils or pens; but that can be written in the soul with a revolver to the chest."

With that, Mishka turned his back on Maxim Gorky and the Central House of Writers, and he went instead to the offices of *Goslitizdat*. There, he mounted the stairs, brushed past the receptionist, and opened door after door until he found the ferret in a conference room, presiding over an editorial meeting. In the center of the table were platters of cheese and figs and cured herring, the very sight of which, for some unaccountable reason, filled Mishka with fury. Turning from Shalamov in order to see who had barged through the door were the junior editors and assistant editors, all young and earnest—a fact that only infuriated Mishka more.

"Very good!" he shouted. "I see you have your knives out. What will you be cutting in half today? *The Brothers Karamazov*?"

"Mikhail Fyodorovich," said Shalamov in shock.

"What is *this*!" Mishka proclaimed, pointing to a young woman who happened to have a slice of bread topped with herring in her hand. "Is that bread from Berlin? Be careful, comrade. If you take a single bite, Shalamov will shoot you from a cannon."

Mishka could see that the young girl thought he was mad; but she put the piece of bread back on the table nonetheless.

"Aha!" Mishka exclaimed in vindication.

Shalamov rose from his chair, both unnerved and concerned.

"Mikhail," he said. "You are clearly upset. I would be happy to speak with you later in my office about whatever is on your mind. But as you can see, we are in the midst of a meeting. And we still have hours of business to attend to. . . ."

"Hours of business. Of that I have no doubt."

Mishka began ticking off the rest of the day's business, and with each item he picked up a manuscript from in front of one of the staff members and flung it across the room in Shalamov's direction.

"There are statues to be moved! Lines to be elided! And at five o'clock, you mustn't be late for your bath with comrade Stalin. For if you are, who will be there to scrub his back?"

"He's raving," said a young man with glasses.

"Mikhail," Shalamov pleaded.

"The future of Russian poetry is the haiku!" Mishka shouted in conclusion, then, with great satisfaction, he slammed the door on his way out. In fact, so satisfying was this gesture that he slammed every door that stood between him and the street below.

And what, to borrow a phrase, was the fallout of that?

Within a day, the gist of Mishka's comments were shared with the authorities; within a week, they were set down word for word. In August, he was invited to the offices of the NKVD in Leningrad for questioning. In November, he was brought before one of the extrajudicial troikas of the era. And in March 1939, he was on a train bound for Siberia and the realm of second thoughts.

. . . . .

The Count was presumably right to be concerned for Nina, though we will never know for certain—for she did not return to the Metropol within the month, within the year, or ever again. In October, the Count made some efforts to discover her whereabouts, all of them fruitless. One assumes that Nina made her own efforts to communicate with the Count, but no word was forthcoming, and Nina Kulikova simply disappeared into the vastness of the Russian East.

The Count was also right to worry that Sofia's residency would be noted. For not only was her presence remarked, within a fortnight of her arrival a letter was sent to an administrative office within the Kremlin stating that a Former Person living under house arrest on the top floor of the Metropol Hotel was caring for a five-year-old child of unknown parentage.

Upon its receipt, this letter was carefully read, stamped, and forwarded to a higher office—where it was counterstamped and directed up another two floors. There, it reached the sort of desk where with the swipe of a pen, matrons from the state orphanage could be dispersed.

It just so happened, however, that a cursory examination of this Former Person's recent associates led to a certain willowy actress—who for years had been the reputed paramour of a round-faced Commisar recently appointed to the Politburo. Within the walls of a small, drab office in an especially bureaucratic branch of government, it is generally difficult to accurately imagine the world outside. But it is never hard to imagine what might occur to one's career were one to seize the illegitimate daughter of a Politburo member and place her in a home. Such initiative would be rewarded with a blindfold and a cigarette.

As a result, only the most discreet inquiries were made. Indications were obtained that this actress had in all likelihood been in a relationship with the Politburo member for at least six years. In addition, an employee of the hotel confirmed that on the very day the young girl arrived at the hotel, the actress was also in residence. As such, all of the information that had been gathered in the course of the investigation was placed in a drawer under lock and key (on the off chance it might prove useful one day). While the pernicious little letter that had launched the inquiry in the first place was set on fire and dropped in the waste bin where it belonged.

So yes, the Count had every reason to be concerned about Mishka, Nina, and Sofia. But did he have cause to be anxious about the following morning?

As it turned out, once they had made their beds and nibbled their biscuits, Sofia did climb up into the desk chair; but rather than stare at the Count expectantly, she unfurled a litany of additional questions about Idlehour and his family, as if she had been composing them in her sleep.

And in the days that followed, a man who had long prided himself on his ability to tell a story in the most succinct manner with an emphasis on the most salient points, by necessity became a master of the digression, the parenthetical remark, the footnote, eventually even learning to anticipate Sofia's relentless inquiries before she had the time to phrase them.

Popular wisdom tells us that when the reel of our concerns interferes with our ability to fall asleep, the best remedy is the counting of sheep in a meadow. But preferring to have his lamb encrusted with herbs and served with a red wine reduction, the Count chose a different methodology altogether. As he listened to Sofia breathing, he went back to the moment that he woke on the hardwood floor, and by systematically reconstructing his various visits to the lobby, the Piazza, the Boyarsky, Anna's suite, the basement, and Marina's office, he carefully calculated how many flights of stairs he had climbed or descended over the course of the day. Up and down he went in his mind, counting one flight after another, until with the final ascent to the twice-tolling clock he reached a grand total of fifty-nine—at which point he slipped into a well-deserved sleep.

Addendum

"Uncle Alexander . . . ?"

. . .

"Sofia . . . ?"

. . .

"Are you awake, Uncle Alexander?"

. . .

"I am now, my dear. What is it?"

. . .

. . .

"I left Dolly in Aunt Marina's room . . ."

. . .

. . .

"Ah, yes . . ."

1946

On Saturday, the twenty-first of June 1946, as the sun rose high over the Kremlin, a lone figure climbed slowly up the steps from the Moskva River embankment, continued past St. Basil's Cathedral, and made his way onto Red Square.

Dressed in a ragged winter coat, he swung his right leg in a small semicircle as he walked. At another time, the combination of the ragged coat and hobbled leg might have made the man stand out on such a bright summer day. But in 1946, there were men limping about in borrowed clothes in every quarter of the capital. For that matter, they were limping about in every city of Europe.

That afternoon, the square was as crowded as if it were a market day. Women in floral dresses lingered under the arcades of the old State Department Store. Before the gates of the Kremlin, schoolboys climbed on two decommissioned tanks as soldiers in white fitted jackets standing at regular intervals watched with their hands clasped loosely behind their backs. And from the entrance of Lenin's tomb snaked a line 150 citizens long.

The man in the ragged coat paused for a moment to admire the orderly behavior of his far-flung countrymen waiting in the queue. At the front stood eight Uzbeks with drooping moustaches dressed in their best silk coats; then came four girls from the east with long braids and brightly embroidered caps; then ten muzhiks from Georgia, and so on, and so on—one constituency waiting patiently behind the next to pay their respects to the remains of a man who died over twenty years before.

If we have learned nothing else, the lone figure reflected with a crooked smile, *at least we have learned to stand in line.*

To a foreigner, it must have seemed that Russia had become the land of ten thousand lines. For there were lines at the tram stops, lines before the grocer, lines at the agencies of labor, education, and housing. But in point of fact, there were not ten thousand lines, or even ten. There was one all-encompassing line, which wound across the country and back through time. This had been Lenin's greatest innovation: a line that, like the Proletariat itself, was universal and infinite. He established it by decree in 1917 and personally took the first slot as his comrades jostled to line up behind him. One by one every Russian took his place, and the line grew longer and longer until it shared all of the attributes of life. In it friendships were formed and romances kindled; patience was fostered; civility practiced; even wisdom attained.

If one is willing to stand in line for eight hours to purchase a loaf of bread, the lone figure thought, what is an hour or two to see the corpse of a hero free of charge?

Passing the spot where Kazan Cathedral had once seen fit to stand, he turned right and walked on; but as he entered Theatre Square he came to a stop. For as his gaze moved from the Palace of Unions, to the Bolshoi, to the Maly Theatre, and finally to the Metropol Hotel, he had to marvel to find so many of the old facades unspoiled.

Five years before to the day, the Germans had launched Operation Barbarossa—the offensive in which more than three million soldiers deployed from Odessa to the Baltic crossed the Russian frontier.

When the operation commenced, Hitler estimated the Wehrmacht would secure Moscow within four months. In fact, having captured Minsk, Kiev, and Smolensk, by late October the German forces had already advanced nearly six hundred miles and were approaching Moscow from the north and south in a classic pincer formation. Within a matter of days, the city would be in range of their artillery.

By this time, a measure of lawlessness had broken out in the capital. The streets were crowded with refugees and deserters who were sleeping in makeshift encampments and cooking looted food over open fires. With the relocation of the seat of government to Kuybyshev underway, the sixteen bridges of the city were mined so that they could be demolished on a moment's notice. Columns of smoke rose above the Kremlin walls from the bonfires of classified files, while in the streets municipal and factory workers, who had not been paid in months, watched with seasoned foreboding as the eternally lit windows of the old fortress began to go dark one by one.

But on the afternoon of the thirtieth of October, an observer—standing in the very spot where our ragged itinerant now stood—would have witnessed a bewildering sight. A small cadre of laborers under the direction of the secret police were carrying chairs out of the Bolshoi on their way to the Mayakovsky Metro Station.

Later that night, the full membership of the Politburo assembled on the platform, one hundred feet below the surface of the city. Safe from the reach of German artillery, they took their seats at nine o'clock at a long table lined with food and wine. Shortly thereafter, a single train pulled into the station, its doors opened, and out stepped Stalin in full military dress. Assuming his rightful position at the head of the table, Marshal Soso said that his purpose in convening the Party leadership was twofold. First, it was to declare that while those assembled were welcome to make their way to Kuybyshev, he, for one, had no intention of going anywhere. He would remain in Moscow until the last drop of Russian blood had been spilled. Second, he announced that on the seventh of November the annual commemoration of the Revolution would be celebrated on Red Square as usual.

Many Muscovites would come to remember that parade as something of a turning point. To hear the heart-swelling sound of "The Internationale" to the accompaniment of fifty thousand boots while their leader stood defiant on the rostrum bolstered their confidence and hardened their resolve. On that day, they would recall, the tide decidedly turned.

Others, however, would point to the seven hundred thousand soldiers whom Soso had held in reserve in the Far East and who, even as the celebration was taking place, were being spirited across the country to Moscow's aid. Still others would note that it snowed on twenty-eight of the thirty-one days that December, effectively grounding the Luftwaffe. It certainly didn't hurt that the average temperature fell to minus 20°—a climate as alien to the Wehrmacht as it had been to the forces of Napoleon. Whatever the cause, although it took Hitler's troops just five months to march from the Russian frontier to the outskirts of Moscow, they would never pass through the city's gates. Having taken over one million prisoners and one million lives, they would begin their retreat in January 1942, leaving the city surprisingly intact.

Stepping from the curb, our lone figure gave way to a young officer driving a motorcycle with a girl in a bright orange dress in his sidecar; he passed between the two captured German fighter planes on display in the defoliated square; then skirting the Metropol's main entrance, he wound around the corner and disappeared down the alley at the back of the hotel.

Antics, Antitheses, an Accident

At 1:30, in the manager's office of the Metropol Hotel, Count Alexander Ilyich Rostov took the chair across the desk from the man with the narrow head and superior demeanor.

When the Count had received the Bishop's summons in the Piazza, he had assumed the matter must be urgent because the messenger had waited for him to finish his demitasse and then led him promptly to the executive suite. But once the Count had been ushered through the manager's door, the Bishop barely glanced up from the papers he was signing. Rather, he waved his pen toward the empty chair in the manner of one who wishes to indicate that he will be with you in a moment.

"Thank you," said the Count, accepting this perfunctory offer of a chair with a perfunctory bow of the head.

Not one to sit idly about, the Count made use of the empty minutes by surveying the office, which had undergone something of a transformation since Jozef Halecki had occupied it. While the desk of the former manager remained, it was no longer impressively bare. Along with six piles of paper, it now boasted a stapler, a penholder, and *two* telephones (presumably so the Bishop could put the Central Committee on hold while he dialed up the Politburo). In place of the burgundy chaise where the old Pole had allegedly reclined, there were now three gray filing cabinets with stainless-steel locks standing at attention. And the delightful hunting scenes that had once adorned the mahogany panels had been replaced, of course, with portraits of Messrs. Stalin, Lenin, and Marx.

Having inscribed his signature on twelve sheets of paper to his perfect satisfaction, the Bishop established a seventh pile at the edge of his desk, replaced the pen in its stand, and for the first time looked the Count in the eye.

"I gather you are an early riser, Alexander Ilyich," he said after a moment of silence.

"Men of purpose usually are."

The corner of the Bishop's mouth rose ever so slightly.

"Yes, of course. Men of purpose."

He reached across his desk to straighten his newest pile of papers.

"And you breakfast in your room at around seven . . . ?"

"That's right."

"Then at eight, it is your habit to read the papers in the lobby."

Confound the fellow, thought the Count. He interrupts the conclusion of a perfectly delightful lunch with a hand-delivered summons. Clearly, there is something on his mind. But must it always be on the bias with him? Has he no facility with the direct question? No appreciation for it? Were they to sit there reviewing the Count's typical day minute by minute—when the Triumvirate was scheduled to meet in less than an hour?

"Yes," confirmed the Count a little impatiently. "I read the morning papers in the morning."

"But in the lobby. You come down to the lobby."

"Without fail, I walk down the stairs to read in the comfort of the lobby."

The Bishop sat back in his chair and offered the briefest of smiles.

"Then perhaps you are aware of the incident that occurred this morning in the fourth-floor corridor at a quarter to eight. . . ."

For the record, the Count had risen shortly after seven. Having completed fifteen squats and fifteen stretches, having enjoyed his coffee, biscuit, and a piece of fruit (today a tangerine), having bathed, shaved, and dressed, he kissed Sofia on the forehead and departed from their bedroom with the intention of reading the papers in his favorite lobby chair. Descending one flight, he exited the belfry and traversed the hall to the main stair, as was his habit. But as he turned on the fifth-floor landing, he heard sounds of commotion coming from below.

The immediate impression was of fifteen voices shouting in twenty languages. These were accompanied by the slamming of a door, the shattering of a plate, and a rather insistent squawking that seemed distinctly avian in character. When he reached the fourth floor at approximately 7:45, the Count, in fact, discovered a genuine state of upheaval.

Nearly every door was open and every guest in the hall. Among those assembled were two French journalists, a Swiss diplomat, three Uzbek fur traders, a representative of the Roman Catholic Church, and a repatriated opera tenor with his family of five. Still in their pajamas, most of the members of this convention were waving their arms and expressing themselves emphatically—as three adult geese scurried between their legs, honking and beating their wings.

Several of the women were acting as terrorized as if they had been descended upon by Harpies. The wife of the tenor was cowering behind her husband's prodigious torso, and Kristina, one of the hotel's chambermaids, was backed against a wall, clutching an empty tray to her chest while at her feet lay a confusion of cutlery and kasha.

When the tenor's three sons displayed their fortitude by giving chase to the three different birds in three different directions, the ambassador from the Vatican advised the tenor on the proper behavior of children. The tenor, who spoke only a few words of Italian, informed the prelate (*fortissimo*) that he was not a man to be toyed with. The Swiss diplomat, who spoke both Russian and Italian fluently, exemplified his nation's reputation for neutrality by listening to both men with his mouth shut. When the prelate stepped forward to make his point more pontifically, one of the geese, which had been cornered by the tenor's eldest son, shot through his legs into his apartment—at which point, a young woman, who was decidedly not a representative of the Roman Catholic Church, came racing into the hallway wrapped only in a blue kimono.

By this point, the commotion had apparently awakened the guests on the fifth floor, as several came tromping down the stairs to see what all the fuss was about. At the forefront of this contingent was the American general—a no-nonsense figure who hailed from what is reportedly known as "The Great State of Texas." Having quickly assessed the situation, the general grabbed one of the geese by the throat. The speed with which he captured the bird gave those assembled a boost of confidence. Several even cheered him on. That is, until he wrapped his second hand around the goose's neck with the clear intention of snapping it. This elicited a scream from the young woman in the blue kimono, tears from the tenor's daughter, and a stern reproach from the Swiss diplomat. Stymied at the very instant of decisive action, the general expressed his exasperation with the fecklessness of civilians, walked into the prelate's apartment, and tossed the goose out the window.

Committed to restoring order, the general returned a moment later and deftly seized a second goose. But when he held up this bird to assure the assembly of his peaceful intent, the tie at his waist unraveled and his robe flew open, revealing a seasoned pair of olive green briefs, prompting the wife of the tenor to faint.

As the Count watched these proceedings from the landing, he became aware of a presence at his side. Turning, he found it was the general's aide-de-camp, a gregarious fellow who had become something of a fixture in the Shalyapin. Taking in the scene at a glance, the aide-de-camp issued a sigh of satisfaction and then remarked to no one in particular:

"How I love this hotel."

So, was the Count "aware" of what took place in the fourth-floor corridor at a quarter to eight? One might just as well ask if Noah was aware of the Flood, or Adam the Apple. Of course he was aware. No man on earth was *more* aware. But what aspect of his awareness could possibly warrant the interruption of a demitasse?

"I am familiar with this morning's events," confirmed the Count, "as I happened to be rounding the landing at the very moment they occurred."

"So you witnessed the mayhem *in person* . . . ?"

"Yes. I saw the antics unfolding firsthand. Even so, I am not entirely certain as to why I am here."

"You are in the dark, as it were."

"In point of fact, I am flummoxed. Mystified."

"Of course."

Following a moment of silence, the Bishop offered his most ecclesiastical smile. Then, as if it were perfectly normal to wander about an office in the middle of a conversation, he rose and crossed to the wall, where he gingerly straightened the portrait of Mr. Marx, who, having slipped on his hook, was admittedly undermining the ideological authority of the room.

Turning back, the Bishop continued.

"I can see why in describing these unfortunate events you chose to discard *mayhem* in favor of *antics*. For *antics* do seem to suggest a certain childishness . . ."

The Count considered this for a moment.

"You don't suspect the tenor's boys?"

"Hardly. After all, the geese had been locked in a cage in the pantry of the Boyarsky."

"Are you suggesting that Emile had something to do with it?"

The Bishop ignored the Count's question and resumed his place behind the desk.

"The Metropol Hotel," he informed the Count unnecessarily, "is host to some of the world's most eminent statesmen and prominent artistes. When they pass through our doors, they have the right to expect unparalleled comfort, unsurpassed service, and mornings free of mayhem. Needless to say," he concluded, reaching for his pen, "I shall get to the bottom of this."

"Well," replied the Count, rising from his chair, "if getting to the bottom is what is called for, I am sure there is no man better suited for the job."

A certain childishness, muttered the Count as he exited the executive suite. *Mornings of mayhem . . .*

Did the Bishop think him a fool? Did he imagine for one second that the Count couldn't see what he was angling at? What he was insinuating? That little Sofia was somehow involved?

Not only could the Count tell *exactly* what the Bishop was driving at, he could have countered with a few insinuations of his own—and in iambic pentameter, no less. But the notion of Sofia's involvement was so unfounded, so preposterous, so outrageous, it did not *deserve* a response.

Now, the Count could not deny that Sofia had a certain playful streak, just as any child of thirteen should. But she was no gadabout. No gadfly. No ne'er-do-well. In fact, as the Count was returning from the manager's office, there she was sitting in the lobby bent over some weighty textbook. It was a tableau familiar to any member of the Metropol staff. For hours on end she sat in that very chair memorizing capitals, conjugating verbs, and solving for x or y. With an equal sense of dedication she studied her sewing with Marina and her sauces with Emile. Why, ask anyone who knew Sofia to describe her and they would tell you that she was studious, shy, and well behaved; or in a word, *demure*.

As he mounted the stairs to the upper floors, the Count enumerated the relevant facts like a jurist: In eight years, Sofia had not thrown a single tantrum; every day she had brushed her teeth and headed off to school without a fuss; and whether it was time to bundle up, buckle down, or eat her peas, she had done so without complaint. Even that little game of her own invention, which she had grown so fond of playing, was founded on a quality of poise that was beyond her years.

Here is how it was played:

The two of them would be sitting somewhere in the hotel—say, reading in their study on a Sunday morning. At the stroke of twelve, the Count would set his book down and excuse himself to pay his weekly visit to the barber. After descending one flight in the belfry and traversing the hall to the main stair, he would continue his journey down five flights to the subfloor, where, having passed the flower shop and newsstand, he would enter the barbershop only to discover—Sofia reading quietly on the bench by the wall.

Naturally, this resulted in the calling of the Lord's name in vain and the dropping of whatever happened to be in one's hand (three books and a glass of wine so far this year).

Setting aside the fact that such a game could prove fatal to a man approaching his sixties, one had to marvel at the young lady's expertise. She could seemingly transport herself from one end of the hotel to the other in the blink of an eye. Over the years, she must have mastered all of the hotel's hidden hallways, back passages, and connecting doors, while developing an uncanny sense of timing. But what was particularly impressive was her otherworldly repose upon discovery. For no matter how far or how fast she had traveled, there was not a hint of exertion about her. Not a patter of the heart, not a panting of the breath, not a drop of perspiration on her brow. Nor would she emit a giggle or exhibit the slightest smirk. On the contrary. With an expression that was studious, shy, and well behaved, she would acknowledge the Count with a friendly nod, and looking back at her book, turn the page, demurely.

The notion that a child so composed would conspire to the releasing of geese was simply preposterous. One might as well accuse her of toppling the Tower of Babel or knocking the nose off the Sphinx.

True, she had been in the kitchen eating her supper when the chef du cuisine first received word that a certain Swiss diplomat, who had ordered the roast goose, had questioned the freshness of the poultry. And admittedly, she was devoted to her Uncle Emile. Even so, how was a thirteen-year-old girl to spirit three adult fowl to the fourth floor of an international hotel at seven in the morning without detection? The very idea, concluded the Count as he opened the door to his rooms, confounded one's reason, offended the laws of nature, and flew in the face of common—

"Iesu Christi!"

Sofia, who the moment before had been in the lobby, was seated at the Grand Duke's desk, leaning diligently over her tome.

"Oh, hello, Papa," she said without looking up.

. . .

"Apparently, it is no longer considered polite to look up from one's work when a gentleman enters a room."

Sofia turned in her chair.

"I'm sorry, Papa. I was immersed in my reading."

"Hmm. And what might that be?"

"It is an essay on cannibalism."

"An essay on cannibalism!"

"By Michel de Montaigne."

"Ah. Yes. Well. That's time well spent, I'm sure," conceded the Count.

But as he headed toward the study, he thought, *Michel de Montaigne . . . ?* Then he shot a glance at the base of their bureau.

. . .

"Is that *Anna Karenina*?"

Sofia followed his gaze.

"Yes, I believe it is."

"But what is she doing down there?"

"She was the closest in thickness to Montaigne."

"The closest in thickness!"

"Is something wrong?"

. . .

"All I can say is that Anna Karenina would never have put *you* under a bureau just because you happened to be as thick as Montaigne."

"The very idea is preposterous," the Count was saying. "How is a thirteen-year-old girl to spirit three fully grown geese up two flights of stairs without the slightest detection? Besides, I ask you: Is such behavior even in her character?"

"Certainly not," said Emile.

"No, not in the least," agreed Andrey.

The three men shook their heads in shared indignation.

One of the advantages of working together for many years is that the daily rigmarole can be dispensed with quickly, leaving ample time for discussions of weightier concerns—such as rheumatism, the inadequacy of public transit, and the petty behavior of the inexplicably promoted. After two decades, the members of the Triumvirate knew a thing or two about the small-minded men who sat behind stacks of paper, and the so-called gourmands from Geneva who couldn't tell a goose from a grouse.

"It's outrageous," said the Count.

"Unquestionably."

"And to summon me half an hour before our daily meeting, at which there is never a shortage of important matters to discuss."

"Quite so," agreed Andrey. "Which reminds me, Alexander . . ."

"Yes?"

"Before we open tonight, could you have someone sweep out the dumbwaiter?"

"Certainly. Is it a mess?"

"I'm afraid so. It has somehow become littered with feathers. . . ."

In saying this, Andrey used one of his legendary fingers to scratch his upper lip while Emile pretended to sip at his tea. And the Count? He opened his mouth with every intention of making the perfect rejoinder—the sort of remark that having cut one man to the quick would be quoted by others for years to come.

But there was a knock at the door, and young Ilya entered with his wooden spoon.

Over the course of the Great Patriotic War, Emile had lost the seasoned members of his crew one by one, even the whistling Stanislav. With every able-bodied man eventually in the army, he had been forced to staff his kitchen with adolescents. Thus, Ilya, who had been hired in 1943, had been promoted on the basis of seniority to sous-chef in 1945, at the ripe old age of nineteen. As a reflection of qualified confidence, Emile had bestowed upon him a spoon in place of a knife.

"Well?" said Emile, looking up with impatience.

In response, Ilya hesitated.

Emile looked to the other members of the Triumvirate and rolled his eyes, as much as to say: *You see what I must put up with?* Then he turned back to his apprentice.

"As anyone can see, we are men with business to attend to. But apparently, you have something of such importance that you feel the need to interrupt. Well then, out with it—before we expire from anticipation."

The young man opened his mouth, but then rather than explain himself, he simply pointed his spoon toward the kitchen. Following the direction of the utensil, the members of the Triumvirate looked through the office window and there, near the door to the back stair, stood an unfortunate-looking soul in a ragged winter coat. At the sight of him, Emile grew crimson.

"Who let him in here?"

"I did, sir."

Emile stood so abruptly he nearly knocked over his chair. Then, just as a commander will tear the epaulettes from the shoulders of an errant officer, Emile grabbed the spoon from Ilya's hand.

"So, you're the Commissar of Nincompoops now, is that it? Eh? When I had my back turned, you were promoted to the General Secretary of Bunglers?"

The young man took a step back.

"No, sir. I have not been promoted."

Emile smacked the table with the spoon, nearly cracking it in two.

"Of course you haven't! How often have I told you not to let beggars in the kitchen? Don't you see that if you give him a crust of bread today, there will be five of his friends here tomorrow, and fifty the day after that?"

"Yes, sir, but . . . but . . ."

"But but but what?"

"He didn't ask for food."

"Eh?"

The young man pointed to the Count.

"He asked for Alexander Ilyich."

Andrey and Emile both looked to their colleague in surprise. The Count in turn looked through the window at the beggar. Then without saying a word, he rose from his chair, exited the office, and embraced this boon companion whom he had not seen in eight long years.

Though Andrey and Emile had never met the stranger, as soon as they heard his name they knew exactly who he was: the one who had lived with the Count above the cobbler's shop; the one who had paced a thousand miles in increments of fifteen feet; the lover of Mayakovsky and Mandelstam who, like so many others, had been tried and sentenced in the name of Article 58.

"Why don't you make yourselves comfortable," suggested Andrey with a gesture of his hand. "You can use Emile's office."

"Yes," agreed Emile. "By all means. My office."

With his impeccable instincts, Andrey led Mishka to the chair with its back to the kitchen while Emile placed bread and salt on the table—that ancient Russian symbol of hospitality. A moment later he returned with a plate of potatoes and cutlets of veal. Then the chef and maître d' excused themselves, closing the door so that the two old friends could speak undisturbed.

Mishka looked at the table.

"Bread and salt," he said with a smile.

As the Count looked across at Mishka, he was moved by two contrary currents of emotion. On the one hand, there was that special joy of seeing a friend from youth unexpectedly—a welcome event no matter when or where. But at the same time, the Count was confronted by the irrefutable facts of Mishka's appearance. Thirty pounds lighter, dressed in a threadbare coat, and dragging one leg behind him, it was no wonder that Emile had mistaken him for a beggar. Naturally, the Count had watched in recent years as age began to take its toll on the Triumvirate. He had noticed the occasional tremor in Andrey's left hand and the creeping deafness in Emile's right ear. He had noticed the graying of the former's hair and the thinning of the latter's. But with Mishka, here were not simply the ravages of time. Here were the marks of one man upon another, of an era upon its offspring.

Perhaps most striking was Mishka's smile. In their youth, Mishka had been almost earnest to a fault and never spoke with irony. Yet when he said "bread and salt" he wore the smile of the sarcast.

"It is so good to see you, Mishka," the Count said after a moment. "I can't tell you how relieved I was when you sent word of your release. When did you return to Moscow?"

"I haven't," his friend replied with his new smile.

Upon the dutiful completion of his eight years, Mishka explained, he had been rewarded with a Minus Six. To visit Moscow, he had borrowed a passport from a sympathetic soul with a passing likeness.

"Is that wise?" the Count asked with concern.

Mishka shrugged.

"I arrived this morning from Yavas by train. I'll be returning to Yavas later tonight."

"Yavas . . . Where is that?"

"Somewhere between where the wheat is grown and the bread is eaten."

"Are you teaching . . . ?" the Count asked tentatively.

"No," Mishka said with a shake of the head. "We are not encouraged to teach. But then, we are not encouraged to read or write. We are hardly encouraged to eat."

So it was that Mishka began to describe his life in Yavas; and as he did so, he used the first person plural so often that the Count assumed he must have moved there with a fellow inmate from the camps. But slowly, it became clear that in saying "we" Mishka had no one person in mind. For Mishka, "we" encompassed *all* his fellow prisoners—and not simply those he had known in Arkhangelsk. It encompassed the million or more who had toiled on the Solovetsky Islands or in Sevvostlag or on the White Sea Canal, whether they had toiled there in the twenties, or the thirties, or toiled there still.*

---

*Stripped of their names and family ties, of their professions and possessions, herded together in hunger and hardship, the residents of the Gulag—the *zeks*—became indistinguishable from one another. That, of course, was part of the

Mishka was silent.

"It is funny what comes to one at night," he said after a moment. "After dropping our shovels and trudging to the barracks, we would swallow our gruel and pull our blankets to our chins eager for sleep. But inevitably some unexpected thought would come, some uninvited memory that wanted to be sized up, measured, and weighed. And many was the night I found myself thinking of that German you encountered in the bar—the one who claimed that vodka was Russia's only contribution to the West and who challenged anyone to name three more."

"I remember it well. I borrowed your observation that Tolstoy and Chekhov were the bookends of narrative, invoked Tchaikovsky, and then ordered the brute a serving of caviar."

"That's it."

Mishka shook his head and then looked at the Count with his smile.

"One night some years ago, I thought of another, Sasha."

"A fifth contribution?"

"Yes, a fifth contribution: The burning of Moscow."

The Count was taken aback.

"You mean in 1812?"

Mishka nodded.

"Can you imagine the expression on Napoleon's face when he was roused at two in the morning and stepped from his brand-new bedroom in the Kremlin only to find that the city he'd claimed just hours before had been set on fire by its citizens?" Mishka gave a quiet laugh. "Yes, the burning of Moscow was *especially* Russian, my friend. Of that there can be no doubt. Because it was not a discrete event; it was the *form* of an

---

point. Not content with the toll exacted by means of incarceration and forced labor in inhospitable climes, the supreme authorities sought to *efface* the Enemies of the People.

But an unanticipated consequence of this strategy was the creation of a new polis. Having been stripped of their identities, henceforth the *zeks*—though millions in number—would move in perfect unison, sharing in their privations as well as their will to persist. Henceforth, they would know each other whenever and wherever they met. They would make room for each other under their roofs and at their tables, addressing each other as *brother* and *sister* and *friend*; but never, ever, under any circumstance, as *comrade*.

event. One example plucked from a history of thousands. For as a people, we Russians have proven unusually adept at destroying that which we have created."

Perhaps because of his limp, Mishka no longer got up to pace the room; but the Count could see that he was pacing it with his eyes.

"Every country has its grand canvas, Sasha—the so-called masterpiece that hangs in a hallowed hall and sums up the national identity for generations to come. For the French it is Delacroix's *Liberty Leading the People*; for the Dutch, Rembrandt's *Night Watch*; for the Americans, *Washington Crossing the Delaware*; and for us Russians? It is a pair of twins: Nikolai Ge's *Peter the Great Interrogating Alexei* and Ilya Repin's *Ivan the Terrible and His Son*. For decades, these two paintings have been revered by our public, praised by our critics, and sketched by our diligent students of the arts. And yet, what do they depict? In one, our most enlightened Tsar studies his oldest son with suspicion, on the verge of condemning him to death; while in the other, unflinching Ivan cradles the body of *his* eldest, having already exacted the supreme measure with a swing of the scepter to the head.

"Our churches, known the world over for their idiosyncratic beauty, for their brightly colored spires and improbable cupolas, we raze one by one. We topple the statues of old heroes and strip their names from the streets, as if they had been figments of our imagination. Our poets we either silence, or wait patiently for them to silence themselves."

Mishka picked up his fork, stuck it in the untouched veal, and raised it in the air.

"Do you know that back in '30, when they announced the mandatory collectivization of farming, half our peasants slaughtered their own livestock rather than give them up to the cooperatives? Fourteen million head of cattle left to the buzzards and flies."

He gently returned the cut of meat to its plate, as if in a show of respect.

"How can we understand this, Sasha? What is it about a nation that would foster a willingness in its people to destroy their own artworks, ravage their own cities, and kill their own progeny without compunction? To foreigners it must seem shocking. It must seem as if we Russians have such a brutish indifference that nothing, not even the fruit of our loins, is viewed as sacrosanct. And how that notion pained me. How it unsettled me. Exhausted as I was, the very thought of it could keep me tossing until dawn.

"Then one night, he came to me in a dream, Sasha: Mayakovsky himself. He quoted some lines of verse—beautiful, haunting lines that I had never heard before—about the bark of a birch tree glinting in the winter sun. Then he loaded his revolver with an exclamation point and put the barrel to his chest. When I awoke, I suddenly understood that this propensity for self-destruction was not an abomination, not something to be ashamed of or abhorred; it was our greatest strength. We turn the gun on ourselves not because we are more indifferent and less cultured than the British, or the French, or the Italians. On the contrary. We are prepared to destroy that which we have created because we believe more than any of them in the power of the picture, the poem, the prayer, or the person."

Mishka shook his head.

"Mark my words, my friend: We have not burned Moscow to the ground for the last time."

As in the past, Mishka talked with a fevered intensity, almost as if he were making his points to himself. But once he had spoken his piece, he looked across the table and saw the distressed expression on the Count's face. Then he suddenly laughed in a heartfelt manner, without bitterness or irony, and reached across the table to squeeze his old friend's forearm.

"I see that I have unsettled you, Sasha, with my talk of revolvers. But don't worry. I am not through yet. I still have something to attend to. In fact, that is why I slipped into the city: to visit the library for a little project that I am working on. . . ."

With a sense of relief, the Count recognized the old spark in Mishka's eye—the one that inevitably flashed before he threw himself headlong into a scrape.

"Is it a work of poetry?" asked the Count.

"Poetry? Yes, in a manner of speaking, I suppose it is. . . . But it is also something more fundamental. Something that can be built upon. I'm not ready to share it just yet; but when I am, you shall be the first."

By the time they came out of the office and the Count led Mishka to the back stair, the kitchen was in full swing. On the counter were onions being minced, beets being sliced, hens being plucked. From the stove where six pots simmered, Emile signaled to the Count that he should wait a moment. After wiping his hands on his apron, he came to the door with some food wrapped in brown paper.

"A little something for your journey, Mikhail Fyodorovich."

Mishka looked taken aback by the offering, and for a moment the Count thought his friend was going to refuse it on principle. But Mishka thanked the chef and took the parcel in hand.

Andrey was there too now, to express his pleasure at finally meeting Mishka and to wish him well.

Having returned the sentiments, Mishka opened the door to the stairwell, but then paused. Having taken a moment to look over the kitchen with all of its activity and abundance, to look from gentle Andrey to heartfelt Emile, he turned to the Count.

"Who would have imagined," he said, "when you were sentenced to life in the Metropol all those years ago, that you had just become the luckiest man in all of Russia."

At 7:30 that evening, when the Count entered the Yellow Room, Osip tamped out his cigarette and leapt from his chair.

"Ah! Here you are, Alexander. I thought a quick trip to San Franchesko was in order. We haven't been back in a year. Get the lights, will you?"

As Osip hurried to the back of the room, the Count absently took his seat at the table for two and put his napkin in his lap.

. . .

"Alexander . . ."

The Count looked back.

"Yes?"

"The lights."

"Oh. My apologies."

The Count rose, switched off the lights, and lingered by the wall.

. . .

"Are you going to take your seat again?" asked Osip.

"Ah, yes. Of course."

The Count returned to the table and sat in Osip's chair.

. . .

"Is everything all right, my friend? You do not seem yourself. . . ."

"No, no," assured the Count with a smile. "Everything is excellent. Please proceed."

Osip waited for a moment to be sure, then he threw the switch and hurried back to the table as the grand old shadows began to flicker on the dining room wall.

Two months after what Osip liked to refer to as "The de Tocqueville Affair," he had appeared in the Yellow Room with a projector and an uncensored print of *A Day at the Races*. From that night onward, the two men left the tomes of history on the bookshelves where they belonged and advanced their studies of America through the medium of film.

Osip Ivanovich had actually mastered the English language right down to the past perfect progressive as early as 1939. But American movies still deserved their careful consideration, he argued, not simply as windows into Western culture, but as unprecedented mechanisms of class repression. For with cinema, the Yanks had apparently discovered how to placate the entire working class at the cost of a nickel a week.

"Just look at their Depression," he said. "From beginning to end it lasted ten years. An entire decade in which the Proletariat was left to fend for itself, scrounging in alleys and begging at chapel doors. If ever there had been a time for the American worker to cast off the yoke, surely that was it. But did they join their brothers-in-arms? Did they shoulder their axes and splinter the doors of the mansions? Not even for an afternoon. Instead, they shuffled to the nearest movie house, where the latest fantasy was dangled before them like a pocket watch at the end of a chain. Yes, Alexander, it behooves us to study this phenomenon with the utmost diligence and care."

So study it they did.

And the Count could confirm that Osip approached the task with the utmost diligence and care, for when a movie was playing he could hardly sit still. During the westerns, when a fight broke out in a saloon, he would clench his fists, fend off a blow, give a left to the gut, and an upper-cut to the jaw. When Fyodor Astaire danced with Gingyr Rogers, his fingers would open wide and flutter about his waist while his feet shuf-fled back and forth on the carpet. And when Bela Lugosi emerged from the shadows, Osip leapt from his seat and nearly fell to the floor. Then, as the credits rolled, he would shake his head with an expression of moral disappointment.

"Shameful," he would say.

"Scandalous."

"Insidious!"

Like the seasoned scientist, Osip would coolly dissect whatever they had just observed. The musicals were "pastries designed to placate the impoverished with daydreams of unattainable bliss." The horror movies were "sleights of hand in which the fears of the workingman have been displaced by those of pretty girls." The vaudevillian comedies were "prepos-terous narcotics." And the westerns? They were the most devious propa-ganda of all: fables in which evil is represented by collectives who rustle and rob; while virtue is a lone individual who risks his life to defend the sanctity of someone else's private property. In sum? "Hollywood is the single most dangerous force in the history of class struggle."

Or so Osip argued, until he discovered the genre of American mov-ies that would come to be known as *film noir*. With rapt attention he watched the likes of *This Gun for Hire*, *Shadow of a Doubt*, and *Double Indemnity*.

"What is this?" he would ask of no one in particular. "Who is making these movies? Under what auspices?"

From one to the next, they seemed to depict an America in which corruption and cruelty lounged on the couch; in which justice was a beg-gar and kindness a fool; in which loyalties were fashioned from paper, and self-interest was fashioned from steel. In other words, they provided an unflinching portrayal of Capitalism as it actually was.

"How did this happen, Alexander? Why do they allow these movies to be made? Do they not realize they are hammering a wedge beneath their own foundation stones?"

But no single star of the genre captivated Osip more than Humphrey

Bogart. With the exception of *Casablanca* (which Osip viewed as a woman's movie), they had watched all of Bogart's films at least twice. Whether in *The Petrified Forest*, *To Have and Have Not*, or, especially, *The Maltese Falcon*, Osip appreciated the actor's hardened looks, his sardonic remarks, his general lack of sentiment. "You notice how in the first act he always seems so removed and indifferent; but once his indignation is roused, Alexander, there is no one more willing to do what is necessary—to act clear-eyed, quick, and without compunction. Here truly is a Man of Intent."

In the Yellow Room, Osip took two mouthfuls of Emile's braised veal with caviar sauce, a gulp of Georgian wine, and looked up just in time to see the image of the Golden Gate Bridge.

In the minutes that followed, once again the services of Sam Spade were enlisted by the alluring, if somewhat mysterious, Miss Wonderly. Once again, Spade's partner was gunned down in an alley just hours before Floyd Thursby met a similar fate. And once again Joel Cairo, the Fat Man, and Brigid O'Shaughnessy, having surreptitiously joined forces, drugged Spade's whiskey and headed for the wharf, their elusive quest finally within reach. But even as Spade was nursing his head, a stranger in a black coat and hat stumbled into his office, dropped a bundle to the floor, and collapsed dead on the couch!

"Do you think Russians are particularly brutish, Osip?" asked the Count.

"What's that?" Osip whispered, as if there were others in the audience whom he didn't want to disturb.

"Do you think we are essentially more brutish than the French, or the English, or these Americans?"

"Alexander," Osip hissed (as Spade was washing the stranger's blood from his hands). "What on earth are you talking about?"

"I mean, do you think we are more apt than others to destroy that which we have created?"

Osip, who had not yet torn his eyes from the screen, now turned to stare at the Count in disbelief. Then he abruptly rose, stomped to the projector, and froze the film at the very moment that Spade, having placed the roughly wrapped bundle on his desk, was taking his penknife from his pocket.

"Is it possible that you don't see what is happening?" he demanded while pointing at the screen. "Having traveled from the Orient to the docks of San Franchesko, Captain Jacoby has been shot five times. He has jumped from a burning ship, stumbled through the city, and used his final breaths to bring comrade Spadsky this mysterious package wrapped in paper and bound in string. And you choose this moment to engage in metaphysics!"

The Count, who had turned around, was holding up a hand to cut the glare from the projection.

"But, Osip," he said, "we have watched him open the bundle on at least three occasions."

"What difference does that make? You have read *Anna Karenina* at least ten times, but I'd wager you still cry when she throws herself under the train."

"That's something else altogether."

"Is it?"

There was silence. Then with an expression of exasperation, Osip turned off the projector. He flicked on the lights and returned to the table.

"All right, my friend. I can see that you are vexed by something. Let's see if we can make sense of it, so we can get on with our studies."

Thus, the Count described for Osip the conversation he'd had with Mishka. Or rather, he relayed Mishka's views on the burning of Moscow, and the toppling of statues, and the silencing of poets, and the slaughter of fourteen million head of cattle.

Osip, having already aired his frustrations, now listened to the Count attentively, occasionally nodding his head at Mishka's various points.

"All right," he said, once the Count had finished. "So, what is it exactly that is bothering you, Alexander? Does your friend's assertion shock you? Does it offend your sensibilities? I understand that you are worried about his state of mind; but isn't it possible that he is right in his opinions while being wrong in his sentiments?"

"What do you mean?"

"It is like the Maltese Falcon."

"Osip. Please."

"No, I am quite serious. What is the black bird if not a symbol of Western heritage itself? A sculpture fashioned by knights of the Crusades from gold and jewels as tribute to a king, it is an emblem of the church and the monarchies—those rapacious institutions that have served as the foundation for all of Europe's art and ideas. Well, who is to say that their love of that heritage isn't as misguided as the Fat Man's for his falcon? Perhaps that is *exactly* what must be swept aside before their people can hope to progress."

His tone grew softer.

"The Bolsheviks are not Visigoths, Alexander. We are not the barbarian hordes descending upon Rome and destroying all that is fine out of ignorance and envy. It is the opposite. In 1916, Russia was a barbarian state. It was the most illiterate nation in Europe, with the majority of its population living in modified serfdom: tilling the fields with wooden plows, beating their wives by candlelight, collapsing on their benches drunk with vodka, and then waking at dawn to humble themselves before their icons. That is, living exactly as their forefathers had lived five hundred years before. Is it not possible that our reverence for all the statues and cathedrals and ancient institutions was precisely what was holding us back?"

Osip paused, taking a moment to refill their glasses with wine.

"But where do we stand now? How far have we come? By marrying American tempo with Soviet aims, we are on the verge of *universal* literacy. Russia's long-suffering women, our second serfdom, have been elevated to the status of equals. We have built whole new cities and our industrial production outpaces that of most of Europe."

"But at what cost?"

Osip slapped the table.

"At the greatest cost! But do you think the achievements of the Americans—envied the world over—came without a cost? Just ask their African brothers. And do you think the engineers who designed their illustrious skyscrapers or built their highways hesitated for one moment to level the lovely little neighborhoods that stood in their way? I guarantee you, Alexander, they laid the dynamite and pushed the plungers themselves. As I've said to you before, we and the Americans will lead the rest of this century because we are the only nations who have learned to brush the past aside instead of bowing before it. But where they have done so in service of their beloved individualism, we are attempting to do so in service of the common good."

When he parted company with Osip at ten, rather than climbing the stairs to the sixth floor, the Count headed to the Shalyapin in the hopes of finding it empty. But as he entered the bar, he discovered a raucous group composed of journalists, members of the diplomatic corps, and two of the young hostesses in their little black dresses—and at the center of the commotion, for the third night in a row, was the American general's aide-de-camp. Hunched over with his arms outstretched, shifting back and forth on the balls of his feet, he was relaying his tale like a wrestler on the mat.

". . . Sidestepping the Monsignor, old Porterhouse slowly advanced upon the second goose, waiting for his prey to look him in the eye. That's the secret, you see: the looking in the eye. That's the moment Porterhouse lets his adversaries imagine for a second that they are his equals. Having taken two steps to the left, Porterhouse suddenly took three to the right. Thrown off balance, the goose met the old boy's gaze—and that's when Porterhouse leapt!"

The aide-de-camp leapt.

The two hostesses shrieked.

Then giggled.

When the aide-de-camp stood back to his full height, he was holding a pineapple. With one hand around its throat and the other under its tail, the captain displayed the fruit for all to see, just as the general had displayed the second goose.

"And it was at this fateful juncture that the good general's sash unsashed and his robe disrobed, revealing a regulation pair of U.S. Army–issue briefs—at the sight of which, Madame Veloshki fainted."

As the audience applauded, the aide-de-camp gave a bow. Then he set the pineapple gently on the bar and lifted his drink.

"Madame Veloshki's response seems perfectly understandable," said one of the journalists. "But what did *you* do when you saw the old man's briefs?"

"What did I do?" exclaimed the aide-de-camp. "Why, I saluted them, of course."

As the others laughed, he emptied his drink.

"Now, gentlemen, I suggest we head out into the night. I can tell you from personal experience that over at the National can be heard the sorriest samba in the Northern Hemisphere. The drummer, who is blind in one eye, can't hit his cymbals. And the bandleader hasn't the slightest sense of a Latin tempo. The closest he has come to South America is when he fell down a flight of mahogany stairs. But he has excellent intentions and a toupee that has descended from heaven."

With that, the motley assembly stumbled into the night, leaving the Count to approach the bar in relative peace and quiet.

"Good evening, Audrius."

"Good evening, Count Rostov. What is your pleasure?"

"A glass of Armagnac, perhaps."

A moment later, as the Count gave the brandy in his snifter a swirl, he found himself smiling at the aide-de-camp's portrayal—which in turn led him to reflect on the personality of Americans in general. In his persuasive fashion, Osip had argued that during the Depression, Hollywood had undermined the inevitable forces of revolution by means of its elaborate chicanery. But the Count wondered if Osip didn't have his analysis upside down. Certainly, it seemed true that glittering musicals and slapstick comedies had flourished during the 1930s in America. But so too had jazz and skyscrapers. Were these also narcotics designed to put a restless nation to sleep? Or were they signs of a native spirit so irrepressible that even a Depression couldn't squelch it?

As the Count gave another swirl of his brandy, a customer sat three stools to his left. To the Count's surprise, it was the aide-de-camp.

Ever attentive, Audrius leaned with his forearm on the bar. "Welcome back, Captain."

"Thank you, Audrius."

"What can I do for you?"

"Same as before, I suppose."

As Audrius turned away to prepare the drink, the captain drummed his hands on the bar and looked idly about. When he met the Count's gaze, he gave a nod and a friendly smile.

"You're not headed for the National?" the Count couldn't help but ask.

"It seems my friends were in such a hurry to accompany me that they left me behind," the American replied.

The Count gave a sympathetic smile. "I'm sorry to hear it."

"No. Please don't be. I'm quite fond of being left behind. It always gives me a whole new perspective on wherever it was I thought I was leaving. Besides, I'm off first thing in the morning to head home for a spell, so it's probably for the best."

He extended his hand to the Count.

"Richard Vanderwhile."

"Alexander Rostov."

The captain gave another friendly nod and then, having looked away, suddenly looked back.

"Weren't you my waiter last night at the Boyarsky?"

"Yes, I was."

The captain let out a sigh of relief.

"Thank God. Otherwise, I would have had to cancel my drink."

As if on cue, Audrius placed it on the bar. The captain took a sip and gave another sigh, this one of satisfaction. Then he studied the Count for a moment.

"Are you Russian?"

"To the core."

"Well then, let me say at the outset that I am positively enamored with your country. I love your funny alphabet and those little pastries stuffed with meat. But your nation's notion of a cocktail is rather unnerving. . . ."

"How so?"

The captain pointed discreetly down the bar to where a bushy-eyebrowed apparatchik was chatting with a young brunette. Both of them were holding drinks in a striking shade of magenta.

"I gather from Audrius that that concoction contains ten different ingredients. In addition to vodka, rum, brandy, and grenadine, it boasts an extraction of rose, a dash of bitters, and a melted lollipop. But a cocktail is not meant to be a mélange. It is not a potpourri or an Easter parade. At its best, a cocktail should be crisp, elegant, sincere—and limited to two ingredients."

"Just two?"

"Yes. But they must be two ingredients that complement each other; that laugh at each other's jokes and make allowances for each other's faults; and that never shout over each other in conversation. Like gin and tonic," he said, pointing to his drink. "Or bourbon and water . . . Or whiskey and soda . . ." Shaking his head, he raised his glass and drank from it. "Excuse me for expounding."

"That's quite all right."

The captain nodded in gratitude, but then after a moment inquired, "Do you mind if I make an observation? I mean of the personal sort."

"Not at all," said the Count.

The captain slid his drink down the bar and moved a stool closer.

"You seem like something is weighing on your mind. I mean, you set that brandy in motion about half an hour ago. If you're not careful, the vortex you've created will drill a hole right through the floor and we'll all end up in the basement."

The Count set the snifter down with a laugh.

"I suppose you're right. Something must be weighing on my mind."

"Well then," said Richard, gesturing to the empty bar, "you have come to the right place. Since days of old, well-mannered men have assembled in watering holes such as this one in order to unburden themselves in the company of sympathetic souls."

"Or strangers?"

The captain raised a finger in the air.

"There are no more sympathetic souls *than* strangers. So, what say we skip the preambling. Is it women? Money? Writer's block?"

The Count laughed again; and then like other well-mannered men since days of old, he unburdened himself to this sympathetic soul. He described Mishka and his notion that Russians were somehow unusually adept at destroying that which they have created. Then he described Osip and his notion that Mishka was perfectly right, but that the destruction of monuments and masterpieces was essential to the progress of a nation.

"Oh, so that's it," said the captain, as if this would have been his fourth guess.

"Yes. But what conclusions would you draw from it all?" asked the Count.

"What conclusions?"

Richard took a drink.

"I think that both of your friends are very sharp. I mean it takes a good bit of dexterity to pull a thread out of the fabric all in one piece. But I can't help feeling that they're missing something. . . ."

He drummed his fingers on the bar as he tried to formulate his thoughts.

"I understand that there's a little history of dismantling here in Russia; and that the razing of a beautiful old building is bound to engender a little sorrow for what's gone and some excitement for what's to come. But when all is said and done, I can't help suspecting that grand things persist.

"Take that fellow Socrates. Two thousand years ago, he wandered around the marketplace sharing his thoughts with whomever he bumped into; and he wouldn't even take the time to write them down. Then, in something of a fix, he punched his own ticket; pulled his own plug; collapsed his own umbrella. Adios. Adieu. Finis.

"Time marched on, as it will. The Romans took over. Then the barbarians. And then we threw the whole Middle Ages at him. Hundreds of years of plagues and poisonings and the burning of books. And somehow, after all of that, the grand things this fellow happened to say in the marketplace are still with us.

"I guess the point I'm trying to make is that as a species we're just no good at writing obituaries. We don't know how a man or his achievements will be perceived three generations from now, any more than we know what his great-great-grandchildren will be having for breakfast on a Tuesday in March. Because when Fate hands something down to posterity, it does so behind its back."

They were both silent for a moment. Then the captain emptied his glass and pointed a finger at the Count's brandy.

"Tell me, though, is that thing pulling its weight?"

When the Count left the Shalyapin an hour later (having joined Captain Vanderwhile for two rounds of Audrius's magenta-colored concoction), he was surprised to see Sofia still reading in the lobby. Catching her eye, he gave a little wave and she gave a little wave back before returning to her book, demurely. . . .

It took all of the Count's presence of mind to cross the lobby at a stroll. With the undeniable appearance of a man at ease, he carefully mounted the stairs and slowly began to ascend. But the moment he turned the corner, he broke into a sprint.

As he vaulted upward, he could barely contain his sense of glee. The hidden genius of Sofia's game had always been that she chose when it was played. Naturally, she would wait for those moments when he was distracted or off his guard, such that the game was generally over before he even knew it had begun. But tonight, things were going to be different—because by the casualness of Sofia's wave, the Count could tell the game was afoot.

I've got her now, he thought as he passed the second floor with a sinister little laugh. But as he turned the landing on the third floor, he was forced to acknowledge a second advantage that Sofia had in this game: her youth. For without question, his pace had begun to slow considerably. If his shortness of breath was any indication, he would be crawling by the time he reached the sixth floor—assuming he reached it alive. To be on the safe side, when he got to the fifth floor he slowed his pace to a purposeful walk.

Opening the door to the belfry, he paused to listen. Looking down the stairs, he couldn't see a thing. Could she have already flown past? Impossible. She hadn't the time. Still, on the off chance that she had transported herself by means of witchcraft, the Count climbed the final flight on the tips of his toes and when he opened their door, he did so with an affect of indifference—only to find that, in fact, the room was empty.

Rubbing his hands together, he wondered: *Where should I place myself?* He considered climbing into bed and acting like he was asleep, but he wanted to see the expression on her face. So he sat in the desk chair, tilted it back on two legs, and grabbed the closest book at hand, which happened to be Monsieur Montaigne. Opening the tome at random, he landed on the essay "Of the Education of Children."

"Just so," he said with a wily smile. Then he adopted an expression of perfect erudition as he pretended to read.

But after five minutes, she hadn't appeared.

"Ah, well. I must have been mistaken," he was conceding with some disappointment, when the door flung open. But it wasn't Sofia.

It was one of the chambermaids. In a state of distress.

"Ilana. What is it?"

"It's Sofia! She has fallen!"

The Count leapt from his chair.

"Fallen! Where?"

"In the service stair."

The Count brushed past the chambermaid and bolted down the belfry. After two flights of empty stairs, a voice in some corner of his mind began to reason that Ilana must have been mistaken; but as he rounded the third-floor landing, there Sofia was—splayed across the steps, her eyes closed, her hair matted with blood.

"Oh, my God."

The Count fell to his knees.

"Sofia . . ."

She didn't respond.

Gently raising her head, the Count could see the gash above her brow. Her skull did not appear compromised, but she was bleeding and unconscious.

Ilana was behind him now, in tears.

"I will go for a doctor," she said.

But it was after eleven. Who could say how long that would take?

The Count slid his arms under Sofia's neck and knees, lifted her off the steps, and carried her down the remaining flights. At the ground floor, he pushed the door open with his shoulder and cut through the lobby. Only in the most remote sense was he aware of a middle-aged couple waiting for the elevator; of Vasily at his desk; of voices in the bar. And suddenly, he found himself on the steps of the Metropol in the warm summer air—for the first time in over twenty years.

Rodion, the night doorman, looked at the Count in shock.

"A taxi," the Count said. "I need a taxi."

Over the doorman's shoulder, he could see four of them parked fifty feet from the entrance, waiting for the last of the Shalyapin's customers. Two drivers at the front of the line were smoking and chatting.

Before Rodion could raise his whistle to his lips, the Count was running toward them.

When the drivers noted the Count's approach, the expression on one's face was a knowing smirk and on the other's a look of condemnation—having both concluded that the gentleman had a drunken girl in his arms. But they stood to attention when they saw the blood on her face.

"My daughter," said the Count.

"Here," said one of the drivers, throwing his cigarette on the ground and running to open the back door of the cab.

"To St. Cyprian's," said the Count.

"St. Cyprian's . . . ?"

"As fast as you can."

Putting the car in gear, the driver pulled onto Theatre Square and headed north as the Count, pressing a folded handkerchief against Sofia's wound with one hand and combing her hair with the other, murmured assurances that went unheard—while the streets of the city raced past unregarded.

In a matter of minutes, the cab came to a stop.

"We're here," said the driver. He got out and opened the back door.

The Count carefully slipped out with Sofia in his arms then suddenly stopped. "I have no money," he said.

"What money! For God's sake, go."

The Count crossed the curb and rushed toward the hospital, but even as he passed through its doors, he knew that he had made a terrible mistake. In the entry hall, there were grown men sleeping on benches, like refugees in a railway station. Hallway lights flickered as if powered by a faulty generator, and in the air was the smell of ammonia and cigarette smoke. When the Count had been a young man, St. Cyprian's had been among the finest hospitals in the city. But that was thirty years ago. By now, the Bolsheviks had presumably built new hospitals—modern, bright, and clean—and this old facility had been left behind as some sort of clinic for veterans, the homeless, and the otherwise forsaken.

Sidestepping a man who appeared to be asleep on his feet, the Count approached a desk where a young nurse was reading.

"It is my daughter," he said. "She has been injured."

Looking up, the nurse dropped her magazine. She disappeared

through a door. After what seemed like an eternity, she returned with a young man in the white jacket of an internist. The Count held Sofia out while pulling back the blood-soaked handkerchief to show the wound. The internist ran his hand across his mouth.

"This girl should be seen by a surgeon," he said.

"Is there one here?"

"What? No, of course not." He looked at a clock on the wall. "At six, perhaps."

"At six? Surely, she needs attention now. You must do something."

The internist rubbed his hand across his mouth again and then turned to the nurse.

"Find Dr. Kraznakov. Have him report to Surgery Four."

As the nurse disappeared again, the internist wheeled over a gurney.

"Lay her here and come with me."

With the Count at his side, the internist pushed Sofia down a hall and into an elevator. Once on the third floor, they passed through a pair of swinging doors into a long hallway in which there were two other gurneys, each with a sleeping patient.

"In there."

The Count pushed open the door and the internist wheeled Sofia into Surgery Four. It was a cold room, tiled from floor to ceiling. In one corner, the tiles had begun falling from the plaster. There was a surgical table, craning lights, and a standing tray. After some minutes, the door opened and an ill-shaven physician entered with the young nurse. He looked as if he had just been wakened.

"What is it?" he said in a weary voice.

"A young girl with a head injury, Dr. Kraznakov."

"All right, all right," he said. Then waving a hand at the Count, he added: "No visitors in the surgery."

The internist took the Count by the elbow.

"Wait a second," the Count said. "Is this man capable?"

Looking at the Count, Kraznakov grew red in the face. "What did he say?"

The Count continued to address the young internist.

"You said she needed to be seen by a surgeon. Is this man a surgeon?"

"Get him out of here, I tell you!" shouted Kraznakov.

But the door to the surgery swung open again and a tall man in his late forties entered in the company of a primly dressed associate.

"Who is in charge here?" he asked.

"I am in charge," said Kraznakov. "Who are you? What is this?"

Brushing Kraznakov aside, the newcomer approached the table and leaned over Sofia. He gingerly parted her hair to examine the wound. He raised one of her eyelids with a thumb and then took her pulse by holding her wrist and glancing at his watch. Only then did he turn to Kraznakov.

"I'm Lazovsky, chief of surgery at First Municipal. I will be seeing to this patient."

"What's that? Now listen here!"

Lazovsky turned to the Count.

"Are you Rostov?"

"Yes," said the Count, astounded.

"Tell me when and how this happened. Be as precise as you can."

"She fell while running up a staircase. I think she hit her head on the edge of the landing. It was at the Metropol Hotel. It couldn't have been more than thirty minutes ago."

"Had she been drinking?"

"What? No. She's a child."

"How old?"

"Thirteen."

"Her name?"

"Sofia."

"All right. Very good."

Ignoring Kraznakov's ongoing protests, Lazovsky turned his attention to the primly dressed associate and began giving her instructions: that she find scrubs for the team and a suitable place to wash; that she gather the necessary surgical tools; that she sterilize everything.

The door swung open and a young man appeared, wearing the cavalier expression of one who has just come from a ball.

"Good evening, comrade Lazovsky," he said with a smile. "What a charming place you have here."

"All right, Antonovich. That'll be enough of that. It's a fracture at the front of the left parietal bone with a likely risk of subdural hematoma. Suit up. And see if you can do something about this lighting."

"Yes, sir."

"But first, get them out of here."

As Antonovich began corralling the two resident physicians out of the surgery with his carefree smile, Lazovsky pointed at the young nurse who had been manning the desk downstairs.

"Not you. Get yourself ready to assist."

Then he turned to the Count.

"Your daughter has taken quite a crack, Rostov, but she hasn't fallen headfirst from a plane. The skull was designed to withstand a certain amount of rough treatment. In these sorts of cases, the greatest risk is from swelling rather than direct damage. But that's nothing we haven't dealt with before. We're going to attend to your daughter immediately. In the meantime, you will need to sit outside. I will come and report to you as soon as I can."

The Count was led to a bench right outside the surgery. It took him a few moments to realize that in the preceding minutes the hallway had been cleared: the two gurneys with their sleeping patients were gone. The door at the end of the hallway suddenly swung open to admit Antonovich, who was now in scrubs and whistling. As the door swung closed, the Count could see that a man in a black suit had held the door open for him. When Antonovich went back into Surgery Four, the Count was alone in the empty hallway.

How did he spend the ensuing minutes? How would any man spend them.

He prayed for the first time since childhood. He allowed himself to imagine the worst, then assured himself that everything would be all right, reviewing the surgeon's few remarks over and over.

"The skull was designed for rough treatment," he repeated to himself.

Yet against his will, he was visited by contrary examples. He recalled a genial woodsman from the village of Petrovskoye, for instance, who had been hit in the head in the prime of his life by a falling limb. When he regained consciousness, he was as strong as ever, but sullen; on occasion he failed to recognize his friends; and without the slightest provocation he could explode in anger toward his own sisters—as if he'd been put to bed one man and had risen from bed another.

The Count began to chastise himself: How could he have let Sofia play such a reckless game? How could he while away an hour in a bar fretting over history paintings and statues—while Fate was preparing to hold his daughter's life in the balance?

For all the varied concerns attendant to the raising of a child—over schoolwork, dress, and manners—in the end, a parent's responsibility could not be more simple: To bring a child safely into adulthood so that she could have a chance to experience a life of purpose and, God willing, contentment.

Untold minutes passed.

The door to the surgery opened and Dr. Lazovsky appeared. He had his mask pulled below his chin. His hands were bare but there was blood on his smock.

The Count leapt up.

"Please, Rostov," said the surgeon. "Have a seat."

The Count sat back on the bench.

Lazovsky didn't join him; rather he put his fists on his hips and looked down at the Count with an unmistakable expression of competence.

"As I told you, in these situations the greatest risk is swelling. We have alleviated that risk. Nonetheless, she has suffered a concussion, which is basically a bruising of the brain. She is going to have headaches and will need a good deal of rest. But in a week, she will be up and about."

The surgeon turned to go.

The Count extended a hand.

"Dr. Lazovsky . . . ," he said, in the manner of one who wishes to ask a question, yet suddenly can't find the means of doing so.

But the surgeon, who had stood in this spot before, understood well enough.

"She's going to be every bit herself, Rostov."

As the Count began to offer his thanks, the man in the black suit opened the door at the end of the hall once again, only this time it was for Osip Glebnikov.

"Excuse me," said the surgeon to the Count.

Meeting halfway down the hall, Osip and Lazovsky conferred for a minute in lowered voices while the Count watched in astonishment.

When the surgeon disappeared into the surgery, Osip joined the Count on the bench.

"Well, my friend," he said with his hands on his knees. "Your little Sofia has given us quite a scare."

"Osip . . . What are you doing here?"

"I wanted to make sure that you were both all right."

"But how did you come to find us?"

Osip smiled.

"As I've told you, Alexander, it is my business to keep track of certain men of interest. But that doesn't matter at the moment. What does matter is that Sofia's going to be fine. Lazovsky is the best surgeon in the city. Tomorrow morning, he will be taking her to First Municipal, where she can recover in comfort. But I'm afraid that you can't stay here any longer."

The Count began to protest, but Osip raised a calming hand.

"Listen to me, Sasha. If I know what has happened tonight, others will soon know too. And it would not be in your best interest, or *Sofia's* for that matter, if they were to find you sitting here. So this is what you must do: There is a staircase at that end of this hall. You need to go down to the ground floor and through the black metal door, which leads to the alley behind the hospital. In the alley, there will be two men waiting who will take you back to the hotel."

"I can't leave Sofia," said the Count.

"You have to, I'm afraid. But your concern is perfectly understandable. So I have arranged for someone to stay with Sofia in your stead until she is ready to go home."

At this remark, the door was opened to admit a middle-aged woman looking bewildered and frightened. It was Marina. Behind the seamstress was a matron in uniform.

"Ah," said Osip, standing. "Here she is."

Because Osip stood, Marina looked to him first. Having never seen him before, she met his gaze with anxiety. But then she saw the Count sitting on the bench and ran forward.

"Alexander! What has happened? What are you doing here? They wouldn't tell me a thing."

"It's Sofia, Marina. She had a bad fall on the service stairs of the hotel, but a surgeon is with her now. She is going to be all right."

"Thank God."

The Count turned to Osip as if he were about to introduce him, but Osip preempted.

"Comrade Samarova," he said with a smile. "We haven't met, but I too am a friend of Alexander's. I'm afraid that he needs to return to the Metropol. But it would be such a comfort to him if you could remain with Sofia until her recovery. Isn't that so, my friend?"

Osip laid a hand on the Count's shoulder without taking his gaze off Marina.

"I know it is a great deal to ask, Marina," said the Count. "But . . ."

"Not another word, Alexander. Of course I will stay."

"Excellent," said Osip.

He turned to the uniformed woman.

"You'll see that comrade Samarova receives everything that she requires?"

"Yes, sir."

Osip offered Marina one more reassuring smile and then took the Count by the elbow.

"This way, my friend."

Osip led the Count down the hall and into the back staircase. They descended a flight together without speaking and then Osip stopped on the landing.

"This is where we part. Remember: down another flight and out the black metal door. Naturally, it would be best if you never mentioned to anyone that either of us were here."

"Osip, I don't know how to repay you."

"Alexander," he said with a smile, "you have been at my service for over fifteen years. It is a pleasure for once to be at yours." Then he was gone.

The Count descended the last flight and went through the black metal door. It was nearly dawn and, despite finding himself in an alley, the Count could sense the gentleness of spring in the air. Across the alley, there was a white van with the words *Red Star Baking Collective* painted in large letters on its side. An ill-shaven young man was leaning against the passenger door smoking. When he saw the Count, he tossed his cigarette and thumped the door behind him. Without asking the Count who he was, he went behind the van and opened the rear door.

"Thank you," said the Count as he climbed inside, receiving no reply.

It was only when the door closed and the Count found himself bent over at the waist in the back of the van that he became aware of an extraordinary sensation: the smell of freshly baked bread. When he had seen the insignia of the baking collective, he had assumed it was a ruse. But on the shelves that ran along one side of the van were over two hundred loaves in orderly arrangement. Gently, almost in disbelief, the Count reached out to lay a hand on one and found it to be soft and warm. It couldn't have been more than an hour from the oven.

Outside, the passenger door slammed shut and the van's engine started. The Count quickly sat on the metal bench that faced the shelves and they were underway.

In the silence, the Count listened to the gears of the van shifting. Having sped up and slowed down as it came into and out of various turns, the van's engine now accelerated to the speed of an open road.

Shuffling to the rear of the van with his back hunched, the Count looked out the little square window in the door. As he watched the buildings and canopies and shop signs flying past, for a moment he couldn't tell where he was. Then suddenly he saw the old English Club and realized that they must be on Tverskaya—the ancient road that radiated from the Kremlin in the direction of St. Petersburg, and that he had strolled a thousand times before.

In the late 1930s, Tverskaya Street had been widened to accommodate the official parades that ended in Red Square. While at the time, some of the finer buildings had been lifted and set back, most had been razed and replaced with towers, in accordance with a new ordinance that buildings on first-rate streets stand at least ten stories tall. As a result, the Count would have had to strain to pick out other familiar landmarks as the van moved along. But he had stopped looking for what was familiar, and instead was watching the blur of facades and street lamps receding rapidly from his view, as if they were being pulled into the distance.

Back in the attic of the Metropol, the Count found his door still open and Montaigne on the floor. Picking up his father's book, the Count sat down on Sofia's bed. Then for the first time that night, he let himself weep, his chest heaving lightly with the release. But if tears fell freely down his face, they were not tears of grief. They were the tears of the luckiest man in all of Russia.

After a few minutes, the Count breathed deeply and felt a sense of peace. Realizing that his father's book was still in his hand, he rose from Sofia's bed to set it down—and that's when he saw the black leather case that had been left on the Grand Duke's desk. It was about a foot square and six inches high with a handle in leather and clasps of chrome. Taped on top was a note addressed to him in an unfamiliar script. Pulling the note free, the Count unfolded it and read:

Alexander,

What a pleasure meeting you tonight. As I mentioned, I am headed home for a spell. In the meantime, I thought you could make good use of this. You might pay special attention to the contents in the uppermost sleeve, as I think you will find it very apropos of our chat.

With warm regards till next we meet,
Richard Vanderwhile

Throwing the clasps, the Count opened the lid of the case. It was a portable phonograph. Inside there was a small stack of records in brown paper sleeves. Per Richard's suggestion, the Count singled out the uppermost disc. On the label at the center, it was identified as a recording of Vladimir Horowitz playing Tchaikovsky's First Piano Concerto at Carnegie Hall in New York.

The Count had seen Horowitz perform in Moscow in 1921, less than four years before the pianist traveled to Berlin for an official concert—with a wad of foreign currency tucked in his shoes. . . .

At the back of the case, the Count found a small compartment in which the electrical cord was folded away. Unraveling it, he plugged the player into the wall socket. He removed the record from its sleeve, placed it on the turntable, threw the switch, cued the needle, and sat back on Sofia's bed.

At first, he heard muted voices, a few coughs, and the last rustling of

an audience settling in; then silence; then heartfelt applause as the performer presumably took the stage.

The Count held his breath.

After the trumpets sounded their first martial notes, the strings
swelled, and then his countryman began to play, evoking for the American
audience the movement of a wolf through the birches, the wind across the
steppe, the flicker of a candle in a ballroom, and the flash of a cannon at
Borodino.

Addendum

On the twenty-third of June at four in the afternoon, Andrey Duras was riding the bus back to his apartment in the Arbat, having taken advantage of his day off to visit Sofia at First Municipal Hospital.

The next day, he looked forward to reporting at the daily meeting of the Triumvirate that she was in good spirits. Housed in a special wing of the hospital, she had a private room full of sunlight, and constant attention from a battalion of nurses. Emile would be pleased to learn that his cookies were well received and that Sofia promised to send word the minute she had run out. While for his part, Andrey had brought a book of adventure stories that had always been a favorite of his son's.

At Smolenskaya Square, Andrey gave his seat to an older woman. He would be disembarking in a few blocks anyway—to get some cucumbers and potatoes at the peasant market in the square. Emile had given him half a pound of minced pork, and he was going to make kotlety for his wife.

Andrey and his wife lived in a narrow four-story apartment building in the middle of the block. Theirs was one of the smallest of the sixteen apartments, but they had it to themselves. At least, for now.

Having completed his errand at the market, Andrey climbed the stairs to the third floor. As he passed the other doors along the hallway, he could smell onions being sautéed in one apartment and hear voices on the radio in another. Shifting the bag of groceries to his left arm, he took out his key.

Letting himself inside, Andrey called out to his wife, though he knew she wouldn't be home. She would be waiting in line at the new milk store that had opened in a decommissioned church on the other side of the neighborhood. She said the milk there was fresher and the line was shorter, but Andrey knew this wasn't true. Like so many others, she went there because the small chapel at the back of the church had a mosaic of *Christ and the Woman at the Well* that no one had bothered to dismantle; and the women who waited in line for their milk were willing to hold your place while you slipped away to pray.

Andrey carried his groceries into the little room overlooking the street, which served as both kitchen and sitting room. On the small counter he laid out the vegetables. After washing his hands, he washed the cucumbers and sliced them. He peeled the potatoes and put them in a pot of water. He mixed the meat from Emile with chopped onion, formed the kotlety, and covered them with a towel. He put the frying pan on the stove and poured in some oil, for later. Having cleared off the counter, he washed his hands again, set the table, and then went down the hallway with the intention of lying down. But without quite thinking about it, he passed their bedroom door and went into the next room.

Many years before, Andrey had visited Pushkin's apartment in St. Petersburg—the one where he'd lived in his final years. The rooms of the apartment had been preserved just as they'd been on the day the poet died. There was even an unfinished poem and pen sitting on the desk. At the time, standing behind the little rope and gazing at the poet's desk, Andrey had thought the whole venture rather preposterous—as if by keeping a few belongings in place, one might actually protect a moment from the relentless onslaught of time.

But when Ilya, their only child, was killed in the Battle of Berlin— just months before the end of the war—he and his wife had done the same thing: leaving every blanket, every book, every piece of clothing exactly where it had been on the day that they'd received the news.

Initially, Andrey had to admit, this had been a great comfort. When he was alone in the apartment, he would find himself visiting the room; and when he did so, he could see from the depression on the bed where his wife must have been sitting while he was at work. Now, though, he worried that this carefully preserved room had begun to sustain rather than alleviate their grief; and he knew the time had come for them to rid themselves of their son's belongings.

Though he knew this, he didn't raise the matter with his wife. For he also knew that soon enough, someone in the building would draw the attention of the housing authorities to their son's death; then they would be moved to an even smaller apartment or required to take in a stranger, and life would reclaim the room as its own.

But even as he had this thought, Andrey walked over to the bed and smoothed out the blankets where his wife had been sitting; and only then, did he turn out the light.

BOOK FOUR

BOOK FOUR

1950

Adagio, Andante, Allegro

In the blink of an eye."

That was how, on the twenty-first of June, Count Alexander Rostov summed up his daughter's journey from thirteen to seventeen, when Vasily remarked on how much she had grown.

"One moment she is scampering up and down the stairwells—a veritable gadabout, a gadfly, a ne'er-do-well—and the next, she is a young woman of intelligence and refinement."

And this was largely true. For if the Count had been premature in characterizing Sofia as demure when she was thirteen, he had perfectly anticipated her persona on the cusp of adulthood. With fair skin and long black hair (but for the white stripe that fell from the spot of her old injury), Sofia could sit for hours listening to music in their study. She could stitch for hours with Marina in the stitching room, or chat for hours with Emile in the kitchen without shifting once in her chair.

When Sofia was just five, the Count had assumed, naively perhaps, that she would grow up to be a dark-haired version of her mother. But while Sofia shared Nina's clarity of perception and confidence of opinion, she was entirely different in demeanor. Where her mother was prone to express her impatience with the slightest of the world's imperfections, Sofia seemed to presume that if the earth spun awry upon occasion, it was generally a well-intentioned planet. And where Nina would not hesitate to cut someone off in midassertion in order to make a contrary point and then declare the matter decided once and for all, Sofia would listen so attentively and with such a sympathetic smile that her interlocutor, having been given free rein to express his views at considerable length, often found his voice petering out as he began to question his own premises. . . .

Demure. That was the only word for it. And the transition had occurred in the blink of an eye.

"When you reach our age, Vasily, it all goes by so quickly. Whole seasons seem to pass without leaving the slightest mark on our memory."

"How true . . . ," agreed the concierge (as he sorted through an allotment of tickets).

"But surely, there is a comfort to be taken from that," continued the Count. "For even as the weeks begin racing by in a blur for us, they are making the greatest of impressions upon our children. When one turns seventeen and begins to experience that first period of real independence, one's senses are so alert, one's sentiments so finely attuned that every conversation, every look, every laugh may be writ indelibly upon one's memory. And the friends that one happens to make in those impressionable years? One will meet them forever after with a welling of affection."

Having expressed this paradox, the Count happened to look across the lobby, where Grisha was lugging the luggage of one guest toward the front desk as Genya lugged the luggage of another toward the door.

"Perhaps it is a matter of celestial balance," he reflected. "A sort of cosmic equilibrium. Perhaps the aggregate experience of Time is a constant and thus for our children to establish such vivid impressions of this particular June, we must relinquish our claims upon it."

"So that they might remember, we must forget," Vasily summed up.

"Exactly!" said the Count. "So that they might remember, we must forget. But should we take umbrage at the fact? Should we feel short-changed by the notion that their experiences for the moment may be richer than ours? I think not. For it is hardly our purpose at this late stage to log a new portfolio of lasting memories. Rather, we should be dedicating ourselves to ensuring that *they* taste freely of experience. And we must do so without trepidation. Rather than tucking in blankets and buttoning up coats, we must have faith in them to tuck and button on their own. And if they fumble with their newfound liberty, we must remain composed, generous, judicious. We must encourage them to venture out from under our watchful gaze, and then sigh with pride when they pass at last through the revolving doors of life. . . ."

As if to illustrate, the Count gestured generously and judiciously toward the hotel's entrance, while giving an exemplary sigh. Then he tapped the concierge's desk.

"By the way. Do you happen to know where she is?"

Vasily looked up from his tickets.

"Miss Sofia?"

"Yes."

"She is in the ballroom with Viktor, I believe."

"Ah. She must be helping him polish the floors for an upcoming banquet."

"No. Not Viktor Ivanovich. Viktor Stepanovich."

"Viktor Stepanovich?"

"Yes. Viktor Stepanovich Skadovsky. The conductor of the orchestra at the Piazza."

If in part, the Count had been trying to express to Vasily how in our golden years a passage of time can be so fleet and leave so little an impression upon our memory, that it is almost as if it never occurred—well then, here was a perfect example.

For the three minutes it took the Count to travel from a delightful conversation at the concierge's desk to the ballroom, where he had grabbed a scoundrel by the lapels, had also passed in the blink of an eye. Why, it had passed so quickly, that the Count did not remember knocking the luggage from Grisha's grip as he marched down the hall; nor did he remember throwing open the door and shouting *Aha!*; nor yanking the would-be Casanova up off the loveseat, where he had intertwined his fingers with Sofia's.

No, the Count did not remember any of it. But to ensure a celestial balance and the equilibrium of the cosmos, this moustachioed scoundrel in evening clothes was sure to remember every single second for the rest of his life.

"Your Excellency," he implored, as he dangled in the air. "There has been a terrible misunderstanding!"

Looking up at the startled face above his fists, the Count confirmed that there had been no misunderstanding. It was definitely the very same fellow who waved his baton so blithely on the bandstand in the Piazza. And though he apparently knew how to produce an honorific in a timely fashion, he was clearly as villainous a viper as had ever slithered from the underbrush of Eden.

But whatever his level of villainy, the current situation did pose a quandary. For once you have hoisted a scoundrel by the lapels, what are you to do with him? At least when you have a fellow by the scruff of the neck, you can carry him out the door and toss him down the stairs. But when you have him by the lapels, he isn't so easy to dispense with. Before the Count could solve his conundrum, Sofia expressed a conundrum of her own.

"Papa! What are you doing?"

"Go to your room, Sofia. This gentleman and I have a few matters to discuss—before I give him the drubbing of a lifetime."

"The drubbing of a lifetime? But Viktor Stepanovich is my instructor."

Keeping one eye on the scoundrel, the Count glanced at his daughter with the other.

"Your what?"

"My instructor. He is teaching me piano."

The so-called instructor nodded four times in quick succession.

Without releasing his hold on the cad's lapels, the Count leaned his head back so that he could study the *mise-en-scène* with a little more care. Upon closer inspection, the loveseat the two had been sitting on did, in fact, appear to be the bench of a piano. And in the spot where their hands had been intertwined there was an orderly row of ivory keys.

The Count tightened his grip.

"So that's your game, is it? Seducing young women with jitterbugs?"

The so-called instructor looked aghast.

"Absolutely not, Your Excellency. I have never seduced a soul with a jitterbug. We have been playing scales and sonatas. I myself trained at the Conservatory—where I received the Mussorgsky Medal. I only conduct in the restaurant in order to make ends meet." Taking advantage of the Count's hesitation, he gestured toward the piano with his head. "Let us show you. Sofia, why don't you play the nocturne that we have been practicing?"

The nocturne . . . ?

"As you wish, Viktor Stepanovich," Sofia replied politely, then turned to the keyboard in order to arrange her sheet music.

"Perhaps . . . ," the instructor said to the Count with another nod toward the piano. "If I could just . . ."

"Oh," said the Count. "Yes, of course."

The Count set him back on the ground and gave his lapels a quick brushing.

Then the instructor joined his student on the bench.

"All right, Sofia."

Straightening her posture, Sofia laid her fingers on the keys; then with the utmost delicacy, she began to play.

At the sound of the first measure, the Count took two steps back.

Were those eight notes familiar to him? Did he recognize them in the least? Why, he would have known them if he hadn't seen them in thirty years and they happened to enter his compartment on a train. He would have known them if he bumped into them on the streets of Florence at the height of the season. In a word, he would have known them anywhere.

It was Chopin.

Opus 9, number 2, in E-flat major.

As she completed the first iteration of the melody in a perfect pianissimo and transitioned to the second with its suggestion of rising emotional force, the Count took another two steps back and found himself sitting in a chair.

Had he felt pride in Sofia before? Of course he had. On a daily basis. He was proud of her success in school, of her beauty, of her composure, of the fondness with which she was regarded by all who worked in the hotel. And that is how he could be certain that what he was experiencing at that moment could not be referred to as pride. For there is something knowing in the state of pride. *Look*, it says, *didn't I tell you how special she is? How bright? How lovely? Well, now you can see it for yourself.* But in listening to Sofia play Chopin, the Count had left the realm of knowing and entered the realm of astonishment.

On one level he was astonished by the revelation that Sofia could play the piano at all; on another, that she tackled the primary and subordinate melodies with such skill. But what was truly astonishing was the sensitivity of her musical expression. One could spend a lifetime mastering the technical aspects of the piano and never achieve a state of musical expression— that alchemy by which the performer not only comprehends the sentiments of the composer, but somehow communicates them to her audience through the manner of her play.

Whatever personal sense of heartache Chopin had hoped to express through this little composition—whether it had been prompted by a loss of love, or simply the sweet anguish one feels when witnessing a mist on a meadow in the morning—it was right there, ready to be experienced to its fullest, in the ballroom of the Hotel Metropol one hundred years after the composer's death. But how, the question remained, could a seventeen-year-old girl achieve this feat of expression, if not by channeling a sense of loss and longing of her own?

As Sofia began the third iteration of the melody, Viktor Stepanovich looked over his shoulder with his eyebrows raised, as if to say: *Can you believe it? Have you ever in all your years even imagined?* Then he quickly looked back to the piano and dutifully turned the page for Sofia almost in the manner of an apprentice turning the page for his master.

After the Count had led Viktor Stepanovich into the hall, where they could confer for a moment in private, he returned to the ballroom. Finding Sofia still at the piano, he took a seat at her side with his back to the keys.

They were both silent.

"Why didn't you tell me you were studying piano?" the Count asked after a moment.

"I wanted it to be a surprise," she said. "For your birthday. I didn't mean to upset you. I'm so sorry if I did."

"Sofia, if anyone should be apologizing, it should be me. You have done nothing wrong. On the contrary. That was wonderful—and unambiguously so."

Sofia blushed and looked down at the keyboard.

"It is a lovely composition," she said.

"Well, yes," agreed the Count with a laugh, "it is a lovely composition. But it is also a piece of paper with circles, lines, and dots. Nearly every student of piano for a century has learned to play that little bit of Chopin. But for most of them, it is an act of recitation. Only one in a thousand—or even a hundred thousand—can bring the music to life as you just have."

Sofia continued to look at the keyboard. The Count hesitated. And then with a touch of trepidation, he asked:

"Is everything all right?"

Sofia looked up, a little surprised. Then seeing how grave her father's expression was, she smiled.

"Of course, Papa. Why do you ask?"

The Count shook his head.

"I've never played an instrument in my life, but I understand something of music. To have played the opening measures of that piece with feelings so perfectly evocative of heartache, one can only assume that you have drawn on some wellspring of sorrow within yourself."

"Oh, I see," she said. Then with the enthusiasm of a young scholar she began to explain: "Viktor Stepanovich calls that the *mood*. He says that before one plays a note, one must discover an example of the composition's mood hidden away in one's heart. So for this piece, I think about my mother. I think of how my few memories of her seem to be fading, and then I begin to play."

The Count was quiet, overwhelmed by another wave of astonishment.

"Does that make sense?" Sofia asked.

"Abundantly," he said. Then after a moment of reflection, he added: "As a younger man, I used to feel the same way about my sister. Every year that passed, it seemed a little more of her had slipped away; and I began to fear that one day I would come to forget her altogether. But the truth is: No matter how much time passes, those we have loved never slip away from us entirely."

They were both quiet now. Then looking about him, the Count gestured with his hand.

"This was a favorite room of hers."

"Of your sister's?"

"No, no. Of your mother's."

Sofia looked around with some surprise.

"The ballroom . . . ?"

"Most definitely. After the Revolution, all the old ways of doing things were abandoned—which was the point, I suppose. But the new ways of doing things had yet to be established. So all across Russia, all manner of groups—trade unions, citizens' committees, commissariats—gathered in rooms like this one in order to hash things out."

The Count pointed to the balcony.

"When your mother was nine, she would crouch up there behind the balustrade to watch these Assemblies for hours on end. She found it all very thrilling. The shuffling of chairs and the heartfelt speeches and the pounding of the gavel. And in retrospect, she was perfectly right. After all, a new course for the country was being charted right before our eyes. But at the time, what with the crawling and the hunching, it just gave me a crick in the neck."

"You would go up there too?"

"Oh, she insisted."

The Count and Sofia both smiled.

"Come to think of it," added the Count after a moment, "that's how I came to know your Aunt Marina. Because every other visit to the balcony, I'd split the seat of my pants."

Sofia laughed. Then the Count wagged a finger in the manner of one who has remembered something else.

"Later, when your mother was thirteen or fourteen, she would come here to enact experiments . . ."

"Experiments!"

"Your mother was not one to take anything on faith. If she hadn't witnessed a phenomenon with her own eyes, then as far as she was concerned it was a hypothesis. And that included all the laws of physics and mathematics. One day, I found her here testing the principles of Galileo and Newton by dropping various objects from the balcony and timing their descent with a sprinter's watch."

"Is that even possible?"

"It was for your mother."

They were quiet for another moment, then Sofia turned and kissed the Count on the cheek.

When Sofia had gone off to meet a friend, the Count went to the Piazza and treated himself to a glass of wine with lunch—something that he had done on a daily basis in his thirties and had rarely done since. Given the morning's revelations, it seemed only appropriate. In fact, when his plate had been cleared and he had dutifully declined dessert, he ordered a second glass.

As he leaned back with his wine in hand, he regarded the young man at the neighboring table, who was sketching in his sketchbook. The Count had noticed him in the lobby the day before with the book in his lap and a small tin of colored pencils at his side.

The Count leaned a little to his right.

"Landscape, portrait, or still life?"

The young man looked up with a touch of surprise.

"Excuse me?"

"I couldn't help but notice you sketching away. I was just wondering if it was a landscape, a portrait, or a still life."

"None of the above, I'm afraid," the young man replied politely. "It is an interior."

"Of the restaurant?"

"Yes."

"May I see?"

The young man hesitated then handed the Count his book.

As soon as the Count had it in hand, he regretted his reference to *sketching*. The word hardly did justice to the young man's skills as an artist, for he had captured the Piazza perfectly. The guests at the tables were rendered with the short, bright strokes of Impressionism, adding to the sense that they were engaged in lively conversations; while the waiters moving deftly between the tables were rendered in something of a blur. But the suggestive style with which the young man had drawn the people was sharply contrasted by the level of detail with which he had drawn the room itself. The columns, the fountain, the arches were all realized in perfect perspective to perfect proportion, with every ornament in place.

"It's a wonderful drawing," said the Count. "But I must say, your sense of space is particularly exquisite."

The stranger smiled a little wistfully.

"That's because I'm an architect by training, not an artist."

"Are you designing a hotel?"

The architect gave a laugh.

"The way things stand, I'd be happy to design a birdhouse."

Given the Count's expression of curiosity, the young man elaborated: "For the time being, there are a lot of buildings being built in Moscow, but little need for architects. So I have taken a job with Intourist. They're putting together a brochure of the city's finer hotels and I'm drawing the interiors."*

"Ah," said the Count. "Because a photograph cannot capture the *feeling* of a place!"

---

*What sort of topsy-turvy circumstances could lead to a boom for builders and a bust for architects? Simple:

In January, the mayor of Moscow had called a convention of the city's architects to discuss the needs of the capital given the rapid growth in its population. Over the course of three days, an excited consensus had quickly formed across the various committees that the time had come for bold new steps. Taking advantage of the latest materials and technologies, they proposed that the city erect towers forty stories high with elevators that shot from the lobby to the roof, and apartments that could be configured to suit every individual need, each with a modern kitchen and private bath and plate-glass windows admitting natural light!

At the closing ceremony of the convention, the mayor—a bald and brutish sort, whom we will have reason to revisit later—thanked the attendees for their artistry, their ingenuity, and their dedication to the Party. "It is satisfying to discover that we are all in agreement," he concluded. "In order to house our fellow comrades as quickly and economically as possible, we must, indeed, pursue bold new steps. So, let us not get bogged down with elaborate designs or bow to aesthetic vanities. Let us apply ourselves instead to a universal ideal that is fitting for our times."

Thus was born the golden age of the prefabricated, cement-walled, five-story apartment building—and the four-hundred-square-foot living spaces with ready access to communal bathrooms boasting four-foot tubs (after all, who has time to lie down in a bath when your neighbors are knocking at the door).

So ingenious was the design of these new apartment buildings, so intuitive their architecture, they could be built from a single page of specifications—regardless of which way the page was oriented! Within six months, thousands of them had sprung up on the outskirts of Moscow, like mushrooms after a rain. And so systematic was their realization, you could mistakenly enter any apartment on your block and feel immediately at home.

"Actually," replied the architect, "because a photograph too readily captures the *condition* of a place."

"Oh, I see," said the Count, feeling a little insulted on the Piazza's behalf. In its defense, he couldn't help pointing out that while the restaurant had been celebrated for its elegance in its time, the room's grandeur had never been defined by its furnishings or architectural details.

"By what then?" the young man asked.

"The citizenry."

"How do you mean?"

The Count turned his chair so that he could better face his neighbor.

"In my day, I had the luxury of doing a good bit of travel. And I can tell you from personal experience that the majority of hotel restaurants—not simply in Russia, you understand, but across Europe—were designed for and have served the guests of the hotel. But this restaurant wasn't and hasn't. It was designed to be and has been a gathering place for the entire city of Moscow."

The Count gestured toward the center of the room.

"For most of the last forty years, on a typical Saturday night you could find Russians cut from every cloth crowded around that fountain, stumbling into conversations with whosoever happened to be at the neighboring table. Naturally, this has led to impromptu romances and heartfelt debates on the merits of Pushkin over Petrarch. Why, I've watched cabbies rub elbows with commisars and bishops with black marketeers; and on at least one occasion, I have actually seen a young lady change an old man's point of view."

The Count pointed to a spot about twenty feet away.

"You see those two tables there? One afternoon in 1939 I watched as two strangers, finding each other vaguely familiar, spent their appetizer, entrée, and dessert going over their entire lives step by step in search of the moment when they must have met."

Looking around the restaurant with renewed appreciation, the architect observed:

"I suppose a room is the summation of all that has happened inside it."

"Yes, I think it is," agreed the Count. "And though I'm not exactly sure what has come of all the intermingling in this particular room, I am fairly certain that the world has been a better place because of it."

The Count was quiet for a moment as he too looked around. Then pointing a finger, he directed the architect's attention to the bandstand on the far side of the room.

"Have you ever happened to see the orchestra play here in the evening?"

"No, I haven't. Why?"

"The most extraordinary thing happened to me today. . . ."

"Apparently, he was walking down the hallway when he happened to hear a Mozart Variation emanating from the ballroom. Intrigued, he poked his head inside and discovered Sofia at the keyboard."

"No!" exclaimed Richard Vanderwhile.

"Naturally, the fellow asked where she was studying. He was taken aback to learn that she hadn't been studying with anyone. She had taught herself to play the piece by listening to one of the recordings you had given me and then sounding out the notes one by one."

"Incredible."

"The fellow was so impressed with her natural abilities that he took her on as a student right then and there; and he has been teaching her the classical repertoire in the ballroom ever since."

"And this is the chap from the Piazza, you say?"

"None other."

"The one who waves the baton?"

"The very same."

Richard shook his head in wonder. "Audrius, have you heard all of this? We've got to raise a glass to the young lady, and as soon as possible. Two Goldenrods, my good man."

The ever-attentive tender at bar was already lining up bottles of various sizes including yellow chartreuse, bitters, honey, and a vodka infused with lemon. On that night in 1946 when the Count and Richard had first become acquainted over Audrius's magenta concoction, the American had challenged the bartender to design a cocktail in each of the colors of St. Basil's Cathedral. Thus were born the Goldenrod, the Robin's Egg, the Brick Wall, and a dark green potion called the Christmas Tree. In addition, it had become generally known in the bar that anyone who could drink all four cocktails back to back earned the right to be called "The Patriarch of All Russia"—as soon as he regained consciousness.

Though Richard, who was now attached to the State Department, tended to stay at the embassy when in Moscow, he would still stop by the Metropol on occasion in order to have a nightcap with the Count. Thus, the Goldenrods were poured and the two gentlemen clinked their glasses with the toast: "To old friends."

Some might wonder that the two men should consider themselves to be old friends having only known each other for four years; but the tenure of friendships has never been governed by the passage of time. These two would have felt like old friends had they met just hours before. To some degree, this was because they were kindred spirits—finding ample evidence of common ground and cause for laughter in the midst of effortless conversation; but it was also almost certainly a matter of upbringing. Raised in grand homes in cosmopolitan cities, educated in the liberal arts, graced with idle hours, and exposed to the finest things, though the Count and the American had been born ten years and four thousand miles apart, they had more in common with each other than they had with the majority of their own countrymen.

This, of course, is why the grand hotels of the world's capitals all look alike. The Plaza in New York, the Ritz in Paris, Claridge's in London, the Metropol in Moscow—built within fifteen years of each other, they too were kindred spirits, the first hotels in their cities with central heating, with hot water and telephones in the rooms, with international newspapers in the lobbies, international cuisine in the restaurants, and American bars off the lobby. These hotels were built for the likes of Richard Vanderwhile and Alexander Rostov, so that when they traveled to a foreign city, they would find themselves very much at home and in the company of kin.

"I still can't believe it's that fellow from the Piazza," said Richard with another shake of the head.

"I know," said the Count. "But he actually studied at the Conservatory here in Moscow where he was the recipient of the Mussorgsky Medal. He only conducts at the Piazza in order to make ends meet."

"One must make ends meet," confirmed Audrius matter-of-factly, "or meet one's end."

Richard studied the bartender for a moment.

"Well, that's the very essence of it, isn't it?"

Audrius shrugged, acknowledging that the essence-of-it was a bartender's stock-in-trade, and then he excused himself to answer the phone behind the bar. As he walked away, the Count seemed particularly struck by the bartender's remark.

"Are you familiar with the moths of Manchester?" he asked Richard.

"The moths of Manchester . . . Isn't that a soccer team?"

"No," said the Count with a smile. "It is not a soccer team. It is an extraordinary case from the annals of the natural sciences that my father related to me as a child."

But before the Count could elaborate, Audrius returned.

"That was your wife on the phone, Mr. Vanderwhile. She asked me to remind you of your appointment in the morning; and to alert you that your driver is waiting outside."

Though most of the customers in the bar had never met Mrs. Vanderwhile, she was known to be as unflappable as Arkady, as attentive as Audrius, and as aware of whereabouts as Vasily—when it came to drawing Mr. Vanderwhile's evenings to a close.

"Ah, yes," conceded Mr. Vanderwhile.

Agreeing that duty comes first, the Count and Mr. Vanderwhile shook hands and wished each other well till next they met.

When Richard left, the Count looked once around the room to see if there was anyone he knew, and was pleased to discover that the young architect from the Piazza was at a table in the corner, bent over his sketchbook, presumably rendering the bar.

He too, thought the Count, is one of the moths of Manchester.

When the Count was nine years old, his father had sat him down in order to explain Darwin's theory of natural selection. As the Count listened, the essence of the Englishman's idea seemed perfectly intuitive— that over tens of thousands of years a species would slowly evolve in order to maximize its chances of survival. After all, if the claws of the lion grow sharper, the gazelle had best grow more fleet of foot. But what had disconcerted the Count was when his father clarified that natural selection didn't need tens of thousands of years to take place. It didn't even need a hundred. It had been observed unfolding over the course of a few decades.

It was true, his father said, that in a relatively static environment the pace of evolution should decelerate, as individual species have little new to adapt to. But environments are never static for long. The forces of nature inevitably unleash themselves in such a manner that the necessity for adaptation will be stirred. An extended drought, an unusually cold winter, a volcanic eruption, any one of these could alter the balance between those traits that improve a species' chance for survival and those that hinder it. In essence, this is what had occurred in Manchester, England, in the nineteenth century, when the city became one of the first capitals of the industrial revolution.

For thousands of years, the peppered moths of Manchester had white wings with black flecking. This coloring provided the species with perfect camouflage whenever they landed on the light gray bark of the region's trees. In any generation there might be a few aberrations—such as moths with pitch-black wings—but they were snapped off the trees by the birds before they had a chance to mate.

But when Manchester became crowded with factories in the early 1800s, the soot from the smokestacks began to settle on every conceivable surface, including the bark of the trees; and the lightly speckled wings that had served to protect the majority of peppered moths suddenly exposed them remorselessly to their predators—even as the darker wings of the aberrations rendered them invisible. Thus, the pitch-black varieties that had represented less than 10 percent of the Manchester moth population in 1800, represented over 90 percent by the end of the century. Or so explained the Count's father, with the pragmatic satisfaction of the scientifically minded.

But the lesson did not sit well with the young Count. If this could happen so easily to moths, he thought, then what was to stop it from happening to children? What would happen to him and his sister, for instance, should they be exposed to excess chimney smoke or sudden extremes of weather? Couldn't they become victims of accelerated evolution? In fact, so disconcerted by this notion became the Count that when Idlehour was deluged by rainstorms that September, giant black moths harrowed his dreams.

Some years later, the Count would come to understand that he had been looking at the matter upside down. The pace of evolution was not something to be frightened by. For while nature doesn't have a stake in whether the wings of a peppered moth are black or white, it genuinely hopes that the peppered moth will persist. And that is why nature designed the forces of evolution to play out over generations rather than eons—to ensure that moths and men have a chance to adapt.

Like Viktor Stepanovich, the Count reflected. A husband and father of two, he must make ends meet. So he waves his baton in the Piazza, ostensibly putting the classical repertoire behind him. Then one afternoon, when he happens to stumble upon a young pianist with promise, in what little time he has to spare, he teaches her the nocturnes of Chopin on a borrowed piano. Just so, Mishka has his "project"; and this young architect, unable to build buildings, takes pride and pleasure from the careful drafting of hotel interiors in his sketchbook.

For a moment, the Count considered going over to the young man, but he seemed to be applying his skills with such satisfaction that it would be a crime to interrupt him. So, instead, the Count emptied his glass, tapped the bar twice, and headed upstairs for bed.

Of course, the Count was perfectly right. For when life makes it impossible for a man to pursue his dreams, he will connive to pursue them anyway. Thus, even as the Count was brushing his teeth, Viktor Stepanovich was setting aside an arrangement that he had been working on for his orchestra in order to sort through the Goldberg Variations—in search of one that might be just right for Sofia. While in the village of Yavas, in a rented room not much larger than the Count's, by the light of a candle, Mikhail Mindich was sitting hunched over a table, sewing another signature of sixteen pages. And down in the Shalyapin? The young architect continued to take pride and pleasure in his work. But contrary to the Count's supposition, he was not adding a rendering of the bar to his collection of hotel interiors. In fact, he was working in a different sketchbook altogether.

On the first of this book's many pages was the design for a skyscraper two hundred stories tall—with a diving board on the roof from which the tenants could parachute to a grassy park below. On another page was a cathedral to atheism with fifty different cupolas, several of which could be launched like rockets to the moon. And on another was a giant museum of architecture showcasing life-size replicas of all the grand old buildings that had been razed in the city of Moscow to make way for the new.

But at this particular moment, what the architect was working on was a detailed drawing of a crowded restaurant that looked very much like the Piazza. Only, under the floor of this restaurant was an elaborate mechanics of axles, cogs, and gears; and jutting from an outside wall was a giant crank, at the turn of which, each of the restaurant's chairs would pirouette like a ballerina on a music box, then spin around the space until they came to a stop at an entirely different table. And towering over this tableau, peering down through the glass ceiling, was a gentleman of sixty with his hand on the crank, preparing to set the diners in motion.

1952

America

On a Wednesday evening in late June, the Count and Sofia walked arm in arm into the Boyarsky, where it was their custom to dine on the Count's night off.

"Good evening, Andrey."

"Bonsoir, mon ami. Bonsoir, mademoiselle. Your table awaits."

As Andrey ushered them into the dining room with a gesture of his hand, the Count could see it was another busy night. On the way to table ten, they passed the wives of two commissars seated at table four. Dining alone at table six was an eminent professor of literature—who they say had single-handedly wrestled the works of Dostoevsky to the ground. And at table seven was none other than the beguiling Anna Urbanova in the company of the beguiled.

Having successfully returned to the silver screen in the 1930s, in 1948 Anna had been lured back to the stage by the director of the Maly Theatre. This was a stroke of good fortune for the fifty-year-old actress, for while the silver screen showed a distinct preference for young beauties, the theater seemed to understand the virtues of age. After all, Medea, Lady Macbeth, Irina Arkadina—these were not roles for the blue-eyed and blushing. They were roles for women who had known the bitterness of joy and the sweetness of despair. But Anna's return to the stage also proved fortunate for the Count because instead of visiting the Metropol a few days a year, she was now in residence for months at a time, which allowed our seasoned astronomer to chart the newest of her constellations with the utmost care. . . .

Once the Count and Sofia had been seated, the two carefully studied their menus (working backward from entrées to appetizers as was their custom), placed their orders with Martyn (who, at the Count's recommendation, had been promoted to the Boyarsky in 1942), and then finally turned their attention to the business at hand.

Surely, the span of time between the placing of an order and the arrival of appetizers is one of the most perilous in all human interaction. What young lovers have not found themselves at this juncture in a silence so sudden, so seemingly insurmountable that it threatens to cast doubt upon their chemistry as a couple? What husband and wife have not found themselves suddenly unnerved by the fear that they might not ever have something urgent, impassioned, or surprising to say to each other again? So it is with good reason that most of us meet this dangerous interstice with a sense of foreboding.

But the Count and Sofia? They looked forward to it all day long—because it was the moment allotted for *Zut*.

A game of their own invention, *Zut's* rules were simple. Player One proposes a category encompassing a specialized subset of phenomena—such as stringed instruments, or famous islands, or winged creatures other than birds. The two players then go back and forth until one of them fails to come up with a fitting example in a suitable interval of time (say, two and a half minutes). Victory goes to the first player who wins two out of three rounds. And why was the game called *Zut*? Because according to the Count, *Zut alors!* was the only appropriate exclamation in the face of defeat.

Thus, having searched throughout their day for challenging categories and carefully considered the viable responses, when Martyn reclaimed the menus father and daughter faced each other at the ready.

Having lost the previous match, the Count had the right to propose the first category and did so with confidence: "Famous foursomes."

"Well chosen," said Sofia.

"Thank you."

They both took a drink of water, then the Count began.

"The four seasons."

"The four elements."

"North, South, East, and West."

"Diamonds, clubs, hearts, and spades."

"Bass, tenor, alto, and soprano."

Sofia reflected.

. . .

"Matthew, Mark, Luke, and John—the Four Evangelists."

"Boreas, Zephyrus, Notos, and Euros—the Four Winds."

. . .

. . .

With an inward smile, the Count began counting the seconds; but he counted prematurely.

"Yellow bile, black bile, blood, and phlegm—the Four Humors," said Sofia.

"*Très bien!*"

"*Merci.*"

Sofia took a sip of water in order to obscure the hint of gloating on her lips. But now it was she who was celebrating prematurely.

"The Four Horsemen of the Apocalypse."

"Ah," said Sofia with the sigh of one receiving the *coup de grâce*, just as Martyn arrived with the Château d'Yquem. Having presented the bottle, the waiter pulled the cork, poured a taste, and served the table.

"Round two?" asked Sofia when Martyn had departed.

"With pleasure."

"Animals that are black and white—such as the zebra."

"Excellent," said the Count.

For a moment, he rearranged his silverware. He took a sip of wine and slowly returned his glass to the table.

"Penguin," he said.

"Puffin."

"Skunk."

"Panda."

The Count reflected; then smiled.

"Killer whale."

"The peppered moth," countered Sofia.

The Count sat up in indignation.

"But that's *my* animal!"

"It is not your animal; but it is your turn. . . ."

The Count frowned.

. . .

"Dalmatian!" he exclaimed.

Now it was Sofia who arranged her silver and sipped her wine.

. . .

. . .

"Time is passing . . . ," said the Count.

. . .

. . .

"Me," said Sofia.

"What!"

With a tilt of her head she held out the white stripe from her long black hair.

"But you're not an animal."

Sofia smiled sympathetically then said: "You're up."

. . .

. . .

Is there a black-and-white fish? the Count asked himself. *A black-and-white spider? A black-and-white snake?*

. . .

. . .

"Tick, tock, tick, tock," said Sofia.

"Yes, yes. Wait a moment."

. . .

. . .

I know there is another black-and-white animal, thought the Count. *It is something reasonably common. I've seen it myself. It's on the very tip of my—*

"Do I have the pleasure of addressing Alexander Rostov?"

The Count and Sofia both looked up in surprise. Standing before them was the eminent professor from table six.

"Yes," said the Count, rising from the table. "I am Alexander Rostov. This is my daughter, Sofia."

"I am Professor Matej Sirovich from Leningrad State University."

"Of course you are," said the Count.

The professor gave a quick bow of the head in gratitude.

"Like so many others," he continued, "I am an admirer of your verse. Perhaps you would do me the honor of joining me for a glass of cognac after your meal?"

"It would be my pleasure."

"I am in suite 317."

"I will be there within the hour."

"Please, don't rush."

The professor smiled and gently backed away from the table.

Resuming his seat, the Count casually placed his napkin in his lap. "Matej Sirovich," he informed Sofia, "is one of our most revered professors of literature; and apparently, he would like to discuss poetry with me over a glass of cognac. What do you think of that?"

"I think your time is up."

The Count lowered his eyebrows.

"Yes. Well. I had an answer sitting right on the tip of my tongue. I should have expressed it in another moment, if we hadn't been interrupted. . . ."

Sofia nodded, in the friendly manner of one who has no intention of considering the merits of an appeal.

"All right," conceded the Count. "One round apiece."

The Count took a kopek from the ticket pocket of his vest and laid it on his thumbnail so that they could determine by toss who would get to choose the tie-breaking category. But before he could flip the coin, Martyn appeared with their first course: Emile's interpretation of the Olivier salad for Sofia and goose-liver pâté for the Count.

Since they never played while they ate, the two turned their attention to an enjoyable discussion of the day's events. It was while the Count was spreading the last of his pâté on a corner of toast that Sofia observed, rather casually, that Anna Urbanova was in the restaurant.

"What's that?" asked the Count.

"Anna Urbanova, the actress. She's seated over there at table seven."

"Is she?"

The Count raised his head to look across the dining room with the curiosity of the idle; then returned to his spreading.

"Why don't you ever invite her to join us for dinner?"

The Count looked up with an expression of mild shock.

"Invite her to dinner! Shall I invite Charlie Chaplin as well?" The Count gave a laugh and a shake of the head: "It is customary to be acquainted with someone before you invite them to dinner, my dear." Then he finished off the pâté, just as he had finished off the conversation.

"I think you're worried that I would be scandalized in some way," continued Sofia. "But Marina thinks it's because—"

"Marina!" exclaimed the Count. "Marina has an opinion on why I would or wouldn't invite this . . . this Anna Urbanova to dine with us?"

"Naturally, Papa."

The Count leaned back in his chair.

"I see. So what is this opinion that Marina so *naturally* has?"

"She thinks it's because you like to keep your buttons in their boxes."

"My buttons in their boxes!"

"You know: your blue buttons in one box, your black buttons in another, your red buttons in a third. You have your relationships here, your relationships there, and you like to keep them distinct."

"Is that so. I had no idea that I was known to treat people like buttons."

"Not all people, Papa. Just your friends."

"What a relief."

"May I?"

It was Martyn, gesturing at the empty plates.

"Thank you," snapped the Count.

Sensing that he had interrupted a heated exchange, Martyn quickly cleared the first course, returned with two servings of veal Pojarski, topped up the wine glasses, and disappeared without a word. The Count and Sofia both breathed in the woody fragrance of the mushrooms then began to eat in silence.

"Emile has outdone himself," the Count said after a few bites.

"He has," Sofia agreed.

The Count took a generous swallow of the Château d'Yquem, which was a 1921 and perfectly suited to the veal.

"Anna thinks it's because you're set in your ways."

The Count commenced to cough into his napkin, as he had determined long ago that this was the most effective means of removing wine from his windpipe.

"Are you all right?" asked Sofia.

The Count put his napkin in his lap and waved a hand in the general direction of table seven.

"And how, may I ask, do you know what this Anna Urbanova thinks?"

"Because she told me so."

"So the two of you are acquainted."

"But, of course we are. We have known each other for years."

"Well, that's just perfect," said the Count in a huff. "Why don't *you* invite her to dinner. In fact, if I am such a button in a box, perhaps you, Marina, and Miss Urbanova should all have dinner on your own."

"Why, that's exactly what Andrey suggested!"

"How is everything tonight?"

"Speak of the devil!" shouted the Count as he dumped his napkin on his plate.

Taken aback, Andrey looked from the Count to Sofia with concern.

"Is something wrong?"

"The food at the Boyarsky is superior," replied the Count, "and the service is excellent. But the gossip? It is truly unsurpassed."

The Count stood.

"I think you have some piano practice to see to, young lady," he said to Sofia. "Now if you'll both excuse me, I am expected upstairs."

As the Count marched down the hallway, he could not help but observe to himself that there was a time, not long before, when a gentleman could expect a measure of privacy in his personal affairs. With reasonable confidence, he could place his correspondence in a desk drawer and leave his diary on a bedside table.

Although, on the other hand, since the beginning of time men in pursuit of wisdom had routinely retreated to mountaintops, caves, and cabins in the woods. So, perhaps that is where one must eventually head, if one has any hopes of achieving enlightenment without the interference of meddlers. Case in point: As the Count headed for the stairwell, who did he happen to bump into waiting for an elevator? None other than that renowned expert on human behavior, Anna Urbanova.

"Good evening, Your Excellency . . ." she said to the Count with a suggestive smile. But then her eyebrows rose in inquiry when she noted the expression on his face. "Is everything all right?"

"I can't believe that you have been having clandestine conversations with Sofia," the Count said in a hushed voice, though no one else was about.

"They weren't clandestine," Anna whispered back. "They just happened to be while you were at work."

"And you think that is somehow appropriate? To foster a friendship with my daughter in my absence?"

"Well, you do like your buttons in their boxes, Sasha. . . ."

"So I gather!"

The Count turned to go, but then came back.

"And if, perchance, I do like my buttons in their boxes, is there anything wrong with that?"

"Certainly not."

"Would the world be a better place if we kept all the buttons in a big glass jar? In such a world, whenever you tried to reach in for a button of a particular color, the tips of your fingers would inevitably push it down below the other buttons until you couldn't see it. Eventually, in a state of exasperation, you would end up pouring all of the buttons on the floor— and then spend an hour and a half having to pick them back up."

"Are we talking about actual buttons now?" asked Anna with genuine interest. "Or is this still an allegory?"

"What is not an allegory," said the Count, "is my appointment with an eminent professor. Which, by the way, will necessitate the cancellation of any further appointments for the evening!"

Ten minutes later, the Count was knocking on that door which he had answered a thousand times, but upon which he had never knocked.

"Ah, here you are," said the professor. "Please come in."

The Count had not been in his old suite in over twenty-five years— not since that night in 1926 when he had stood at the parapet.

Still styled in the manner of a nineteenth-century French salon, the rooms remained elegant, if a little worse for wear. Only one of the two gilded mirrors now hung on the wall; the dark red curtains had faded; the matching couch and chairs needed to be reupholstered; and while his family's clock still stood guard near the door, its hands were stopped at 4:22—having become an aspect of the room's décor, rather than an essential instrument for the keeping of engagements. But if one no longer heard the gentle sound of time advancing in the suite, in its place were the strains of a waltz emanating from an electric radio on the dining room mantel.

Following the professor into the sitting room, the Count habitually glanced at the northwest corner with its privileged view of the Bolshoi—and there, framed by the window, was the silhouette of a man gazing out into the night. Tall, thin, with an aristocratic bearing, it could have been a shadow of the Count from another time. But then the shadow turned and crossed the room with its hand outstretched.

"Alexander!"

. . .

"Richard?"

It was none other. Dressed in a tailored suit, Richard Vanderwhile smiled and took hold of the Count's hand.

"It's good to see you! How long has it been? Almost two years?"

From the dining room, the strains of the waltz grew a little louder. The Count looked over just in time to see Professor Sirovich closing the doors to his bedroom and turning the brass latch. Richard gestured to one of the chairs by the coffee table, on which was an assortment of zakuski.

"Have a seat. I gather you've eaten, but you won't mind if I dig in, will you? I'm absolutely starving." Sitting on the couch, Richard put a slice of smoked salmon on a piece of bread and chewed it with relish even as he spread caviar on a blini. "I saw Sofia from across the lobby this afternoon and I couldn't believe my eyes. What a beauty she's become! You must have all the boys in Moscow knocking at your door."

"Richard," said the Count with a wave at the room, "what are we doing here?"

Richard nodded, brushing the crumbs from his hands.

"I apologize for the theatrics. Professor Sirovich is an old friend, and generous enough to loan me his sitting room on occasion. I'm only in town for a few days, and I didn't want to miss the opportunity to speak with you in private, as I'm not exactly sure when I'll be back."

"Has something happened?" the Count asked with concern.

Richard put up both hands.

"Not at all. In fact, they tell me it's a promotion. I'll be working out of the embassy in Paris for the next few years overseeing a little initiative of ours, which is likely to keep me tied to a desk. Actually, Alexander, that's why I wanted to see you. . . ."

Richard sat a little forward on the couch, putting his elbows on his knees.

"Since the war, relations between our countries may not have been especially chummy, but they have been predictable. We launch the Marshall Plan, you launch the Molotov Plan. We form NATO; you form the Cominform. We develop an atom bomb, you develop an atom bomb. It's been like a game of tennis—which is not only a good form of exercise, but awfully entertaining to watch. Vodka?"

Richard poured them both a glass.

"*Za vas*," he said.

"*Za vas*," replied the Count.

The men emptied their glasses and Richard refilled them.

"The problem is that your top player has played the game so well, for so long, he's the only player we know. Were he to quit tomorrow, we'd have no idea which fellow would pick up his racket, and whether he'd play from the baseline or the net."

Richard paused.

"You do play tennis?"

"I'm afraid not."

"Ah. Right. The point is, comrade Stalin appears to be on his last legs, and when he gives up his ghost, things are going to become very unpredictable. And not just in matters of international diplomacy. I mean right here in Moscow. Depending on who ends up in charge, the doors of the city could either be flung open to the world, or slammed shut and bolted from the inside."

"We must hope for the former," the Count declared.

"Absolutely," agreed Richard. "We certainly have no business praying for the latter. But whatever happens, it is preferable to anticipate. Which brings us to the point of my visit. You see, the group I'll be heading in Paris is in the intelligence field. A sort of research unit, as it were. And we are looking for some friends here and there who might be in a position now and then to shed some light on this or that. . . ."

"Richard," said the Count in some surprise, "you're not asking me to spy on my country."

"What? Spy on your country? Absolutely not, Alexander. I like to think of it more as a form of cosmopolitan gossip. You know: who was invited to the dance and who showed up uninvited; who was holding hands in the corner; and who got hot under the collar. The typical topics of a Sunday morning breakfast anywhere in the world. And in exchange for these sorts of trifles, we could prove generous to a fault. . . ."

The Count smiled.

"Richard, I am no more inclined to gossip than I am to spy. So, let's not speak of this again and we shall remain the best of friends."

"To the best of friends then," said Richard, clinking the Count's glass with his own.

And for the next hour, the two men set aside the game of tennis and spoke instead of their lives. The Count spoke of Sofia, who was making wonderful strides at the Conservatory, and who remained so thoughtful and quiet. Richard spoke of his boys, who were making wonderful strides in the nursery, and who remained neither thoughtful nor quiet. They spoke of Paris and Tolstoy and Carnegie Hall. Then at nine o'clock, these two kindred spirits rose from their seats.

"It's probably best if you see yourself out," said Richard. "Oh, and should it ever come up, you and Professor Sirovich had a lengthy debate on the future of the sonnet. You were in favor, he was against."

After they'd shaken hands, the Count watched Richard disappear into the bedroom, then he turned toward the door to let himself out. But as he passed the grandfather clock, he hesitated. How loyally it had stood in his grandmother's drawing room and sounded the time for tea, for supper, for bed. On Christmas Eve, it had signaled the moment when the Count and his sister could slide apart the seamless doors.

Opening the narrow glass door in the clock's cabinet, the Count reached inside and found the little key still on its hook. Inserting it into the keyhole, the Count wound the clock to its limit, set the time, and gave the pendulum a nudge, thinking: *Let the old man keep time for a few hours more.*

Almost nine months later, on the fifth of March 1953, the man known variously as Dear Father, Vozhd, Koba, Soso, or simply Stalin would die in his Kuntsevo residence in the aftermath of a stroke.

The following day, workmen and trucks laden down with flowers arrived at the Palace of Unions on Theatre Square, and within a matter of hours the building's facade was adorned with a portrait of Stalin three stories high.

On the sixth, Harrison Salisbury, the new Moscow bureau chief of *The New York Times*, stood in the Count's old rooms (now occupied by the Mexican chargé d'affaires), to watch as members of the Presidium arrived in a cavalcade of ZIM limousines and as Soso's coffin, taken from a bright blue ambulance, was borne ceremoniously inside. And on the seventh, when the Palace of Unions was opened to the public, Salisbury watched in some amazement as the line of citizens waiting to pay their respects stretched five miles across the city.

Why, many Western observers wondered, would over a million citizens stand in line to see the corpse of a tyrant? The flippant said it must have been to ensure that he was actually dead; but such a remark did not do justice to the men and women who waited and wept. In point of fact, legions mourned the loss of the man who had led them to victory in the Great Patriotic War against the forces of Hitler; legions more mourned the loss of the man who had so single-mindedly driven Russia to become a world power; while others simply wept in recognition that a new era of uncertainty had begun.

For, of course, Richard's prediction proved perfectly right. When Soso breathed his last, there was no plan of succession, no obvious designee. Within the Presidium there were eight different men who could reasonably claim the right to lead: Minister of Security Beria, Minister of the Armed Forces Bulganin, Deputy Chairman of the Council of Ministers Malenkov, Minister of Foreign Trade Mikoyan, Foreign Minister Molotov, Secretariat members Kaganovich and Voroshilov, and even former mayor of Moscow Nikita Khrushchev—that blunt, brutish, and bald apparatchik who not long before had perfected the five-story concrete apartment building.

Much to the relief of the West, it seemed in the aftermath of the funeral that the man most likely to prevail was the progressive internationalist and outspoken critic of nuclear arms, Malenkov—because, like Stalin, he was appointed as both Premier of the Party and General Secretary of the Central Committee. But a consensus quickly formed within the Party's upper ranks that no one man should ever be allowed to simultaneously hold both of these positions again. So ten days later, Party Premier Malenkov was forced to pass his chairmanship of the Secretariat to the conservative Khrushchev, setting the stage for a duumvirate of antagonists—a delicate balance of authority between two men of contrary views and ambiguous alliances, which would keep the world guessing for a few years to come.

"How can anyone live his life in expectation of the Latter?"

Despite having announced that he would have no more time for appointments that evening, when the Count asked this question, he was in Anna Urbanova's bed. . . .

"I know there is something quixotic in dreaming of the Former," he continued, "but when all is said and done, if the Former is even a remote possibility, then how can one submit to the likelihood of the Latter? To do so would be contrary to the human spirit. So fundamental is our desire to catch a glimpse of another way of life, or to share a glimpse of our way of life with another, that even when the forces of the Latter have bolted the city's doors, the forces of the Former will find a means to slip through the cracks."

The Count reached over, borrowed Anna's cigarette, and took a puff. Having thought for a moment, he waved the cigarette at the ceiling.

"In recent years, I have waited on Americans who have traveled all the way to Moscow to attend one performance at the Bolshoi. Meanwhile, our haphazard little trio in the Shalyapin will take a stab at any little bit of American music they've heard on the radio. These are unquestionably the forces of the Former on display."

The Count took another puff.

"When Emile is in his kitchen, does he cook the Latter? Of course not. He simmers, sears, and serves the Former. A veal from Vienna, a pigeon from Paris, or a seafood stew from the south of France. Or consider the case of Viktor Stepanovich—"

"You're not going to start in on the moths of Manchester again?"

"No," said the Count peevishly. "I am making a different point entirely. When Viktor and Sofia sit down at the piano, do they play Mussorgsky,

Mussorgsky, and Mussorgsky? No. They play Bach and Beethoven, Rossini and Puccini, while at Carnegie Hall the audience responds to Horowitz's performance of Tchaikovsky with thunderous applause."

The Count turned on his side to study the actress.

"You're keeping unusually quiet," he said, returning her cigarette. "Perhaps you don't agree?"

Anna took a drag and slowly exhaled.

"It's not that I disagree with you, Sasha. But I'm not so sure that one can simply dance away one's life to the tune of the Former, as you call it. Certain realities must be faced wherever you live, and in Russia that may mean a bit of bending to the Latter. Take your beloved bouillabaisse, or that ovation in Carnegie Hall. It is no coincidence that the cities from which your examples spring are port cities: Marseille and New York. I daresay, you could find similar examples in Shanghai and Rotterdam. But Moscow is not a port, my love. At the center of all that is Russia—of its culture, its psychology, and perhaps, its destiny—stands the Kremlin, a walled fortress a thousand years old and four hundred miles from sea. Physically speaking, its walls are no longer high enough to fend off attack; and yet, they still cast a shadow across the entire country."

The Count rolled onto his back and stared at the ceiling.

"Sasha, I know you don't want to accept the notion that Russia may be inherently inward looking, but do you think in America they are even having this conversation? Wondering if the gates of New York are about to be opened or closed? Wondering if the Former is more likely than the Latter? By all appearances, America was founded on the Former. They don't even know what the Latter is."

"You sound as if you dreamed of living in America."

"Everyone dreams of living in America."

"That's ridiculous."

"Ridiculous? Half of the inhabitants of Europe would move there tomorrow just for the conveniences."

"Conveniences! What conveniences?"

Turning on her side, Anna tamped out her cigarette, opened the drawer in the bedside table, and produced a large American magazine, which, the Count noted, was rather presumptuously entitled *LIFE*. Flipping through the pages, Anna began pointing to various brightly colored photographs.

Each one seemed to show the same woman in a different dress smiling before some newfangled contraption.

"Dishwashing machines. Clothes-washing machines. Vacuum cleaners. Toasters. Televisions. And look here, an automatic garage door."

"What is an automatic garage door?"

"It is a garage door that opens and closes itself on your behalf. What do you think of that?"

"I think if I were a garage door, I should rather miss the old days."

Anna lit another cigarette and handed it to the Count. He took a drag and watched the smoke spiral toward the ceiling where the Muses looked down from the clouds.

"I'll tell you what is convenient," he said after a moment. "To sleep until noon and have someone bring you your breakfast on a tray. To cancel an appointment at the very last minute. To keep a carriage waiting at the door of one party, so that on a moment's notice it can whisk you away to another. To sidestep marriage in your youth and put off having children altogether. These are the greatest of conveniences, Anushka—and at one time, I had them all. But in the end, it has been the inconveniences that have mattered to me most."

Anna Urbanova took the cigarette from the Count's fingers, dropped it in a water glass, and kissed him on the nose.

1953

Apostles and Apostates

L ike the wheeling of the stars," muttered the Count as he paced.

That is how time passes when one is left waiting unaccountably. The hours become interminable. The minutes relentless. And the seconds? Why, not only does every last one of them demand its moment on the stage, it insists upon making a soliloquy full of weighty pauses and artful hesitations and then leaps into an encore at the slightest hint of applause.

But hadn't the Count once waxed poetic over how slowly the stars advanced? Hadn't he rhapsodized over how the constellations seemed to halt in their course when on a warm summer's night one lay on one's back and listened for footsteps in the grass—as if nature itself were conspiring to lengthen the last few hours before daybreak, so that they could be savored to the utmost?

Well, yes. Certainly that was the case when one was twenty-two and waiting for a young lady in a meadow—having climbed the ivy and rapped on the glass. But to keep a man waiting when he is sixty-three? When his hair has thinned, his joints have stiffened, and his every breath might be his last? There is such a thing as courtesy, after all.

It must be nearly one in the morning, calculated the Count. The performance was scheduled to end by eleven. The reception by twelve. They should have been here half an hour ago.

"Are there no taxis left in Moscow? No trolley cars?" he wondered aloud.

Or had they stopped somewhere on the way home . . . ? Was it possible that in passing a café they could not resist the impulse to slip inside and share a pastry while he waited and waited and waited? Could they have been so heartless? (If so, they dare not attempt to hide the fact, for he could tell if a pastry had been eaten from a distance of fifty feet!)

The Count paused in his pacing to peek behind the Ambassador, where he had carefully hidden the Dom Pérignon.

Preparing for a *potential* celebration is a tricky business. If Fortune smiles, then one must be ready to hit the ceiling with the cork. But if Fortune shrugs, then one must be prepared to act as if this were just another night, one of no particular consequence—and then later sink the unopened bottle to the bottom of the sea.

The Count stuck his hand into the bucket. The ice was nearly half melted and the temperature of the water a perfect 50°. If they did not return soon, the temperature would become so tepid that the bottle *belonged* at the bottom of the sea.

Well, it would serve them right.

But as the Count withdrew his hand and stood to his full height, he heard an extraordinary sound emanating from the next room. It was the chime of the twice-tolling clock. Reliable Breguet announcing the stroke of midnight.

Impossible! The Count had been waiting for at least two hours. He had paced over twenty miles. It had to be half past one. Not a minute earlier.

"Perhaps reliable Breguet was no longer quite so reliable," muttered the Count. After all, the clock was over fifty years old, and even the finest time-pieces must be subject to the ravages of Time. Cogs will eventually lose their coginess just as springs will lose their springiness. But as the Count was having this thought, through the little window in the eaves he heard a clock tower in the distance tolling once, then twice, then thrice. . . .

"Yes, yes," he said, collapsing into his chair. "You've made your point."

Apparently, this was destined to be a day of exasperations.

Earlier that afternoon, the Boyarsky's staff had been assembled by the assistant manager so that he could introduce new procedures for the taking, placing, and billing of orders.

Henceforth, he explained, when a waiter took an order, he would write it on a pad designed for this purpose. Leaving the table, he would bring the order to the bookkeeper, who, having made an entry in his ledger, would issue a cooking slip for the kitchen. In the kitchen, a corresponding entry would be made in the cooking log, at which point the cooking could commence. When the food was ready for consumption, a confirmation slip would be issued by the kitchen to the bookkeeper, who in turn would provide a stamped receipt to the waiter authorizing the retrieval of the food. Thus, a few minutes later, the waiter would be able to make the appropriate notation on his notepad confirming that that dish which had been ordered, logged, cooked, and retrieved was finally on the table. . . .

Now, in all of Russia, there was no greater admirer of the written word than Count Alexander Ilyich Rostov. In his time, he had seen a couplet of Pushkin's sway a hesitant heart. He had watched as a single passage from Dostoevsky roused one man to action and another to indifference—in the very same hour. He certainly viewed it as providential that when Socrates held forth in the agora and Jesus on the Mount, someone in the audience had the presence of mind to set their words down for posterity. So let us agree that the Count's concerns with this new regimen were not grounded in some distaste for pencils and paper.

Rather, it was a matter of context. For if one has chosen to dine at the Piazza, one should expect to have one's waiter leaning over the table and scratching away on his little pad. But ever since the Count had become headwaiter of the Boyarsky, its customers could expect their server to look them in the eye, answer their questions, offer recommendations, and flawlessly record their preferences—without ever taking his hands from behind his back.

Sure enough, when the new regimen was put into practice that evening, the Boyarsky's customers were shocked to find a clerk sitting at a little desk behind the maître d's podium. They were bemused to watch pieces of paper flitting about the room as if it were the floor of a stock exchange. But they were beside themselves to find their cutlets of veal and asparagus spears arriving at their table as cold as aspic.

Naturally, this would not do.

As luck would have it, in the middle of the second seating the Count noticed the Bishop stopping momentarily at the Boyarsky's door. So, having been raised on the principle that civilized men should share their concerns and proceed in the spirit of collegial common sense, the Count crossed the dining room and followed the Bishop into the hall.

"Manager Leplevsky!"

"Headwaiter Rostov," said the Bishop, showing a hint of surprise at being hailed by the Count. "What can I do for you . . . ?"

"It's really such a small matter that I hardly wish to trouble you with it."

"If the matter concerns the hotel, then it concerns me."

"Just so," agreed the Count. "Now, I assure you, Manager Leplevsky, that in all of Russia there is no greater admirer of the written word . . ." And having thus broached the subject, the Count went on to applaud the couplets of Pushkin, the paragraphs of Dostoevsky, and the transcriptions of Socrates and Jesus. Then he explained the threat that pencils and pads posed to the Boyarsky's tradition of romantic elegance.

"Can you imagine," concluded the Count with a glint in his eye, "if when you sought your wife's hand, you had to issue your proposal with the stamp of a presiding agency, and were then required to take down her response on a little pad of paper in triplicate—so that you could give one copy to her, one to her father, and one to the family priest?"

But even as the Count was delivering this quip, he was reminded by the expression on the Bishop's face that one should generally avoid quips in which a man's marriage played a part. . . .

"I don't see that my wife has anything to do with this," said the Bishop.

"No," agreed the Count. "That was poorly put. What I am trying to say is that Andrey, Emile, and I—"

"So you are bringing this grievance on behalf of Maître d' Duras and Chef Zhukovsky?"

"Well, no. I have hailed you of my own accord. And it is not a grievance per se. But the three of us are dedicated to ensuring the satisfaction of the Boyarsky's customers."

The Bishop smiled.

"Of course. And I am sure that all three of you have your own special concerns given your specific duties. But as *manager* of the Metropol, I am the one who must ensure that *every* aspect of the hotel meets a standard of perfection; and *that* requires a vigilant attention to the elimination of all discrepancies."

The Count was confused.

"Discrepancies? What sort of discrepancies?"

"All kinds of discrepancies. One day, there may be a discrepancy between how many onions arrived in the kitchen and how many were served in the stew. On another, there may be a discrepancy between how many glasses of wine were ordered and how many poured."

The Count grew cold.

"You are speaking of thievery."

"Am I?"

The two men stared at each other for a moment, then the Bishop smiled narrowly.

"Given your shared dedication, please feel free to relate our conversation to Chef Zhukovsky and Maître d' Duras at your earliest convenience."

The Count gritted his teeth.

"Rest assured, I shall do so word for word tomorrow at our daily meeting."

The Bishop studied the Count.

"You have a daily meeting . . . ?"

Suffice it to say that at the Boyarsky's second seating, the customers were shocked, bemused, and beside themselves once again as slips of paper flew about the dining room like pheasants at the crack of a rifle. And after enduring all of that, here was the Count sitting alone in his study counting the minutes.

After drumming his fingers on the armrest of his chair, the Count rose and recommenced his pacing while humming Mozart's Piano Sonata No. 1 in C major.

"Dum de dum de dum," he hummed.

It was a delightful composition, you had to admit, and one quite well suited to his daughter's personality. The first movement had the tempo of Sofia coming home from school at the age of ten with fifteen things to relate. Without taking the time to explain who was who or what was what, she would zip along, punctuating her report with *and then, and then, and then, and then*. In the second movement, the sonata transitioned to an andante tempo more in keeping with Sofia at seventeen, when she would welcome thunderstorms on Saturday afternoons so that she could sit in their study with a book in her lap or a recording on the phonograph. In the third movement, with its fleet pace and pointillist style, you could almost hear her at the age of thirteen, running down the hotel's stairs, freezing on a landing momentarily to let someone pass, and then bolting brightly ahead.

Yes, it was a delightful composition. There was no debating that. But was it *too* delightful? Would it be viewed by the judges as insufficiently weighty for the times? When Sofia had selected the composition, the Count had attempted to signal his concerns diplomatically, by referring to the piece as "pleasant" and "quite diverting"; and then he had kept his peace. For it is the role of the parent to express his concerns and then take three steps back. Not one, mind you, not two, but three. Or maybe four. (But by no means five.) Yes, a parent should share his hesitations and then take three or four steps back, so that the child can make a decision by herself—even when that decision may lead to disappointment.

But wait!

What was that?

As the Count turned, the closet door swung open and Anna charged into the study, dragging Sofia behind her.

"She won!"

For the first time in twenty years, the Count let out a shout: "Ha-ha!"

He embraced Anna for delivering the news.

Then he embraced Sofia for winning.

Then he embraced Anna again.

"We're sorry we're so late," said Anna breathlessly. "But they wouldn't let her leave the reception."

"Don't think of it for a minute! I hadn't even noticed the time. But sit, sit, sit, and tell me everything."

Offering the ladies the high-back chairs, the Count perched himself on the edge of the Ambassador and trained his gaze on Sofia, expectantly. Smiling shyly, Sofia deferred to Anna.

"It was incredible," said the actress. "There were five performers before Sofia. Two violinists, a cellist—"

"Where was it? Which venue?"

"In the Grand Hall."

"I know it well. Designed by Zagorsky at the turn of the century. How crowded was it? Who was there?"

Anna furrowed her brow. Sofia laughed.

"Papa. Let her tell it."

"All right, all right."

So the Count did as he was instructed: He let Anna tell it. And she told how there were five performers before Sofia: two violinists, a cellist, a French-horn player, and another pianist. All five had done the Conservatory proud, comporting themselves professionally and playing their instruments with precision. Two pieces by Tchaikovsky, two by Rimsky-Korsakov, and something by Borodin. But then it was Sofia's turn.

"I tell you, Sasha, there was an audible gasp when she appeared. She crossed the stage to the piano without the slightest rustle of her dress. It was as if she were floating."

"You taught me that, Aunt Anna."

"No, no, Sofia. The manner in which you entered is *unteachable*."

"Without a doubt," agreed the Count.

"Well. When the director announced that Sofia would be playing Mozart's Piano Sonata No. 1, there was some muttering and a shifting of chairs. But the moment she began to play, they were overcome."

"I knew it. Didn't I say so? Didn't I say that a little Mozart is never out of step?"

"Papa . . ."

"She played with such tenderness," Anna continued, "such joy, that the audience was won over from the start. There was a smile on every face in every row, I tell you. And the applause when she finished! If only you could have heard it, Sasha. It shook the dust from the chandeliers."

The Count clapped his own hands and rubbed them together.

"How many musicians performed after Sofia?"

"It didn't matter. The competition was over and everyone knew it. The poor boy who was up next practically had to be dragged onstage. And then, she was the belle of the reception, being toasted from every corner."

"*Mon Dieu!*" exclaimed the Count, leaping to his feet. "I nearly forgot!"

He shoved aside the Ambassador and produced the bucket with the champagne.

"*Voilà!*"

As his hand dipped in the water, the Count could tell the temperature had climbed to 53°, but what did *that* matter. With a single twist of the fingers he spun the foil off the bottle, then to the ceiling with the cork! The champagne flowed over his hands and they all laughed. He filled two flutes for the ladies and a wine glass for himself.

"To Sofia," he said. "Let tonight mark the beginning of a grand adventure—one that is sure to take her far and wide."

"Papa," she said with a blush. "It was just a school competition."

"Just a school competition! It is one of the intrinsic limitations of being young, my dear, that you can never tell when a grand adventure has just begun. But as a man of experience, you may take my word that—"

Suddenly Anna silenced the Count by holding up her hand. She looked to the closet door.

"Did you hear that?"

The three stood motionless. Sure enough, though muffled, they could hear the sound of a voice. Someone must have been at the bedroom door.

"I'll find out who it is," whispered the Count.

Setting down his glass, he slipped between his jackets, opened the closet door, and stepped into his bedroom only to discover—Andrey and Emile at the foot of the bed in the midst of a hushed debate. Emile was holding a ten-layered cake in the shape of a piano, and Andrey must have just suggested they leave it on the bed with a note, because Emile was replying that one does not "dump a Dobos torte on a bedcover"—when the closet door opened and out popped the Count.

Andrey let out a gasp.

The Count drew in a breath.

Emile dropped the cake.

And the evening might have come to an end right then and there, but for Andrey's instinctive inability to let an object fall to the floor. With the lightest of steps and his fingers outstretched, the onetime juggler caught the torte in midair.

As Andrey breathed a sigh of relief and Emile stared with his mouth open, the Count attempted to act matter-of-factly.

"Why, Andrey, Emile, what a pleasant surprise. . . ."

Taking his cue from the Count, Andrey acted as if nothing out of the ordinary had just happened. "Emile made a little something for Sofia in anticipation of her victory," he said. "Please give her our heartfelt congratulations." Then placing the cake gently on the Grand Duke's desk, Andrey turned to the door.

But Emile didn't budge.

"Alexander Ilyich," he demanded: "What in the name of Ivan were you doing in the closet?"

"In the closet?" asked the Count. "Why, I . . . I was . . ." His voice trailed off diminuendo.

Andrey offered a sympathetic smile and then made a little sweeping motion with his hands, as if to say: *The world is wide, and wondrous are the ways of men. . . .*

But Emile furrowed his brow at Andrey, as if to say: *Nonsense.*

The Count looked from one member of the Triumvirate to the other.

"Where are my manners?" he said at last. "Sofia will be delighted to see you both. Please. Come this way." Then he gestured with a welcoming hand to the closet.

Emile looked at the Count as if he'd lost his mind. But Andrey, who could never hesitate before a well-mannered invitation, picked up the cake and took a step toward the closet door.

Emile let out a grunt of exasperation. "If we're going in," he said to Andrey, "then you'd better watch out for the frosting on the sleeves." So the maître d' passed Emile the cake and carefully parted the Count's jackets with his delicate hands.

Emerging on the other side, Andrey's surprise at seeing the Count's study for the first time was immediately displaced by the sight of Sofia. "*Notre champion!*" he said, taking her by the arms and kissing her on both cheeks. For Emile, however, the surprise at seeing the Count's study was displaced by the even greater surprise of finding the film star Anna Urbanova standing inside it. For unbeknownst to the Triumvirate, the chef had seen every single one of her movies, and generally from the second row.

Noting Emile's starstruck expression, Andrey took a quick step forward and put his hands under the cake. But Emile did not lose his grip this time. Rather, he suddenly thrust the cake toward Anna, as if he had baked it for her.

"Thank you so much," she said. "But isn't that for Sofia?"

Emile blushed from his shoulders to the top of his balding head and turned to Sofia.

"I made your favorite," he said. "A Dobos torte with chocolate cream."

"Thank you, Uncle Emile."

"It is in the shape of a piano," he added.

As Emile produced his chopper from his apron string and proceeded to slice the cake, the Count took two more glasses from the Ambassador and filled them with champagne. The story of Sofia's victory was told again and the perfection of her performance was compared by Anna to the perfection of Emile's cake. As the chef began explaining to the actress the intricate process by which one makes such a torte, Andrey was recalling for Sofia's benefit the night many years ago when he and several others had toasted the Count's arrival on the sixth floor.

"Do you remember, Alexander?"

"As if it were yesterday," replied the Count with a smile. "You did the honors with the brandy that night, my friend; and Marina was here along with Vasily. . . ."

As if by an act of magic, at the very instant the Count said Vasily's name, the concierge stepped through the closet door. In military fashion, he clicked his heels and greeted those assembled in rapid succession without showing the slightest indication of surprise as to their whereabouts:

"Miss Urbanova. Sofia. Andrey. Emile." Then turning to the Count, he said: "Alexander Ilyich, may I have a word . . . ?"

From the manner in which Vasily asked the question, it was clear that he wished to take the Count aside. But as the Count's study was but a hundred foot square, they could only step about three feet away from the others in order to secure their privacy—an action that was immediately rendered inconsequential when the other four members of the party moved a similar distance in a similar direction.

"I wish to inform you," said Vasily (in a manner sort of *entre nous*), "that the hotel's manager is on his way."

It was the Count's turn to express surprise.

"On his way where?"

"On his way here. Or rather . . . there," said Vasily, pointing back toward the Count's bedroom.

"But for what possible reason?"

Vasily explained that as he was reviewing the next night's reservations, he happened to notice the Bishop lingering in the lobby. When a few minutes later a rather *petit* gentleman wearing a brimmed hat approached the front desk and asked for the Count by name, the Bishop introduced himself, indicated that he had been expecting the visitor, and offered to show him personally to the Count's room.

"When was this?"

"They were just entering the elevator when I took to the stairs; but they were accompanied by Mr. Harriman from suite 215 and the Tarkovs from room 426. Accounting for the stops at the second and fourth floors, I suspect they should be here any second."

"Good God!"

The members of the party looked to one another.

"No one make a sound," said the Count. Entering the closet, he closed the study door behind him, then he opened the door to his bedroom a little more cautiously than he had the last time. Relieved to find the room empty, he shut the closet door, took up Sofia's copy of *Fathers and Sons*, sat in his desk chair, and tilted back on two legs just in time to hear the knock on the door.

"Who is it?" called out the Count.

"It is Manager Leplevsky," called back the Bishop.

The Count let the front legs of his chair drop with a thump and opened the door to reveal the Bishop and a stranger in the hall.

"I hope we are not disturbing you," said the Bishop.

"Well, it is a rather unusual hour for paying a call. . . ."

"Of course," said the Bishop with a smile. "But allow me to introduce you to comrade Frinovsky. He was asking after you in the lobby, so I took the liberty of showing him the way, what with your room's . . . remoteness."

"How considerate of you," replied the Count.

When Vasily had noted that comrade Frinovsky was *petit*, the Count had assumed the concierge was being colorful in his choice of adjectives. But in point of fact, the word *small* would not have been sufficiently diminutive to suggest comrade Frinovsky's size. When the Count addressed the visitor, he had to resist the temptation of getting down on his haunches.

"How can I be of service to you, Mr. Frinovsky?"

"I am here in regards to your daughter," Frinovsky explained, taking his little hat from his head.

"Sofia?" asked the Count.

"Yes, Sofia. I am the director of the Red October Youth Orchestra. Your daughter was recently brought to our attention as a gifted pianist. In fact, I had the pleasure of attending her performance tonight, which accounts for the lateness of my visit. But with the greatest pleasure, I come to confer upon her a position as our second pianist."

"The Youth Orchestra of Moscow!" exclaimed the Count. "How wonderful. Where are you housed?"

"No. I'm sorry if I haven't been clear," explained Frinovsky. "The Red October Youth Orchestra is not in Moscow. It is in Stalingrad."

After a moment of bewilderment, the Count attempted to compose himself.

"As I said, it is a wonderful offer, Mr. Frinovsky. . . . But I am afraid that Sofia would not be interested."

Frinovsky looked to the Bishop as if he hadn't understood the Count's remark.

The Bishop simply shook his head.

"But it is not a matter of interest," Frinovsky said to the Count. "A requisition has been made and an appointment has been granted—by the regional undersecretary of cultural affairs." The director took a letter from his jacket, handed it to the Count, and reached over to point to the undersecretary's signature. "As you can see, Sofia is to report to the orchestra on the first of September."

With a feeling of nausea, the Count read over this letter that, in the most technical of language, welcomed his daughter to an orchestra in an industrial city six hundred miles away.

"The Youth Orchestra of Stalingrad," the Bishop said. "How exciting this must be for you, Alexander Ilyich. . . ."

Looking up from the letter, the Count saw the flash of spite in the Bishop's smile, and just like that the Count's feelings of nausea and bewilderment were gone—having been replaced by a cold fury. Standing to his full height, the Count took a step toward the Bishop with every intention of grabbing him by the lapels, or better yet the throat—when the door to the closet opened and Anna Urbanova stepped into the room.

The Count, the Bishop, and the *petit* musical director all looked up in surprise.

Crossing gracefully to the Count's side and delicately placing her hand at the small of his back, Anna studied the expressions of the two men in the doorway then addressed the Bishop with a smile.

"Why, Manager Leplevsky, you look as if you've never seen a beautiful woman step from a closet before."

"I haven't," sputtered the Bishop.

"Of course," she said sympathetically. Then she turned her attention to the stranger. "And who have we here?"

Before the Bishop or the Count could reply, the little man piped up:

"Comrade Ivan Frinovsky, director of the Red October Youth Orchestra of Stalingrad. It is an honor and a privilege to meet you, comrade Urbanova!"

"An honor and a privilege," echoed Anna with her most disarming smile. "You exaggerate, comrade Frinovsky; but I shan't hold it against you."

Comrade Frinovsky returned the actress's smile with a blush.

"Here," she added, "let me help you with your hat."

For, as a matter of fact, the musical director had folded his hat two times over. Taking it from his hands, Anna gently restored the crown, snapped the brim, and returned the hat in a manner that would be retold by the director a few hundred times in the years to come.

"So, you are the musical director of the Youth Orchestra in Stalingrad?"

"I am," he said.

"Then perhaps you know comrade Nachevko?"

At the mention of the round-faced Minister of Culture, the director stood up so straight he added an inch to his stature.

"I have never had the honor."

"Panteleimon is a delightful man," assured Anna, "and a great supporter of youthful artistry. In fact, he has taken a personal interest in Alexander's daughter, young Sofia."

"A personal interest . . . ?"

"Oh, yes. Why, just last night at dinner, he was telling me how exciting it will be to watch her talent develop. I sense he has great plans for her here in the capital."

"I wasn't aware. . . ."

The director looked to the Bishop with the expression of one who has been put in an uncomfortable position due to no fault of his own. Turning back to the Count, he delicately retrieved his letter. "If your daughter should ever be interested in performing in Stalingrad," he said, "I hope you will not hesitate to contact me."

"Thank you, comrade Frinovsky," said the Count. "That's very gracious of you."

Looking from Anna to the Count and back again, Frinovsky said, "I am so sorry that we have inconvenienced you at such an unsuitable hour." Then he placed his hat on his head and hurried to the belfry with the Bishop hot on his heels.

When the Count had quietly closed the door, he turned to Anna, whose expression was unusually grave.

"When did the Minister of Culture start taking a personal interest in Sofia?" he asked.

"Tomorrow afternoon," she replied. "At the latest."

If those gathered in the Count's study had good cause to celebrate before the Bishop's visit, they had even more cause to do so after his departure. In fact, as the Count opened a bottle of brandy, Anna found an American jazz record that Richard had slipped among the classical recordings, and cued it on the phonograph. In the minutes that followed, the brandy was poured liberally, Emile's cake was eaten in its entirety, the jazz record was played repeatedly, and each of the gentlemen had his turn scuffing the parquet with the ladies in attendance.

When the last of the brandy was dispensed, Emile—who given the hour was nearly in a state of ecstasy—suggested they all head downstairs for another round, a little more dancing, and to bring the festivities to Viktor Stepanovich, who was still on the bandstand in the Piazza.

Emile's motion was immediately seconded and passed by unanimous vote.

"But before we go," said Sofia, who was a little flushed, "I would like to make a toast: To my guardian angel, my father, and my friend, Count Alexander Rostov. A man inclined to see the best in all of us."

"Hear! Hear!"

"And you needn't worry, Papa," Sofia continued. "For no matter who comes knocking at our door, I have no intention of ever leaving the Metropol."

After joining in a cheer, the members of the gathering emptied their glasses, stumbled through the closet, and exited into the hall. Opening the door to the belfry, the Count gave a slight bow and gestured for everyone to proceed. But just as the Count was about to follow the others into the stairwell, a woman in late middle age with a satchel on her shoulder and a kerchief in her hair stepped from the shadows at the end of the hall. Though the Count had never seen her before, it was clear from her demeanor that she had been waiting to speak with him alone.

"Andrey," the Count called into the belfry, "I've forgotten something in the room. You all go ahead. I'll be down in a moment. . . ."

Only when the last sound of voices had receded down the stairs did the woman approach. In the light, the Count could see that she had an almost severe beauty about her—like one for whom there would be no half measures in matters of the heart.

"I'm Katerina Litvinova," she said without a smile.

It took a moment for the Count to realize that this was none other than Mishka's Katerina, the poet from Kiev whom he had lived with back in the 1920s.

"Katerina Litvinova! How extraordinary. To what do I owe—"

"Is there somewhere we could talk?"

"Why, yes . . . Of course . . ."

The Count led Katerina into the bedroom and then, after a moment's hesitation, took her through the jackets into the study. Apparently, he needn't have hesitated, for she looked around the room as one who had heard descriptions of it before, nodding lightly to herself as her gaze shifted from the bookcase to the coffee table to the Ambassador. Taking her satchel from her shoulder, she suddenly appeared tired.

"Here," said the Count, offering a chair.

She sat down, putting the satchel in her lap. Then passing a hand over her head, she removed her kerchief, revealing light brown hair cut as short as a man's.

"It's Mishka, isn't it . . . ," the Count said after a moment.

"Yes."

"When?"

"A week ago today."

The Count nodded, as one who had been expecting the news for some time. He didn't ask Katerina how his old friend had died, and she didn't offer to tell him. It was plain enough that he had been betrayed by his times.

"Were you with him?" asked the Count.

"Yes."

"In Yavas?"

"Yes."

. . .

"I was under the impression that . . ."

"I lost my husband some time ago."

"I'm sorry. I didn't know. Do you have children . . . ?"

"No."

She said it curtly, as if in response to a foolish question; but then she continued more softly. "I received word from Mikhail in January. I went to him in Yavas. We have been together these last six months." After a moment, she added: "He spoke of you often."

"He was a loyal friend," said the Count.

"He was a man of devotions," corrected Katerina.

The Count had been about to remark on Mishka's propensity for getting into scrapes and his love of pacing, but she had just described his old friend better than he ever had. Mikhail Fyodorovich Mindich was a man of devotions.

"And a fine poet," the Count added, almost to himself.

"One of two."

The Count looked to Katerina as if he didn't understand. Then he offered a wistful smile.

"I've never written a poem in my life," he said.

Now, it was Katerina who didn't understand.

"What do you mean? What about *Where Is It Now?*"

"It was Mishka who wrote that poem. In the south parlor at Idlehour . . . In the summer of 1913 . . ."

As Katerina still looked confused, the Count elaborated.

"What with the revolt of 1905 and the repressions that followed, when we graduated it was still a dangerous time for writing poems of political impatience. Given Mishka's background, the Okhrana would have swept him up with a broom. So one night—after polishing off a particularly good bottle of Margaux—we decided to publish the poem under my name."

"But why yours?"

"What were they going to do to Count Alexander Rostov—member of the Jockey Club and godson of a counselor to the Tsar?" The Count shook his head. "The irony, of course, is that the life which ended up being saved was mine, not his. But for that poem, they would have shot me back in 1922."

Katerina, who had listened to this story intently, was suddenly holding back tears.

"Ah, but there you have him," she said.

They were both silent as she regained her composure.

"I want you to know," said the Count, "how much I appreciate your coming to tell me in person." But Katerina dismissed his gratitude.

"I came at Mikhail's request. He asked me to bring you something."

From her satchel she took out a rectangular package wrapped in plain brown paper and tied with twine.

Taking the package in hand, the Count could tell from its weight that it was a book.

"It is his project," said the Count with a smile.

"Yes," she said. Then she added with pointed emphasis: "He slaved over it."

The Count nodded to express his understanding and to assure Katerina that he did not take the bestowal lightly.

Katerina looked once more around the room with a light shake of the head as if it somehow exemplified the mystery of outcomes; then she said that she should go.

The Count rose to his feet with her, setting Mishka's project on the chair.

"Are you going back to Yavas?" he asked.

"No."

"Will you be staying in Moscow?"

"No."

"Where then?"

"Does it matter?"

She turned to go.

"Katerina . . ."

"Yes?"

"Is there anything I can do for you?"

Katerina looked surprised at first by the Count's offer, then ready to dismiss it. But after a moment, she said: "Remember him."

Then she went out the door.

Returning to his chair, the Count sat in silence. After a few minutes, he took up Mishka's legacy, untied the twine, and folded back the paper. Inside there was a small volume bound in leather. Tooled into the cover was a simple geometric design, at the center of which was the work's title: *Bread and Salt*. From the roughly cut pages and loose threads, one could tell that the binding was the work of a dedicated amateur.

After running his hand over the surface of the cover, the Count opened the book to the title page. There, tucked in the seam, was the photograph that had been taken in 1912 at the Count's insistence, and much to Mishka's chagrin. On the left, the young Count stood with a top hat on his head, a glint in his eye, and moustaches that extended beyond the limits of his cheeks; while on the right stood Mishka, looking as if he were about to sprint from the frame.

And yet, he had kept the picture all these years.

With a sorrowful smile, the Count set the photograph down and then turned the title leaf to the first page of his old friend's book. All it contained was a single quotation in a slightly uneven typeset:

And to Adam he said, "Because you have listened to the voice of your wife, and have eaten of the tree of which I commanded you, 'You shall not eat of it,' cursed is the ground because of you . . . In the sweat of your face you shall eat **BREAD** till you return to the ground, for out of it you were taken; you are dust, and to dust you shall return."

Genesis
3:17–19

The Count turned to the second page, on which there was also one quotation:

> And the tempter came and said to him, "If you are the Son of God, command these stones to become loaves of **BREAD**." But he answered, "It is written, 'Man shall not live by **BREAD** alone, but by every word that proceeds from the mouth of God.'"
>
> *Matthew*
> *4:3–4*

And then to the third . . .

> And he took **BREAD**, and when he had given thanks he broke it and gave it to them, saying, "This is my body which is given for you. Do this in remembrance of me."
>
> *Luke*
> *22:19*

As the Count continued turning slowly through the pages, he found himself laughing. For here was Mishka's project in a nutshell: a compendium of quotations from seminal texts arranged in chronological order, but in each of which the word *bread* had been capitalized and printed in bold. Beginning with the Bible, the citations proceeded right through the works of the Greeks and Romans onto the likes of Shakespeare, Milton, and Goethe. But particular tribute was paid to the golden age of Russian literature:

> For the sake of propriety, Ivan Yakovlevich put his tailcoat on over his undershirt and, settling at the table, poured out some salt, prepared two onions, took a knife in his hands, and, assuming a significant air, began cutting the **BREAD**. Having cut the loaf in two, he looked into the middle and, to his surprise, saw something white. Ivan Yakovlevich poked cautiously with his knife and felt with his finger. "Firm!" he said to himself. "What could it be?"
>
> He stuck in his fingers and pulled out—a nose!
>
> *"The Nose"*
> Nikolai Gogol
> (1836)

When a man isn't meant to live upon the earth, the sunshine doesn't warm him as it does others, and **BREAD** doesn't nourish him and make him strong.

A Sportsman's Sketches
Ivan Turgenev
(1852)

The past and the present merged together. He was dreaming he had reached the promised land flowing with milk and honey, where people ate **BREAD** they had not earned and went clothed in gold and silver. . . .

Oblomov
Ivan Goncharov
(1859)

"It's all nonsense," he said hopefully, "and there was nothing to be troubled about! Just some physical disorder. One glass of beer, a piece of dry **BREAD**, and see—in an instant the mind gets stronger, the thoughts clearer, the intentions firmer!"

Crime and Punishment
Fyodor Dostoevsky
(1866)

I, the vile Lebedev, do not believe in the carts that deliver **BREAD** to mankind! For carts that deliver **BREAD** to all mankind, without any moral foundations for their action, may quite cold-bloodedly exclude a considerable part of mankind from enjoying what they deliver.

The Idiot
Fyodor Dostoevsky
(1869)

And do you know, do you know that mankind can live without the Englishman, it can live without Germany, it can live only too well without the Russian man, it can live without science, without **BREAD**, and it only cannot live without beauty. . . .

Demons
Fyodor Dostoevsky
(1872)

All this happened at the same time: a boy ran up to a pigeon and, smiling, looked at Levin; the pigeon flapped its wings and fluttered off, sparkling in the sun amidst the air trembling with snowdust, while the smell of baked **BREAD** wafted from the window as the rolls appeared in it. All this together was so extraordinarily good that Levin laughed and wept from joy.

Anna Karenina
Leo Tolstoy
(1877)

Do you see these stones in this bare, scorching desert? Turn them into **BREAD** and mankind will run after you like sheep, grateful and obedient. . . . But you did not want to deprive man of freedom and rejected the offer, for what sort of freedom is it, you reasoned, if obedience is bought with loaves of **BREAD**?

From "The Grand Inquisitor"
The Brothers Karamazov
Fyodor Dostoevsky
(1880)

As the Count turned the pages, he smiled in recognition of the characteristic feistiness that Mishka's project expressed. But following the quote from "The Grand Inquisitor," there was a second citation from *The Brothers Karamazov* from a scene the Count had all but forgotten. It related to the little boy, Ilyushechka—the one who was hounded by his schoolmates until falling dangerously ill. When the boy finally dies, his heartstricken father tells the saintly Alyosha Karamazov that his son had made one final request:

Papa, when they put the dirt on my grave, crumble a crust of **BREAD** on it so the sparrows will come, and I'll hear that they've come and be glad that I'm not lying alone.

Upon reading this, Alexander Rostov finally broke down and wept. Certainly, he wept for his friend, that generous yet temperamental soul who only briefly found his moment in time—and who, like this forlorn child, was disinclined to condemn the world for all its injustices.

But, of course, the Count also wept for himself. For despite his friendships with Marina and Andrey and Emile, despite his love for Anna, despite Sofia—that extraordinary blessing that had struck him from the blue—when Mikhail Fyodorovich Mindich died, there went the last of those who had known him as a younger man. Though, as Katerina had so rightfully observed, at least he remained to remember.

Taking a deep breath, the Count attempted to restore his composure, determined to read through the final pages of his old friend's final discourse. The progression of citations, which had spanned over two thousand years, did not continue much further. For rather than extending into the present, the survey ended in June 1904, with the sentences that Mishka had cut from Chekhov's letter all those years ago:

> Here in Berlin, we've taken a comfortable room in the best hotel. I am very much enjoying the life here and haven't eaten so well and with such an appetite in a long time. The **BREAD** here is amazing, I've been stuffing myself with it, the coffee is excellent, and the dinners are beyond words. People who have never been abroad don't know how good **BREAD** can be. . . .

Given the hardships of the 1930s, the Count supposed he could understand why Shalamov (or his superiors) had insisted upon this little bit of censorship—having presumed that Chekhov's observation could only lead to feelings of discontent or ill will. But the irony, of course, was that Chekhov's observation was no longer even accurate. For surely, by now, the Russian people knew better than anyone in Europe how good a piece of bread could be.

When the Count closed Mishka's book, he did not head straight downstairs to join the others. Instead, he remained in his study, lost in thought.

Given the circumstances, an observer might understandably have drawn the conclusion that as the Count sat there he was dwelling on memories of his old friend. But, in fact, he was no longer thinking about Mishka. He was thinking about Katerina. In particular, he was thinking—with a sense of foreboding—that in the course of twenty years this firefly, this pinwheel, this wonder of the world had become a woman who, when asked where she was going, could answer without the slightest hesitation: *Does it matter?*

BOOK FIVE

BOOK FIVE

Applause and Acclaim

Paris . . . ?"

Or so asked Andrey in the manner of one who cannot quite believe what he has heard.

"Yes," said Emile.

"Paris . . . *France?*"

Emile furrowed his brow. "Are you drunk? Have you been knocked on the head?"

"But how?" asked the maître d'.

Emile sat back in his chair and nodded. For here was a question that was worthy of a man of intelligence.

It is a well-known fact that of all the species on earth *Homo sapiens* is among the most adaptable. Settle a tribe of them in a desert and they will wrap themselves in cotton, sleep in tents, and travel on the backs of camels; settle them in the Arctic and they will wrap themselves in sealskin, sleep in igloos, and travel by dog-drawn sled. And if you settle them in a Soviet climate? They will learn to make friendly conversation with strangers while waiting in line; they will learn to neatly stack their clothing in their half of the bureau drawer; and they will learn to draw imaginary buildings in their sketchbooks. That is, they will adapt. But certainly one aspect of adaptation for those Russians who had seen Paris before the Revolution was the acceptance that they would never, ever see Paris again. . . .

"Here he is now," said Emile as the Count came through the door. "Ask him yourself."

Having taken his seat, the Count confirmed that six months hence, on the twenty-first of June, Sofia would be in Paris, France. And when asked how this could possibly have come about, with a shrug the Count responded: "VOKS." That is, the All-Union Society for Cultural Relations with Foreign Countries.

It was now Emile's turn to express disbelief: "Do we have cultural relations with foreign countries?"

"Apparently, we are now sending our artists all around the world. In April we are sending the ballet to New York; in May we are sending a dramatic ensemble to London; and in June we are sending the orchestra of the Moscow Conservatory to Minsk, Prague, and Paris—where Sofia will be performing Rachmaninov at the Palais Garnier."

"It's incredible," said Andrey.

"Fantastical," said Emile.

"I know."

The three men laughed, until Emile pointed his chopper at his colleagues:

"But well deserved."

"Oh, absolutely."

"Without a doubt."

The three were quiet, each lost for a moment in their respective memories of the City of Light.

"Do you think it has changed?" wondered Andrey.

"Yes," said Emile. "As much as the pyramids."

And here, the three members of the Triumvirate might have waded into the rose-colored past, but for the fact that the door to Emile's office swung open and in walked the newest member of the Boyarsky's daily meeting: the Bishop.

"Good afternoon, gentlemen. I'm sorry to keep you waiting. There was business at the front desk that demanded my immediate attention. In the future, please don't feel the need to congregate until I have arrived."

Emile grunted, semiaudibly.

Ignoring the chef, the Bishop turned to the Count.

"Headwaiter Rostov, isn't this your day of rest? You shouldn't feel the need to be in attendance at the daily meeting when you are not scheduled to work."

"Well informed is well prepared," said the Count.

"Of course."

Some years before, the Bishop had helpfully explained to the Count that while the Metropol's employees each had their narrow little tasks, the manager alone had to ensure a standard of excellence for the entire hotel. And to be fair, the Bishop's personality made him perfectly suited to the task. For whether in the guest rooms, the lobby, or the linen closet on the second floor, no detail was too small, no flaw too immaterial, no moment too inopportune to receive the benefit of the Bishop's precious, persnickety, and mildly dismissive interference. And that was certainly the case within the walls of the Boyarsky.

The daily meeting commenced with a detailed description of the evening's special offerings. Naturally, the Bishop had dispensed with the tradition of tasting the specials, on the grounds that the chef knew perfectly well what his food tasted like, and to prepare samples for the staff was both indiscriminate and wasteful. Instead, Emile was instructed to write out a description of the specials by hand.

With another grunt, the chef slid his menu across the table. After inscribing a series of circles, arrows, and x's, the Bishop's pencil paused.

"I should think that beets would accompany the pork quite as well as apples," he reflected. "And if I am not mistaken, Chef Zhukovsky, you still have a bushel of beets in the pantry."

As the Bishop inserted this improvement into Emile's menu, the chef cast a furious glance across the table at the man he now referred to as Count Blabbermouth.

Handing the corrected menu back to the chef, the Bishop now turned his attention to the maître d', who slid the Book across the table. Despite the fact that it was one of the last days of 1953, the Bishop opened the Book to the first page and turned through the weeks of the year one by one. Finally arriving at the present, he scrutinized the evening's reservations with the tip of his pencil. Then he provided seating instructions to Andrey and slid the Book back. As a final piece of business, the Bishop alerted the maître d' to the fact that the flowers in the dining room's centerpiece had begun to wilt.

"I noted that as well," said Andrey. "But I am afraid our flower shop has not been carrying the inventory necessary to ensure a frequent refreshing of the arrangement."

"If you cannot secure flowers of sufficient freshness from Florist Eisenberg, then perhaps it is time to switch to a silk arrangement. That would obviate the necessity for refreshing the arrangement and should have the added benefit of proving more economical."

"I shall speak with Florist Eisenberg today," said Andrey.

"Of course."

Once the Bishop had concluded the meeting and Emile had gone off grumbling in search of his bushel of beets, the Count accompanied Andrey to the main staircase.

"*À tout à l'heure*," said the maître d', as he headed down to the flower shop.

"*À bientôt*," said the Count as he headed up to his rooms.

But as soon as Andrey had disappeared from sight, the Count was back on the second-floor landing. Spying around the corner to confirm that his friend was gone, the Count hurried to the Boyarsky. Having locked the door behind him, he peeked into the kitchen to confirm that Emile and his staff were otherwise engaged. Only then did he approach the maître d's podium, open the drawer, cross himself twice, and pull out the 1954 edition of the Book.

Within minutes he had reviewed all the reservations in January and February. He paused at one event scheduled for the Yellow Room in March and at another scheduled for the Red Room in April, but neither would do. As he moved farther into the future, the pages of the Book became increasingly bare. Whole weeks passed without a single entry. The Count began flipping the pages with a quicker pace, and even a hint of desperation—that is, until he landed on the eleventh of June. Having studied the marginal notes written in Andrey's delicate script, the Count tapped the entry twice. A combined dinner of the Presidium and the Council of Ministers—two of the most powerful bodies in the Soviet Union.

Returning the Book to its drawer, the Count climbed the stairs to his bedroom, pushed his chair aside, sat on the floor, and for the first time in almost thirty years opened one of the hidden doors in the legs of the Grand Duke's desk. For while the Count may have resolved to take action on the night of Katerina's visit six months before, it was only with news of the Conservatory's goodwill tour that the clock had begun to tick.

When the Count arrived at the Shalyapin at six o'clock that night, the denizens of the bar were celebrating the misadventures of "Pudgy" Webster, a gregarious if somewhat hapless American who had recently arrived in the capital. Twenty-nine years old and still suffering from that affliction for which he had been nicknamed as a boy, Pudgy had been sent to Russia by his father—the owner of the American Vending Machine Company of Montclair, New Jersey—with strict instructions that he not come home until he had sold a thousand machines. After three weeks, he had finally secured his first meeting with a Party official (the assistant to the manager of the skating rink in Gorky Park), and had thus been convinced by several journalists to sponsor a round of champagne.

Taking a stool at the other end of the bar, the Count accepted a flute from Audrius with a grateful nod and the smile of one who has his own cause for celebration. The designs of men are notoriously subservient to happenstance, hesitation, and haste; but had the Count been given the power to engineer an optimal course of events, he could not have done a better job than Fate was doing on its own. So with a smile on his lips, he raised his glass.

But to toast Fate is to tempt Fate; and sure enough, even as the Count set his flute down on the bar, a gust of frozen air brushed against the nape of his neck, followed by an urgent whisper.

"Your Excellency!"

Turning on his stool, the Count was surprised to find Viktor Stepanovich standing behind him with frost on his shoulders and snow on his cap. A few months before, Viktor had joined a chamber orchestra and thus was rarely at the hotel in the evening. What's more, he was panting as if he had just sprinted across the city.

"Viktor!" exclaimed the Count. "What is it? You look in a state."

Viktor ignored the remark and began to speak with uncharacteristic impatience.

"I know that you are protective of your daughter, Your Excellency, and rightfully so. Such is the prerogative of any parent, and the duty of one who is raising a tender heart. But with all due respect, I think you are making a terrible mistake. She will be graduating in six months, and her chances of receiving a worthy position will only be hampered by your decision."

"Viktor," said the Count, rising from his stool. "I have no idea what you are talking about."

Viktor studied the Count.

"You did not instruct Sofia to withdraw her name?"

"Withdraw her name from what?"

"I just received a call from Director Vavilov. He informed me that she has declined the invitation to travel with the Conservatory's orchestra."

"Declined the invitation! I assure you, my friend, that I had no idea. In fact, I agree with you hares, hounds, and horses that the brightness of her future *depends* upon her performing on that tour."

The two men looked at each other, dumbfounded.

"She must have acted of her own accord," said the Count after a moment.

"But to what end?"

He shook his head.

"I fear it may be my fault, Viktor. Yesterday afternoon, when we received the news, I made so much of it: *The chance to play Rachmaninov before an audience of thousands in the Palais Garnier!* I must have triggered feelings of trepidation. She has a tender heart, as you say; but she also has spunk. She is bound to come around in the weeks ahead."

Viktor took the Count by the sleeve.

"But there are no weeks ahead. On Friday, a public announcement will be made describing the orchestra's itinerary and the musical program. The director will need to have all of his performers in place before the announcement. Assuming that the decision to withdraw Sofia was yours, I gained his assurance that he would wait twenty-four hours before making a new appointment—so that I could try to persuade you. If she has made this decision on her own, then you must speak to her tonight and change her mind. She must come to the defense of her own talent!"

One hour later at table ten of the Boyarsky, with menus perused and orders placed, Sofia looked to the Count expectantly—as it was his turn to play first in *Zut*. But, despite the fact that he had prepared a promising category (common uses for wax),* the Count opted instead to summon an untold story from the past.

---

*The making of candles; the sealing of letters; the sculpting of maquettes; the polishing of parquet; the removal of hair; the shaping of moustaches!

"Have I ever told you about Ribbon Day at the academy?" he began.

"Yes," Sofia said. "You have."

Furrowing his brow, the Count reviewed all of the conversations that he had ever had with his daughter in chronological order and could find no evidence of having told her the tale before.

"I may have mentioned something about Ribbon Day once or twice," he conceded, to be polite, "but I am quite sure that I have never told you this *particular* story. You see, as a boy I had a certain aptitude for marksmanship. And one spring—when I was about your age—there was a Ribbon Day at the academy in which we were all chosen to compete in different events—"

"Weren't you closer to thirteen?"

"What's that?"

"Weren't you thirteen when this happened?"

The Count's eyes went back and forth as he completed certain calculations.

"Well, yes," he continued somewhat impatiently, "I suppose I was something like thirteen. The *important* point is that given my marksmanship, I was generally regarded throughout the school as the favorite in the archery competition, and I looked forward to the event with great anticipation. But the closer we got to Ribbon Day, the worse my marksmanship became. Well known for piercing grapes at fifty paces, I suddenly couldn't hit the hide of an elephant at fifteen feet. Just the sight of my bow made my hands shake and my eyes water. Suddenly, I—a Rostov—found myself flirting with the notion of inventing an illness and checking into the infirmary—"

"But you didn't."

"That's right. I didn't."

The Count took a sip of wine and paused for dramatic effect.

"At last the dreaded day arrived; and with all the spectators assembled on the sporting fields, the time came for the archery event. Even as I faced the target, I could anticipate the humiliation that was sure to follow when—despite my reputation—my arrow would shoot wide of its mark. But as with trembling hands I drew back my bow, from the corner of my eye I happened to see old Professor Tartakov trip over his walking stick and topple into a pile of manure. Well, the sight filled me with such joy that my fingers released the bow of their own accord—"

"And having sailed through the air, your arrow landed in the center of the target."

"Well, yes. That's right. The very center. So perhaps I have told you this story before. But did you know that ever since that day, when I have been anxious about my aim, I have thought of old Professor Tartakov tumbling into the manure and have reliably hit my mark."

The Count turned his hand in the air in a concluding flourish.

Sofia smiled but with a perplexed expression, as if she wasn't quite sure why the renowned marksman had chosen to relay this particular tale at this particular time. So, the Count elaborated.

"In life, it is the same for all of us. We are bound to face moments of trepidation whether we venture onto the floor of the senate, the field of athletics, or . . . the stage of a concert hall."

Sofia stared at the Count, for a moment then let out a bright laugh.

"The stage of a concert hall."

"Yes," said the Count, a little offended. "The stage of a concert hall."

"Someone has told you about my conversation with Director Vavilov."

The Count rearranged his fork and knife, which had somehow become misaligned.

"I may have heard something from someone," he said noncommittally.

"Papa. I am not afraid of performing with the orchestra before an audience."

"Can you be so sure?"

"Positively."

"You have never performed in a hall as large as the Palais Garnier. . . ."

"I know."

"And the French are notoriously exacting as an audience. . . ."

Sofia laughed again.

"Well, if you're trying to set me at ease, you're not doing a very good job of it. But honestly, Papa, feelings of anxiety have nothing to do with my decision."

"Then what?"

"I simply don't want to go."

"How could you *not* want to go?"

Sofia looked down at the table and moved her own silver.

"I like it here," she said at last—gesturing to the room and, by extension, the hotel. "I like it here with you."

The Count studied his daughter. With her long black hair, fair skin, and dark blue eyes, she seemed serene beyond her years. And therein, perhaps, lay the problem. For if serenity should be a hallmark of maturity, then impetuousness should be a hallmark of youth.

"I want to tell you a different story," he said, "a story that I am sure you have never heard. It took place in this very hotel some thirty years ago—on a snowy night in December, much like this one. . . ."

And the Count went on to tell Sofia about the Christmas that he had celebrated with her mother in the Piazza in 1922. He told her about Nina's hors d'oeuvre of ice creams, and her reluctance to sit in scholarly rows, and her argument that if one wished to broaden one's horizons, one would best be served by venturing *beyond* the horizon.

The Count suddenly grew somber.

"I fear I have done you a great disservice, Sofia. From the time you were a child, I have lured you into a life that is principally circumscribed by the four walls of this building. We all have. Marina, Andrey, Emile, and I. We have ventured to make the hotel seem as wide and wonderful as the world, so that you would opt to spend more time in it with us. But your mother was perfectly right. One does not fulfill one's potential by listening to *Scheherazade* in a gilded hall, or by reading the *Odyssey* in one's den. One does so by setting forth into the vast unknown—just like Marco Polo when he traveled to China, or Columbus when he traveled to America."

Sofia nodded in understanding.

The Count continued.

"I have had countless reasons to be proud of you; and certainly one of the greatest was the night of the Conservatory competition. But the moment I felt that pride was not when you and Anna brought home news of your victory. It was earlier in the evening, when I watched you heading out the hotel's doors on your way to the hall. For what matters in life is not whether we receive a round of applause; what matters is whether we have the courage to venture forth despite the uncertainty of acclaim."

"If I *am* to play the piano in Paris," said Sofia after a moment, "I only wish that you could be there in the audience to hear me."

The Count smiled.

"I assure you, my dear, were you to play the piano on the moon, I would hear every chord."

Achilles Agonistes

"Greetings, Arkady."

"Greetings to you, Count Rostov. Is there something I can do for you this morning?"

"If it wouldn't be too much trouble, could you spare a bit of stationery?"

"Certainly."

Standing at the front desk, the Count penned a one-sentence note under the hotel's moniker and addressed the envelope in an appropriately slanted script; he waited until the bell captain was otherwise occupied, casually crossed the lobby, slipped the note onto the bell captain's desk, and then headed downstairs for his weekly visit to the barber.

It had been many years since Yaroslav Yaroslavl had worked his magic in the barbershop of the Metropol, and in the interim any number of successors had attempted to fill his shoes. The most recent fellow—Boris Something-or-other-ovich—was perfectly qualified to shorten a man's hair; but he was neither the artist nor the conversationalist that Yaroslav had been. In fact, he went about his business with such mute efficiency, one suspected he was part machine.

"Trim?" he asked the Count, wasting no time with subjects, verbs, or the other superfluities of language.

Given the Count's thinning hair and the barber's predisposition to efficiency, a trim might take all of ten minutes.

"Yes, a trim," said the Count. "But perhaps a shave as well. . . ."

The barber furrowed his brow. The man in him, no doubt, was inclined to point out that the Count had obviously shaved a few hours before; but the machinery in him was so finely tuned, it was already putting down the scissors and reaching for the shaving brush.

Having whipped a sufficient lather, Boris dabbed it on those areas of the Count's face where whiskers would have been had the Count been in need of a shave. He sharpened one of his razors on his strop, leaned over the chair, and with an unflinching hand shaved the Count's right upper cheek in a single pass. Wiping the blade on the towel at his waist, he then leaned over the Count's left upper cheek, and shaved it with equal alacrity.

At this rate, fretted the Count, he'll be done in a minute and a half.

Using a bent knuckle, the barber now raised the Count's chin. The Count could feel the metal of the razor make contact with his throat. And that's when one of the new bellhops appeared in the door.

"Excuse me, sir."

"Yes?" said the barber with his blade held fast at the Count's jugular.

"I have a note for you."

"On the bench."

"But it is urgent," said the young man with some anxiety.

"Urgent?"

"Yes, sir. From the manager."

The barber looked back at the bellhop for the first time.

"The manager?"

"Yes, sir."

After an extended exhalation, the barber removed the blade from the Count's throat, accepted the missive, and—as the bellhop disappeared down the hall—slit the envelope open with his razor.

Unfolding the note, the barber stared at it for a full minute. In those sixty seconds, he must have read it ten times over because it was composed of only four words: *Come see me immediately!*

The barber exhaled again then looked at the wall.

"I can't imagine," he said to no one. Then having thought it over for another minute, he turned to the Count: "I must see to something."

"By all means. Do what you must. I am in no hurry."

To underscore his point, the Count leaned back his head and closed his eyes as if to nap; but when the barber's footsteps had receded down the hall, the Count leapt from the chair like a cat.

When the Count was a young man, he prided himself on the fact that he was unmoved by the ticking of the clock. In the early years of the twentieth century, there were those of his acquaintance who brought a new sense of urgency to their slightest endeavor. They timed the consumption of their breakfast, the walk to their office, and the hanging of their hat on its hook with as much precision as if they were preparing for a military campaign. They answered the phone on the first ring, scanned the headlines, limited their conversations to whatever was most germane, and generally spent their days in pursuit of the second hand. God bless them.

For his part, the Count had opted for the life of the purposefully unrushed. Not only was he disinclined to race toward some appointed hour—disdaining even to wear a watch—he took the greatest satisfaction when assuring a friend that a worldly matter could wait in favor of a leisurely lunch or a stroll along the embankment. After all, did not wine improve with age? Was it not the passage of years that gave a piece of furniture its delightful patina? When all was said and done, the endeavors that most modern men saw as urgent (such as appointments with bankers and the catching of trains), probably could have waited, while those they deemed frivolous (such as cups of tea and friendly chats) had deserved their immediate attention.

Cups of tea and friendly chats! the modern man objects. *If one is to make time for such idle pursuits, how could one ever attend to the necessities of adulthood?*

Luckily, the answer to this conundrum was provided by the philosopher Zeno in the fifth century B.C. Achilles, a man of action and urgency, trained to measure his exertions to the tenth of a second, should be able to quickly dispense with a twenty-yard dash. But in order to advance a yard, the hero must first advance eighteen inches; and in order to advance eighteen inches, he must first advance nine; but to advance nine, he must first advance four and a half, and so on. Thus, on his way to completing the twenty-yard dash, Achilles must traverse an infinite number of lengths—which, by definition, would take an infinite amount of time. By extension (as the Count had liked to point out), the man who has an appointment at twelve has an infinite number of intervals between now and then in which to pursue the satisfactions of the spirit.

Quod erat demonstrandum.

But ever since Sofia returned home that night in late December with word of the Conservatory's tour, the Count had had a very different perspective on the passage of time. Before they'd even finished celebrating the news, he'd calculated that less than six months remained before she was scheduled to depart. One hundred and seventy-eight days, to be exact; or 356 chimings of the twice-tolling clock. And in that brief span, there was so much to be done. . . .

Given the Count's membership as a younger man to the ranks of the purposefully unrushed, one might have expected the ticking of this clock to buzz around his ears like a mosquito in the night; or prompt him, like Oblomov, to turn on his side and face the wall in a state of malaise. But what occurred was the opposite. In the days that followed, it brightened his step, sharpened his senses, and quickened his wits. For just like the rousing of Humphrey Bogart's indignation, the clock's ticking revealed the Count to be a Man of Intent.

In the last week of December, one of the Catherines the Count had retrieved from the Grand Duke's desk was brought by Vasily to the basement of TsUM and cashed in for store credit. With the proceeds, the concierge purchased a small tan valise along with other necessities of travel, such as a towel, soap, toothpaste, and a toothbrush. These were wrapped in festive paper and presented to Sofia on Christmas Eve (at midnight).

Per Director Vavilov, Sofia's performance of Rachmaninov's Second Piano Concerto was to be the penultimate piece on the program, followed by a violin prodigy's performance of a Dvorak concerto, both with full orchestra. The Count had no doubt that Rachmaninov's Second was well within Sofia's grasp; but even Horowitz had his Tarnowsky. So in early January, the Count hired Viktor Stepanovich to help her rehearse.

In late January, the Count commissioned Marina to fashion a new dress for the concert. After a design meeting that included Marina, Anna, and Sofia—and which, for some incomprehensible reason, excluded the Count—Vasily was dispatched back to TsUM for a bolt of blue taffeta.

Over the years, the Count had done an adequate job of teaching Sofia the rudiments of conversational French. Nonetheless, beginning in February, father and daughter set aside games of *Zut* in order to review the more practical applications of the French language while they awaited their appetizers.

"Pardonnez-moi, Monsieur, avez-vous l'heure, s'il vous plaît?"

"Oui, Mademoiselle, il est dix heures."

"Merci. Et pourriez-vous me dire où se trouvent les Champs-Élysées?"

"Oui, continuez tout droit dans cette direction."

"Merci beaucoup."

"Je vous en prie."

Early in March, for the first time in years, the Count visited the Metropol's basement. Passing by the furnace and electrical rooms, he made his way to the little corner where the hotel stowed those items left behind by guests. Kneeling before the shelf of books, he scanned the spines, paying special attention to those little red volumes with gold lettering: the *Baedekers*. Naturally enough, the majority of travel guides in the basement were dedicated to Russia, but a few were for other countries, having presumably been discarded at the end of an extended tour. Thus, scattered among the abandoned novels, the Count discovered one *Baedeker* for Italy; one for Finland; one for England; and, finally, two for the city of Paris.

Then on the twenty-first of March, the Count penned the slanted one-sentence insistence under the hotel's moniker, slipped it on the bell captain's desk, went on his weekly visit to the barber, and waited for the note to arrive. . . .

Having poked his head into the hallway in order to watch Boris mount the stairs, the Count closed the barbershop door and turned his attention to Yaroslav's renowned glass cabinet. At the front of the cabinet were two rows of large white bottles bearing the insignia of the Hammer and Sickle Shampoo Company. But behind these soldiers in the fight for universal cleanliness, all but forgotten, was a selection of the brightly colored bottles from the old days. Taking out several of the shampoo bottles, the Count surveyed the tonics, soaps, and oils—but couldn't find what he was looking for.

It must be here, he thought.

The Count began moving the bottles about like chess pieces—to see what was hiding behind what. And there, tucked in the corner behind two vials of French cologne, covered in dust, was that little black bottle that Yaroslav Yaroslavl had referred to with a wink as the Fountain of Youth.

The Count put the bottle in his pocket, reloaded the cabinet, and closed its doors. Scurrying back into his chair, he smoothed his smock and leaned back his head; but even as he closed his eyes, he was struck by the image of Boris slitting open the envelope with his razor. Leaping again from the chair, the Count snatched one of the spares from the counter, slipped it into his pocket, and resumed his place—just as the barber came through the door grumbling about fools' errands and wasted time.

Upstairs in his room, the Count put the little black bottle at the back of his drawer then sat at his desk with the Paris *Baedeker*. Consulting the table of contents, he turned to the fiftieth page, where the section on the 8th arrondissement began. Sure enough, before the descriptions of the Arc de Triomphe and the Grand Palais, of the Madeleine and Maxim's, was a thin paper foldout with a detailed map of the neighborhood. Taking Boris's razor from his pocket, the Count used the edge to cut the map cleanly from its guide; then with a red pen he carefully drew a zigzagging line from the Avenue George V to Rue Pierre Charron and down the Champs-Élysées.

When he was done with the map, the Count went to his study and retrieved his father's copy of Montaigne's *Essays* from the bookcase where it had resided in comfort ever since Sofia had liberated it from under the bureau. Taking the book back to the Grand Duke's desk, the Count began turning through the pages, stopping here and there to read the passages his father had underlined. As he was lingering over a particular section in "Of the Education of Children," the twice-tolling clock began to signal the hour of noon.

One hundred and seventy-three chimings to go, thought the Count.

Then issuing a sigh, he shook his head, crossed himself twice, and with Boris's razor began removing the text from two hundred pages of the masterpiece.

Arrivederci

One evening in early May, as the Count sat in the high-back chair between the potted palms, over the top of his newspaper he spied the young Italian couple exiting the elevator. She was a long, dark beauty in a long, dark dress, and he a shorter man in slacks and jacket. The Count wasn't certain what had brought the couple to Moscow, but they reliably left the hotel every evening at seven o'clock, presumably to avail themselves of the city's nightlife. Case in point, when they stepped off the elevator at 6:55 they walked straight to the concierge's desk, where Vasily was ready with two tickets for *Boris Godunov* and a reservation for a late supper. Then the couple swung by the front desk in order to drop off their key, which Arkady stowed in the twenty-eighth slot of the fourth row.

Laying his newspaper on the table, the Count rose, yawned, and stretched. He strolled toward the revolving door as one who wishes to gauge the weather. Outside on the steps, Rodion exchanged greetings with the young couple, signaled a taxi, and held the back door open for them. When they drove off, the Count spun on his heels and crossed the lobby to the stairs. Taking the steps one at a time (as had been his habit since 1952), he ascended to the fourth floor, traversed the hallway, and stopped before the twenty-eighth door. Easing two fingers into the ticket pocket of his vest, he extracted Nina's key. Then with a look left and a look right, he let himself inside.

The Count had not been in room 428 since the early 1930s—when Anna was attempting to revive her career—but he wasted no time in assessing how the décor of the little sitting room had changed. Rather, he went straight into the bedroom and opened the left closet door. It was filled with dresses exactly like the one the dark beauty had been wearing tonight: ankle length, short sleeved, monochromatic. (It was a look that suited her well, after all.) Closing her side of the closet, the Count opened the companion door. Inside were slacks and jackets on hangers, and the flat cap of a newsboy on a hook. Selecting a pair of tan pants, he closed the door. In the second drawer of the bureau, he found a white oxford. Removing a folded pillowcase from his pocket, he stuffed the clothes inside. He returned to the sitting room, opened the door a crack, confirmed the hallway was empty, and slipped out.

Only with the click of the latch did it occur to the Count that he should have taken the cap. But even as he poked his fingers back into his vest pocket, he heard the unmistakable sound of squeaking wheels. Taking three strides down the hallway, the Count disappeared into the belfry—just as Oleg from room service turned the corner, pushing his cart before him.

At eleven o'clock that night, the Count was in the Shalyapin reviewing his checklist over a snifter of brandy. The Catherines, the *Baedeker*, the Fountain of Youth, the slacks and shirt, a heavy-duty needle and thread from Marina were all in hand. There were still a few things to accomplish, but only one significant loose end: the matter of notice. From the beginning, the Count had known that this would prove the most difficult element of the plan to achieve. After all, one could not simply send a telegram. But it wasn't absolutely essential. If left no alternative, the Count was prepared to proceed without it.

The Count emptied his glass with the intention of heading upstairs, but before he rose from his stool Audrius was there with the bottle.

"A splash on the house?"

Ever since turning sixty, the Count had generally refrained from alcohol after eleven, having found that late-night drinks, like unsettled children, were likely to wake you at three or four in the morning. But it would have been rude for the Count to refuse the bartender's offer, especially after he had gone to the trouble of uncorking the bottle. So, accepting the splash with an appropriate expression of gratitude, the Count made himself comfortable and turned his attention to the small group of Americans laughing at the other end of the bar.

Once again, the source of good humor was the hapless salesman from Montclair, New Jersey. Having initially struggled to get anyone of influence on the phone, in April the American began securing face-to-face meetings with senior bureaucrats in every conceivable branch of government. He had met personally with officials at the People's Commissariats of Food, Finance, Labor, Education, and even Foreign Affairs. Knowing that a vending machine had as much chance of selling in the Kremlin as a portrait of George Washington, the journalists had watched this turn of events in amazement. That is, until they learned that to better illustrate the function of his machines, Webster had asked his father to send him fifty cases of American cigarettes and chocolate bars. Thus, the salesman who had not been able to secure an appointment was suddenly welcomed into a hundred offices with open arms—and ushered out empty-handed.

"I really thought I had one on the line today," he was saying.

As the American launched into the particulars of his near success, the Count was inevitably reminded of Richard, who was almost as wide-eyed as Webster, equally gregarious, and just as ready to tell a humorous tale at his own expense.

The Count set his glass down on the bar.

I wonder, he thought. Could it be possible?

But before the Count could answer his own question, the pudgy American waved a friendly hand at someone in the lobby—and who should return the wave but a certain eminent professor. . . .

Shortly after midnight, the American settled his bill at the bar, patted his companions on the shoulder, and wound up the stairs whistling an approximation of "The Internationale." In the hallway on the fourth floor, he fumbled with his keys. But once the door to his room was closed, his posture became a little more straight, his expression a little more sober.

That's when the Count switched on the lamp.

Though presumably startled to find a stranger sitting in one of his chairs, the American didn't jump back or shout.

"Excuse me," he said with the smile of the inebriated. "I must be in the wrong room."

"No," said the Count. "You are in the right room."

"Well, if I am in the right room, then it must be you who are in the wrong room. . . ."

"Perhaps," said the Count. "But I don't think so."

The American took a step forward and studied his uninvited guest with a little more care.

"Aren't you the waiter in the Boyarsky?"

"Yes," said the Count. "I am the waiter."

The American nodded slowly.

"I see. Mr. . . . ?"

"Rostov. Alexander Rostov."

"Well, Mr. Rostov, I'd offer you a drink, but the hour is late and I have a rather early appointment. Is there something else I can do for you?"

"Yes, Mr. Webster, I suspect that there is. You see, I have a letter that I need delivered to a friend in Paris, whom I think that you might know. . . ."

Despite the late hour and early appointment, Pudgy Webster ended up offering the Count a glass of whiskey, after all.

Now if, as a rule, the Count generally avoided drinking after eleven, he absolutely never drank after midnight. In fact, he had even found himself quoting his father to Sofia on the subject, asserting that the only things that came from the practice were foolhardy acts, ill-advised liaisons, and gambling debts.

But having snuck into the room of this American and arranged for a message to be delivered, it suddenly struck the Count that Humphrey Bogart would never turn down an offer of a drink after midnight. In fact, all evidence suggested that Bogart *preferred* his drinking after midnight— when the orchestra had stopped playing, the barstools had emptied, and the revelers had stumbled off into the night. That was the hour when, with the saloon doors closed, the lights turned low, and a bottle of whiskey on the table, Men of Intent could speak without the distractions of love and laughter.

"Yes, thank you," said the Count to Mr. Webster. "A glass of whiskey might just hit the spot."

And as it turned out, the Count's instincts had been perfectly right, for the glass of whiskey hit the spot. As did the second.

So when he finally bid Mr. Webster goodnight (with a package of

American cigarettes for Anna in one pocket and a chocolate bar for Sofia in the other), the Count headed homeward in an elevated frame of mind.

The fourth-floor hallway was empty and still. Behind the line of closed doors slept the practical and predictable, the cautious and comfortable. Tucked under their covers, they dreamt of breakfast, leaving the hallways of night to be walked by the likes of Samuel Spadsky and Philip Marlov and Alexander Ilyich Rostov. . . .

"Yes," said the Count as he weaved down the hall: "*I* am the waiter."

Then with the finely attuned senses of his brotherhood, the Count noticed something suggestive out of the corner of his eye. It was the door to room 428.

Boris Godunov was a production of three and a half hours. A post-theater supper would last an hour and a half. So, in all likelihood, the Italians would not return to the hotel for another thirty minutes. The Count knocked and waited; he knocked again to be sure; then retrieving the key from his vest, he unlocked the door and crossed the threshold clear-eyed, quick, and without compunction.

In a glance, he could see that the night service had already visited the suite, for everything was in its proper place: the chairs, the magazines, the carafe of water and glasses. In the bedroom, he found the corners of the bed turned down at an angle of forty-five degrees.

Opening the right closet door, he was about to take the newsboy's cap off its hook when he noticed something he'd missed before. On the shelf above the clothes was a bundle wrapped in paper and tied with twine—a bundle about the size of a small statuette. . . .

Putting the newsboy's cap on his head, the Count took the bundle off the shelf and laid it on the bed. He untied the string and carefully peeled back the paper—only to find a set of Russian nesting dolls. Painted in a simple if traditional style, available in a hundred Moscow shops, the *matryoshka* was just that sort of whimsical toy that two parents would bring home to their child from a trip to Russia.

And in which they could easily hide something . . .

Sitting on the bed, the Count opened the largest of the nesting dolls. Then he opened the second largest of the nesting dolls. Then he opened the third largest of the nesting dolls. And he was about to open the fourth, when he heard a key in the lock.

For a moment, the Man of Intent was a Man Who Didn't Know What to Do. But at the sound of the hallway door opening and the two Italian voices, the Count swept up the halves of the dolls, slipped into the closet, and quietly closed the door.

The shelf that ran above the hanging bar must have been less than six feet off the ground, because in order to fit in the closet, the Count had to bend his head like a penitent. (Point taken.)

It took only a few moments for the couple to shed their coats and come into the bedroom. If they went into the bathroom to perform their nightly toilette together, thought the Count, he would have the perfect opportunity to escape. But room 428 had only a small bath, and rather than crowd each other at the sink, the husband and wife chose to take turns.

Listening closely, the Count could hear the brushing of respective teeth, the opening of drawers, and the donning of pajamas. He could hear the bedsheets being pulled back. He could hear some quiet conversation, the lifting of books, and the turning of pages. After fifteen minutes, or an eternity, there was an exchange of endearments, a delicate kiss, and the lights went out. By the grace of God, this fine-looking couple opted for rest over intimacy. . . .

But how long, the Count wondered, would it take for them to fall asleep? Being careful not to move a muscle, he listened to their breathing. He heard a cough; a sniff; a sigh. Then someone rolling on their side. He might have worried about falling asleep himself, if it weren't for the crippling pain in his neck and the creeping realization that he would soon need a toilette of his own.

Well, there you have it, thought the Count: one more reason not to drink after midnight . . .

"Che cos 'era questo?! Tesoro, svegliati!"

  "Cos'è?"

  "C'è qualcuno nella stanza!"

  . . .

  [Bump]

  "Chi è la?"

"Scusa."

"Claudio! Accendi la luce!"

[Bam]

"Scusa."

[Crash]

"Arrivederci!"

Adulthood

"A re you ready?" asked Marina.

The Count and Anna, who were sitting side by side on the couch in the actress's suite, answered in the affirmative.

With a fitting sense of ceremony, Marina opened the bedroom door to reveal Sofia.

The dress that the seamstress had fashioned for the concert was a long-sleeved gown in the trumpet style—fitted above the waist and flared below the knee. The blue of the fabric, which recalled the depths of the ocean, provided an otherworldly contrast to the fairness of Sofia's skin and the blackness of her hair.

Anna let out a gasp.

Marina beamed.

And the Count?

Alexander Rostov was neither scientist nor sage; but at the age of sixty-four he was wise enough to know that life does not proceed by leaps and bounds. It unfolds. At any given moment, it is the manifestation of a thousand transitions. Our faculties wax and wane, our experiences accumulate, and our opinions evolve—if not glacially, then at least gradually. Such that the events of an average day are as likely to transform who we are as a pinch of pepper is to transform a stew. And yet, for the Count, when the doors to Anna's bedroom opened and Sofia stepped forward in her gown, at that very moment she crossed the threshold into adulthood. On one side of that divide was a girl of five or ten or twenty with a quiet demeanor and a whimsical imagination who relied upon him for companionship and counsel; while on the other side was a young woman of discernment and grace who need rely on no one but herself.

"Well? What do you think?" asked Sofia shyly.

"I'm speechless," said the Count with unabashed pride.

"You look magnificent," said Anna.

"Doesn't she, though?" said Marina.

Gay with the compliments and the sound of Anna's applause, Sofia spun once on her feet.

And that is when the Count discovered, to his utter disbelief, that there was no back to the dress. The taffeta (which had been purchased by the bolt, mind you) fell away from her shoulders in a vertiginous parabola that reached its nadir at the base of Sofia's spine.

The Count turned upon Anna.

"I suppose this was *your* doing!"

The actress stopped clapping.

"What was my doing?"

He waved his hand in Sofia's direction.

"This dressless dress. No doubt it was drawn from one of your *convenient* magazines."

Before Anna could respond, Marina stomped her foot.

"This was *my* doing!"

Startled by the seamstress's tone, the Count saw with some trepidation that while one of her eyes had rolled toward the ceiling in exasperation, the other was bearing down on him like a cannonball.

"It is a dress of *my* design," she said, "fashioned from *my* handiwork for *my* Sofia."

Recognizing that he may have unintentionally insulted an artist, the Count adopted a more conciliatory tone.

"It is unquestionably a beautiful dress, Marina. One of the finest I have ever seen; and I have seen many fine dresses in my time." Here the Count gave an awkward little laugh in the hopes of clearing the air and then continued in a tone of fellowship and common sense. "But after months of preparation, Sofia will be performing Rachmaninov at the Palais Garnier. Wouldn't it be a pity if, instead of listening to her play, the audience was staring at her back?"

"Perhaps we should drape her in sackcloth," suggested the seamstress. "To ensure that the audience is not distracted."

"I would never counsel sackcloth," protested the Count. "But there is such a thing as moderation, even within the bounds of glamour."

Marina stomped her foot again.

"Enough! We have no interest in your scruples, Alexander Ilyich. Just because you witnessed the Comet of 1812, does not mean that Sofia must wear a petticoat and bustle."

The Count began to object, but Anna intervened.

"Perhaps we should hear what Sofia has to say."

They all looked to Sofia who, oblivious to the course of the debate, was admiring herself in the mirror. She turned and took Marina's hands.

"I think it's splendid."

Marina looked at the Count in triumph; then turning back to Sofia, she tilted her head and studied her handiwork with a more critical eye.

"What is it?" asked Anna, taking up a position beside the seamstress.

"It needs something. . . ."

"A cape?" muttered the Count.

All three women ignored him.

"I know," Anna said after a moment. Slipping into her bedroom, she returned with a choker that had a sapphire pendant. She handed it to Marina, who fastened it around Sofia's neck, then the two older women stepped back.

"Perfect," they agreed.

"Is it true?" asked Anna, as she and the Count walked down the hallway after the fitting.

"Is what true?"

"Did you really see the Comet of 1812?"

The Count harrumphed.

"Just because I am a man of decorum does not mean that I am stodgy."

Anna smiled.

"You do realize that you just harrumphed."

"Maybe so. But I am still her father. What would you have me do? Abdicate my responsibilities?"

"Abdicate!" replied Anna with a laugh. "Certainly not, Your Highness."

The two had reached the point in the hallway where the door to the service stair was hidden in plain sight. Stopping, the Count turned to Anna with the smile of the artificially polite.

"It is time for the Boyarsky's daily meeting. As a result, I am afraid that I must now bid you *adieu*." Then with a nod the Count disappeared behind the door.

Once he was descending the stairs, he felt a sense of relief. With its precise geometry and pervading silence, the belfry was much like a chapel or reading room—a place designed to provide one with solitude and respite. That is, until the door opened and Anna stepped onto the landing.

In a state of disbelief, the Count remounted the stairs.

"What are you doing?" he whispered.

"I need to go to the lobby," she replied. "I thought I'd keep you company on the way down."

"You can't keep me company. This is the service stair!"

"But I am a guest in the hotel."

"That is my point exactly. The service stair is reserved for those who serve. Right down the hallway is a glamorous staircase reserved for the glamorous."

Anna smiled and took a step toward the Count.

"What's gotten your goat?"

"Nothing has gotten my goat. My goat is not gotten."

"I suppose it's understandable," she continued philosophically. "A father is bound to be a little unnerved by the discovery that his daughter has become a beautiful young woman."

"I was not unnerved," the Count said, taking a step back. "My only point was that the back of the dress did not have to be cut quite as low."

"You must admit that her back is lovely."

"That may be so. But the world needn't be presented with every single one of her vertebrae."

Anna took another step forward.

"You have often admired my vertebrae. . . ."

"That's something else entirely." The Count tried to take another step back, but came up against the wall.

"I'll give you the Comet of 1812," Anna said.

"Shall we begin?"

This shockingly straightforward question came from none other than the man who ate, drank, and slept on the bias.

With a grunt, Emile slid his menu across the desk.

The Count and Andrey shifted in their chairs.

Having begun attending the Boyarsky's daily meeting in the summer of 1953, in April of 1954 the Bishop had switched the venue from Emile's office to his own, on the grounds that the activity in the kitchen was proving a distraction. To accommodate the members of the Triumvirate, the manager had three French chairs lined up in front of his desk. The chairs had such delicate proportions one could only assume that they had originally been designed for handmaidens in the court of Louis XIV. Which is to say, it was virtually impossible for grown men to sit in them at ease, especially when tucked in a tight little row. The general effect was to make the Boyarsky's maître d', chef, and headwaiter feel like schoolboys called before their principal.

Accepting the menu, the Bishop squared it with the edge of his desk. Then with the tip of his pencil he reviewed each item in the manner of a banker double-checking the sums of his apprentice.

Naturally enough, in the interim the three schoolboys found themselves looking about. If only the walls had been decorated with maps of the world or a periodic table, they could have made fruitful use of the time—by imagining they were Columbus crossing the Atlantic or an alchemist in ancient Alexandria. With only the portraits of Stalin, Lenin, and Marx to consider, the three men had no choice but to fidget.

When the Bishop had edited Emile's menu and returned it to the chef, with a sniff he turned to Andrey, who dutifully delivered the Book. As usual, the Bishop opened to the beginning and the Triumvirate watched in mute exasperation as he turned through the pages until he finally reached the last night of May.

"Here we are," he said.

Again, the tip of the banker's pencil moved from entry to entry, column by column, row by row. The Bishop provided Andrey with seating instructions for the night and set down his pencil.

Sensing the meeting was about to end, the members of the Triumvirate moved to the edge of their chairs. But rather than close the Book, the Bishop suddenly flipped ahead to survey the upcoming weeks. After turning a few pages, he paused.

"How are preparations coming for the combined dinner of the Presidium and the Council of Ministers . . . ?"

Andrey cleared his throat.

"All is in order. At official request, the dinner is to be held not in the Red Room but in suite 417, which Arkady has arranged to be free; Emile has just finalized the menu; and Alexander, who will be overseeing the dinner, has been working closely with comrade Propp, our liaison from the Kremlin, to ensure the evening runs smoothly."

The Bishop looked up from the Book.

"Given the importance of the event, shouldn't you be overseeing it personally, Maître d' Duras?"

"It was my intention to stay in the Boyarsky, as usual. But I could certainly attend to the dinner, if you thought that preferable."

"Excellent," said the Bishop. "Then Headwaiter Rostov can stay at the restaurant to ensure that all goes accordingly there."

As the Bishop closed the Book, the Count went cold.

The dinner for the Presidium and Council of Ministers was tailor made to his intentions. He could not conceive of a better occasion. But even if there were one, with just sixteen days until the Conservatory's tour, the Count was simply out of time.

The Bishop slid the Book back across his desk and the meeting was concluded.

As usual, the members of the Triumvirate walked from the principal's office to the stairwell in silence. But at the landing, when Emile began climbing the stairs to the second floor, the Count took Andrey by the sleeve.

"Andrey, my friend," he said under his breath. "Can you spare a moment . . . ?"

An Announcement

At 6:45 on the eleventh of June, Count Alexander Rostov stood in suite 417 dressed in the white jacket of the Boyarsky, ensuring that the place settings were properly arranged and his men properly attired before opening the doors for the 1954 combined dinner of the Presidium and the Council of Ministers.

Eleven days earlier, as we know, the Count had been excused from this duty rather unceremoniously. But early on the afternoon of the tenth of June, Maître d' Duras arrived at the Boyarsky's daily meeting with distressing news. For some time, he said, he had been experiencing a tremor of the hands consistent with the onset of palsy. After a troubled night's sleep, he had awakened to discover that the condition had grown considerably worse. By way of illustration, he held his right hand over the table where it trembled like a leaf.

Emile looked on with an expression of shock. *What sort of Divinity*, he seemed to be thinking, *would devise a world in which an aging man's malady afflicts the very attribute that has set him apart from his fellow men and elevated him in the eyes of all?*

What sort of Divinity, Emile? The very same who rendered Beethoven deaf and Monet blind. For what the Lord giveth, is precisely what he cometh later to taketh away.

But if Emile's face expressed an almost sacrilegious indignation at his friend's condition, the Bishop's expressed the grimace of the inconvenienced.

Noting the manager's annoyance, Andrey sought to set his mind at ease.

"You needn't worry, Manager Leplevsky. I have already contacted comrade Propp at the Kremlin and assured him that while I cannot oversee tomorrow night's event, Headwaiter Rostov will be assuming my responsibilities. Needless to say," the maître d' added, "comrade Propp was greatly relieved by the news."

"Of course," said the Bishop.

. . . . .

In reporting that comrade Propp was greatly relieved to have Headwaiter Rostov at the helm of this dinner of state, Andrey was not exaggerating. Born ten years after the Revolution, comrade Propp didn't know that Headwaiter Rostov was under house arrest at the Metropol; he didn't even know that Headwaiter Rostov was a Former Person. What he did know—and from personal experience—was that Headwaiter Rostov could be counted upon to attend to every detail on the table and respond immediately to the slightest hint of a customer's dissatisfaction. And though comrade Propp was still relatively inexperienced in the ways of the Kremlin, he was experienced enough to know that any shortcomings in the evening would be laid at his door as surely as if he had set the table, cooked the meal, and poured the wine himself.

Comrade Propp personally communicated his relief to the Count during a brief meeting on the morning of the event. At a table for two in the Boyarsky, the young liaison reviewed with the Count, quite unnecessarily, all the details of the evening: the timing (the doors were to be opened promptly at 9:00); the layout of the tables (a long U with twenty seats on either side and six at the head); the menu (Chef Zhukovsky's interpretation of a traditional Russian feast); the wine (a Ukrainian white); and the necessity of dousing the candles at exactly 10:59. Then, perhaps to emphasize the evening's importance, comrade Propp gave the Count a glimpse of the guest list.

While it's true that the Count generally hadn't concerned himself with the inner workings of the Kremlin, that is not to suggest that he was unfamiliar with the names on that piece of paper—for he had served them all. Certainly, he had served them at formal functions in the Red and Yellow Rooms, but he had also served them at the more intimate and less guarded tables of the Boyarsky when they had dined with wives or mistresses, friends or enemies, patrons or protégés. He knew the boorish from the abrupt and the bitter from the boastful. He had seen all of them sober and most of them drunk.

"All will be seen to," said the Count as the young apparatchik stood to go. "But, comrade Propp . . ."

Comrade Propp paused.

"Yes, Headwaiter Rostov? Have I forgotten something?"

"You haven't given me the seating arrangement."

"Ah. Not to worry. Tonight there is to be no seating arrangement."

"Then rest assured," the Count replied with a smile, "the evening is bound to be a success."

Why was the Count so pleased to hear that this dinner of state would have no seating arrangement?

For a thousand years, civilizations the world over have recognized the head of the table as a privileged spot. Upon seeing a formally set table, one knows instinctively that the seat at the head is more desirable than those along the sides—because it inevitably confers upon its occupant an appearance of power, importance, and legitimacy. By extension, one also knows that the farther one sits from the head, the less powerful, important, and legitimate one is likely to be perceived. So, to invite forty-six leaders of a political party to dine around the periphery of an extended U without a seating arrangement was to risk a certain amount of disorder. . . .

Thomas Hobbes, no doubt, would have likened the situation to "Man in a State of Nature" and would have counseled one to expect a scuffle. Born with similar faculties and driven by similar desires, the forty-six men in attendance had equal right to any seat at the table. As such, what was most likely to ensue was a scrum for the head, animated by accusations, recriminations, fisticuffs, and possibly gunfire.

John Locke, on the other hand, would argue that once the dining room's doors were opened, after a brief moment of confusion the better natures of the forty-six men would prevail, and their predisposition to reason would lead them to a fair and orderly process of seat taking. Thus, in all likelihood, the attendees would draw lots to decide their placement, or simply reconfigure the tables into a circle—just as King Arthur had, to ensure the equity of his knights.

Chiming in from the mid-eighteenth century, Jean Jacques Rousseau would inform Messrs. Locke and Hobbes that the forty-six guests—freed at long last from the tyranny of social conventions—would shove the tables aside, gather the fruits of the earth in hand, and share them freely in a state of natural bliss!

But the Communist Party was not a "State of Nature." Quite to the contrary, it was one of the most intricate and purposeful constructions ever manufactured by man. In essence: the hierarchy of all hierarchies.

So, when the guests arrived, the Count was fairly certain that there would be no raising of fists, drawing of lots, or free-spirited sharing of fruits. Rather, with only the slightest jostling and jockeying, each of the forty-six attendees would find their proper place at the table; and this "spontaneous" arrangement would tell the studious observer all he needed to know about the governance of Russia for the next twenty years.

At the Count's signal, the doors to suite 417 were opened at precisely 9:00 P.M. By 9:15, forty-six men of various rank and seniority were taking the seats appropriate to their station. Without a word of orchestration, the head of the table was left to Bulganin, Khrushchev, Malenkov, Mikoyan, Molotov, and Voroshilov—the six most eminent members of the Party— with the two center seats reserved for Premier Malenkov and General Secretary Khrushchev.*

In fact, as if to make the point, when Khrushchev entered the room he didn't even walk in the direction of the table's head. Rather, he exchanged a few remarks with Vyacheslav Malyshev, the rather mundane Minister of Medium Machine Building who was sitting near the table's end. Only when everyone else was comfortable did the former mayor of Moscow pat Malyshev on the shoulder and casually work his way to the seat beside Malenkov—the last empty chair in the room.

---

*The studious reader will recall that upon Stalin's death there were *eight* men of eminence at the pinnacle of the Party. Where were the other two at the time of this dinner? Lazar Kaganovich, a fine old Stalinist in the iron-fisted mold, had been sent on an administrative mission to Ukraine. Within a few years, he would be presiding over a potassium factory a thousand miles from Moscow. But at least he fared better than Lavrentiy Beria. The former head of the secret police, who many Western observers thought well positioned to inherit the throne when Stalin died, instead was decorated by the Party with a pistol shot to the head. And then there were six.

Over the next two hours, the men in attendance ate heartily, drank freely, and gave toasts that ranged in tone from the high-minded to the humorous, but always in the most patriotic of spirits. And in between toasts, as the Count presented courses, refilled glasses, replaced utensils, whisked away plates, and swept crumbs from the linens, the attendees made asides to the men on their left, conferred with the men on their right, or muttered to themselves under the hum of the festivities.

Upon reading this, you may be tempted to ask a little sardonically whether Count Rostov—this self-proclaimed man of propriety—allowed himself to overhear any of the private exchanges around the table? But your question and your cynicism would be entirely misplaced. For as with the best manservants, it is the *business* of capable waiters to overhear.

Consider the example of Grand Duke Demidov's butler. In his day, Kemp could stand for hours at the edge of the library as silent and stiff as a statue. But should one of the Grand Duke's guests even mention that he was thirsty, Kemp was there with an offer of a drink. Should someone complain quietly of a chill, Kemp was at the fireside stirring the coals. And when the Grand Duke observed to a friend that while the Countess Shermatova was "a delight," her son was "unreliable," Kemp would know without being told that should either of the Shermatovas appear at the door unannounced, the Grand Duke was available to the one and indisposed to the other.

So, did the Count overhear any of the private exchanges of the attendees? Did he hear any of the sly observations, pointed asides, or dismissive remarks uttered *sotto voce*?

He heard every single word.

Every man has his own personality at table, and one needn't have waited upon members of the Communist Party for twenty-eight years to know that while comrade Malenkov only toasted upon occasion and then with a glass of white wine, comrade Khrushchev would give four toasts in an evening and always with vodka. Thus, it did not escape the Count's notice that during the course of the meal, the former mayor of Moscow never once rose to his feet. But at ten minutes to eleven, when the meal was nearly over, the General Secretary rapped on his glass with the blade of his knife.

"Gentlemen," he began, "the Metropol is no stranger to historic events.

In fact, in 1918 comrade Sverdlov locked the members of the constitutional drafting committee in the suite two floors below us—informing them that they would not be let out until their work was done."

Laughter and applause.

"To Sverdlov!" someone called and, as Khrushchev emptied his glass with a self-assured grin, all around the table followed suit.

"Tonight," continued Khrushchev, "we have the honor of witnessing another historic event at the Metropol. If you will join me at the windows, comrades, I believe that Minister Malyshev has an announcement. . . ."

With expressions ranging from curious to bemused, the forty-four other attendees pushed back their chairs and approached the great windows overlooking Theatre Square, where Malyshev was already standing.

"Thank you, General Secretary," Malyshev said with a bow toward Khrushchev, followed by a weighty pause: "Comrades, as most of you know, three and a half years ago we began construction of our new power plant in the city of Obninsk. I am proud to announce that on Monday afternoon the Obninsk facility became fully operational—six months ahead of schedule."

Appropriate commendations and the nodding of heads.

"Furthermore," Malyshev continued, "at exactly eleven o'clock tonight—in less than two minutes—the plant will begin providing power to half the city of Moscow. . . ."

With that, Malyshev turned and faced the windows (as the Count and Martyn quietly snuffed the candles on the table). Outside, the lights of Moscow glimmered in the same old fashion, such that as the seconds ticked by, the men in the room began shifting on their feet and exchanging remarks. But suddenly, in the far northwestern corner of the city, the lights in a neighborhood ten blocks square went out all at once. A moment later, the lights went out in the adjacent quarter. Then the darkness began moving across the city like a shadow across a plain, growing closer and closer, until at roughly 11:02, the eternally lit windows of the Kremlin went black, followed a few seconds later by those of the Metropol Hotel.

In the darkness, the mutterings of a moment before rose in volume and shifted in tone, expressing some combination of surprise and consternation. But the attentive observer could see from Malyshev's silhouette that when the darkness fell, he neither spoke nor moved. He continued to stare out the window. Suddenly, in the far northwest corner of the capital, the lights of those initially darkened blocks flickered back on. Now it was luminescence that was moving across the city, growing closer and closer, until the windows of the Kremlin flashed on followed by the chandelier overhead—and the combined dinner of the Presidium and the Council of Ministers erupted into justified applause. For, in fact, the lights of the city seemed to burn brighter with the electricity from the first nuclear power plant in the world.

Without a doubt, the finale to this dinner of state was as fine a piece of political theater as Moscow had ever seen. But when the lights went out, were any of the city's citizens inconvenienced?

Luckily, in 1954 Moscow was not the world capital of electrical appliances. But in the brief course of the outage, at least three hundred thousand clocks stopped, forty thousand radios went silent, and five thousand televisions went black. Dogs howled and cats meowed. Standing lamps were toppled, children cried, parents banged their shins into coffee tables, and more than a few drivers—looking up through their windshields at the suddenly darkened buildings—ran into the fenders of the automobiles in front of them.

In that little gray building on the corner of Dzerzhinsky Street, the little gray fellow who was charged with taking down the eavesdroppings of waitresses kept right on typing. For like any good bureaucrat, he knew how to type with his eyes closed. Although, when a few moments after the lights went out someone stumbled in the hallway and our startled typist looked up, his fingers inadvertently shifted one column of keys to the right, such that the second half of his report was either unintelligible, or in code, depending upon your point of view.

Meanwhile, at the Maly Theatre, where Anna Urbanova—in a wig tinged with gray—was appearing as Irina Arkadina in Chekhov's *The Seagull*, the audience let out muted exclamations of concern. Though Anna and her fellow actors were well practiced at leaving the stage in the dark, they made no move to do so. For having been trained in the methods of

Stanislavsky, they immediately began acting exactly as their characters would have acted had they suddenly found themselves in a blackout:

ARKADINA: [*Alarmed*] The lights have gone out!

TRIGORIN: Stay where you are, my dear. I'll look for a candle.
[*The sound of cautious movement as TRIGORIN exits right, followed by a moment of silence*]

ARKADINA: Oh, Konstantin. I'm frightened.

KONSTANTIN: It is only darkness, Mother—that from which we have come and to which we shall return.

ARKADINA: [*As if she hasn't listened to her son*] Do you think the lights have gone out all over Russia?

KONSTANTIN: No, Mother. They have gone out all over the world. . . .

And at the Metropol? Two waiters in the Piazza carrying trays to their tables collided; four customers in the Shalyapin spilled their drinks and one was pinched; trapped in the elevator between the second and third floors, the American, Pudgy Webster, shared chocolate bars and cigarettes with his fellow passengers; while alone in his office, the hotel's manager vowed "to get to the bottom of this."

But in the dining room of the Boyarsky, where for almost fifty years the ambience had been defined by candlelight, the customers were served without interruption.

Anecdotes

On the night of the sixteenth of June, beside Sofia's empty suitcase and knapsack, the Count laid out all of the various items that he had collected on her behalf. The night before, when she'd returned from rehearsal, he had sat her down and explained exactly what it was that she must do.

"Why have you waited until now to speak of this?" she asked, on the verge of tears.

"I was afraid if I told you earlier, you would object."

"But I do object."

"I know," he said, taking her hands. "But oftentimes, Sofia, our best course of action appears objectionable at the first step. In fact, it almost always does."

What followed was a debate between father and daughter on the whys and wherefores, a contrasting of perspectives, a comparison of time horizons, and heartfelt expressions of conflicting hopes. But in the end, the Count asked Sofia that she trust him; and this proved to be a request that she did not know how to refuse. So, after a moment of shared silence, with the courage that she had shown since the first day they'd met, Sofia listened attentively as the Count went over every detail step by step.

Tonight, as he finished laying out the items, the Count reviewed the same details for himself, to ensure that nothing had been forgotten or overlooked; and he was feeling, at last, that everything was in order, when the door flung open.

"They have changed the venue!" Sofia exclaimed, out of breath.

Father and daughter traded anxious looks.

"To what?"

About to answer, Sofia stopped and closed her eyes. Then opened them with a suggestion of distress.

"I can't remember."

"It's all right," assured the Count, knowing full well that distress was no friend to recollection. "What did the director say exactly? Do you remember anything about the new location? Any aspect of its neighborhood or name?"

Sofia closed her eyes again.

"It was a hall, I think . . . , a *salle*."

"The Salle Pleyel?"

"That's it!"

The Count breathed a sigh of relief.

"We needn't worry. I know the spot well. A historic venue with fine acoustics—which also happens to be in the 8th. . ."

So, as Sofia packed her bags, the Count went down to the basement. Having found the second Paris *Baedeker*, he tore out the map, climbed the stairs, sat at the Grand Duke's desk, and drew a new red line. Then when all the straps were tightened and the latches snapped, with a touch of ceremony the Count ushered Sofia through the closet door into the study, much as he had sixteen years before. And just as on that occasion, Sofia said: "Ooo."

For since she had set out earlier that afternoon to attend her last rehearsal, their secret study had been transformed. On the bookcase a candelabra burned brightly. The two high-back chairs had been set at either end of the Countess's oriental coffee table, which in turn had been draped with linen, decorated with a small arrangement of flowers, and set with the hotel's finest silver.

"Your table awaits," said the Count with a smile, pulling out Sofia's chair.

"Okroshka?" she asked as she put her napkin in her lap.

"Absolutely," said the Count, taking his seat. "Before one travels abroad, it is best to have a simple, heartwarming soup from home, so that one can recall it fondly should one ever happen to feel a little low."

"I shall be sure to do so," said Sofia with a smile, "the minute I become homesick."

As they were finishing their soup, Sofia noticed that tucked beside the arrangement of flowers was a little silver lady in an eighteenth-century dress.

"What is that?" she asked.

"Why don't you see for yourself."

Sofia picked up the little lady and, hearing the hint of a jangle, waggled it back and forth. At the sound of the resulting chime, the door to the study swung open and in came Andrey pushing a Regency cart topped with a silver dome.

"Bonsoir, Monsieur! Bonsoir, Mademoiselle!"

Sofia laughed.

"I trust you enjoyed the soup," he said.

"It was delicious."

"Très bien."

Andrey whisked the bowls from the table and stowed them on the bottom shelf of his cart as the Count and Sofia looked to the silver dome with anticipation. But when Andrey stood back up, instead of revealing what Chef Zhukovsky had in store for them, he produced a pad.

"Before I serve the next course," he explained, "I will need you to confirm your satisfaction with the soup. Please sign here and here and here."

The look of shock on the Count's face prompted a burst of laughter from both Andrey and Sofia. Then with a flourish, the maître d' raised the dome and presented Emile's newest specialty: Goose à la Sofia. "In which," he explained, "the goose is hoisted in a dumbwaiter, chased down a hall, and thrown from a window before being roasted."

Andrey carved the bird, served the vegetables, and poured the Château Margaux all in a single motion of the hands. Then he wished the diners *"Bon appétit"* as he backed out the door.

While the two enjoyed Emile's latest creation, the Count recalled for Sofia in some detail the commotion he had found on the fourth floor that morning in 1946—including the army-issue briefs that Richard Vanderwhile had saluted. And this somehow led to a retelling of the time that Anna Urbanova threw all her clothes out the window, only to gather them back up in the middle of the night. Which is to say, they shared those humorous little stories of which family lore is made.

Perhaps some will find this surprising, having supposed that the Count would reserve this particular dinner for an offering of Polonial advice or expressions of heartache. But the Count had quite intentionally chosen to see to all of that the night before, after their discussion of what was to be done.

Showing a sense of personal restraint that was almost out of character, the Count had restricted himself to two succinct pieces of parental advice. The first was that if one did not master one's circumstances, one was bound to be mastered by them; and the second was Montaigne's maxim that the surest sign of wisdom is constant cheerfulness. But when it came to expressing admissions of heartache, the Count had not held back. He told her exactly how sad he would be in her absence, and yet, how joyful he would feel at the slightest thought of her grand adventure.

Why was the Count so careful to ensure that all of this was covered on the night before Sofia's journey? Because well he knew that when one is traveling abroad for the first time, one does not wish to look back on laborsome instructions, weighty advice, or tearful sentiments. Like the memory of the simple soup, when one is homesick what one will find most comforting to recall are those lighthearted little stories that have been told a thousand times before.

That said, when their plates were finally empty, the Count attempted to broach a new subject that had clearly weighed on his mind.

"I was thinking . . . ," he began rather haltingly. "Or rather, it occurred to me, that you might like . . . Or at some point, perhaps . . ."

Amused to see her father so uncharacteristically flummoxed, Sofia laughed.

"What is it, Papa? What might I like?"

Reaching into his jacket, the Count sheepishly removed the photograph that Mishka had tucked into the pages of his project.

"I know how you treasure the photograph of your parents, so I thought . . . you might like a picture of me, as well." Blushing for the first time in over forty years, he handed her the picture, adding: "It's the only one I have."

Genuinely moved, Sofia accepted the photograph with every intention of expressing her deepest gratitude; but getting a look at the picture, she clapped a hand over her mouth and began to laugh.

"Your moustaches!" she blurted.

"I know, I know," he said. "Although, believe it or not, at one time, they were the envy of the Jockey Club. . . ."

Sofia laughed aloud again.

"All right," said the Count, holding out his hand. "If you don't want it, I understand."

But she gripped the picture to her chest.

"I wouldn't part with it for the world." Smiling, she took another peek at his moustaches then looked up at her father in wonder. "Whatever happened to them?"

"What happened to them, indeed . . ."

Taking a considerable drink of his wine, the Count told Sofia of the afternoon in 1922 when one of his moustaches had been clipped so unceremoniously by a heavyset fellow in the hotel's barbershop.

"What a brute."

"Yes," agreed the Count, "and a glimpse of things to come. But, in a way, I have that fellow to thank for my life with you."

"How do you mean?"

The Count explained how a few days after the incident in the barbershop, her mother had popped up at his table in the Piazza to ask, in essence, the very same question that Sofia had just asked: *Where did they go?* And with that simple inquiry, their friendship had commenced.

Now it was Sofia who took a drink from her wine.

"Do you ever regret coming back to Russia?" she asked after a moment. "I mean after the Revolution."

The Count studied his daughter. If when Sofia had stepped out of Anna's room in her blue dress, the Count had felt she was crossing the threshold into adulthood, then here was a perfect confirmation. For in both tone and intent, when Sofia posed this question she did not do so as a child asks a parent, but as one adult asks another about the choices he has made. So the Count gave the question its due consideration. Then he told her the truth:

"Looking back, it seems to me that there are people who play an essential role at every turn. And I don't just mean the Napoleons who influence the course of history; I mean men and women who routinely appear at critical junctures in the progress of art, or commerce, or the evolution of ideas—as if Life itself has summoned them once again to help fulfill its purpose. Well, since the day I was born, Sofia, there was only one time when Life needed me to be in a particular place at a particular time, and that was when your mother brought you to the lobby of the Metropol. And I would not accept the Tsarship of all the Russias in exchange for being in this hotel at that hour."

Sofia rose from the table to give her father a kiss on the cheek. Then returning to her chair, she leaned back, squinted, and said: "Famous threesomes."

"Ha-ha!" exclaimed the Count.

Thus, as the candles were consumed by their flames and the bottle of Margaux was drunk to its lees, reference was made to the Father, the Son, and the Holy Ghost; Purgatory, Heaven, and Hell; the three rings of Moscow; the three Magi; the three Fates; the Three Musketeers; the gray ladies from *Macbeth*; the riddle of the Sphinx; the heads of Cerberus; the Pythagorean theorem; forks, spoons, and knives; reading, writing, and arithmetic; faith, hope, and love (with the greatest of these being love).

"Past, present, future."

"Beginning, middle, end."

"Morning, noon, and night."

"The sun, the moon, the stars."

And with this particular category, perhaps the game could have gone on all night long, but for the fact that the Count tipped over his own king with a bow of the head when Sofia said:

"Andrey, Emile, and Alexander."

At ten o'clock, when the Count and Sofia snuffed the candles and returned to their bedroom, there was a delicate knock at the door. The two looked at each other with the wistful smiles of those who know the hour has come.

"Enter," said the Count.

It was Marina, in her hat and coat.

"I'm sorry if I'm late."

"No, no. You're right on time."

As Sofia took a jacket from the closet, the Count picked up her suitcase and knapsack from the bed. Then the three of them headed down the belfry to the fifth floor, where they exited, crossed the hallway, and continued their descent on the main staircase.

Earlier that day, Sofia had already said her good-byes to Arkady and Vasily; nonetheless, they came out from behind their desks to see her off, and they were joined a moment later by Andrey in his tuxedo and Emile in his apron. Even Audrius appeared from behind the bar of the Shalyapin, leaving his customers unattended for a change. This little assembly gathered around Sofia in a circle of well-wishing, while feeling that touch of envy which is perfectly acceptable among family and friends, from one generation to the next.

"You'll be the belle of Paris," one of them said.

"We can't wait to hear all about it."

"Someone get her suitcase for her."

"Yes, her train is leaving within the hour!"

When Marina went outside to call for a taxi, as if by prior agreement Arkady, Vasily, Audrius, Andrey, and Emile all fell a few paces back—so that the Count and Sofia could have a few final words alone. Then father and daughter embraced, and Sofia, despite being uncertain of acclaim, passed through the endlessly spinning doors of the Metropol Hotel.

Returning to the sixth floor, the Count spent a moment looking around his bedroom from corner to corner, finding that it already seemed unnaturally quiet.

So this is an empty nest, he thought. What a sad state of affairs.

Pouring himself a glass of brandy and taking a good swallow, he sat down at the Grand Duke's desk and wrote five letters on the hotel's stationery. When he was done, the Count put the letters in the drawer, he brushed his teeth, he donned his pajamas, and then, despite the fact that Sofia was gone, he slept on the mattress under the bedsprings.

An Association

With the coming of the Second World War, many eyes in imprisoned Europe turned hopefully, or desperately, toward the freedom of the Americas. Lisbon became the great embarkation point. But not everybody could get to Lisbon directly, and so, a tortuous, roundabout refugee trail sprang up. Paris to Marseilles, across the Mediterranean to Oran, then by train, or auto, or foot, across the rim of Africa to Casablanca in French Morocco. Here, the fortunate ones, through money, or influence, or luck, might obtain exit visas and scurry to Lisbon, and from Lisbon to the New World. But the others wait in Casablanca— and wait—and wait—and wait. . . .

I've got to hand it to you, Alexander," whispered Osip. "This was an excellent choice. I'd quite forgotten how exciting it is."

"Shhh," said the Count. "It's beginning. . . ."

Having initiated their studies in 1930 with monthly meetings, over the years the Count and Osip had met with less frequency. In the way of these things, the two men began meeting quarterly, then semiannually, then suddenly they weren't meeting at all.

Why? you might ask.

But does there need to be a reason? Do you still dine with all of the friends with whom you dined twenty years ago? Suffice it to say that the two shared a fondness for each other and despite their best intentions, life intervened. So, when Osip happened to visit the Boyarsky with a colleague one night in early June, as he was leaving the restaurant he approached the Count in order to remark that it had been too long.

"Yes, it has," agreed the Count. "We should get together for a film."

"The sooner the better," said Osip with a smile.

And the two men might have left it at that, but as Osip turned to join his colleague at the door, the Count was struck by a notion.

"What is an intention when compared to a plan?" he said, catching Osip by the sleeve. "If *the sooner the better*, then why not next week?"

Turning back, Osip considered the Count for a moment.

"You know, you're absolutely right, Alexander. How about the nineteenth?"

"The nineteenth would be perfect."

"What shall we watch?"

Without hesitation the Count said, "*Casablanca*."

"*Casablanca* . . . ," Osip groaned.

"Isn't Humphrey Bogart your favorite?"

"Of course he is. But *Casablanca* isn't a Humphrey Bogart movie. It's just a love story in which he happens to appear."

"On the contrary, I suggest to you that *Casablanca* is *the* Humphrey Bogart movie."

"You just think that because he wears a white dinner jacket for half the film."

"That's preposterous," the Count replied a little stiffly.

"Maybe it's a little preposterous," conceded Osip, "but I don't *want* to watch *Casablanca*."

Not one to be outmaneuvered by another man's childishness, the Count pouted.

"All right," Osip sighed. "But if you get to pick the film, I get to pick the food."

As it turned out, once the film was flickering Osip was rapt. After all, there was the murder of two German couriers in the desert, then the rounding up of suspects in the marketplace, the shooting of a fugitive, the pickpocketing of a Brit, the arrival by plane of the Gestapo, music and gambling at Rick's Café Américain, as well as the stashing of two letters of transit in a piano—and that was in the first ten minutes!

In minute twenty, when Captain Renault instructed his officer to take Ugarte quietly and the officer saluted, Osip saluted too. When Ugarte cashed in his winnings, Osip cashed in his. And when Ugarte dashed between the guards, slammed the door, drew his pistol, and fired four shots, Osip dashed, slammed, drew, and fired.

[With nowhere to hide, Ugarte runs madly down the hallway. Seeing
    Rick appear from the opposite direction, he grabs him.]
UGARTE: Rick! Rick, help me!
RICK: Don't be a fool. You can't get away.
UGARTE: Rick, hide me. Do something! You must help me, Rick.
    Do something! Rick! Rick!
[Rick stands impassively as guards and gendarmes drag Ugarte off.]
CUSTOMER: When they come to get me, Rick, I hope you'll be
    more of a help.
RICK: I stick my neck out for nobody.
[Moving casually among the tables and disconcerted customers, some of
    whom are on the point of leaving, Rick speaks to the room in a calm
    voice.]
RICK: I'm sorry there was a disturbance, folks, but it's all over
    now. Everything's all right. Just sit down and have a good
    time. Enjoy yourself. . . . All right, Sam.

As Sam and his orchestra began to play, restoring something of a
carefree mood to the saloon, Osip leaned toward the Count.

"You may have been right, Alexander. This may be Bogart at his best.
Did you see the indifference he expressed as Ugarte was practically pulled
from his lapels? And when that superior American makes his smug
remark, Bogart doesn't even deign to look at him when he replies. Then
after instructing the piano player to play, he goes about his business as if
nothing has happened."

Listening to Osip with a frown, the Count suddenly stood and switched
off the projector.

"Are we going to watch the movie, or talk about it?"

Taken aback, Osip assured his friend: "We're going to watch."

"Until the end?"

"Until the credits roll."

Thus, the Count switched the projector back on while Osip paid his
utmost attention to the screen.

If the truth be told, having made such a fuss about attentiveness, the
Count did not pay *his* utmost attention to the progress of the movie. Yes,
he was watching closely enough when at minute thirty-eight Sam finds

Rick drinking whiskey alone in the saloon. But when the smoke from Rick's cigarette dissolves into a montage of his days in Paris with Ilsa, the Count's thoughts dissolved into a Parisian montage of his own.

Unlike Rick's, however, the Count's montage did not draw on his memories; it drew instead on his imaginings. It began with Sofia disembarking in the Gare du Nord as steam from the locomotive billowed across the platform. Moments later, she was outside the station with her bags in hand, preparing to board the bus with her fellow musicians. Then she was looking out the window at the sights of the city as they drove to the hotel, where the young musicians would remain until their concert—under the watchful gaze of two members of the Conservatory staff, two representatives from VOKS, a cultural attaché, and three "chaperones" in the employ of the KGB. . . .

When the movie returned from Paris to Casablanca, so did the Count. Setting aside thoughts of his daughter, he followed the action while noting through the corner of his eye Osip's complete submission to the plights of the principals.

But the Count took particular pleasure in his friend's engagement during the final minutes of the film. For with the plane to Lisbon in the air and Major Strasser dead on the ground, when Captain Renault frowned at the bottle of Vichy water, dropped it in a wastebasket, and kicked it across the floor, Osip Glebnikov, the former Red Army colonel and high official of the Party, who was sitting on the edge of his seat, poured, frowned, dropped, and kicked.

Antagonists at Arms
(And an Absolution)

"**G**ood evening and welcome to the Boyarsky," began the Count in Russian, as the middle-aged couple with blond hair and blue eyes looked up from their menus.

"Do you speak English?" the husband asked in English, though with a decidedly Scandinavian cadence.

"Good evening and welcome to the Boyarsky," the Count translated accordingly. "My name is Alexander and I will be your waiter tonight. But before describing our specials, may I offer you an aperitif?"

"I think we are ready to order," said the husband.

"We have just arrived in the hotel after a long day of travel," explained the wife with a weary smile.

The Count hesitated.

"And where, if I may ask, have you been traveling from . . . ?"

"Helsinki," said the husband with a hint of impatience.

"Well then, *tervetuloa Moskova*," said the Count.

"*Kiitos*," replied the wife with a smile.

"Given your long journey, I will see to it that you are served a delightful meal without delay. But before I take your order, would you be so kind as to give me your room number . . . ?"

From the beginning, the Count had determined that he would need to filch a few things from a Norwegian, a Dane, a Swede, or a Finn. On the face of it, this task should not have posed a significant challenge, as Scandinavian visitors were reasonably common at the Metropol. The problem was that the visitor in question was sure to notify the hotel's manager as soon as he discovered that his pocket had been picked, which in turn might lead to the notification of authorities, the official interviewing of hotel staff, perhaps even the searching of rooms and the posting of guards at railway stations. So, the pocket picking would have to take place at the very last minute. In the meantime, the Count could only cross his fingers that a Scandinavian man would be residing in the hotel at the critical juncture.

With grim attention, he had watched as a salesman from Stockholm checked out of the hotel on the thirteenth of June. Then on the seventeenth, a journalist from Oslo had been recalled by his paper. In no small terms, the Count berated himself for not acting sooner. When, lo and behold, with only twenty-four hours to spare, a pair of beleaguered Finns came into the Boyarsky and sat right at his table.

But there remained one small complication: The primary item that the Count hoped to secure was the gentleman's passport. And as most foreigners in Russia carried their passports about on their person, the Count would not be able to pay a visit to the Finns' suite on the following morning when they were touring about the city; he would need to visit the suite tonight—while they were in it.

As much as we hate to admit the fact, Fate does not take sides. It is fair-minded and generally prefers to maintain some balance between the likelihood of success and failure in all our endeavors. Thus, having put the Count in the challenging position of having to lift a passport at the very last minute, Fate offered the Count a small consolation: for at 9:30, when he asked the Finns if they would like to see the dessert cart, they declined on the grounds that they were exhausted and ready for bed.

Shortly after midnight, when the Boyarsky was closed and the Count had bid goodnight to Andrey and Emile, he climbed the stairs to the third floor, went halfway down the hall, took off his shoes, and then by means of Nina's key slipped into suite 322 in his stocking feet.

Many years before, under a spell cast by a certain actress, the Count had dwelt for a time among the ranks of the invisible. So, as he tiptoed into the Finns' bedroom, he called upon Venus to veil him in a mist—just as she had for her son, Aeneas, when he wandered the streets of Carthage—so that his footfalls would be silent, his heartbeat still, and his presence in the room no more notable than a breath of air.

As it was late in June, the Finns had drawn their curtains to block out the glow of the white nights, but a sliver of light remained where the two drapes met. By this narrow illumination, the Count approached the foot of the bed and took in the sleeping forms of the travelers. Thanks be to God, they were about forty years old. Fifteen years younger, they would not have been asleep. Having stumbled back from a late dinner in the Arbat at which they had ordered two bottles of wine, they would now be in each other's arms. Fifteen years older, they would be tossing and turning, getting up twice a night to visit the loo. But at forty? They had enough appetite to eat well, enough temperance to drink in moderation, and enough wisdom to celebrate the absence of their children by getting a good night's sleep.

Within a matter of minutes the Count had secured the gentleman's passport and 150 Finnish marks from the bureau, tiptoed through the sitting room, and slipped back into the hallway, which was empty.

In fact, it was so empty that even his shoes weren't in it.

"Confound it," said the Count to himself. "They must have been picked up by the night service for shining."

After issuing a litany of self-recriminations, the Count took comfort that in all likelihood on the following morning his shoes would simply be returned by the Finns to the main desk, where they would be cast into the hotel's collection of unidentifiable misplaced possessions. As he climbed the stairs of the belfry he took additional comfort that all else had gone according to plan. *By this time tomorrow night . . .* , he was thinking as he opened his bedroom door—only to discover the Bishop, sitting at the Grand Duke's desk.

Naturally enough, the Count's first instinct at the sight was a feeling of indignation. Not only had this accountant of discrepancies, this stripper of wine labels entered the Count's quarters without invitation, he had actually rested his elbows on that dimpled surface where once had been written persuasive arguments to statesmen and exquisite counsel to friends. The Count was just opening his mouth to demand an explanation, when he saw that a drawer had been opened, and that a sheet of paper was in the Bishop's hand.

The letters, the Count realized with a feeling of dread.

Oh, if it had only been the letters. . . .

Carefully written expressions of fondness and fellowship may not have been common between colleagues, but they were hardly suspicious in and of themselves. A man has every right—and some responsibility—to communicate his good feelings to his friends. But it was not one of the recently written letters that the Bishop was holding. It was the first of the *Baedeker* maps—the one on which the Count had drawn the bright red line connecting the Palais Garnier to the American Embassy by way of the Avenue George V.

Then again, perhaps whether it was a letter or a map mattered not. For when the Bishop had turned at the sound of the door, he had witnessed the transition in the Count's expression from indignation to horror—a transition that confirmed a state of guilt even before an accusation had been made.

"Headwaiter Rostov," said the Bishop, as if surprised to see the Count in his own room. "You truly are a man of many interests: Wine . . . Cuisine . . . The streets of Paris . . ."

"Yes," said the Count while attempting to compose himself. "I have been reading a bit of Proust lately, and thus have been reacquainting myself with the arrangement of the city's arrondissements."

"Of course," said the Bishop.

Cruelty knows that it has no need of histrionics. It can be as calm and quiet as it likes. It can sigh, or lightly shake its head in disbelief, or offer a sympathetic apology for whatever it must do. It can move slowly, methodically, inevitably. Thus, the Bishop, having gently laid the map on the dimpled surface of the Grand Duke's desk, now rose from the chair, walked across the room, and slipped past the Count without a word.

What went through the mind of the Bishop as he descended the five flights from the attic to the ground floor? What emotion did he feel?

Perhaps it was gloating. Having felt belittled by the Count for over thirty years, perhaps he now felt the pleasure of finally putting this pretentious polymath in his place. Or perhaps it was righteousness. Maybe comrade Leplevsky was so dedicated to the brotherhood of the Proletariat (from which he'd sprung), that the persistence of this Former Person in the new Russia galled his sense of justice. Or maybe it was simply the cold satisfaction of the envious. For those who had difficulty in school or at making friends when they were young will forever recognize with a bitter glance those for whom life has seemed to come easy.

Gloating, righteousness, satisfaction, who can say? But the emotion the Bishop felt upon opening the door to his office was almost certainly that of shock—for the adversary that he had left in the attic just minutes before was now sitting behind the manager's desk with a pistol in his hand.

How was this possible?

When the Bishop left the Count's bedroom, the Count was frozen in place by a torrent of emotions—by feelings of fury, incredulity, self-recrimination, and fear. Rather than burn the map, like a fool he had slipped it in his drawer. Six months of the most careful planning and painstaking execution overturned by a single misstep. And what was worse, he had put Sofia at risk. What price was she to pay for his carelessness?

But if the Count was frozen in place, he was frozen for all of five seconds. For these perfectly understandable sentiments, which threatened to drain the blood from his heart, were swept aside by resolve.

Turning on his heels, the Count went to the head of the belfry and listened until the Bishop had descended the first two flights of stairs. Still in his stocking feet, the Count began to follow in the Bishop's footsteps; but when he got to the fifth floor, he exited the belfry, sped down the hallway, and ran down the main staircase, just as Sofia had at the age of thirteen.

As if he were still enshrouded in a mist, when the Count alit from the stairs, he ran down the hall and entered the executive offices without being seen by a soul; but upon reaching the Bishop's door, he discovered it was locked. Even as he was taking the Lord's name in vain, the Count slapped his hands against his vest with relief. For he still had Nina's passkey in his pocket. Letting himself in, the Count relocked the door and crossed to the wall where the filing cabinets had taken the place of Mr. Halecki's chaise. Counting from the portrait of Karl Marx, the Count placed his hand in the center of the second panel to the right, gave a push, and popped it open. Taking the inlaid box from its chamber, the Count set it on the desk and opened the lid.

"Simply marvelous," he said.

Then sitting in the manager's chair, the Count removed the two pistols, loaded them, and waited. He guessed that he had only a matter of seconds before the door would open, but he used them as best he could to moderate his breathing, lower his heart rate, and calm his nerves; such that by the time the Bishop's key turned in the lock, he was as cold as a killer.

So unanticipated was the Count's presence behind the desk that the Bishop had swung the door closed before even noticing that he was there. But if every man has his strengths, one of the Bishop's was that he was never more than a step away from petty protocol and an inherent sense of superiority.

"Headwaiter Rostov," he said almost peevishly, "you have no business being in this office. I insist that you leave immediately."

The Count raised one of the pistols.

"Sit down."

"How dare you!"

"Sit down," the Count repeated more slowly.

The Bishop would be the first to admit that he had no experience with firearms. In fact, he could barely distinguish between a revolver and a semiautomatic. But any fool could see that what the Count was holding was an antique. A museum piece. A curiosity.

"You leave me no choice but to alert the authorities," he said. Then stepping forward, he took up the receiver from one of his two telephones.

The Count shifted his aim from the Bishop to the portrait of Stalin and shot the former Premier between the eyes.

Shocked by either the sound or the sacrilege, the Bishop jumped back, dropping the receiver with a clatter.

The Count raised the second pistol and leveled it at the Bishop's chest.

"Sit down," he said again.

This time, the Bishop obliged.

With the second gun still trained on the Bishop's chest, the Count now stood. He replaced the telephone receiver in its cradle. He backed around the Bishop's chair and locked the office door. Then he returned to his seat behind the desk.

The two men were quiet as the Bishop restored his sense of superiority.

"Well, Headwaiter Rostov, it seems that by threat of violence, you have succeeded in keeping me against my will. What do you intend to do now?"

"We're going to wait."

"Wait for what?"

The Count didn't answer.

After a few moments, one of the telephones began to ring. Instinctively, the Bishop reached for it, but the Count shook his head. It rang eleven times before it went silent.

"How long do you expect to hold me here?" insisted the Bishop. "An hour? Two? Until morning?"

It was a good question. The Count looked around the walls of the room for a clock, but couldn't find one.

"Give me your watch," he said.

"Excuse me?"

"You heard me."

The Bishop removed the watch from his wrist and tossed it on the desk. Generally speaking, the Count was not in favor of relieving men of their possessions at gunpoint, but having prided himself on ignoring the second hand for so many years, the time had come for the Count to attend to it.

According to the Bishop's watch (which was probably set five minutes fast to ensure that he was never late for work), it was almost 1:00 A.M. There would still be a few of the hotel's guests returning from late suppers, a few stragglers in the bar, the clearing and setting up of the Piazza, the vacuuming of the lobby. But by 2:30, the hotel would be quiet in every corner.

"Make yourself comfortable," said the Count. Then to pass the time, he began to whistle a bit of Mozart from *Cosi fan tutte*. Somewhere in the second movement, he became conscious of the fact that the Bishop was smiling dismissively.

"Is there something on your mind?" asked the Count.

The left upper corner of the Bishop's mouth twitched.

"Your sort," he sneered. "How convinced you have always been of the rightness of your actions. As if God Himself was so impressed with your precious manners and delightful way of putting things that He blessed you to do as you pleased. What vanity."

The Bishop let out what must have passed in his household for a laugh.

"Well, you have had your time," he continued. "You have had your chance to dance with your illusions and act with impunity. But your little orchestra has stopped playing. Whatever you say or do now, whatever you think, even if it is at two or three in the morning behind a locked door, will come to light. And when it does, you will be held to account."

The Count listened to the Bishop with genuine interest and a touch of surprise. His sort? The Lord's blessing that he could do as he pleased? While dancing with his illusions? The Count had no idea what the Bishop was talking about. After all, he had now lived under house arrest in the Metropol Hotel for over half his life. He almost smiled, on the verge of making some quip about the large imaginations of small men—but his expression instead grew sober, as he considered the Bishop's smug assurance that all would "come to light."

His gaze shifted to the filing cabinets, of which there were now five.

With the barrel of the pistol still trained on the Bishop, the Count crossed to the filing cabinets and pulled at the left uppermost drawer. It was locked.

"Where is the key?"

"You have no business opening those cabinets. They contain my personal files."

The Count went around to the back of the desk and opened the drawers. They were surprisingly empty.

Where would a man like the Bishop keep the key to his personal files? Why, on his person. Of course.

The Count came around the desk and stood over the Bishop.

"You can give me that key," he said, "or I can take it from you. But there is no third way."

When the Bishop looked up with an expression of mild indignation, he saw that the Count had raised the old pistol in the air with the clear intention of bringing it down across his face. The Bishop took a small ring of keys from a pocket and threw it on the desk.

Even as they landed in a jangle, the Count could see that the Bishop had undergone something of a transformation. He had suddenly lost his sense of superiority, as if all along it had been secured by his possession of these keys. Picking up the ring, the Count sorted through them until he found the smallest, then he unlocked all of the Bishop's filing cabinets one by one.

In the first three cabinets, there was an orderly collection of reports on the hotel's operations: revenues; occupancy rates; staffing; maintenance expenditures; inventories; and yes, discrepancies. But in the remainder of the cabinets, the files were dedicated to individuals. In addition to files on various guests who had stayed in the hotel over the years, in alphabetical arrangement were files on members of the staff. On Arkady, Vasily, Andrey, and Emile. Even Marina. The Count needed no more than a glance at them to know their purpose. They were a careful accounting of human flaws, noting specific instances of tardiness, impertinence, disaffection, drunkenness, sloth, desire. One could not exactly call the contents of these files spurious or inaccurate. No doubt, all of the aforementioned had been guilty of these human frailties at one point or another; but for any one of them the Count could have compiled a file fifty times larger that cataloged their virtues. Having pulled the files of his friends and dumped them on the desk, the Count returned to the cabinets and double-checked among the Rs. When he found his own file, he was pleased to discover that it was among the thickest.

The Count looked at his watch (or rather the Bishop's). It was 2:30 in the morning: the hour of ghosts. The Count reloaded the first pistol, tucked it through his belt, and then pointed the other at the Bishop.

"It's time to go," he said, then he waved at the files on the desk with the pistol. "They're your property, you carry them."

The Bishop gathered them up without protest.

"Where are we going?"

"You'll see soon enough."

The Count led the Bishop through the empty offices, into an enclosed stairwell, and down two flights below street level.

For all his persnickety command of the hotel's minutiae, the Bishop had obviously never been in the basement. Coming through the door at the bottom of the stairs, he looked around with a mixture of fear and disgust.

"First stop," the Count said, pulling open the heavy steel door that led into the boiler room. The Bishop hesitated, so the Count poked him with the barrel of the gun. "Over there." Taking a handkerchief from his pocket, the Count opened the small door in the furnace. "In they go," he said.

Without a word, the Bishop fed the flames with his files. Perhaps it was his proximity to the furnace, or the exertion of carrying the stack of dossiers down two flights of stairs, but the Bishop had begun to sweat in a manner that was distinctly out of character.

"Come on," said the Count. "Next stop."

Once outside the boiler room, the Count prodded the Bishop down the hall to the cabinet of curiosities.

"There. On the lower shelf. Get that small red book."

The Bishop did as he was told and handed the Count the *Baedeker* for Finland.

The Count nodded his head to indicate they were headed farther into the basement. The Bishop now looked quite pale, and after a few steps it seemed his knees might buckle beneath him.

"Just a little farther," coaxed the Count. And a moment later they were at the bright blue door.

Taking Nina's key from his pocket, the Count opened it. "In you go," he said.

The Bishop stepped in and turned. "What are you going to do with me?"

"I'm not going to do anything with you."

"Then when are you coming back?"

"I am never coming back."

"You can't leave me here," said the Bishop. "It could be weeks before someone finds me!"

"You attend the daily meeting of the Boyarsky, comrade Leplevsky. If you were listening at the last one, you'd recall that there is a banquet on Tuesday night in the ballroom. I have no doubt that someone will find you then."

At which point, the Count closed the door and locked the Bishop into that room where pomp bides its time.

They should get along just famously, thought the Count.

It was three in the morning when the Count entered the belfry on the lobby floor. As he climbed, he felt the relief of the narrow escape. Reaching in his pocket, he removed the stolen passport and the Finnish marks and tucked them in the *Baedeker*. But when he turned the corner on the fourth floor, a shiver ran down his spine. For on the landing just above him was the ghost of the one-eyed cat. From his elevated position, the cat looked down upon this Former Person—who was standing there in his stocking feet with pistols in his belt and stolen goods in his hand.

It has been said that Admiral Lord Nelson, having been blinded in one eye during the Battle of the Nile in 1798, three years later during the Battle of Copenhagen held his telescope to his dead eye when his commander raised the signal for retreat—thus continuing his attack until the Danish navy was willing to negotiate a truce.

Though this story was a favorite of the Grand Duke's and often retold to the young Count as an example of courageous perseverance in the face of impossible odds, the Count had always suspected it was a little apocryphal. After all, in the midst of armed conflicts, facts are bound to be just as susceptible to injury as ships and men, if not more so. But at the onset of the summer solstice of 1954, the one-eyed cat of the Metropol turned his blind eye upon the Count's ill-gotten gains, and without the slightest expression of disappointment, disappeared down the stairs.

Apotheoses

Despite having gone to bed at four in the morning, on the twenty-first of June the Count rose at his usual hour. He did five squats, five stretches, and took five deep breaths. He breakfasted on coffee, a biscuit, and his daily fruit (today an assortment of berries), after which he went downstairs to read the papers and chat with Vasily. He lunched in the Piazza. In the afternoon, he paid a visit to Marina in the stitching room. As it was his day off, at seven o'clock he had an aperitif at the Shalyapin, where he marveled at the arrival of summer with the ever-attentive Audrius. And at eight, he dined at table ten in the Boyarsky. Which is to say, he treated the day much as he treated any other. Except that when he left the restaurant at ten, having told Nadja that the manager wished to see her, he slipped inside the empty coatroom in order to borrow the raincoat and fedora of the American journalist, Salisbury.

Back on the sixth floor, the Count dug to the bottom of his old trunk in order to retrieve the rucksack that he had used in 1918 on his trek from Paris to Idlehour. As on that journey, this time he would travel only with the bare necessities. That is, three changes of clothing, a toothbrush and toothpaste, *Anna Karenina*, Mishka's project, and, finally, the bottle of Châteauneuf-du-Pape that he intended to drink on the fourteenth of June 1963—ten years to the day after his old friend's death.

Gathering up his things, the Count paid one last visit to his study. So many years before, he had bid *adieu* to a whole household. Then a few years later he had bid *adieu* to a suite. Now, he was to bid *adieu* to a room that was one hundred square feet. It was, without question, the smallest room that he had occupied in his life; yet somehow, within those four walls the world had come and gone. With that thought, the Count tipped his hat to Helena's portrait and switched out the light.

At the same time that the Count was descending to the lobby, Sofia was concluding her performance on the stage of the Salle Pleyel in Paris. Rising from the piano, she turned to the audience almost in a state of wonder—for whenever Sofia performed, she so fully immersed herself in her playing, that she tended to forget there was anyone listening. But having been brought back to her senses by the sound of applause, she did not forget to gesture graciously toward the orchestra and her conductor before taking one final bow.

Immediately offstage, Sofia received a formal congratulations from the cultural attaché and a heartfelt embrace from Director Vavilov. It was her finest performance yet, he said. But then the two men turned their attention back to the stage, where the violin prodigy was taking his place before the conductor. The hall grew so quiet that all assembled could hear the tap of the conductor's baton. Then after that universal moment of suspension, the musicians began to play and Sofia made her way to the dressing room.

The Conservatory's orchestra performed Dvorak's concerto in just over thirty minutes. Sofia would allow herself fifteen to reach the exit.

Taking up her knapsack, she went straight to one of the bathrooms reserved for the musicians. Locking the door behind her, she kicked off her shoes and shed the beautiful blue dress that Marina had made. She took off the necklace that Anna had given her and dropped it on the dress. She donned the slacks and oxford shirt that her father had purloined from the Italian gentleman. Then looking into the small mirror above the sink, she took out the scissors that her father had given her and began to cut her hair.

This little implement in the shape of an egret, which had been so prized by her father's sister, had clearly been designed for snipping, not shearing. The rings cut into the knuckles of Sofia's thumb and forefinger as she tried and failed to cut through lengths of her hair. Beginning to shed tears of frustration, Sofia closed her eyes and took a breath. *There is no time for that*, she told herself. Wiping the tears from her cheeks with the back of her hand, she began again—cutting smaller amounts of hair, working systematically around her head.

When she was finished, she swept up the hair with her hands and flushed it down the toilet, just as her father had instructed. Then from a side pocket in the knapsack she took the little black bottle that the barber of the Metropol had once used to dye those first gray hairs that appeared in his customers' beards. The cap of the bottle had a small brush attached to it. Taking in hand the strip of white hair that had virtually defined her appearance since the age of thirteen, Sofia leaned over the sink and carefully brushed it with the dye until it was as black as the rest of her hair.

When she was done, she returned the bottle and the scissors to her pack. She took out the Italian's cap and set it on the sink. Then she shifted her attention to the pile of clothes on the floor—and that is when she realized they had never considered her shoes. All she had was the elegant pair of high-heeled pumps that Anna had helped pick out for the Conservatory competition the year before. With little choice, she dumped them in the trash.

She scooped up the dress and necklace to dispose of them as well. Yes, Marina had made the dress and Anna had given her the necklace, but she couldn't take them with her—of that, her father had left no doubt. If for any reason she was stopped and her bag was searched, these glamorous feminine items would give her away. Sofia hesitated for a moment, then she stuffed the dress into the trash with the shoes; but the necklace, she slipped into her pocket.

Securing the straps of the knapsack and swinging it onto her back, Sofia pulled the cap tightly onto her head, opened the bathroom door, and listened. The strings were beginning to swell, signaling the end of the third movement. Leaving the bathroom, she turned away from the dressing rooms and headed toward the back of the building. The music grew louder as she passed directly behind the stage. Then with the first notes of the final movement, she passed through the exit at the rear of the hall and went barefoot into the night.

Walking quickly, but not running, Sofia circled the Salle Pleyel to the Rue du Faubourg Saint-Honoré, where the well-lit entrance of the concert hall was located. Crossing the street, she stepped into a doorway and took off the Italian's cap. From under the brim, she pulled out the little map that her father had cut from the *Baedeker* and folded into the size of a matchbook. Opening it, she oriented herself and then began following the red line half a block along Faubourg Saint-Honoré, down the Avenue Hoche to the Arc de Triomphe, and then left onto the Champs-Élysées, headed toward the Place de la Concorde.

In drawing this zigzagging line from the doors of the Salle Pleyel to the American Embassy, the Count had not chosen the most direct route. That would have been ten blocks straight along Faubourg Saint-Honoré. But the Count had wanted to get Sofia away from the concert hall as quickly as possible. This slight detour would add only a few minutes to Sofia's journey, but it would allow her to disappear into the anonymity of the Champs-Élysées; and she should still have enough time to reach the embassy before her absence was discovered.

But when the Count had made this calculation, what he had failed to take into account was the impact upon a twenty-one-year-old girl of seeing the Arc de Triomphe and the Louvre lit up at night for the very first time. True, Sofia had seen them both the day before, along with plenty of other sights; but just as the Count had imagined, she had seen them through the window of a bus. It was a different thing altogether to see them at the onset of summer, having received an ovation, changed one's appearance, and escaped into the night. . . .

For while in the classical tradition there was no Muse of architecture, I think we can agree that under the right circumstances, the appearance of a building can impress itself upon one's memory, affect one's sentiments, and even change one's life. Just so, risking minutes that she did not have to spare, Sofia came to a stop at the Place de la Concorde and turned slowly in place, as if in a moment of recognition.

On the night before she had left Moscow, when Sofia had expressed her distress at what her father wanted her to do, he had attempted to console her with a notion. He had said that our lives are steered by uncertainties, many of which are disruptive or even daunting; but that if we persevere and remain generous of heart, we may be granted a moment of supreme lucidity—a moment in which all that has happened to us suddenly comes into focus as a necessary course of events, even as we find ourselves on the threshold of a bold new life that we had been meant to lead all along.

When her father had made this claim, it had seemed so outlandish, so overblown that it had not assuaged Sofia's distress in the least. But turning in place on the Place de la Concorde, seeing the Arc de Triomphe, and the Eiffel Tower, and the Tuileries, and the cars and Vespas zipping around the great obelisk, Sofia had an inkling of what her father had been trying to say.

"Was it like this all night?"

Richard Vanderwhile, who was standing in his apartment in the embassy, had just noticed the angle of his bow tie in the bedroom mirror. It was at a slant of twenty-five degrees.

"Your tie is always like that, my dear."

Richard turned to his wife in shock.

"Always! Why on earth haven't you ever said anything?"

"Because I think it makes you look rakish."

Giving the nod of one who could make do with "rakish," Richard took another look in the mirror, then pulled the tie loose, hung his tuxedo jacket on the back of his chair, and was about to suggest a nightcap when there was a knock at the door. It was Richard's attaché.

"What is it, Billy?"

"I'm sorry to bother you at this hour, sir. But there is a young man asking for you."

"A young man?"

"Yes. Apparently, he is seeking asylum. . . ."

Richard raised his eyebrows.

"Asylum from what?"

"I'm not certain, sir. But he isn't wearing any shoes."

Mr. and Mrs. Vanderwhile exchanged looks.

"Well then, I guess you had better show him in."

The attaché returned a minute later with a young man in a newsboy's cap who was, in fact, barefoot. In the manner of the polite but anxious, the young man took off his cap and held it at his waist in both hands.

"Billy," said Mrs. Vanderwhile, "this is not a young man."

The attaché's eyes widened.

"Well, I'll be damned," said Richard. "Sofia Rostov."

Sofia smiled with an expression of relief: "Mr. Vanderwhile."

Richard told his attaché he could go, then he approached Sofia with a grin and took her by the elbows.

"Let me get a good look at you." Without letting go of Sofia, Richard turned to his wife. "Didn't I tell you she was a beauty?"

"You certainly did," said Mrs. Vanderwhile with a smile.

Although from Sofia's perspective, it was Mrs. Vanderwhile who was the beauty.

"What a terrific turn of events," said Richard.

"You weren't . . . expecting me?" asked Sofia tentatively.

"Of course we were! But your father has grown quite fond of all this cloak-and-dagger business. He assured me that you were coming, but he wouldn't let me know when, where, or how. And he certainly didn't tell me you'd be arriving as a barefoot boy." Richard pointed to Sofia's knapsack. "Is that all you brought with you?"

"I'm afraid so."

"Are you hungry?" asked Mrs. Vanderwhile.

Before Sofia could respond, Richard chimed in: "Of course she's hungry. I'm hungry and I've just returned from a dinner. I'll tell you what, my dear: Why don't you see if you can scare up some clothes for Sofia, while she and I have a chat. Then we can all rendezvous in the kitchen."

While Mrs. Vanderwhile went in search of clothes, Richard led Sofia into his study and sat on the edge of his desk.

"I can't tell you how excited we are to have you in house, Sofia. And I do so hate putting business before pleasure. But once we sit down to eat, I suspect we'll be swept away with stories of your adventures. So, before we go to the kitchen, your father mentioned that you might have something for me. . . ."

Sofia looked shy and hesitant.

"My father said that you might have something for me first. . . ."

Richard laughed and slapped his hands together.

"Right you are! I'd forgotten all about it."

Richard crossed the room to one of the bookcases. Standing on his tiptoes, he reached to the uppermost shelf and removed what looked like a large book—but which turned out to be a package wrapped in brown paper. Richard set it down on his desk with a thud.

In turn, Sofia began to reach into her knapsack.

"Before giving anything to me," Richard cautioned, "you should probably make sure that this is what it's supposed to be. . . ."

"Oh, yes. I see."

"Besides," he added, "I've been dying of curiosity."

Joining Richard at his desk, Sofia untied the strings and pulled back the folds of paper. Inside was an old edition of Montaigne's *Essays*.

"Well," said Richard a little bemused, "you've got to give that old Frenchman credit. He's substantially heavier than Adam Smith or Plato. I really had no idea."

But then Sofia opened the book, revealing a rectangular cavity cut into the pages, in which there were eight small stacks of gold coins.

"Naturally," said Richard.

Sofia closed the book and retied the strings. Then taking off her knapsack, she emptied its contents onto a chair and handed the empty bag to Richard.

"Father said you should cut the seam at the top of the straps."

There was a knock at the door and Mrs. Vanderwhile poked in her head.

"I've got some clothes to show you, Sofia. Are you ready?"

"Perfect timing," said Richard while giving a nod to Sofia. "I'll follow you in a minute."

Left alone, Richard took a penknife from his pocket. He switched out the blade and carefully cut the seam that had been expertly sewn along the top of the shoulder straps. In the narrow gap that ran behind the length of one of the straps had been slipped a tightly rolled piece of paper.

Easing the roll from its hiding place, Richard sat down and spread it across his desk. On the top side there was a diagram entitled "Combined Dinner of Council of Ministers and Presidium, June 11, 1954." The diagram itself depicted a long U with forty-six names inscribed around its periphery. Under the name of each person was their title and a summation of their personality in three words. On the verso was a detailed description of the evening in question.

Certainly, the Count described the announcement concerning the Obninsk nuclear power plant and the theatric display of its connection to the Moscow grid. But what he emphasized in the course of his report were the evening's social nuances.

First, the Count observed that when the guests appeared at the dinner, virtually all were surprised by the venue. They had obviously arrived at the hotel expecting they would be dining in one of the Boyarsky's formal rooms, only to be directed instead to suite 417. The one exception was Khrushchev—who entered the room with the cool satisfaction of one who not only knew where the dinner would be held, but was pleased to see that everything was perfectly in order. The General Secretary erased any doubt as to his personal involvement in the planning of the evening when, having been unusually quiet, he stood at ten minutes to eleven to make a toast that referenced the history of the suite two floors below.

But for the Count, the genius of the evening was in Khrushchev's casual display of his alignment with Malyshev. In recent months, Malenkov had made no secret of his disagreement with Khrushchev regarding nuclear armament. Malenkov foresaw that a nuclear arms race with the West could only have devastating results, referring to it as an "apocalyptic policy." But with this little event of political theater, Khrushchev had performed the perfect sleight of hand—switching out the threat of nuclear Armageddon for the uplifting sight of a city sparkling with nuclear power. In a stroke, the conservative hawk had cast himself as a man of the future and his progressive opponent as a reactionary.

Sure enough, with the lights of the city shining brightly and freshly chilled bottles of vodka on the table, Malyshev crossed the room to confer with the General Secretary. As most of the others were still milling about with smiles on their faces, Malyshev quite naturally took the empty chair at Khrushchev's side. So, when everyone began to resume their places, Malenkov found himself stranded behind Khrushchev and Malyshev; and as the Premier of the Communist Party waited awkwardly for them to finish their conversation so that he could reclaim his seat, no one at the table even batted an eye.

As Richard finished reading the Count's description, he leaned back in his chair and smiled, thinking he could use a hundred men like

Alexander Rostov. And that's when he noticed the small, slightly curled piece of paper lying on his desk. Picking it up, Richard immediately recognized the Count's cursive. The note, which had presumably been rolled up in the report, included a straightforward instruction of how to confirm that Sofia had arrived at the embassy safely, followed by a long sequence of seven-digit numbers.

Richard jumped to his feet.

"Billy!"

After a moment the door swung open and the attaché stuck in his head.

"Sir?"

"If it is almost ten in Paris, what time is it almost in Moscow?"

"Midnight."

"How many girls are on the switchboard?"

"I'm not certain," admitted the lieutenant, a little flustered. "At this hour, two; maybe three?"

"That's not enough! Go to the typing pool, the decoding room, the kitchen. Round up everyone with a finger on their hand!"

When the Count arrived in the lobby with his rucksack on his shoulder and sat in his chair between the potted palms, he didn't fidget. He didn't get up and walk about, or read the evening edition. Nor did he check the time on the Bishop's watch.

If asked in advance to imagine what sitting there under these circumstances would feel like, the Count would have predicted a definite sense of anxiety. But as the minutes ticked away, the Count didn't find the wait distressing at all; he found it surprisingly peaceful. With a patience that was almost otherworldly, he watched the guests of the hotel come and go. He saw the elevator doors open and close. He heard the sound of music and laughter emanating from the Shalyapin Bar.

At that moment, it somehow seemed to the Count that no one was out of place; that every little thing happening was part of some master plan; and that within the context of that plan, he was meant to sit in the chair between the potted palms and wait. And almost exactly at midnight, the

Count's patience was rewarded. For in accordance with the instructions he'd written to Richard, every telephone on the first floor of the Metropol began to ring.

All four telephones at the main desk rang. The two house phones that were on a side table by the elevator rang. The telephones at Vasily's desk and the bell captain's station rang. As did the four telephones in the Piazza, the three in the coffeehouse, the eight in the executive offices, and the two on the Bishop's desk. All told, there must have been thirty phones ringing at once.

What a simple thing in concept, the simultaneous ringing of thirty phones. And yet, it immediately created a sense of pandemonium. Those who were in the lobby began looking from corner to corner. What could bring about the ringing of thirty phones at twelve o'clock at night? Had the Metropol been struck by lightning? Was Russia under attack? Or were the spirits of the past exacting their toll on the present?

Whatever the cause, the sound was utterly disconcerting.

When a single telephone rings, our immediate instinct is to pick up the receiver and say hello. But when thirty ring at once, our instinct is to take two steps back and stare. The limited crew of the night shift found themselves running from phone to phone without the fortitude to answer a single one. The drunken crowd in the Shalyapin began spilling into the lobby, as guests, who had been awakened on the second floor, came marching down the stairs. And in the midst of this commotion, Count Alexander Ilyich Rostov quietly donned the journalist's hat and coat, shouldered his rucksack, and walked out of the Metropol Hotel.

AFTERWORD

Afterwards . . .

On the twenty-first of June 1954, Viktor Stepanovich Skadovsky left his apartment shortly before midnight in order to keep an appointment.

His wife had urged him not to go. What good could come from an appointment at this hour, she wanted to know. Did he think the police didn't walk the streets at midnight? The police *made a point* of walking the streets at midnight. Because since the beginning of time, that's when fools have kept their appointments!

Viktor responded to his wife that this was nonsense; that she was being melodramatic. But when he left their building, he walked ten blocks to the Garden Ring before boarding a bus, and he took comfort from the indifference with which the others on the bus received him.

Yes, his wife was upset that he had an appointment at midnight. But if she had known the purpose of the appointment, she would have been beside herself. And if, upon learning of his intentions, she had demanded to know why on earth he had agreed to do something so foolhardy, he wouldn't have been able to answer her. He wasn't certain himself.

It wasn't simply because of Sofia. Of course, he felt an almost fatherly pride in her achievement as a pianist. The very notion of helping a young artist discover her talent was a fantasy that Viktor had long since abandoned; and to experience it so unexpectedly was beyond description. What's more, it was the hours of teaching Sofia that had ultimately led him to pursue another abandoned dream: playing the classical repertoire in a chamber orchestra. But even so, it wasn't simply because of her.

To a greater degree, it was because of the Count. For, however unaccountably, Viktor felt a profound sense of loyalty to Alexander Ilyich Rostov; a sense of loyalty that was grounded in feelings of respect that Viktor could hardly articulate—and that his wife, for all her virtues, would never have understood.

But perhaps most of all, he had agreed to the Count's request because it felt right to do so; and that feeling of conviction, in itself, was a pleasure that had become increasingly rare.

With that thought, Viktor stepped off the bus, entered the old St. Petersburg Station, and walked across the central hall toward the brightly lit café where he had been instructed to wait.

Viktor was sitting in a booth in the corner—watching an old accordion player move from table to table—when the Count entered the café. He was wearing an American trench coat and a dark gray fedora. Seeing Viktor, he crossed the café, set down his rucksack, shed the coat and hat, and joined him in the booth. When a moment later the waitress appeared, he ordered a cup of coffee and then waited for the coffee to arrive before sliding a little red book across the table.

"I want to thank you for doing this," he said.

"You needn't thank me, Your Excellency."

"Please, Viktor. Call me Alexander."

Viktor was about to ask if the Count had received any word from Sofia, but he was interrupted by a scuffle on the other side of the café. Two haggard-looking fruit sellers carrying woven baskets had gotten into a territorial dispute. Given that it was so late, both men were down to a few sorry pieces of produce; and while this may have lent an air of futility to their argument in the eyes of the observers, it in no way diminished the stakes for the principals. To that end, after a brief exchange of insults, one struck the other in the face. With blood on his lip and fruit on the floor, the assaulted man responded in kind.

As the customers in the café stopped their conversations to watch the skirmish with weary, knowing expressions, the café's manager rounded the bar and dragged the combatants out by their collars. For a moment, the room was silent while everyone stared out the café window to the spot where the two fruit sellers remained sitting on the ground a few feet apart. Then all of a sudden, the old accordion player—who had stopped performing during the scuffle—struck up a friendly tune, presumably in the hopes of restoring some sense of goodwill.

As Viktor took a sip from his coffee, the Count watched the accordion player with interest.

"Have you ever seen *Casablanca*?" he asked.

Somewhat bewildered, Viktor admitted that he had not.

"Ah. You must see it one day."

And so the Count told Viktor about his friend Osip and their recent viewing of the movie. In particular, he described the scene in which a small-time crook was dragged away by the police and how the American saloonkeeper, having assured his customers that everything was all right, casually instructed his bandleader to play on.

"My friend was very impressed with this," explained the Count. "He saw the saloonkeeper's instruction to the piano player to start playing so soon after the arrest as evidence of his indifference to the fates of other men. But I wonder. . . ."

The following morning at half past eleven, two officers of the KGB arrived at the Metropol Hotel in order to question Headwaiter Alexander Rostov on an undisclosed matter.

Having been escorted by a bellhop to Rostov's room on the sixth floor, the officers found no sign of him there. Nor was he receiving a trim in the barbershop, lunching at the Piazza, or reading the papers in the lobby. Several of Rostov's closest associates, including Chef Zhukovsky and Maître d' Duras, were questioned, but none had seen Rostov since the previous night. (The officers also endeavored to speak with the hotel's manager, only to find that he had not yet reported to work—a fact that was duly noted in his file!) At one o'clock, two additional KGB men were summoned so that a more thorough search could be made of the hotel. At two, the senior officer conducting the investigation was encouraged to speak with Vasily, the concierge. Finding him at his desk in the lobby (where he was in the midst of securing theater tickets for a guest), the officer did not beat about the bush. He put his question to the concierge unambiguously:

"Do you know the whereabouts of Alexander Rostov?"

To which the concierge replied: "I haven't the slightest idea."

Having learned that both Manager Leplevsky and Headwaiter Rostov had gone missing, Chef Zhukovsky and Maître d' Duras convened at 2:15 for their daily meeting in the chef's office, where they immediately engaged in close conversation. To be perfectly frank, there was little time spent on consideration of Manager Leplevsky's absence. But there was a good deal of time spent on Headwaiter Rostov's. . . .

Initially concerned when they had received word of their friend's disappearance, the two members of the Triumvirate took comfort from the KGB's obvious frustration—for it confirmed that the Count was not in their grips. But the question remained: *Where could he possibly be?*

Then a certain rumor began to spread among the hotel's staff. For though the officers of the KGB were trained to be inscrutable, gestures, language, and facial expressions have a fundamentally unruly syntax. Thus, over the course of the morning, implications had slipped out and inferences had been made that Sofia had gone missing in Paris.

"Is it possible . . . ?" wondered Andrey aloud, clearly implying to Emile that their friend may also have escaped into the night.

As it was only 2:25, and Chef Zhukovsky had yet to turn the corner from pessimist to optimist, he curtly replied: "Of course not!"

This led to a debate between the two men on the differences between what was probable, plausible, and possible—a debate that might have gone on for an hour, but for a knock at the door. Responding with an irritated "Yes?" Emile turned, expecting to find Ilya with his wooden spoon, but it was the clerk from the mail room.

The chef and maître d' were so confounded by his sudden appearance that they simply stared.

"Are you Chef Zhukovsky and Maître d' Duras?" he asked after a moment.

"Of course we are!" declared the chef. "Who else would we be?"

Without a word, the clerk presented two of the five envelopes that had been dropped in his slot the night before (having already made visits to the seamstress's office, the bar, and the concierge's desk). A professional through and through, the clerk showed no curiosity as to the contents of these letters despite their unusual weight; and he certainly didn't wait around for them to be opened, having plenty of his own work to attend to, thank you very much.

With the mail clerk's departure, Emile and Andrey looked down at their respective envelopes in wonder. In an instant, they could see that the letters had been addressed in a script that was at once proper, proud, and openhearted. Meeting each other's gaze, they raised their eyebrows then tore the envelopes open. Inside, they each found a letter of parting that thanked them for their fellowship, assured them that the Night of the Bouillabaisse would never be forgotten, and asked that they accept the enclosed as a small token of undying friendship. The "enclosed" happened to be four gold coins.

The two men, who had opened their letters at the same time, and read them at the same time, now dropped them on the table at the same time.

"It's true!" gasped Emile.

A man of discretion and civility, Andrey did not for one second consider saying: *I told you so.* Although with a smile he did observe: "So it seems . . ."

But when Emile had recovered from these happy surprises (four pieces of gold *and* an old friend purposefully at large!), he shook his head as one forlorn.

"What is it?" asked Andrey in concern.

"With Alexander gone and you afflicted with palsy," the chef said, "what is to become of me?"

Andrey looked at the chef for a moment then smiled.

"Afflicted with palsy! My friend, my hands are as agile as they have ever been."

Then to prove his point, Andrey picked up the four gold Catherines and sent them spinning in the air.

At five o'clock that afternoon, in a nicely appointed office of the Kremlin (with a view of the lilacs in the Alexander Gardens, no less), the Chief Administrator of a special branch of the country's elaborate security apparatus sat behind his desk reviewing a file. Dressed in a dark gray suit, the Chief Administrator might have been described as relatively indistinguishable when compared to any other balding bureaucrat in his early sixties, were it not for the scar above his left ear where, by all appearances, someone had once attempted to cleave his skull.

When there was a knock at his door, the Chief Administrator called, "Come in."

The knocker was a young man in a shirt and tie bearing a thick brown folder.

"Yes?" said the Chief Administrator to his lieutenant, while not looking up from his work.

"Sir," the lieutenant replied. "Word was received early this morning that a student on the Moscow Conservatory's goodwill tour has gone missing in Paris."

The Chief Administrator looked up.

"A student from the Moscow Conservatory?"

"Yes, sir."

"Male or female?"

"A young woman."

. . .

"What is her name?"

The lieutenant consulted the folder in his hands.

"Her given name is Sofia and she resides in the Metropol Hotel, where she has been raised by one Alexander Rostov, a Former Person under house arrest; although there appears to be some question as to her paternity. . . ."

"I see. . . . And has this Rostov been questioned?"

"That is just it, sir. Rostov cannot be found either. An initial search of the hotel's premises proved fruitless, and no one who has been questioned has admitted to seeing him since last night. However, a second and more thorough search this afternoon resulted in the discovery of the hotel's manager, locked in a storeroom in the basement."

"Not comrade Leplevsky . . ."

"The very same, sir. It appears that he discovered the plan of the girl's defection and was on his way to inform the KGB when Rostov overcame him and forced him into the storeroom at gunpoint."

"At gunpoint!"

"Yes, sir."

"Where did Rostov get a firearm?"

"It appears that he had a pair of antique dueling pistols—and the will to use them. In fact, it has been confirmed that he shot a portrait of Stalin in the manager's office."

"Shot a portrait of Stalin. Well. He does sound like a rather ruthless fellow. . . ."

"Yes, sir. And, if I may say so, wily. For it appears that two nights ago a Finnish passport and Finnish currency were stolen from one of the hotel's Finnish guests. Then last night, a raincoat and hat were stolen from an American journalist. This afternoon, investigators were sent to Leningradsky Railway Station, where confirmation was obtained that a man wearing the hat and coat in question was seen boarding the overnight train to Helsinki. The hat and coat were discovered in a washroom at the Russian terminus in Vyborg, along with a travel guide for Finland from which the maps had been removed. Given the tightness of security at the railway crossing into Finland, it is presumed that Rostov disembarked in Vyborg in order to cross the border on foot. Local security has been alerted, but he may already have slipped through their fingers."

"I see . . . ," said the Chief Administrator again, accepting the file from his lieutenant and putting it on his desk. "But tell me, how did we make the connection between Rostov and the Finnish passport in the first place?"

"Comrade Leplevsky, sir."

"How so?"

"When comrade Leplevsky was led to the basement, he witnessed Rostov taking the Finnish guide from a collection of abandoned books. With that piece of information in hand, the connection was quickly made to the theft of the passport, and officers were dispatched to the station."

"Excellent work all around," said the Chief Administrator.

"Yes, sir. Though it does make one wonder."

"Wonder what?"

"Why Rostov didn't shoot Leplevsky when he had the chance."

"Obviously," said the Chief Administrator, "he didn't shoot Leplevsky, because Leplevsky isn't an aristocrat."

"Sir?"

"Oh, never mind."

As the Chief Administrator tapped the new folder with his fingers, the lieutenant lingered in the doorway.

"Yes? Is there something else?"

"No, sir. There is nothing else. But how shall we proceed?"

The Chief Administrator considered this question for a moment and then, leaning back in his chair with the barest hint of a smile, replied:

"Round up the usual suspects."

It was Viktor Stepanovich, of course, who left the damning evidence in the Vyborg terminal washroom.

An hour after bidding the Count good-bye, he boarded the Helsinki-bound train wearing the journalist's hat and coat with the *Baedeker* in his pocket. When he disembarked in Vyborg, he tore out the maps and left the guide with the other items on a counter in the station's washroom. Then he traveled back on the next train bound for Moscow empty-handed.

It was almost a year later when Viktor finally had the opportunity to watch *Casablanca*. Naturally, when the scene shifted to Rick's Café and the police began closing in on Ugarte, his interest was piqued, because he remembered his conversation with the Count in the railway station café. So with utmost attention, he watched as Rick disregarded Ugarte's pleas for help; he saw the saloonkeeper's expression remain cool and aloof when the police dragged Ugarte from his lapels; but then, as Rick began making his way through the disconcerted crowd toward the piano player, something caught Viktor's eye. Just the slightest detail, not more than a few frames of film: In the midst of this short journey, as Rick passes a customer's table, without breaking stride or interrupting his assurances to the crowd, he sets upright a cocktail glass that had been knocked over during the skirmish.

Yes, thought Viktor, that's it, exactly.

For here was Casablanca, a far-flung outpost in a time of war. And here at the heart of the city, right under the sweep of the searchlights, was Rick's Café Américain, where the beleaguered could assemble for the moment to gamble and drink and listen to music; to conspire, console, and most importantly, hope. And at the center of this oasis was Rick. As the Count's friend had observed, the saloonkeeper's cool response to Ugarte's arrest and his instruction for the band to play on could suggest a certain indifference to the fates of men. But in setting upright the cocktail glass in the aftermath of the commotion, didn't he also exhibit an essential faith that by the smallest of one's actions one can restore some sense of order to the world?

And Anon

On one of the first afternoons of summer in 1954, a tall man in his sixties stood in the high grass among some ragged apple trees somewhere in the Nizhny Novgorod Province. The beginnings of a beard on his chin, the dirt on his boots, and the rucksack on his back all contributed to the impression that the man had been hiking for several days, though he didn't look weary from the effort.

Pausing among the trees, the traveler looked a few paces ahead to where he could just make out the suggestion of a road that had become overgrown long ago. As the man turned onto this old road with a smile at once wistful and serene, a voice came down from the heavens to ask: *Where are you going?*

Stopping in his tracks, the man looked up as—with a rustle of branches—a boy of ten dropped to the ground from an apple tree.

The eyes of the old man widened.

"You're as silent as a mouse, young man."

With a look of self-assurance, the boy took the man's remark very much as a compliment.

"I am too," said a timid voice from among the leaves.

The traveler looked up to discover a girl of seven or eight perched on a branch.

"Indeed, you are! Would you like a hand coming down?"

"I don't need one," said the girl. But she angled herself to drop into the traveler's arms, just the same.

Once the girl was on the ground beside the boy, the traveler could see that the two were siblings.

"We're pirates," the boy said matter-of-factly, while looking off toward the horizon.

"I could tell," said the man.

"Are you going to the mansion?" the little girl asked with curiosity.

"Most no one goes there," cautioned the boy.

"Where is it?" the man asked, having seen no sign of it through the trees.

"We'll show you."

The boy and girl led the man along the old, overgrown road, which turned in a long, lazy arc. After they had walked about ten minutes, the mystery of the mansion's invisibility was solved: for having been burned to the ground decades before, it consisted now of two tilting chimneys at either end of a clearing still dusted here and there with ash.

If one has been absent for decades from a place that one once held dear, the wise would generally counsel that one should never return there again.

History abounds with sobering examples: After decades of wandering the seas and overcoming all manner of deadly hazards, Odysseus finally returned to Ithaca, only to leave it again a few years later. Robinson Crusoe, having made it back to England after years of isolation, shortly thereafter set sail for that very same island from which he had so fervently prayed for deliverance.

Why after so many years of longing for home did these sojourners abandon it so shortly upon their return? It is hard to say. But perhaps for those returning after a long absence, the combination of heartfelt sentiments and the ruthless influence of time can only spawn disappointments. The landscape is not as beautiful as one remembered it. The local cider is not as sweet. Quaint buildings have been restored beyond recognition, while fine old traditions have lapsed to make way for mystifying new entertainments. And having imagined at one time that one resided at the very center of this little universe, one is barely recognized, if recognized at all. Thus do the wise counsel that one should steer far and wide of the old homestead.

But no counsel, however well grounded in history, is suitable for all. Like bottles of wine, two men will differ radically from each other for being born a year apart or on neighboring hills. By way of example, as this traveler stood before the ruins of his old home, he was not overcome by shock, indignation, or despair. Rather, he exhibited the same smile, at once wistful and serene, that he had exhibited upon seeing the overgrown road. For as it turns out, one can revisit the past quite pleasantly, as long as one does so expecting nearly every aspect of it to have changed.

.   .   .   .   .

Having wished the young pirates well, our traveler made his way into the local village about five miles away.

Though he didn't mind seeing that so many of the old landmarks had disappeared, he was greatly relieved to find that the inn at the edge of town was still there. Ducking his head as he came through the front door and taking his rucksack from his shoulder, he was greeted by the innkeeper—a middle-aged woman who appeared from the back wiping her hands on her apron. She asked if he was looking for a room. He confirmed that he was, but said he'd like to have something to eat first. So she gestured with her head toward the doorway that led to the tavern.

Ducking his head again, he went inside. Given the hour, there were but a few citizens seated here and there at the old wooden tables, eating a simple stew of cabbage and potatoes, or drinking a glass of vodka. Offering a friendly nod to those who bothered to look up from their meals, the man headed to the little room with the old Russian stove at the back of the tavern. And there in the corner, at a table for two, her hair tinged with gray, the willowy woman waited.

Rules of Civility

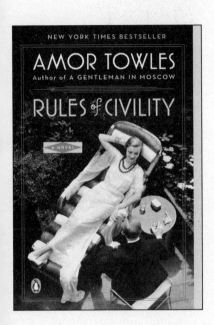

NEW YORK TIMES BESTSELLER

AMOR TOWLES
Author of A GENTLEMAN IN MOSCOW

RULES of CIVILITY

A NOVEL

On the last night of 1937, twenty-five-year-old Katey Kontent is in a second-rate Greenwich Village jazz bar when Tinker Grey, a handsome banker, happens to sit down at the neighboring table. This chance encounter and its startling consequences propel Katey on a year-long journey into the upper echelons of New York society—where she will have little to rely upon other than a bracing wit and her own nerve.

"With this snappy period piece, Towles resurrects the cinematic black-and-white Manhattan of the golden age."
—*The New York Times Book Review*